My Dangerous Duke

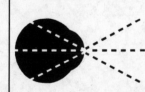

This Large Print Book carries the
Seal of Approval of N.A.V.H.

MY DANGEROUS DUKE

GAELEN FOLEY

THORNDIKE PRESS

A part of Gale, Cengage Learning

Farmington Hills, Mich • San Francisco • New York • Waterville, Maine
Meriden, Conn • Mason, Ohio • Chicago

GALE
CENGAGE Learning®

Thorndike Press® Large Print Romance.
The text of this Large Print edition is unabridged.
Other aspects of the book may vary from the original edition.
Set in 16 pt. Plantin.

LIBRARY OF CONGRESS CATALOGING-IN-PUBLICATION DATA

Foley, Gaelen.
    My dangerous duke / by Gaelen Foley. — Large print edition.
        pages ; cm. — (Thorndike Press large print romance)
    ISBN 978-1-4104-6999-1 (hardcover) — ISBN 1-4104-6999-9 (hardcover)
    1. Aristocracy (Social class)—England—Fiction. 2. Secret societies—England—Fiction. 3. Aristocracy (Social class)—England—Fiction. 4. Large type books. I. Title.
PS3556.O3913M85 2014
813'.54—dc23   2014010545

Published in 2014 by arrangement with Avon, an imprint of HarperCollins Publishers

Printed in Mexico
1 2 3 4 5 6 7 18 17 16 15 14

And my good master, though I had not asked, urged me: "Look at that mighty one who comes and does not seem to shed a tear of pain."
— Dante's *Inferno,* Canto XVIII, II. 82–84

Nothing great enters the life of mortals without a curse.
— Sophocles

CHAPTER 1

Cornwall, 1816

She was to be given to him as a gift — a plaything for some powerful, dark stranger. How her life had come to this, Kate Madsen could barely comprehend, but her rage at this horrifying fate was muted by the drug her kidnappers forced down her throat.

The tincture of the poppy soon dissolved her will to fight.

Within half an hour of being made to swallow it, it had tamed her temper, blurred her mind, quelled the usual sharp-tongued retorts she blasted at her captors, and left her hands limp instead of her usual clenched fists when the smugglers' wives came in to prepare her for her doom.

Barely two-thirds conscious, capable only of dull-witted yes's and no's, she was uncharacteristically docile as the women washed her roughly and dressed her like a harlot for their lord.

Kate did not know what the smugglers had done to anger the dread Duke of Warrington, but from what she could glean, she was to be the virgin sacrifice by which they hoped to appease his wrath.

His appetite for women was known to be voracious.

This, along with his expertise in all manner of violence, was, she had heard, why the locals privately called their landlord "the Beast."

None of it felt real. When she saw her reflection clad in the indecent shred of white muslin they had made her wear, she could only laugh bitterly. She knew she did not have a prayer. Half-naked, she shivered uncontrollably — not so much from the cold but in terror of the night ahead.

Only the sedative offered sweet refuge, carrying her fears away to oblivion, like so much chimney smoke torn asunder by the winter wind that even now was howling through the seaside village.

The women nearly scalped her while combing out the tangles in her long brown hair. They sprinkled her with cheap perfume, then stood back to admire their work.

"Right pretty," one weathered sea-wife declared. "She don't clean up too badly."

"Aye, the Beast should fancy her."

"Still too pale," another said. "Put some rouge on her, Gladys."

It all seemed to be happening to someone else. A slimy daub of pink-tinted cream rubbed into her cheeks none too gently, then her lips.

"There." This done, they pulled Kate to her feet and started herding her toward the door.

Through her dulled, distorted senses, the prospect of exiting the cramped room that had been her recent prison roused Kate slightly from her stupor. "Wait," she forced out in a mumble. "I . . . don't have any shoes."

"That's so you won't try runnin' away again, Miss Clever!" Gladys snapped. "Here, finish your wine. I'd take it if I were you. He's like to be rough with ye."

Kate stared at her, her glassy eyes widening at the warning, but she did not argue. She took the cup and gulped down the last swallow of drugged red wine, while the crude harpies cackled with laughter to think they had finally succeeded in breaking her will.

Lord knew, if not for the strong dose of laudanum they had given her, she would have been screaming bloody murder and fighting them like a wild thing, just as she had on the night of her abduction about a month ago.

Instead, she simply finished the cup and handed it back to them with a grim, lost gaze.

The women bound her wrists with some rope, then took her downstairs to the ground floor of the cluttered little house.

In the room below, grizzled old Caleb Doyle and the other male leaders of the smugglers' ring were waiting to take her up to the castle. She could not bear to make eye contact with anyone, humiliated by the way they had made her look like a whore — she, who had always valued herself for her brains, not her looks.

Thank God, none of them saw fit to mock her. She did not think what was left of her pride could have borne it.

Despite the heavy, rolling fog that hung over her mind, she noticed how somber the men's mood was. There was none of the cheerful vulgarity she had come to expect from the citizens of the smugglers' village.

Tonight, she could almost smell their fear, and it multiplied her own exponentially.

Good God, what manner of man were they taking her to, that he could make these rough criminals tremble like whipped dogs at their master's approach?

"Finally made a lady of the little hoyden, have ye?" Caleb, the smugglers' chieftain, grunted at his wife.

"Aye. She'll show some manners now. Don't worry, 'usband," Gladys added. "She'll soften his anger."

"Let's just hope he takes the bait," Caleb muttered. He turned away, but Gladys grasped his arm and pulled her husband aside.

"You're sure you want to risk this?"

He scoffed. "What choice do I have?"

Though the couple kept their voices down, Kate stood close enough to hear their tense exchange — not that she was able to make much sense of it, with her usually sharp wits deliberately dulled, as was no doubt their plan.

"Why don't you just talk to him, Caleb? Aye, he'll be furious, but if ye explain what happened —"

"I'm done groveling to him!" her husband shot back angrily. "Look at the answer our fine duke sent back the last time we asked for help! Coldhearted bastard. Rubbin' elbows with princes and czars, wrapped up in God-knows-what dark dealings on the Continent. His Grace is too important to be bothered with the likes of us these days," he said bitterly. "I can't even remember the last time he troubled himself with a visit to Cornwall. Can you?"

"It's been a long time," she admitted.

"Aye, and he only came back this time on account of the blasted shipwreck! He don't care about us anymore, never mind we're his own people. You ask me, he's forgot where he came from. But this little lesson ought to help remind him."

"Caleb!"

"I ain't afraid of 'im! Don't worry. Once he's had the girl, he'll be up to his neck in this, too, whether he likes it or not. Then he'll have no choice but to help us."

"Aye, and if you're wrong, there will be hell to pay."

"I expect there will be," he replied with a hard glitter in his shrewd old eyes. "But look at my choices, Gladys. Better the devil you know."

"Right, well, if you're sure, then. Off ye go." Gladys folded her arms across her chest.

Caleb turned away, his weathered face taut as he gestured to his men. "Come on. Bring the girl. Let's not keep His Grace waitin'!"

Two of the grubby smugglers took hold of Kate's arms and, without further ado, ushered her out into the biting cold of the

12

pitch-black January night.

Her brain seethed as she tried to sort out the sketchy information in the Doyles' exchange. This was the first sort of explanation she had heard about what was going on, but with the laudanum working in her blood, her wits were too slugging to weigh it all out. She rose and fell on waves between euphoria and dread; following one train of thought simply took too much effort. It was easier just to drift . . .

Meanwhile, the smugglers lifted her limp body and deposited her in the second of three battered, waiting carriages. Caleb threw her a flimsy blanket to keep her from catching her death. He locked her in with a wary look, as if he suspected her of eavesdropping.

A moment later, they set out for Kilburn Castle, the ancestral home of the Beast.

As their caravan rumbled out of the wind-whipped village, Kate stared blankly out the carriage window.

Above, the hooked moon tore like a claw through the smoky scattered clouds, revealing pinprick stars; winter constellations marched down over the horizon into the glossy onyx English Channel.

Feeble lanterns on the smugglers' boats bobbed in the harbor, riding out the frigid night at anchor.

Ahead, the road hugged the hill as their small caravan ascended. And far up on the distant crest, the black tower of Kilburn Castle loomed.

Kate rested her forehead for a moment against the carriage window, staring dully at the castle. She had already had plenty of time to contemplate what she might find there, for through the window of the tiny bedchamber that had been her prison cell for the past few days, she had been able to see the stark tower standing alone a few miles away on the bleak cliff top.

According to local legend, the castle was haunted, its master's bloodlines cursed.

She shook her head in woozy annoyance. *Ignorant peasant superstitions.* The Duke of Warrington was not cursed, merely evil, she could have explained to these unlettered brutes. What other sort of man would participate in such iniquity?

From the snatches of gossip she had overheard among the smugglers' women over the past few weeks, the duke sounded like the very worst sort of aristocrat — rich, powerful, corrupt. Steeped in sheer debauchery. She had also heard the women say His Grace belonged to some unspeakable libertines' society in London called the

14

Inferno Club.

How he amused himself there made her shudder even to wonder.

Hating him, however, seemed as futile as wondering why all this was happening to her.

She had never really understood from the start why she had been kidnapped. She lived so quietly at the edge of the moors with her books and writings; she kept to herself, never bothered anyone. She had no enemies that she knew of.

Nor many friends, admittedly.

Why would somebody target her?

For all her love of logic puzzles since she was a child, she could not riddle this one out, until at length, she had drawn her own conclusions based on the few facts she possessed.

The smugglers dealt in black markets, which, since the end of the war, had ceased to exist. Now that there was peace, there were no more tariffs on French luxury goods.

Lean times had come to Cornwall. Ergo, to make a living, the smugglers must have broadened their interests by venturing into a darker sort of commodity.

Oh, she had read about so-called white slavery before. The newspapers spoke of criminal rings that abducted young females without any family, and sold them in secrecy to decadent noblemen and other rich perverts to rape at will, as though inflicting pain and terror was its own expensive form of depraved amusement.

Though she had heard of it, Kate had never dreamed it was anything more than a lurid myth, the stuff of the Gothic novels that were her secret vice. Yet somehow, to her horror, here she was, caught up in it.

This was the only explanation that seemed to fit at all.

The Doyles' tense conversation of a few moments ago offered new bits of insight, but in her current muddled state, she did not have the wherewithal to assimilate it into her working theory. Whatever their words had meant, it did not bode well.

More important than knowing *why,* at any rate, was figuring some way out of this.

The castle was getting closer. Her fear mounted with every yard of road the carriages covered. Rallying herself with a mighty effort against the heaviness of the laudanum, Kate sat up and tried the door handle. She rattled it with some vague notion of escape, but it did not budge.

Even if she could succeed in breaking free, she realized that exposed to the elements, half-naked as she was, the wet, brutal cold would kill her within hours.

She could not even hope for justice someday, she thought in a flood of despair. Everyone knew that a duke was practically immune to prosecution for any form of criminal barbarity.

Besides, whom would she tell? For that matter, who would believe her? She barely believed it herself. For all she knew, this man might kill her in his pursuit of twisted pleasure.

No, her only hope at this point was that when he was finally done with her, he might let her live, might let her just go home.

The thought of her cozy thatched cottage at the edge of Dartmoor brought tears of nearly unbearable homesickness to her eyes, all of her emotions intensified by the opiates. By God, if she ever made it home, she swore she would never complain again about her rural isolation out there on the heath. For she had discovered lately that there were worse things in the world than loneliness.

The hardest part was thinking that stupid O'Banyon had not even kidnapped the right girl!

On the night of her abduction, the ringleader, O'Banyon, kept calling her by the wrong name — Kate Fox instead of Kate Madsen.

Her name was Kate Madsen!

With failing hope, she thought perhaps it might all be an outrageous case of mistaken identity. Perhaps she could convince the duke that this was never supposed to happen, not to her.

And yet . . . a glimmer of a childhood memory, a tiny incident she had almost forgotten poked a hole in her neat little theory about the white slavers, spawning a fearful bewilderment that shook her to the core.

But there was no time left to ponder the question.

Her fate was at hand. They had come to Kilburn Castle.

Surrounded by a landscape of bleakly frosted rock, its rugged stone face was silvered by moonlight, contoured with charcoal shadows.

Kate turned, looking this way and that as the three carriages pounded over the drawbridge and gusted under the archway of the barbican gatehouse, a bristling portcullis hanging overhead. A pair of burly guards there waved them through without stopping them.

So. We are expected.

She stared out the carriage window at the castle's outer walls. They stretched out on either side and disappeared into the night, like a steely embrace she would never escape.

Her pulse slammed. *Escape from here? No. There is no way.* Even if she were warmly dressed and in her right mind, there were armed men everywhere.

Why? Why does he keep all these guards?

It seemed to be more evidence that the duke had plenty to hide.

She had already drawn a few conclusions about his dealings with the smugglers. As the aristocratic patron of these criminals, she had ascertained that the duke allowed the smugglers to operate freely along his coastal lands, no doubt in exchange for a cut of their ill-gotten gains. The smugglers probably supplied the girls that fed the demon appetites of the Inferno Club.

No wonder he kept all these guards, she thought. Even drugged, she could see it was only logical that a wealthy peer who dabbled in the criminal underworld would want to take added measures to ensure his security.

Perhaps he was merely as paranoid as every tyrant in history, she thought, missing her dusty historical tomes. Caesar and his Praetorian Guards — and the modern-day

Caesar, Napoleon, with his elite Grande Armée, or what was left of it, after Waterloo last summer.

Lord, if the duke was this paranoid, her situation might be even more dire than she had thought.

Ahead, the Norman keep with its four rounded towers rose against the darkness. The carriages filed into the mighty quadrangle, arriving in a formal courtyard at the center of the inner bailey.

As the horses clattered to a halt, a fresh wave of terror gripped her, any hope of some miraculous reprieve dwindling by the second.

Quickly, the smugglers began jumping out of their three vehicles. The door to the middle one flew open abruptly; a burst of frigid air rushed in.

"Come on," Caleb ordered gruffly. Reaching into the carriage, the smugglers' chieftain pulled her out.

Kate clutched the too-small blanket, trying to protect herself from the elements, but he ripped it away, leaving her exposed again in her harlot gown. "You don't need that."

When he set her on her feet, she let out a small cry of pain, for the thin white stockings she wore offered no protection against the coating of frost on the flagstones.

Doyle nodded to a pair of his underlings. "Help her walk."

"Aye, sir." The two men grabbed her by her elbows and began steering her toward the yawning Gothic entrance.

Teeth chattering, her body shivering violently, Kate did her best to keep up, but her legs were wobbly with fear, her almost-bare feet smarting with every step.

Still dizzy and disoriented, she thought surely anyone who saw her at this moment would believe she was indeed just a common drunken trollop. Oh, God, her high-born French mama would be turning over in her grave to see her now.

Fortunately, however, the cold served one purpose in Kate's favor. It cleared away some of her stupor, forcing her to stay relatively alert and aware of her surroundings.

She kept a bleary eye out for any means of escape, either now or in the future. Scanning the smugglers who had come along, she did not see any of the three who had burst into her cottage on the night of her kidnapping.

She especially hated O'Banyon. *Filthy, leering brute.*

She had overheard the ringleader's name

21

on the night of her abduction when one of the two younger men had asked him for permission to rob her home after they had taken her captive. O'Banyon had generously allowed his assistants that night to help themselves to whatever money and jewelry they could find. Which wasn't much, anyway.

The possessions Kate valued most of all sat on her bookshelf, but those ruffians were too crude to care about the likes of Aristotle and the Bard.

Just inside the windbreak of the mighty stone entrance, Doyle called a halt. "Untie her hands," he ordered his underlings.

The men holding her arms looked at their chief in surprise.

"His Grace might not like it," Caleb muttered. "Let him tie her up himself if that's how he wants her. Don't worry, she ain't goin' nowhere. Lass barely knows her own name at the moment. Go on, be quick about it!" he ordered, nodding at the ropes around her wrists. "I'm freezin' me arse off."

To Kate's relief, the man he had spoken to obeyed, removing the knotted rope that bound her wrists.

Before moving on, however, Mr. Doyle stuck his finger in her face and issued a dire warning. "Don't you give His Grace any o' your lip, my girl, or you'll wish you was back in that cellar. Ye mark me? He don't take kindly to insolence. He's a very powerful man. If you're smart, you keep your mouth shut and do as he tells you. Understand?"

She nodded meekly, rubbing her chafed wrists.

The smugglers' chief looked startled by the absence of her usual fighting spirit. The frown on Caleb's lined face deepened to a scowl. "Aw, don't look at me like that — some wee lamb brought to slaughter!" he blustered. "Dozens o' lasses around these parts would give their right arm to spend a few nights in his bed! You'll live."

Kate stiffened, but his rough tone had succeeded in chasing off the threat of tears that stung her eyelids and calling up the last reserves of her courage. She steeled herself the best she could and squared her shoulders, determined to survive. By God, she would not go into this already cringing and defeated.

"Come on, you lot," Doyle muttered to his men, shrugging off her ruin. "Let's give the devil his due." With that, he banged on the iron-studded door with the huge metal knocker.

At once, a wiry, black-clad butler admitted them.

"Evening, Mr. Eldred," Caleb greeted him with all the charm he could muster as they stepped inside.

The butler bowed like an animated skeleton in black clothes. "Mr. Doyle." He had shrewd, deep-set eyes, a bony face, and an air of gaunt, foreboding stillness. Past his receding hairline, a storm cloud of wild gray hair stuck out in all directions at the back of his head.

His expression inscrutable, Eldred the butler glanced at Kate, but was apparently too shrewd to ask any questions. He turned away, lifting his lantern high. "This way, please. The master is expecting you."

Their whole party followed as Eldred led them down a tall, shadowy corridor, all stone and aged plaster and carved dark wood. Kate stumbled along on her frozen feet, staring all around her. She had never been in a castle before, but it was hard to believe that anyone could actually live in such a place.

It was not a home, it was a fortress, a mighty barracks left over from the days of knights and dragons.

Everything was dark and hard, cold and threatening. Ancient weapons, shields and pieces of armor, tattered battle flags hung on the walls instead of paintings. There was not one cozy thing about it, yet perversely, despite its unwelcoming atmosphere, the castle's historical significance made her forget her dread for one or two seconds as her scholar's unquenchable curiosity was roused about the place, the battles it had seen, and all the other mysterious things that might have happened here over the centuries.

Then she noticed her captors becoming increasingly nervous.

" 'Hoy, Eldred." Caleb leaned toward the butler as they trudged down a darkly paneled corridor. "How's his mood tonight?"

"I beg your pardon, sir?"

"The Beast!" he whispered. "Is he in a foul temper?"

The butler eyed him in disapproval. "I'm sure I couldn't say."

"So, that's a yes," Caleb muttered.

Then Eldred led them into a cavernous great hall with a soaring vaulted ceiling.

Darkness clustered thickly between the arching beams. Moldering tapestries draped the side walls here and there. Overlooking the room, a small balcony — the minstrel's gallery — jutted out slightly from the far wall. Closer to hand, several pieces of thick, ancient furniture provided barren comfort.

Two black-clad guards, like those stationed at the gatehouse, were posted in the nearest corners. They stood at attention, as immovable as the ancient suits of armor that adorned the great hall.

The only real sign of life glowed from the blazing bonfire in the yawning fireplace, far away down at the dais end of the hall — and it was there that Kate caught her first glimpse of the Beast.

She knew at once that it was he.

The huge, crackling power of his presence filled the hall before he even turned around. His back to them, the Duke of Warrington stood before the fire, a towering figure silhouetted against the flames.

He was toying with a large, strange weapon with a long, notched blade, some sort of deadly cross between a lance and a sword. Balancing it on its tip, he twirled it slowly in a most ominous fashion.

Eldred announced them with a polite cough. "Ahem, Your Grace: Caleb Doyle and company."

He lifted the weapon, resting the bar of its long handle on his huge shoulder.

Her heart leaped up into her throat as the iron giant slowly pivoted to face them. He paused, studying them from across the hall with a dissecting stare.

Then he began prowling toward them, his

long paces unhurried yet relentless: a medieval warlord in modern-day clothes. Each fall of his mud-flecked boots boomed in the hollow vastness of the chamber.

Kate's mouth hung open slightly as she stared at him in fear and some degree of awe.

Caleb whipped off his hat and took a couple steps forward, gesturing to his men to do the same.

The smugglers' party advanced in cringing dread, with Kate in the center.

Her stare stayed locked on the warrior duke as he sauntered closer. She searched in vain for any sign of softness in the man, but instead, a capacity for ruthless force emanated from him. He was hard and dark and dangerous, intimidation incarnate.

It was clear he had just arrived, his wild, windblown mane of thick sable hair tied back in a queue. She studied him, wide-eyed. The dark knotted cloth around his neck was nothing so formal as a cravat. His loose white shirt hung open a bit at the neck, disappearing into a black waistcoat that hugged his lean, sculpted torso.

Rain and sleet still dotted his black riding breeches, while the reddish firelight gleamed on the blade that he wielded so idly as he advanced, as though he'd been born with it

27

in his hand.

Heart pounding, Kate could not take her eyes off him.

He appeared to be in his midthirties; she scanned his square, rugged face as he drew closer. He had thick, dark eyebrows with a scar above the left like the mark of a thunderbolt. His skin was unfashionably bronzed, as though he had spent years in sunnier climes. His nose was broad but straight, the grim set of his hard mouth bracketed by lines.

His eyes were terrifying.

Steely in color and expression, they were narrowed with suspicion, their depths gleaming with a banked fury that she realized he was waiting to unleash on the smugglers — and might take out on her, as well, before the night was through.

Dear God, he could kill her easily, she understood at once. The man was huge, nearly six and a half feet tall, with arms of iron, and shoulders like the Cornish cliffs. He looked strong enough to lift a horse, while she only came up to the center of his massive chest.

No wonder the smugglers were terrified of him, despite Caleb's claim to the contrary back at the village. Warrington had the imposing physique of a conqueror, and all the worldly power of the aristocracy's highest rank, save the royal family.

She tried to back away as the duke stalked closer, running a bold stare over the length of her.

"What is this?" he growled softly at Doyle, nodding at her. She reacted instinctively to his notice, pulling against her captors' hold in panic. She tried to run.

They stopped her.

"A gift, Your Grace!" Caleb Doyle exclaimed in forced joviality.

As the smugglers dragged her over to him, Warrington studied her like a predatory wolf.

"A gift?" he echoed in a musing tone.

Caleb thrust her toward him with a cheerful grin. "Aye, sir! A token of our regard, to welcome you back to Cornwall after all this time! A fine young bed warmer for a cold winter's night. Right little beauty, ain't she?"

He was silent for a long moment, perusing her intently. Then he answered barely audibly, his deep voice reverberated like a distant rumble of thunder drawing closer: "Indeed."

Caught in his stare, Kate could not even move. She was lucky she remembered to keep breathing.

When Caleb laughed again nervously, the

others followed suit, but Warrington barely took note of them, his stare trailing over her in appreciation.

"Very thoughtful of you, Doyle," he murmured, taking lecherous note of how the chill affected certain regions of her anatomy.

His brazen stare erased any last remaining hope that he might not be a party to their crimes. Of course he was.

She was naught but merchandise to him.

"We thought you'd like 'er, sir. We brought a few other tokens of our regard, as well —" Doyle gestured hastily to his followers. "Show him. Hurry!" His men leaped into motion, presenting their lord with a case of premium brandy and a selection of fine tobaccos.

He barely glanced at these offerings, however, still studying Kate with a speculative gleam in his eyes.

She barely knew what to do with herself. She had never been looked at this way by a man — inspected, nay, devoured.

Warrington's glance flicked down from her still-damp hair to her stockinged feet, assessing her from top to bottom; then, to her surprise, he stared, hard, into her eyes — but only for a moment.

In that fleeting instant, she was not sure what she read in his penetrating gaze, other

30

than a chilling degree of intelligence, like a man in the midst of a chess game.

"The gift is, er, acceptable, Your Grace?" Caleb ventured in a delicate tone.

The duke flashed a dangerous smile more potent than the laudanum.

"We'll soon find out," he said. Never taking his stare off her, he nodded to his silent guardsmen. "Put her in my chamber."

CHAPTER 2

Kate gasped as two of his black-clad guards took her from the smugglers' hold. She struggled to free her arms, scowling in woozy defiance. Damn and blast!

"Let go of me!" Her angry words came out slightly slurred.

"Is there a problem?" the duke demanded, glancing back in irritation.

"No, sir," the guard on her right answered rather sheepishly as he gripped her elbow again.

"Don't touch me!" Kate yanked away and nearly lost her balance. Steadying herself, she whirled to meet Warrington's gaze with a curse for him on the tip of her tongue like a dart.

"Go upstairs and wait for me," he ordered her.

Kate stopped, taken off guard by the velvet undertones in his deep voice. She forgot her anger for a heartbeat, arrested by the promise of pleasure in his smoky eyes; she stood motionless, staring at him but disoriented when the drug swept her up in its most disturbing side effect yet.

Attraction. *Arousal.*

A fatal fascination with him gripped her. He was beautiful, undeniably, but an utter mystery to her. One she suddenly desired to solve, obsessed as she had always been with finding hidden answers. An impetuous hunger to taste his lips stormed through her blood. As if outside herself, she saw, of course, this was the maddest possible reaction.

She couldn't seem to control it. Dear God, the devilish tincture would almost make her eager for her own ravishment. How humiliating!

At the same time, the satisfaction in his eyes, as if he was thoroughly used to being wanted by women, his air of towering pride, awoke the slumbering fighter within her.

How dare he have this effect on me?

Who did he think he was, the big arrogant brute? A rush of bracing anger slammed her back to her senses, but as she shook off the strange sensation of lust, Caleb's warnings echoed through her mind. *Keep your mouth shut. Do as he tells you.* Kate stifled a low growl. *Easier said than done,* she thought, but at least now her wary sense of self-preservation had returned.

Given that Warrington's pride seemed even larger than his castle, she suddenly realized it would be folly to dare reject him in front of all his men. Only a fool would give him a reason to punish her. *Don't make it worse for yourself.*

"Parker?" he said in a long-suffering tone.

"Yes, Your Grace. Sorry, sir." The guard on her right, apparently Parker, took hold of her arm again. "Come along, miss. His Grace has got business to attend to with these fellows."

Kate suspended her efforts to fight, realizing direct confrontation with such an invincible foe was not going to get her anywhere. She stood a better chance of dashing away from these two guards once they were out of the Beast's vicinity.

Bide your time. Be patient, she told herself.

Though she shot a parting glare at the smugglers, she offered no further objections, but let the duke's black-clad henchmen escort her out of the great hall.

Passing the dais end of the chamber, they exited through the archway beneath the minstrels' gallery.

At once, the two men shepherded her up a lonely staircase carved of stone. The merest glimmer of starlight shone through the stained glass of the tall, pointed window at the landing where the stairwell turned.

Though her brain was still working slowly, she cast about for a ruse of some sort that would help her slip away from the guards. "I-I need to use the necessary," she forced out all of a sudden.

"Don't you get sick on our floors," the man the duke had addressed as "Parker" warned her sternly. "Hold on, the garderobe's right up here."

"Garderobe?" she mumbled.

Reaching the upper floor, they tugged her over to a sort of closet at the end of hallway. Parker took a lantern off a peg on the wall and handed it to her.

"Take this with you. And mind you don't fall into the moat while you're at it." He opened the door to the garderobe for her, but Kate immediately recoiled at the smell — beyond disgusting!

Bringing her hand up to cover her mouth and nose, she shook her head violently, backing away. "Never mind!"

The guards laughed. "That'll clear your head, won't it, you little tosspot?" the other one said.

"Ah, leave 'er alone, Wilkins. She can't help what she is. Come on, you," Parker muttered. "There's a chamber pot in the solar if you're goin' to puke."

Actually, Kate had not felt queasy until now, but the horrible stench of the garde-robe had temporarily routed all thoughts of escape.

Merely happy that she could breathe again, she paid scant attention as they marched her past the top of the stairs, heading down the upper hallway in the opposite direction.

Before she could summon a second idea for how she might evade them, a roar from the great hall below suddenly echoed up to them, its distant reverberations booming through the minstrels' gallery on the mezzanine.

"How dare you disobey me? Did I not make myself perfectly clear?"

The terrifying bellow froze Kate in her tracks. Wide-eyed, she looked back slowly toward the stairwell and blanched. She could not make out every thunderous word, but the Beast was clearly giving the smugglers what for.

"Waste my time . . . bring down this embarrassment on my name? Fools! I should let the hangman have the lot of you!"

The guards exchanged a worried glance, then Parker grumbled at her not to dawdle.

Lifting her by her arms, his henchmen sailed her along down the dark hallway, till they came to a massive arched door.

One man opened it; the other thrust her in.

"Off you go, now. Make yourself comfortable."

Kate stumbled into the solar, then spun around, her heart pounding. "Wait! You can't leave me here!"

"Sorry, miss. Just following orders. His Grace will be with you shortly."

"But I don't —"

They shut the door in her face.

"Hey!"

"Daft chit's conversin' with Pharaoh," she heard Wilkins mutter.

"Aye, well, it's none of our affair."

Hearing a key turn in the lock, Kate lurched forward, falling against the door. "Come back! You don't understand!" She pounded on it. "Please! Mr. Parker! Let me out!"

No answer.

Had they already gone? She knelt quickly and peered with one eye through the keyhole.

There was only darkness. She could hear the businesslike rhythm of the Beast's two disciplined henchmen marching away.

"Oh, God," Kate whispered, closing her eyes and leaning her reeling head against the door. Thankfully, the solidity of its hard planks helped to steady the woozy pounding in her brain.

It was then, quite without warning, she noticed the chamber they had brought her to was . . . wonderfully warm.

Feeling was returning to her cold-numbed feet. She was still shivering, but not so violently now. She opened her eyes, lifted her head, and straightened up by cautious degrees from her spot by the keyhole.

As the sweet thaw spread through her chilled body, she slowly turned and faced the duke's chamber.

To her uneasy surprise, it was not so bad. It wasn't a dungeon cell. She could spy no instruments of torture. No dripping pools of blood on the floor, after all.

A cheery fire in the hearth cast a warm glow through the dark-paneled room, making it seem unexpectedly cozy.

The fire entranced her. She was drawn to it instinctively across a thick carpet woven in rich colors. She did not stop until she stood on the warmed slates before the fireplace, sighing with gratitude while the lovely heat seeped up into her through the soles of her icy feet. Warmth — *at last.*

Keeping her arms wrapped around herself, she glanced down at the leather armchair set before the fireplace, a luxurious white fur throw strewn across it.

It was more temptation than she could resist.

In the next instant, she was curled up on the armchair, huddled under the fur throw, and telling herself that as soon as she was fully warmed, she would rally her wits and find some way to escape.

The thought of fleeing back out into the bitter winter night made her want to weep. But for now, she would just rest here for a few minutes to regain her strength.

In a moment, she would come up with a plan . . .

What she did not realize was that the cold had been the only thing keeping her awake. It alone had been warding off the full effects of the laudanum. The warmth that now enveloped her was richly comforting, lulling her senses.

Moments passed . . . she suddenly jerked awake, having failed to notice herself falling asleep.

Disaster!

Shoving off the fur throw with an angry motion, her heart pounding, she paused for a moment, took a deep, shaky breath, and pondered the ruin that could have befallen her if she had not returned to her senses.

Good God, could she make it any easier on him? Handsome or not, she did not intend to let that man force himself on her tonight. Unsure how much time had passed, she sat up straighter and glanced around for a clock.

Instead, for the first time, she now noticed the giant bed hulking in the deep shadows on the far end of the room.

She stared at it for a long moment: the ornately carved posts of time-blackened wood, the crimson velvet hangings. A chill ran down her spine. It was to be the place of her ruin; even so, she was not immune to its instinctual pull.

The duke's bed was the picture of warm, luxurious softness, safety: pillows, blankets. All seemed to beckon to her, even from where she sat.

No. She was not that weak. She turned forward again and shook her head, trying to clear out the cobwebs, even as the laudanum tormented her with the need for sleep.

Ignoring the bed with a will, she sank back into the armchair, drawing the fur throw back around her, still promising herself she'd look for an exit in a moment. But gazing into the fire, its dancing flames soon mesmerized her.

Nothing seemed to matter anymore.

Her mind drifted hopelessly, the drugged swaying of the room summoning childhood memories of those bygone days, the happiest in her life, when she had lived aboard her father's ship at sea.

With a faint, drugged half smile and a heartbreaking wave of nostalgia at the bright memories, she recalled how Papa used to let her stand at the helm and play the role of his miniature bo'sun. He'd tell her what to say, and she'd repeat his orders, shouting them out to the crew in a high-pitched, child's voice: *"Ahoy, you lazy buggers! Mind the topsail! Trim the main!"*

Strange how the thought of Papa could make her feel safe, even at a time like this.

Too bad he was dead and could not lift a finger to help her. She was on her own.

As usual.

Must get up. I've got to get out of here. Hurry. Find a way out. Before he comes . . . She tried to rise, but her body felt like lead. The dreamworld had begun to claim her in earnest this time. *One more minute,* begged her fading senses. *I'll just close my eyes . . .*

Rohan Kilburn, the Duke of Warrington, trusted he had made his displeasure clear.

41

The great hall still reverberated with the echoes of his wrath, but damn it, this debacle was a waste of critical time.

As one of the Order's top assassins, he burned to be back in London hunting the deadly Promethean operative, Dresden Bloodwell, who had been spotted in Town.

Worse, one of the Order's finest agents had been captured.

As long as Drake remained in enemy hands, all their identities were at risk as members of the ancient warrior brotherhood, the secretive Order of St. Michael the Archangel.

Unfortunately, there was no getting out of this task.

The recent shipwreck had been perpetrated by *his* tenants on *his* stretch of England's coastline; therefore, it was his problem.

And so, here he was, with instructions from his handler back in London not to return until the smugglers' ring had been secured.

Lucky for Caleb Doyle and his motley followers, the smugglers still remained a vital conduit for the Order's secret communications.

For years, the Dukes of Warrington and the local smugglers' ring had shared a cordial but clandestine symbiosis. Just like his father before him, Rohan kept the village rents low and turned a blind eye to the smugglers' black market schemes — within reason.

In exchange, old Caleb Doyle, the smugglers' current chief, made sure that the Order's coded messages were delivered to various foreign ports as swiftly as the wind could carry them, no questions asked.

The bold and speedy smuggler captains had honed their talents at evading Customs; they were a highly useful resource, considering that the Prometheans had spies watching every port in Europe. The smugglers were able to get in and out of any harbor before the enemy even knew they were there.

The end of the war against Napoleon, however, had lifted the trade tariffs, shutting down the lucrative black market that had been the smugglers' bread and butter for twenty years. Devil take them, how many times had he warned the fools not to squander the fortune they were raking in while the fat times lasted? To put some gold aside for later? Had they listened?

Of course not. Indeed, they had infuriated him several months ago with their outrageous plea for yet more money.

The tersely worded letter he had sent back had been the end of it, or so he had thought. Apparently, he had been wrong. Greed, ambition, desperation had driven his unruly tenants to overstep the simple boundaries he had laid down for them.

Now they had drawn themselves to the attention of the Coast Guard with their activities, and he was all that stood between them and the gallows.

Well, rules were rules. If he did not bring down the hammer on them and deal with them privately in his own fashion, it was going to become a public scandal, and the Order could not have that.

There was an old seaside ploy, a trick of the trade, that English smugglers had indulged in for centuries.

By the clever use of multiple large lanterns, they could simulate the signals of a lighthouse, luring unsuspecting ships to wreck on nearby rocks. This done, they would run down onto the beach, steal whatever washed ashore, and even row out and claim whatever booty they could scavenge from the wreckage.

It was a reckless, cutthroat procedure, and, of course, highly illegal. He could hardly believe the fools had done it. They clearly needed reminding of whom they answered to.

Pacing past the row of tattered ruffians lined up before him, he sent each one a glance of dark severity. He still dangled his unusual sword from his hand as casually as a dandy might swing his walking stick.

He paused to stare the largest man into submission, the one they called Ox. The sweaty mountain of a smuggler dropped his gaze.

"How many times have I warned all of you against this sort of thing?" Rohan continued, moving on. "I drew the line for you and bade you not to step over it, and yet you have the temerity to disregard my orders. Then — well!" He let out a sudden, harsh laugh that made them jump; he stopped at the end of the line and pivoted. "You bring me one of your drunken wenches — as if that's going to get you off the hook!

"Don't misunderstand me, she is a fine-looking lass, and I shall use her well. But if you believe that a willing harlot and a few bottles of decent brandy are going to make this go away, then you fail to grasp the seriousness of your situation. There is such a thing as consequences, gentlemen," he added. He swept them with a fiery look, though in truth, he was making more of a show of anger than the irritation he actually felt.

Those who saw him genuinely angry rarely lived to tell about it.

"The most amusing part is that you actually imagined I wouldn't find out. Ah, yes! You must have assumed that I was still abroad. Obviously, you were wrong."

He had returned from his rather bloodthirsty mission to Naples months ago.

Of course, they knew nothing of that. He never explained his long absences to anyone. He let them draw their own conclusions, and usually, they believed he traveled merely to entertain himself, seeking new pastures, new populations of women he had not yet bedded.

There was, perhaps, a grain of truth to that — but a man had to vent his tensions somehow.

"I was at my London house when I received a most enlightening visit from a high-ranking Coast Guard official, come to inform me of my tenants' mischief. Oh, yes, they know all about you," he informed them with a cutting edge to his voice. "As a courtesy to a peer of the realm, he saw fit to warn me in advance of the raid about to be carried out on the village. You should have seen how eager he was for your blood."

The smugglers exchanged uneasy glances.

"We all know what a thorn your gang has been in the side of the Coast Guard. Now they have witnesses, you see. Crewmen from that merchant ship you sank."

"But Your Grace —"

"Silence!"

They cowered.

"I will not hear your excuses!" he boomed. "If even one of those sailors had drowned, I should not have intervened to save your miserable hides, I can assure you. Did I mention that the Coast Guard was even prepared to arrest your wives? Aye, and most of your young sons, as well. It's no secret that these shipwrecks usually involve the whole village. However" — he continued pacing — "given that no lives were lost, I was able, at the cost of a large sum of gold, to bribe the Coast Guard agent into letting me deal with you privately. He agreed to a simple arrangement.

"I promised to hand over the men directly responsible for the shipwreck; these alone will face prosecution. In exchange, the rest of the village will be spared."

He noted their looks of relief.

"Gentlemen, I know it is your great tradition to protect one another with your code of silence. While I admire your loyalty, times have changed now that the war is over," he informed them, scanning the line of them slowly. "The Coast Guard doesn't have to keep watch for Boney anymore. Now they're free to concentrate on *you.*"

A few of them blanched.

"At any rate, the Coast Guard man consented to my proposal, and Mr. Doyle has wisely agreed to cooperate."

Rohan had written to the smugglers' chief before leaving London, giving him the chance to redeem himself by rounding up the guilty party ahead of his arrival.

He cast old Caleb Doyle a dark glance. "I trust you are ready to hand them over now?"

"Aye, sir."

Rohan gave him a curt nod. "Bring them in."

Doyle glanced grimly at his underlings to go and fetch the prisoners, who remained under guard in the carriages outside. The smugglers retreated from the great hall, but Doyle stayed behind; when Rohan looked at him, he could not help noticing the weariness on the old man's face, and perhaps a trace of shame.

No doubt Doyle was aggrieved, considering two of his own nephews were caught up in the scheme. Now it was either the gallows or some hell-hole penal colony for them.

What a waste. But Rohan also suspected that Doyle's look of guilt arose from the fact that, as the smugglers' leader, he was ultimately to blame for failing to keep his people under control.

Rohan knew that Caleb had not authorized the shipwreck. The feckless crime had been the brainchild of a handful of the younger men out to prove their mettle.

That was part of the problem. Doyle was growing older, weaker, losing his authority. It was inevitable that his role as village head would eventually be challenged by the new blood. No doubt Doyle's pride had taken a blow in all this, but Rohan did not intend to throw him to the wolves. The old man was too valuable to lose. Though a trickster by nature, to be sure, Caleb Doyle had proved his loyalty these many years to both Rohan's father and to him.

By now, having arranged the delivery of so many secret communiqués, the grizzled smugglers' chief surely suspected certain things about the Warrington dukes' long-standing involvement in secret government intrigues.

Fortunately, Caleb was too shrewd to let on how much he knew — or guessed.

Indeed, part of Doyle's genius lay in knowing what questions *not* to ask.

The mood in the great hall was tense as they heard Eldred get the front door for the guilty smugglers, who were about to be brought in.

Rohan took a seat on the old, thronelike chair in the center of the great hall and drummed his fingers on his sword's hilt in kingly impatience.

After all, the sooner he finished here, the sooner he could go unwrap his little "present." His eyes gleamed with anticipation as he permitted himself to think about her briefly. Even now, his instincts were wide-awake with a very male awareness of a woman in his house.

Waiting for him in his bed.

He had wanted her gone from the great hall in case stronger measures were needed to remind his unruly tenants of his authority. He did not wish any female to witness his capacity for violence.

Besides, he did not need the distraction of those beautiful breasts clamoring for his attention. He'd get to know them better soon enough, every silky inch of her.

His people knew what he liked; he was decidedly pleased with their peace offering. This luscious young token of their apology

50

left him feeling much more disposed to forgive. Indeed, the prospect of spending the next few nights in this abominable stone crypt of a castle suddenly looked a good deal more agreeable.

Coming out here to the middle of nowhere, he had expected to have to go without his daily dose of sex, a real inconvenience for a man of his elemental nature. He had a rule, after all, against poaching on the locals.

He wanted to be feared, not hated. But, hell, if they were going to offer her up on a silver platter, far be it from him to refuse such a delicious-looking morsel.

On the other hand, cynically, he couldn't help thinking of the Trojan horse. *Beware of Greeks bearing gifts.*

No doubt the head-turning beauty sent to warm his bed was also tasked with spying on him for the smugglers' gang. Certainly, he would not put such a scheme past sly old Caleb.

The smugglers probably reasoned that if they could get one of their girls into position close to him, she could warn them in advance of their lord's comings and goings, the better to help them conceal from him their next round of criminal mischief.

Rohan shook his head to himself in amusement. Whatever their scheme, he wasn't worried. In fact, it might be quite entertaining to play a little game of disinformation on his tenants if they actually thought they were clever enough to fool him.

As for his young present, he'd enjoy her all the same. Amateur spy or no, he was not about to let a little deception get in the way of his pleasure.

Watching the smugglers bring in six of their own, bound and shackled, he had some difficulty chasing the green-eyed harlot out of his mind.

It was difficult to find a woman that did not suit his tastes, true. He had a lusty appreciation for them all — tall, short, curvy, thin, blonde, brunette, commoner, aristocrat. But there was something particularly appealing about that . . . luscious little mess. Her plump, rouged lips and those sweet erect nipples like hard pink candies pressing against her plunging gown had roused in him a mental groan of lust; and yet, the expression in her big, emerald eyes had looked so vulnerable and lost — pathetic, almost — that it had summoned up an even fiercer protective instinct in him.

Quite bewildering.

Something about the shivering, shoeless, tipsy tart had nearly touched the chunk of stone that had once been his heart. In that moment, he had not known which he had wanted more: to gather her onto his lap and comfort her, or to lay her down and ride her into mindless, sweaty ecstasy.

He cast off the question with a restless shrug, deciding to do both as soon as he was done here.

Until he was ready for her, however, she'd find the solar upstairs much more toasty. The girl had been obviously freezing cold — and foxed, to boot. He had not liked seeing her tremble so with the chilly drafts inside the castle. As for her state of inebriation, he had noted that she could barely stand without weaving on her feet.

He scowled, recalling how the little tosspot had even forgotten her shoes. What was it about the harlot breed that they did not know when it was time to quit drinking?

Well, she could sober up while he concluded matters with the smugglers. She was a bed warmer; let her warm his bed until he got through here.

Then he would join her, and they would have some fun.

He still couldn't help wondering, though, why she had stared at him so strangely . . . as though she was scared of him. Those big, green, haunted eyes. Even now, he found himself perturbed by her strange, disquieting allure, plaguing him with equal parts desire and uneasiness.

Maybe her possible mission as a spy for the smugglers had suddenly seemed too difficult for her once she was in his presence. Most people realized on sight he was not to be trifled with, but surely she did not think he would ever hurt a woman.

True, there was the old family curse that might claim otherwise about the men in his line, but surely she didn't believe in that rubbish.

At least he liked to think it was rubbish.

If she was nervous of his size, she needn't have feared that, either. He knew how to safely wield the oversized weapon with which Nature had endowed him.

Perhaps she had never been bedded by an aristocrat before, but if that was the case, she had better get used to it, he thought cynically. She'd soon find out that dukes had the same base needs as any other blackguard.

Forget her, man. There's work to be done! You'll join her soon enough. With that, he dismissed her from his mind, refusing, as ever, to let a woman distract him. They were objects of pleasure, a favorite hobby, the reward for a hard day's work, and nothing more.

He stood as Doyle's men brought in the troublemakers, some of them cursing and struggling as they were marched in. He maintained a stony silence until Caleb had bullied the miscreants into line.

"These are the lads behind it, Yer Grace," Doyle said at last.

Resting his hands on his hips, Rohan searched the faces of the guilty men for a long moment with a brooding stare. Scanning the line of angry, resentful scowls, he took note of Pete and Denny Doyle, Caleb's nephews.

Each about twenty years old, these two alone seemed resigned to their fate. The other four looked prepared to start fighting again.

"Take them to the dungeon," he ordered his black-clad contingent of personally trained guards.

"Yes, sir," said trusty Sergeant Parker. He and his men took the shipwreckers from the chastened smugglers, answering their curses and attempts to writhe free with a rough bit of muscle.

Rohan watched as his soldiers marched the villains out of the great hall in chains.

There now, that wasn't so hard, was it? he

almost said to the remaining smugglers, who were to be spared. But when he looked at them again, he saw they were distraught, faced with their mates' doom, and he managed to curb his sarcasm.

Hopefully, this would at least scare the rest of them back into relatively good behavior. The hall was silent after the guilty had been marched off to the dungeon.

That, God knew, was one place not even he would have wanted to spend a night, not after some of the weird phenomena he had witnessed down there.

Flesh-and-blood enemies were one thing, but even the most invincible warrior could not battle vengeful apparitions.

He refused to say much to anyone about his occasional brushes with the dead around this haunted pile. His brother agents back in London were fond of ribbing him for his superstitions, but he shrugged off their laughter.

He knew what he knew. None of *them* came from cursed bloodlines, after all. In his circumstances, a man did well at least to pay attention to such things.

As if on cue, a burst of howling winter wind slammed the castle, like the Alchemist himself unleashing some dark new spell. Rohan shrugged off the chill, but such eerie thoughts made him all the more glad they had brought him the girl. On so foul a night, it would be good to have a warm body beside him in bed. And beneath him, and on top of him . . .

He cleared his throat, eager to get his hands on her.

"Mr. Doyle, gentlemen, you may go," he said sternly to the remaining smugglers. "You were wise to cooperate. We may now consider this matter resolved. But if I hear of any similar mischief in future," he warned in an ominous tone, "rest assured, you will not find me so forgiving." He waved his hand with an idle motion, signaling their dismissal.

"Aye, sir. Good night, then." Doyle bowed his head to him, then nodded to his followers. They hurried after the old man, no doubt as happy as he to be hastening toward the exit.

"Doyle!" Rohan called after him.

The old chief paused and turned back. "Aye, sir?"

"About the girl." Rohan looked at him wryly, wondering if he could get the old man to admit the truth about her assignment here. "She did not happen to wash ashore along with the rest of the booty your boys picked up on the night of the shipwreck, hm?"

Caleb looked astounded at the accusation. "Nay, sir! Not at all!"

His lips twisted. "Who is she?"

"A village lass, Yer Grace! She's as tired of livin' hand to mouth as we all are, but unlike the rest of us, she's pretty enough to find herself a better life in Town."

Rohan narrowed his eyes, sizing him up in amused vexation. *Why so nervous, Caleb?*

"Many a wench not half so fair as she has made a fine career in London entertainin' highborn gentl'men like yourself," the smugglers' chief hastily explained.

"These are her wishes?" Rohan inquired.

"Aye, the lass aspires to be a rich man's ladybird."

He raised an eyebrow. "Surely you do not expect me to keep her?" He already had more women in London, almost, than even he could handle — a harem, as the scandal sheets preferred to call it. What they saw in him other than a thorough rogering, he was never sure.

Not promises, that was for certain.

Doyle was shaking his head emphatically. "Not at all, sir! It's just that seein' as how Yer Grace is such a favorite with the ladies, she hoped you might be willing to, ah, show her the ropes, if ye don't mind."

A few of Doyle's men stifled coughs.

"Oh, it'll be a sacrifice," Rohan drawled. Doyle grinned — rather in relief. "What is she called?"

"Kate, milord."

"Kate what?"

"Madsen."

"Hm." The name was not familiar. "Had a bit to drink, I take it."

"Nerves, Yer Grace," Doyle answered without blinking an eye. "Well, sir, you do have, er, a certain reputation as a man of high standards. But from what I hear, our Kate should be able to keep up with you, no problem. Quite a hussy in the making, she is. We're awful proud of 'er."

Rohan's lips tilted sardonically. Leave it to a band of criminals to be proud of their daughters who grew up to become notorious London courtesans. "Thank you, Mr. Doyle. That will be all."

"Then we shall leave you to your night's enjoyment!" Doyle's cheery grin faded as he bowed out, hurrying after his men.

Eldred discreetly sent Rohan a wry look before gliding off to show their rustic visitors out.

A hussy in the making, he mused, casting a lusty glance toward the staircase as he rose from his chair. *Sounds like my kind of girl.*

CHAPTER 3

Free at last to turn his full attention to his waiting bedmate, Rohan set his weapon aside and left the great hall, still musing cynically on what Doyle had said about the girl's career ambitions.

So, he mused with a speculative gleam in his eyes, the young temptress desired a little instruction from a man of the world on how she might go about joining London's demimonde.

With her looks, she could make a fortune, and certainly, he could show her the road to perdition. Alas, he knew the route well. As it happened, he was acquainted with two or three grand madams in London discreetly offering high-priced whores to a most selective clientele.

One of these elegant abbesses would no doubt be happy to take on an alluring new girl, especially if she came recommended by him. He could hardly wait to find out if this

Kate possessed the requisite skill for the courtesan's trade. If not, and she proved awkward, why, generous soul that he was, he was perfectly willing to serve as her tutor until the Coast Guard chaps arrived to take their prisoners into custody.

Of course, he still believed Caleb had placed the girl with him to act as their little spy, but given her overindulgence in drink, the smugglers had chosen a poor secret agent. She would soon find the vice a considerable impediment to stealth.

Hopefully, she had sobered up a bit by now, having been left to her own devices for about half an hour.

As he climbed the stairs, bewitching moonlight streamed through the tall, pointed Gothic window and flooded the soaring vault of the cold stone stairwell with its silver glow.

As he reached the landing, blue shadows from the window mullions crisscrossed his rugged countenance like the war paint of his most ancient Celtic ancestors.

He paused at the window, habitually scanning for trouble. From his tower stronghold, he had an excellent view of the surrounding territory. He could see the distant lanterns of the smugglers' carriages heading back down to the village, tiny orange spheres inching down the road.

At closer range, the windows of the gate-house, where his men remained on duty, gave off a cheerful glow.

Before he turned away, his lingering gaze took in the frigid beauty of the winter night. The castle grounds had become an ice kingdom, dark but sparkling in the moon-light; hoarfrost coated the frozen garden statues and topiaries like diamond dust. No doubt, it would melt by morning, and all would be cold and bleak and gray again.

As his slow, warm breath fogged the glass before him, his hard-eyed reflection looked back at him, transparent as a ghost.

His thoughts wandered, the situation back in London gnawing at him, especially concerning their missing agent.

Rohan did not know Drake personally — only the team leaders were allowed to communicate with each other, a structure that helped to secure their covert web as a whole. The Order now believed that Drake was being held by one of the Promethean Council's most powerful members, James Falkirk, and his ever-present bodyguard and assistant, the one-eyed killer known as Talon.

He wondered if any progress had been made to locate Drake since he had left

London, but just then, Rohan felt a draft waft behind him. It raised the hairs on his nape.

Instantly, he whipped around, his heart pounding — but there was no sign of the Gray Lady, no sighting of any vengeful apparition. He had only seen her once in his life, as a youngster, after all.

He could feel . . . something. But, no. There was only darkness, empty air, and the guilt of all the previous dukes in his barbaric lineage.

The Kilburn Curse.

His belligerent posture eased, but the odd, eerie tingle still ran down his arms. He shook it off with a gruff snort and, mocking himself, went on his way, marching up the rest of the stairs with a scowl.

Absurdity. A grown man, an educated man, a peer of the realm, spooked by his own bloody house! Good God, he was a top assassin for one of the deadliest organizations in the world, taken from his boyhood like a Spartan to be turned into the fiercest of warriors.

And so he was. It was in his blood. The Warrington line had always produced the most gifted killers.

That was precisely the problem.

Hundreds of years ago, a medieval ancestor, a typical vainglorious Warrington knight, had incurred the wrath of a Promethean sorcerer, Valerian the Alchemist, who had laid the curse on his line.

"Ye mighty warriors, be ye doomed to kill that which ye love."

Ever since, every few generations, Warrington dukes had exhibited an unfortunate tendency toward killing their wives — mostly by accident, but occasionally on purpose.

This was their doom, allegedly.

Local lore claimed that his forefathers' cherished victims still roamed the silent halls of the castle by moonlight, yearning for revenge on the current duke, for whatever bloody fate had befallen them at the hands of their Warrington husbands.

All he knew was that he would be glad to leave this eerie place as soon as possible.

Good God, he was comfortable anywhere on earth except for here, could sleep soundly in a desert wilderness, indifferent to scorpions and snakes, or doze on a ship's hammock with perfect tranquility in the midst of a tempest. He feared nothing and was damned proud of it.

But here in the seat of his hallowed ancestors, he knew what it was to be haunted, if not by murdered duchesses, then certainly by the thought of what he had willingly become for the sake of the Order.

The Beast.

He never doubted that he fought on the side of good, and no one could ever say he had flinched at his duty, but killing was killing, and with his superstitious nature, he could not help but think that someday, he would have to face some sort of divine retribution for the blood he had shed.

Of course, the targets he hunted were dangerous players in the Promethean hierarchy, corrupt men in positions of power who had to be eliminated.

But some of those men he had finished in Naples had had wives and families. Sometimes he woke up in a sweat with the screams of the children he had orphaned ringing in his ears.

Indeed, he might as well be cursed, for a man such as he, an assassin, a Beast, was not fit for love, in any case.

Fortunately, he had made up his mind a long time ago that he would never allow their family curse to befall him. Especially not after seeing firsthand as a boy how love had nearly destroyed his father.

His own solution was simple: Love no one. *Do not get attached.* Avoiding entanglements was easy if a man channeled his energies toward women he could neither trust nor respect. The world was full of lecherous widows, vain adulteresses, assorted conniving whores.

Like the one waiting for him now.

Yes. Such women served their purpose. Refusing to let his dark thoughts spoil the night's much-needed release, he shrugged them off like a heavy cloak as he reached the upper hallway.

All the while, the bitter wind moaned through the castle's ancient stones like an anguished spirit.

Striding down the dark corridor, he came to the door to the solar and took out his key. Many of the castle's medieval drop-bar doors had been replaced ages ago with modern ones with keyed locks. His men had locked his chamber door to keep the girl from wandering off into certain regions of the castle not meant for prying eyes.

He unlocked the door with a quiet click. *Time to have some fun.*

But even as he turned the handle, he was already on his guard. Given his life in the Order, he was accustomed to people trying to kill him unexpectedly for no apparent reason. He stepped into his bedchamber, ready for anything.

Where is she? Sweeping the room with a

glance, he spotted a dainty white elbow poking out over the arm of the leather wing chair facing the fire.

Tallyho. The quarry had been spotted.

"Kate?" he greeted her softly, not wishing to startle her. He closed the door behind him and locked it again with a sly gleam in his eyes. "I believe you and I have not yet been properly introduced."

He slipped his key back into his waistcoat pocket. Still getting no answer, he stayed on his guard as he crossed the room, approaching her slowly.

In the next moment he saw why she had failed to respond. The girl was curled up in the armchair before the fire, and to his wary dismay, she was passed out cold.

Or was she? He raised an eyebrow. In the world as he knew it, things were not always what they appeared. She could be faking. She could be armed, for all he knew. No way in hell was he about to trust her, given her criminal associations.

"Kate," he said more firmly.

As he lowered himself to the ottoman across from her, staring at her intensely, what he saw before him was the very sketch of young, feminine vulnerability.

And of an excess of wine.

Damn. The toasty fire in the hearth must

have warmed her into a lull, but the liquid courage that Doyle said she had imbibed appeared to have been her undoing.

Someone's going to feel pretty dreadful in the morning, he thought with an ironic tilt of his mouth. She was so still, it occurred to him he had better make sure she had not drunk herself to the point of danger.

"Kate, it's Warrington. Are you all right? Can I get you anything?" he inquired as he slipped his fingers past the soft wavy fall of her light brown hair and pressed them gently to her neck, feeling her pulse.

Normal. *Glad you didn't drink yourself to death, my girl.* "Hullo? Anyone in there?"

No such luck. Impatient to find that his hunger to sample the tantalizing beauty had been so inconveniently thwarted, he studied her for a moment longer. "Very well, then. We'll play tomorrow," he whispered. "Up you go."

He moved forward and gently, ever so carefully, scooped her limp body up off the chair, fur throw and all. He shifted her in his arms, and still, she did not stir.

When her head fell onto his shoulder with an almost childlike innocence, a great wistfulness came over him. He wondered how such a lovely creature could have come to such a life — but then, noting the disturbing direction of his own thoughts, he quickly girded himself against these tender sentiments. Her misfortunes were not his affair.

He was too good an assassin ever to wear his heart on his sleeve. Carrying her over to his bed, he slowly laid her down on it. She sank into the mattress with a dreamy murmur of a sigh.

Though the protective impulse he had felt toward her earlier had returned full force, the soft and sensual moan from her lips filled him with a moment's blinding lust.

Dear God. A tremor of hunger ran through him. His stare traveled over her lax face and down her white neck to her creamy chest. He swallowed hard, gazing at her breasts.

Somehow, he became fixated on them again.

Heart pounding, he moved slowly and with caution sat on the edge of the bed. Desire slammed through his veins, but he only meant to look. She was a harlot, she wouldn't care, as long as he had money, which he did, lots of it. Yet it amazed him that such beauty could be purchased for the taking. She was exquisite, with the dusky fringe of her lashes fanned above her cheeks in sleep.

The thick and wavy cloud of her satiny brown hair flowed back from the pale oval of her face and spilled across his pillow.

He marveled at the creamy shimmer of her complexion by the firelight, her flushed cheeks like delicate pink-tinted porcelain. His gaze traveled over her smooth forehead, the delicate twin arches of her light brown eyebrows, and her small, prettily formed nose.

He would not have guessed her any common sort of wench. Then his attention strayed to her pink lips in ever-growing desire, a gathering smolder darkening his eyes.

She had a very charming chin, slightly pronounced, and hinting at a firm stubbornness of character. He wanted to nibble its smooth rounded curve.

With the drift of his imaginings, Rohan found he had to shut his eyes for a moment. He swallowed hard, took a breath, then exhaled it slowly. He chased away an all-too-vivid fantasy of loving her gently while she slept.

Trying his best to pull himself back from the hinterlands of lechery, he pulled the coverlet up over her with a dutiful motion and cleared his throat a bit. "Do you need anything, Kate," he asked loudly, "or will you be all right?"

But his fingers grazed her shoulder as he

tucked her in, and won from her lips another blissful sigh.

It was more than he could take. Needing one small touch, he let his fingertips alight on her shoulder, merely admiring the delicate bone structure.

"Kate?" he uttered hoarsely. She slept on, more temptation than he could bear. Cursing himself, he glided his fingertips from her shoulder inward along the elegant line of her collarbone.

She responded to him with a sigh of intoxicated pleasure, arching her head back, lifting her breasts slightly as her body rose to his touch. His eyes glazed over as he realized then that she was awake enough to know what she wanted.

He leaned down at once and kissed her shoulder softly, whispering her name. *"Wake to me."* She touched his head in answer, draping her arm weakly over his neck.

He moved onto the bed with her, his heart pounding. He lay beside her, close enough to consume with his lips the small, heady sigh that escaped hers.

He watched the dreamy smile that curved her lips as he began caressing her with seductive reassurance, letting her get accustomed to his touch.

"That's right. You just relax," he breathed.

He skimmed his palm down her arm, but at her elbow, he diverted his explorations to her slender waist. From there, he ran his hand down lower, to her hip.

She stretched a little like a pampered cat under his patient stroking. He bent his head at length and pressed a kiss to the white line of her tender neck.

He was rewarded with another enticing undulation of her body, drawing him closer. As his lips worked his way higher, Kate turned her mouth to his invitingly. She met his gaze for a fleeting instant before he kissed her; her glittering, heavy-lidded eyes teemed with feverish desire.

"Hullo there," he whispered, then he bent his head and claimed her mouth. Her low moan passed from her lips to his. Rohan answered in kind as he deepened the kiss, capturing her chin between his finger and thumb. She clutched two fistfuls of his shirt for a passing instant.

Her mouth tasted of red wine. He drank deeper. As she opened her mouth to his hungry kiss, he skimmed his fingertips down her throat to her chest. He slipped his hand into her gown and cupped her breast.

With tingling hands, he took her nipple between his finger and thumb and held it lightly as he kissed her. Her approving groan asked wordlessly for more. She touched his shoulders, arms, and chest as he moved downward over her body to indulge himself in sampling her breasts.

She made no move to stop him, no longer cold or shivering as she had been in the great hall, but panting, her skin aglow with newfound heat as he undid the bodice of her skimpy gown and bared her lovely breasts.

Closing his eyes, he took her nipple into his mouth and sucked until it swelled to glorious fullness against his tongue. The kiss went on and on, for she was even sweeter than he had already fantasized in the great hall. Now that he had her nipple in his mouth, he could not get enough of her.

But when she began to writhe hungrily beneath him, her moans climbing, he obliged her, taking his hand down slowly over her quivering stomach through her gown. She was wanton, but he stoked her fire by keeping a leisurely pace for now. He put his hand between her legs, giving her a taste of what she craved. She began rubbing restlessly against the snug hold of his hand cupping her mound.

He was rock hard, and enjoyed pleasuring her for a while further, feeling the dampness of her core permeating the thin cloth of her gown, but he stopped short of bringing her to climax. "Let me get undressed."

Somehow he found the strength to pull himself away from the luscious beauty laid before him. Her lips were still parted, her eyes emerald pools of helpless want as she watched him rise from the bed.

He sent her a dark half smile that bade her to be patient just for a moment or two. He shed his waistcoat, lifted his shirt over his head, then turned away and sat down briefly by the fire to take off his boots and thick wool stockings. He stood again and unfastened his breeches, shedding them, along with his warm cotton drawers. He paused to retrieve a condom from the night table, but when he returned to the bed, he halted in dismay to find that his companion was asleep — or more accurately, unconscious.

Well, bloody hell, he'd simply have to wake her up again. He scowled a bit and nudged her as he returned to bed. "Wake up, Kate," he ordered in a chiding whisper. "I've got plans for you."

He lifted her hand and pressed a passionate, craving kiss to her knuckles, waiting for her to rejoin the land of the living. But her eyes stayed closed.

When he released her hand, it fell limply

to the mattress. He groaned. "Come back, sweet. I need you." *Don't do this to me.* Determined to have his way, he tried one more time in aching hunger. Leaning down, he kissed her creamy chest in between her breasts.

There was no response.

So much for his personal charms. Damn it, the girl was elsewhere, sleeping off her drunk after what had no doubt been a very pleasant dream.

As for him, hang it all, he did not need the Order's blasted code to remind him that unconscious demoiselles were strictly off-limits. He was hardly the model of virtue, but he was not yet that far gone.

"Cruel," he reproached her in a sardonic whisper. They were just going to have to pick up this pleasant exchange again tomorrow where they had left off.

If she remembered any of it.

If not, he would be quite happy to show her again all that she had missed. God, she was tempting, he thought, letting his lusty stare roam freely over her. He felt strangely possessive, perhaps because they had given her to him as a gift: Ergo, she was his.

Ah, well, naught to be done for it. *Let the little drunkard sleep it off.* Not trusting himself to spend the night beside her in monkish virtue, Rohan got up from his bed without a sound and pulled the blankets back up over her. He put the condom away with a droll, self-mocking sigh and slipped on his banyan robe.

Still rather dazed with lust, he took one last, longing look at her over his shoulder, then he shook his head and left to sleep in another room.

The noisy drumming of freezing rain pounded the chamber's mullioned windows the next morning and slowly summoned Kate back to awareness.

At first, not quite awake, she merely lay there, enjoying the comfort of the bed and just beginning to note the unpleasant dryness in her mouth.

Strange bits of scarlet dreams drifted back to her. Thrilling sensations aroused by the most indecent liberties, and *dear me,* she thought with a flutter in the pit of her belly, the gorgeous firelit image of a naked man like a demigod coming toward her.

Unfortunately, pain routed the intriguing vision; she felt the crushing headache that awaited her before she even opened her eyes to the gray, wintry daylight filtering through the panes. When her burning eyes focused, she beheld the rumpled covers of an unfamiliar bed.

Where am I?

She shot upright with a bewildered start, only to receive a lightning bolt of pain running up from the back of her skull. She groaned and reached up to touch her throbbing head gingerly. *"Ow."*

Glancing down at herself, she noticed the undone bodice of the scanty dress she was wearing — and her jaw dropped as the night before came flooding back.

Him!

No! *Oh, my God.*

The Beast. It wasn't a dream at all! She was in the Beast's bed.

Kilburn Castle and its formidable owner, the menacingly handsome warrior-duke she had first encountered in the great hall. She remembered him now — somewhat. The details were sketchy, but the overall theme was clear.

Oh, no, no, no! The last image she recalled before she had lost consciousness was watching the Duke of Warrington taking off his clothes in order to have his wicked way with her.

A sickened wave of disbelief washed over her, but, heart pounding, she had to know the outcome. She whipped aside the covers and searched for any telltale signs of maiden blood.

There was none.

Her frantic heartbeat gradually slowed as she realized that, by some miracle, he must have left her alone. No amount of laudanum could make a woman forget having been deflowered by such a man.

How fortunate for her that she had passed out! she thought in shaky relief. Unconscious, perhaps she had not provided him with sufficient sport to hold his interest. Then she realized grimly, *He'll be back.*

At once, the desperate urge to escape sounded the alarm through her entire being. She felt awful, ill with the aftereffects of the drug the smugglers had given her, but she marshaled up all her strength to try to get out before the duke returned. She longed so badly to go home, she could almost taste it.

Scrambling out of his bed, she paused as a wave of dizziness made the room seesaw weightlessly for a second.

"Ugh." She put out a hand and braced herself against the nearest bedpost. She felt horrible, though the morning chill helped a bit. The room was cold; the fire had gone out.

Drawing upon her large reserves of stubborn determination, Kate tore through more of the cobwebs in her brain and realized she had better investigate the door. If she was locked in, she might have to use some imagination to find another exit.

Padding across the room, she grasped the latch without much hope, said a small prayer for mercy, then jerked the handle upward — hard — expecting resistance.

It opened.

She gasped. *He didn't lock it last night when he left!*

Astounded by her good luck, her heart began to race. It was the first occasion in weeks that she had a real chance at escape. There was no time to lose.

She spun around, thinking what to do next, her wild hope tinged with panic that this one chance might somehow slip through her fingers.

Knowing it could be mere moments before he or one of his servants or those blasted guards came back and stopped her, she rushed to the window and looked out to get her bearings. Which way was the village? She did not want to end up there again.

The sea was straight ahead, out beyond the high cliffs atop which the castle sat. Well, with the Continent across the Channel, that would be the south, and the village lay to the west, on lower ground. She would have to sneak off toward the east.

Good. Her home at the edge of Dartmoor was northeast of Cornwall, anyway, though how far away it was, she did not know for sure. Closer to hand, it appeared she was going to have to deal with the gatehouse, for this, as far as she knew, was the only way off the castle grounds.

When she saw the guards on duty, her burst of optimism floundered. Last night, escape had seemed too difficult, and perhaps it would never work, but she had to try.

She counted three guards huddling under the overhanging shelter of the gatehouse. They looked bored and irked by the morning's foul weather; their wet black cloaks flapping in the wind, they sipped from steaming mugs of some hot drink.

Kate shook her head to herself, biting her lower lip. How she was going to get past them, she had no idea. Once she got closer, perhaps she could find some way to divert their attention and slip past them, but how?

Surely they would spot her immediately when it came time for her to run across the open space of the inner courtyard. She would make an absurdly easy target.

There had to be a better way.

Well, she'd have to figure it out as she went, she concluded, for the longer she lingered here, the greater the chances of somebody stopping her before she could even start. In the meantime, the guards were not the only obstacle she would have to contend with. There was also the weather, which was perfectly dreadful this morning.

If she were at home in Devonshire, this precipitation would have brought a foot of snow, but here on the coast, it was warmer, limited to a nasty freezing rain.

The sea wind drove the rain in sheets, buffeting the castle just as it no doubt had for hundreds of years.

She shook her head, uneager to brave it, but not even Cornwall's version of a winter storm would stop her. One thing was certain, however. She'd need warmer clothes.

Sweeping a fierce glance over the chamber, her gaze narrowed in on the chest of drawers. She flew over to it, yanked the drawers open, and quickly helped herself to some of the duke's huge clothing.

She slipped a shirt on over her head, hastening to push up the overlong sleeves. She took a cravat of his and used it for a scarf to keep her neck warm, then absconded with two pairs of his thick woolen stockings. These would have to do instead of shoes.

Lastly, she went over and peeked in his giant armoire, snatching a dark blue jacket off a peg. It was an elegant tailored affair of soft merino wool, no doubt straight from some haughty tailor on Bond Street.

At once, she slipped it on, hurrying back to the door as she fastened the buttons. There was a smell of cologne on the coat that did strange things to her senses.

Very well, the man was not without appeal, but Satan himself could appear as an angel of light, could he not?

Never having been one for vanity, she did not pause to consider that she looked ridiculous in his giant clothes. All that mattered was escaping her captivity at last.

And when she did, she vowed, clenching her jaw, she was going straight to whatever authorities she could find to report what had happened to her. By God, she would expose the criminal goings-on around here!

So what if they didn't believe her? At the moment, she *needed* to believe that one day she might get justice, even if it was probably a pipe dream. It was the only thing that gave her the courage to move.

Ignoring her hunger and dizziness, Kate cracked open the bedchamber door and peered out into the corridor.

No one was in sight.

She slipped out of the solar without a sound, closed the door behind her, then stole down the corridor, moving stealthily along the wall. Her brief encounter with the garderobe came back to her when she spotted the little closet door at the end of the hallway. Her lip curled at the hazy memory, but she pressed on.

She approached the top of the staircase, descending in swift silence to the mezzanine, not quite sure where she was going.

Suddenly, male voices reached her, a casual conversation drifting up through the minstrels' gallery.

Needing to see where the men were so that she could avoid crossing paths with them, she crept over to the minstrels' gallery and ever so carefully peeked down into the great hall.

She drew in her breath, spotting the Beast himself followed by his butler. What was his name again?

Eldred. Oh, yes. Eldred was carrying a tray laden with covered dishes of food and a teapot. He was following Warrington, who was talking to him, but Kate noted that there were a couple of guards posted in the room, just like last night. She wouldn't be going out that way.

"You've got that headache powder?" said the duke.

"Yes, Your Grace."

"No doubt she's going to need it. Maybe now we'll find out what she's really up to." They marched past, heading for the stairs.

Kate blanched — no time to puzzle his words. *They're coming this way! Hide!* She dove out of sight behind a thick stone column that girded an arched window alcove in the mezzanine.

A moment later, Warrington's heavy footfalls marched past, trailed by the lighter, slower ones belonging to Eldred. They turned at the landing, continuing on to the upper hallway.

Oh, no, Kate thought, stealing a covert peek around the column. Wide-eyed, she realized that Warrington was on his way up to the solar. In moments, he'd discover she was gone.

Doubtless, as soon as he found her missing, he would send his minions out to hunt her. She backed out of the alcove, her heart in her throat. Speed was everything now.

As soon as they had passed, she whirled out of the alcove and bolted down the shadowy mezzanine corridor in the opposite direction, her sock-clad feet padding silently over the smooth stone floors.

She had to find a way out. She passed several rooms, but none of them seemed to offer any route of egress.

Slipping around the corner ahead, she entered a long, cloisterlike gallery lined with a row of life-sized statues: snow-white ladies, bygone Warrington duchesses carved from alabaster.

At the end of the statue gallery, however, she spied a small, arched, unobtrusive door. *That has to lead somewhere,* she thought, hurrying toward it at once. The life-sized figures gave her an eerie feeling, almost as if they were living beings watching in silence as she sped past.

She glanced over her shoulder, still dashing toward the door ahead. When she reached it, she had to shake her hands free from the overlong sleeves of the duke's jacket, then she grasped the latch.

Pulling it up, she swung the door open just a crack, with no idea what she might find on the other side.

At once, the wind caught at the door and the cold rushed in, enveloping her; but she drew in her breath, for the door opened onto the walkway atop the castle walls!

Now she would not have to cross the open courtyard — she could follow this high walkway all the way around to the upper floor of the gatehouse. This put her closer to her goal than she had dared to hope. Her heart beat faster with this unexpected encouragement.

As soon as she stepped out into the foul weather and shut the door behind her, she crouched down, using the parapets to shield her from view.

The wind shoved at her from every direction, while the freezing rain drenched her hair. In a trice, it had her shivering violently, but her more pressing concern was the thin layer of ice that coated the stone wall-walk.

Her lack of shoes made the footing even more treacherous — added to that, the frigid breeze continually tried to knock her off balance.

Already dizzy with the aftereffects of the laudanum, she swallowed hard, but she steadied herself and refused to be daunted. Staying hunched down, she began stealing down the long, windy walkway.

Her head throbbed, but she ignored the pain. Escape was everything, the only thing. This was her chance to take back control of her life.

If she failed, heaven only knew what fate might still befall her at the hands of the Beast.

CHAPTER 4

While Eldred stood by with breakfast for Kate on a tray, Rohan rapped on his bedchamber door and waited a moment for courtesy's sake.

Last night, after such extreme temptation, he had tossed and turned and lain awake for restless hours alone in the other room; this morning, he wanted answers — namely, confirmation of his suspicions that she had been sent to spy on him for the smugglers.

Admittedly, part of his impatience to wake up his "present" today came from his frank desire to finish what they had started. He was well aware that the little drunkard must feel like the very devil this morning, but no matter. He was fully prepared to give her some time to recover.

Today was a new day — and tonight would be a new night.

Savoring the memory of her sweetness in his arms, Rohan quit waiting for an invitation and opened the door, taking the initiative, as he was wont to do.

Before going in, he accepted the tray from Eldred, nodding the butler's dismissal. He would deliver her breakfast personally, always happy to play the lover when it came to a woman he had decided would be his next conquest. As he walked in, he masked his genuine eagerness to see her again behind a tone of sardonic amusement. "Rise and shine, my blossom."

He nudged the door shut behind him with his foot, then eyed the rumpled bed in heated anticipation.

Kate was not in it. *Ah.* She must be behind the folded screen in the corner, he thought, making use of the necessary. Lud, he hoped she wasn't back there casting up her accounts.

"How are you this morning?" As he set the tray on the dresser, he noticed one of the drawers hanging open. *Odd.* He shut it. "You may not feel up to eating yet, but I brought you something for the headache."

No answer was returned to him: No sound came from behind the screen.

"Kate?"

There wasn't a sound in his chamber. He suddenly realized that he sensed no other presence in the room. "Kate," he said more firmly, furrowing his brow. He glanced behind the screen, but no one was there.

He walked out into the hallway, resting his hands on his waist. Where the deuce was she?

Perhaps she was hungry and had made her way downstairs to find the kitchens on her own — but he had not passed her on his way up. His frown deepened. He did not like the thought of her wandering around the castle unescorted. Some of the oldest parts of the compound were dangerous. Moreover, there were areas of his home he'd rather a stranger not see.

He suddenly wondered if he should have locked her in last night. After what had happened between them, it had not seemed necessary. True, a tipsy young harlot was not exactly a paragon of virtue, but having met the alluring Kate for himself, and having found her to be not precisely what he'd call a threat, he would've felt like a Beast, indeed, to have locked the girl in his chamber as if she were some sort of prisoner.

He did not want any woman to view him as a monster.

Only the Order's enemies need think that.

He started to walk away to search for her downstairs, but he suddenly paused. She wouldn't have tried to leave the building for some strange reason, would she?

Something made him stop, walk back into the solar, and go to look out the bay window, which offered an excellent view of all the castle grounds.

There! He spotted her at once and narrowed his eyes, leaning closer. *I'll be damned.*

She was sneaking along the walkway atop the castle walls. *What the devil — ?*

She's stolen something, he thought at once. The open drawer. She must have taken something from the room.

Well, she wouldn't have found much more than perhaps a gold watch or a jeweled cravat pin, he thought with a quick glance over his shoulder at his bedchamber.

He certainly did not keep any type of sensitive information in the room. So what was her game? Probably petty thieving, considering where she had come from. Well! How dare she show him such disrespect, raiding his chamber, then sneaking off without so much as a by-your-leave? With whom did she think she was dealing?

With a scowl, he grasped the latch on the ancient window, intent on shouting down to her to stop. It had not been opened in ages, however, considering his usual absence from the castle. Today's freezing rain had further sealed it with a layer of ice.

The thing did not want to open, and he did not want to break the ancient glass panes by using too much brute strength. Growling under his breath, he restrained his frustration, jiggling the stupid latch while Kate made her way stealthily toward the gatehouse tower.

Truly, he could not believe his eyes. Her furtive exit seemed dangerously close to a rejection by a female, an experience almost wholly beyond his understanding of reality. With an indignant bang on the window's frozen seam with the heel of his fist, he dislodged the ice.

The jammed window popped free; he pushed both sides outward. At once, the cold swept in, and the loud clatter of the freezing rain filled the room. Daft little hellion, what was she thinking, going out half-naked in this weather? Was his company so very objectionable? She wasn't even wearing any shoes! She had wrapped herself in one of his coats, which hung down to her knees, but he could see she was already soaked to the skin.

Well, she might have decided that she didn't like him, but he was not about to let the little henwit catch her death running away in this cold, gray, miserable slop. He leaned out the window a bit, cupping his mouth to be heard above the clatter of the ice pellets bulleting out of the sky.

"Kate!" he bellowed. *"Halt!"*

The wind made sport of his command, snatching at his words and tossing them away toward the sea, but she had heard him, all right. She skidded to a precarious halt on the icy flagstones of the walkway, looked over her shoulder, spied him in the window, and blanched as she met his matter-of-fact stare.

"Going somewhere?" he inquired loudly as he rested his hands on the window ledge and raised an eyebrow at her.

She shot back a glare in answer, then she simply ran, no longer bothering to crouch down behind the parapets.

If actions spoke louder than words, her answer was clear, and once more, Rohan was astonished. The saucy tart wanted no part of him. *We'll just see about that!* Noting the way she was headed, he realized her destination was probably the little door still several yards ahead of her, which opened into the upper story of the gatehouse tower.

He took it as confirmation that her goal was to get back to the smugglers' village with whatever booty she had managed to lift from his chamber.

"Findlay!" he shouted, waving his arm to

attract the attention of one of the guards on duty. He could see a few of his men staying out of the weather as best they could while keeping their posts at the gatehouse.

It took a moment for one of the men to hear his shout above the constant loud splatter of the rain.

"Sir?" Findlay shouted back, coming out of their shelter toward him. The men's black cloaks blew every which way as they approached across the inner courtyard.

Shielding their eyes from the needling rain, they gazed up at the window at Rohan.

"The girl! She's coming your way! Stop her!"

"Pardon, Your Grace?"

He pointed angrily at the wall, but even as they followed his gesture and turned to look, Kate slipped into the little side door on the upper story of the gatehouse.

Findlay turned back to him, raising his hands in an eloquent shrug.

Rohan cursed, realizing he had only served to distract the guards, thus making it all the easier for Kate to sneak out the front.

"Get the girl!" he boomed, pointing to the castle gates. *"She's getting away!"*

Bloody hell.

In the blink of an eye, he abandoned the

window, bolted out his chamber door, and went rushing down the stairs to go after the little hoyden himself.

"Sir! What is the matter?" Eldred surged toward him in surprise as Rohan came barreling down the steps.

"The girl's run off. I don't think she likes me," he said wryly, then he dashed down the corridor and pushed the massive door aside.

Without his greatcoat, he was instantly drenched by the pelting rain, though its prickly ice edges melted on contact. Striding out into the courtyard, he saw that his men had finally caught on and now gave chase; Kate raced ahead of the pack like a fox, her short lead already diminishing.

Rohan followed as the whole group moved out of sight beyond the castle walls. The light crusting of ice on the dead winter grass made every step crunch as he jogged after them, wondering what he would say once they'd caught her.

Obviously, she had changed her mind about trying to join the London demimonde. Did she think he'd object? It was all the same to him. Let her do as she pleased.

In the next instant, however, his heart skipped a beat, every protective male instinct in his blood summoned when he suddenly heard her scream.

He sprinted automatically, speeding to the scene as fast as his body could move.

About thirty yards beyond the castle gates, he saw a stand-off that made his blood run cold.

His men had cornered the girl on the edge of a hundred-foot cliff overlooking the sea.

The salt wind buffeted her, whipping the dark, wet cords of her hair around her pale face, while under her sock-clad feet, the weather had slicked the rough folds of rock, making her perch on the cliffside all the more perilous.

He slowed his pace as he approached, his forceful heartbeat easing, his breathing deepening as his training took over, his mind locking into emergency mode.

Details of the whole scene before him sharpened, his men's agitation, yelling at her as if they could not see her vulnerability, or how scared and small she looked in his oversized coat, drooping in the rain.

Behind her, the cold, indifferent, pewter sea stretched to the horizon.

Kate was holding out her cold-reddened hands, warning his men back in fury as Rohan strode into their midst, with one goal — to defuse the situation. She needed to be calmed, and she had to be protected, if only from herself.

She could so easily fall from the precipice, and that spelled certain death. In a most unhurried fashion, Rohan walked past the bristling line of guards, all his focus taking her in.

"What's going on, Kate?" he asked softly.

"Stay back!" she screamed. "I swear I'll jump if you come any closer, I'll do it."

He obeyed, at least for the moment. He stopped about ten feet away, but stared at her intensely, as if he could slow time and the wind itself to keep her secure.

"Easy, now. Come away from there, Kate," he cajoled her as gently as possible.

"Go to Hell!"

"No one is going to hurt you, sweet. I just want to help."

"Oh, really?" Her voice was shaky, but her incredulous glare was fraught with rage. "Then call off your dogs!"

"Fall back!" he commanded at once. He looked over his shoulder to make sure his men backed off far enough to satisfy her. He did not want them frightening her any further. He gazed at her again, wondering if Caleb had saddled him with a madwoman. "All right? You're in control now. We'll do as you say."

She shook her head at him with an angry scoff. "Right!"

"Kate: Listen to me. Come away from the edge. You mustn't stand there. These cliffs are very unstable. They crumble all the time without any warning. This rain has probably weakened them more. It's not safe."

"Safe?" she echoed miserably. "I don't even know what that word means anymore."

Training or no, his heart pounded at the prospect of this beautiful girl with the tragic green eyes killing herself right in front of him. He could not allow it to happen. He just wished he had some idea of what demon was driving her.

Something was obviously very wrong, beyond his earlier assumptions. "Kate. Please." He clenched his jaw, inching forward ever so slightly, but taking pains not to make any sudden moves. "Tell me what is the matter."

"You expect me to trust you?"

"What is it you want?"

"I want to go home!" she wailed.

"Then you shall," he promised softly. "But come away from there, my dear. It isn't worth it. Those rocks are icy. You're soaking wet. Come in and have breakfast —"

"Don't toy with me!" she wrenched out. "God, I can't bear any more cruelty."

"What cruelty?" he asked in amazement. "Has someone on my staff been unkind to you?"

She laughed at him and turned away in disgust, shaking her head.

His heart leaped into his throat because he thought at that moment she was going to do it — going to jump.

His glance homed in, swiftly calculating the distance between them — seven or eight feet, now that he had moved closer — but before he could spring, she looked at him again, this time with hopeless tears in her eyes.

"Please, Your Grace. Just let me go. I swear, I won't tell anyone. But I'm not going back in that cellar," she whispered barely audibly. "And I'd rather die than live as any man's slave."

Rohan stared at her in shock. "What cellar?"

"As if you don't know!" she screamed at him in sudden fury.

"Kate — I don't have the slightest idea what you are talking about!"

At that moment, a loud crack and rumble split the air.

She glanced around wildly and started to rush forward, but she was too late — before his horrified eyes, the ledge crumbled under her weight like a trapdoor.

Before the shriek had even left her lips, he dove forward onto his stomach with a lightninglike move, grabbing her arm as she fell. Flat on his belly at the edge of the broken cliff, he pulled back, counterbalancing his weight, while dimly aware of his men's wild shouts.

In that instant, plagues, fires, wars — all the terrible things he had seen in his thirty-four years flashed through his mind like a deck of cards being expertly shuffled in the hands of a cardsharp . . . all the things that had nearly stripped him of his humanity.

Time bowed, taut with the echo of the various targets he had been sent to kill for the Order. He could still hear them begging in vain for their lives.

Somehow, all of it paled in comparison to the sight of Kate dangling off the cliff's edge — and the prospect of losing his grip on her rain-slicked arm.

His heart slammed as the seconds dripped like the rain off the tip of his nose.

A hundred feet below, the fiercely churning sea yawned, waiting to swallow her. The white waves broke with violent sprays of foam over the jagged boulders.

Gritting his teeth, he clasped her left arm with his right hand, taking a stronger hold.

"Hold on to my arm," he ground out.

She obeyed, her right hand clawing onto his forearm; he braced himself on the ledge with his left hand as Kate looked up into his eyes with a pleading, panicked stare that begged him not to let her go.

"Help me," she choked out.

With a heave of furious strength, Rohan pulled her up, dragging her higher until he was on his knees. She gained the ledge. He fell back, hugging her to him.

She collapsed on his heaving chest, shaking, soaked, and panting. Her slim body felt frozen to the bone atop him; she choked on a sob.

He rolled her onto the wet, frigid, hopefully solid earth beside him, and took approximately three seconds to catch his breath. But years of survival training had begun to drive him now. He stood up, scooping Kate into his arms.

She let out a small cry as he slung her over his shoulder and strode at a swift pace past Eldred and his men, who were standing by to help.

Rohan ignored them. The men parted to let him pass as he carried her into the nearby gatehouse. Some of them followed anxiously, asking if they could help, but he did not answer, marching up the narrow steps to the heated guardroom in the gate tower's upper story.

"Stay out," he ordered them, shutting the door in their faces.

A fire crackled in the hearth. He carried her across the wood-plank floor to the chair in front of the fire. The simple guardroom had a timber-beam ceiling and plain stone walls.

Depositing Kate unceremoniously in the chair, he scanned the room like an eagle-eyed sentry and retrieved a blanket the men kept on a shelf for those long night watches. He shook it open and wrapped it around her shaking body without a word, then noted the kettle hanging over the fire. He took a mug off the rugged wood mantel and poured her a cup of what proved to be mulled cider.

His hands were steady as he poured it, and his mind was crystal clear, but some deep, savage part of him wanted to roar at having just pulled this woman out of the mouth of the monster, death. His old friend! Why, it seemed he had saved a life for once instead of taking it.

How novel, he thought acidly.

Moving with angry, automaton-like precision, he turned and held the steaming mug toward her, but she was staring at nothing, apparently in shock.

He put the cup in her shaking hands. "Drink this," he ordered in a most uncompromising fashion.

Still dazed by her narrow brush with catastrophe, Kate slowly lifted her stunned gaze to his face.

Warrington looked furious.

She took in his taut-lipped expression; the jagged star-shaped scar carved in his skin at the outer corner of his left eyebrow. A small streak of mud slashed across his cheek like war paint.

Iron authority was stamped across his closed, hard face. His pale eyes glittered as he held her gaze.

She had nothing left to fight him with, so she simply bent her head and took an obedient sip of the mulled apple cider, as commanded. It left a warming trail all the way to her belly, but it could not fill her emptiness at the moment. Her heart felt as hollow as a drum.

The Beast turned away, apparently not quite ready to deal with her yet. Kate did not know what to think: The man she had reason to fear the most had just saved her life.

Where did that leave her now?

Wrapping her hands around the mug, she shut her eyes, still hearing the horrific sound of the stone ledge breaking under her.

If not for Warrington, she would be dead.

A tremor ran through her.

She had threatened suicide as a final, desperate measure to gain her freedom, but even the earth itself seemed to be against her, delivering her back to him, whether she liked it or not.

She had been so close to escape! But now her hopes were dashed. She was glad to be alive, of course, but having been recaptured, she feared she might be in for an even darker fate now that she had displeased the man she had been "given" to, had made him risk his own life to save hers. Now Warrington could claim that she *owed* him whatever he might want. Even now, she could feel his silent anger throbbing through the Spartan little room.

Dear heaven, what punishment might she have to endure for her attempt to flee? She let out a long, shaky exhalation, tears threatening behind her closed eyes. As she huddled in her chair and held the mug close, letting the curling steam warm her nose, she searched her heart to find out if there was any fight left in her.

Always, the thought of her seafaring papa

gave her another little ounce of strength to keep holding on.

The memory of the man who had laughed in the face of a tempest, along with the sweet, spicy taste of the cider with its bracing hint of cinnamon began, ever so gradually, to bring her back to the world of the living.

At least she did not deceive herself into some vapid dream that Warrington had pulled her back to safety because he somehow cared. She was not a fool. He had spoken kindly to her outside — the thought of his gentle tone sharpened the sting of unshed tears behind her eyes.

How she longed for someone to be kind to her. But she swallowed hard and thought, *No.* She would not fall for that ruse. She did not dare believe in it. He did not care about her. His heroic rescue was more likely due to the fact that if a dead body were spotted floating in the ocean around here, it could draw unwanted attention to the secret trade in kidnapped women that the smugglers were operating on behalf of the libertine duke and his unspeakable rakehell friends.

Easy, Kate. I just want to help.

Of course, you do, Your Grace.

When she opened her eyes again in bristling uneasiness, he had just stepped past her to throw another log onto the fire.

A discreet knock on the door sounded just then. "Sir?" a voice queried from the other side.

"What is it, Eldred?" the autocrat clipped out.

"Will the young lady require the physician? I can send down to the village straightaway."

Warrington cast her an ominous glance. "Do you want the doctor?"

Kate shook her head vehemently. "No. No one from the village." She was a bit banged up overall, her shoulder wrenched from when the duke had grabbed her arm and stopped her from plunging over the cliff, but other than that, she was none the worse for wear.

He eyed her skeptically but did not argue. "The physician won't be necessary, Eldred. Just some dry clothes for us both."

"Very good, sir, but, er, I am not altogether certain we have any ladies' apparel."

"Improvise then, Eldred! It's not the promenade. Bring boys' clothes if that's all we've got for her. She can hardly go round naked. As much as I might enjoy that," he added in a low, sharp aside to her.

She furrowed her brow.

He looked pleased at having goaded a reaction from her, however mild. Then he passed a bold, leisurely gaze over her body. "One of the younger footmen ought to be about her size," he said in the direction of the door. "Shoes for her, too, Eldred." To her, he drawled: "Ever heard of those? Astonishing new invention."

Kate's frown deepened to a guarded scowl; she was not sure what to make of his sardonic tone. This was hardly a time for rude jests.

"Very good, sir," his butler answered. "I shall return post-haste."

When Eldred withdrew from the other side of the door, Warrington sent a pointed glance in her direction, then he took off his wet, mud-covered jacket and threw it on the hearthstones.

It occurred to Kate that he was cold and soaked with rain, as well. While she took another sip of the cider, doing her best to mind her own business and furtively trying to figure out what he might do next, he unbuttoned his waistcoat and stripped it off, too.

The fine silk was soiled from his lying on his stomach at the edge of the cliff. The memory of it shook her once again, making her hands tremble and the cider slosh.

But when Warrington lifted his shirt off over his head in the next moment and threw it onto the pile, Kate went perfectly still.

She held her breath with an unblinking stare as he crouched down nearby, warming his hands before the flames.

Her gaze traveled over his beautiful back, that glorious expanse of smooth skin she had caressed so eagerly last night — to her shame.

She wished she couldn't remember at all, for what could be worse than to desire a man who meant one's destruction?

Yet she could not deny her awe at his leonine beauty, all dangerous power, his massive, sculpted size balanced by effortless male grace. Her wistful stare followed the sweeping line of his lean sides and stone-carved arms as he warmed his hands before the hearth fire.

Between his broad shoulder blades, his sable hair hung in a thick, glossy queue. Kate watched a droplet of rain run off his wet hair and roll down his back.

As he rubbed his hands together, she was riveted by the complex play of chiseled muscle that flowed through his upper body with the simple motion. She was especially entranced by his fortresslike shoulders and those incredible arms, whose raw strength had saved her life. She looked away, feeling a bit faint. Never in all her days had she seen a physique like that on a man.

Well, except for last night. When he had taken advantage of her in her drugged state — though not as fully as she had feared . . .

Why did he hold back? What is going on? she thought, beginning to feel routed. *Why does a man who looks like that and has his rank and wealth need to buy a woman, anyway?* Surely he could have any female he liked for free with naught but a devilish smile and a crook of his finger.

Because of cruelty, she reminded herself, but with her head finally clearing after the laudanum's aftereffects, her certainty about everything had begun to erode, much like the cliff that had fallen away from beneath her.

Could he ever know how fragile she felt in that moment? How scared? How close to complete despair? How could a man who looked nearly invincible ever relate to her sense of powerlessness? He could not understand it, nor did he care. She was alone. Always alone.

She quite feared she was on the verge of becoming undone, hanging by a thread, even as she sat there quietly.

He, too, was silent, perhaps realizing what a close call that had been. Then, without warning, he turned to her and asked in a low, searing tone: "What cellar?"

She looked at him for a long moment. "You should have let me die."

His black eyebrows drew together in vexed confusion at her answer. "Why did you run?" he demanded.

"Wouldn't anyone have done the same thing in my place?" she wrenched out.

"No, actually!" he retorted, his scowl deepening. "Believe it or not, some women even seek out my company. What cellar?" he repeated more forcefully.

Kate couldn't stand any more of his lies. *What cellar?* she repeated angrily as she set down her drink. Staring at him, something in her snapped. "The one where they kept me all those weeks before they handed me over to you! A gift to the mighty Duke of Warrington . . . from his *filthy criminal minions*!" Her thunderous condemnation echoed through the chamber, but there was no taking back the words once she had let them loose.

On the contrary, she could feel the rising anger breaking from her, cresting, crashing like the waves that had almost been her grave. Perhaps she would never receive justice, but everything in her demanded that at least she make a stand.

"You should be ashamed of yourself," she charged on in trembling wrath as she rose slowly from her chair. "You and all your soulless henchmen."

"What?"

"Oh, feign innocence as you please, Your Grace — but I know now that *you're* the one behind this wicked scheme. The smugglers aren't smart enough to do this on their own!"

He looked at her in slack-jawed astonishment, which only emboldened her more.

So, he wasn't used to anyone standing up to him? Well, he might kill her for her insolence, but by God, now that she had his attention, she would speak her piece!

To the end, she would hold her head high — and go out with a flourish.

Her father would be proud. "Come, who else is a party to this scheme?" she dared to taunt the Beast, though, as he rose from his crouched position, he towered over her.

She didn't care anymore. She refused to live another day in fear. "Your fellow libertines from this Inferno Club I've heard about? A fitting name for you demons, considering you all are bound for Hell!"

"For what, pray tell?" he inquired.

"For abducting innocent girls — to use as your wretched playthings!"

He paled — with guilt, no doubt.

"You make me sick." She began to turn away, but he grasped her arm and turned her around quickly.

"What are you saying, exactly?" he demanded.

She pulled back, but he didn't let go.

"Do you actually claim that you were abducted?"

"Claim?" she nearly screeched. "Oh, what schoolboy lies —"

"Answer me!"

"You know full well I was!" she exploded as she jerked away in rage, then pointed an accusing finger in his face. *"You're* the one who gave the order for it!"

CHAPTER 5

Kate stood her ground in wild courage, but a dark and frightening chill had come over Warrington's demeanor.

He looked absolutely stunned.

"I did nothing of the kind," he ground out, holding her stare. "Nor would I. Ever."

Fists clenched, chest heaving, she eyed him warily. A denial was the last thing she had expected from a man too powerful to care about her objections to his criminal dealings.

Indeed, what she half expected from him was a backhand across the face like O'Banyon had given her, but she would not bow her head. By God, she would not. If the brute was going to strike her, let him look her in the eyes.

She held her chin high while he searched her face.

"Is that why you threatened to kill yourself, why you ran away?" he demanded.

She kept her mouth shut, suddenly not sure what to believe.

"Tell me what happened," he ordered. "If what you claim is true —"

"*If?*" she cut him off in outrage.

"You should've told me this last night!"

"Tell the man I had been given to as a gift? How could I? Why waste my breath, when you were the one behind it?"

"I was *not* — Good God, I would never harm a woman!" he thundered, his deep voice booming through the guardroom. "I had no knowledge of this whatsoever! I'm telling you the truth!"

"You accepted the gift," she pointed out.

"I thought you wanted to be here!" He fell silent, then shook his head in furious amazement. "It appears we both have been deceived." He turned away abruptly and, still shirtless, stalked to the door, all rippling muscle and tense, silent rage. He reached for the handle and nearly tore the door off its hinges, opening it. "*Findlay!*"

"Yes, sir!"

"Take my carriage down to the village and bring me Caleb Doyle. *Go!*" he roared, when the guard did not move fast enough for him. Kate jumped when he whammed the door shut. "How dare they?" he growled under his breath, obviously enraged, but also mortified, perhaps, to learn that he might have been duped by the lowly smugglers. "By God, if this is true . . ."

"It *is* true," she informed him, folding her arms across her chest as he began pacing. "I am not a liar."

He shot her an ominous look with a dark air of utter seething wrath and prowled over to the arched stone tracery window overlooking the inner courtyard. He braced his hands on the window ledge, his brooding stare fixed on the gray day beyond the glass.

She noticed the large, red scrape across the underside of his forearm. He must have got it on the sharp rock edge when he had stopped her from going over the cliff, but he did not even seem aware of the wound.

"Allow me to assure you on my most sacred oath, Miss Madsen, that your accusations of me are in error." He looked over his shoulder at her with a pointed glance. "Caleb Doyle lied to me. And he will be dealt with. He told me you wanted my help to begin a new career in London as a . . ." He closed his eyes and shook his head again with a self-directed epithet.

"A whore?" she finished bluntly for him as she struggled to piece together the bits she could remember through the drug's haze. "Yes. Some of the smugglers' wives made me look like that on purpose, so you would find me — appealing. But that is not at all the kind of person I am. Or was, before all this." She pointed at his arm. "You're hurt."

"I don't care." He turned from the window and looked into her eyes, the cold winter light bathing his iron-sculpted torso in its silver-gray glare. "Who did this to you, Kate? I need you to tell me exactly what happened."

She hesitated. The possibility that he might be telling the truth, that he really wasn't involved in this, gave her a glimmer of hope that maybe, just maybe, all of this could eventually be made right. He was a duke, after all, the smugglers' landlord. He had the power and the authority to help her get justice if he was inclined to.

She did not dare raise her hopes overmuch quite yet.

"A few of the smugglers' wives made me wear this horrid dress and painted my face like a harlot's." She lowered her gaze. "The rest is a bit foggy, I'm afraid, on account of the laudanum they forced down my throat."

"Laudanum?" he asked with a startled, guilty wince.

"They drugged me so I wouldn't fight you."

At this, the fury that flared in his eyes was unlike anything she had ever seen.

He turned away, looking like he wanted to rip someone's head off. He drummed his fingers on the window ledge for a second, then let out a measured exhalation. "I'm sorry, Kate — last night, I did not know. I believed the ruse. I had no reason to suspect them. I simply thought . . . you'd had too much to drink."

She was silent for a long moment, realizing that even under this misapprehension, he had left her alone. Despite thinking her a lowly, drunken whore, the so-called Beast had behaved like a gentleman.

"This is all very confusing," she murmured.

He nodded in sharp-edged agreement, then went to the fireplace and picked up the poker, jabbing at the logs.

As sparks popped in the hearth, he stared into the flames, seeming to take a certain comfort from having something that resembled a weapon in his hand.

Kate watched him in guarded fascination, beginning to wish he would put on a shirt. All that sleek, bare, male flesh was a little too distracting.

Returning the poker to its stand, he turned to her, his rugged face set with determination. "Kate, it's very important that you tell me exactly what happened to you, from the beginning. I'm sure it's difficult to recount, but if my tenants are committing crimes of this magnitude, I need to know the details so I can put a stop to it immediately. You help me get to the bottom of this, and I promise that you will see justice."

That word got her full attention. She met his gaze sharply. Aside from going home to her cottage, justice was the thing she wanted most.

"We will get this sorted out," he assured her. "Now, I've ordered Doyle brought to the castle so you and I both might get some answers. It's hard for me to fathom he would sanction such a thing — I've known the old man since I was a boy. But I also know his authority is being challenged lately by some of the younger men. Perhaps they're the ones behind it. Firstly, I need to know if there were any other girls in that cellar with you, or if you saw any others who might also have been taken, as you were."

She shook her head. "I did not see any, but that doesn't mean they're not there."

"Very well. I'll have my men search the village anyway. We'll tear apart every house from top to bottom if we have to, and every fishing boat, as well, in case there are any girls being kept out there. Now, I'm going to need a clear picture of the facts so I can help you."

When she did not immediately answer, he scanned her face in regret. "You still don't trust me."

She gave a wary shrug as she drew the coarse blanket more tightly around her. "It's just — they told me some rather alarming things about you."

"I can imagine." He shook his head. "Kate, dealing with such tenants as these . . . let's just say they see what I want them to see." He reached out and gently wiped away a spot of dried mud on her cheek that she hadn't known was there. "If I were as bad you were led to believe, would I have left my bed last night so you could sleep in peace?"

The light touch of his fingertips on her face now, and the memory of how she had writhed beneath his skillful caresses last night brought a scarlet blush to her cheeks.

She looked away; he lowered his hand to his side.

He was silent for a moment. "You are in no danger, Kate. I am not going to hurt you. I know you are afraid, but look at my actions if you doubt my words. I saved your life, didn't I? That must count for something."

She looked up slowly, her gaze skimming the chiseled symmetry of his muscled abdomen and the powerful swells of his chest until she met his steady gaze.

The look in his gray-blue eyes seemed sincere, and she desperately longed to believe in him. He might be her only hope. With a reluctant nod, she decided to trust him with her story and see where it might lead. In truth, she had nothing left to lose.

Still shivering a bit from her brush with death, she sat down in her chair once more and took a deep breath. "It was the twenty-seventh of November, about ten o'clock at night. I was sitting at home in my cottage on the southwest edge of Dartmoor, just reading by the fireplace. Waiting for the kettle to boil. I was making tea. How far away are we from there, anyway?"

He considered. "About twenty miles."

"Twenty miles," she echoed in amazement. It was the farthest she had gone in ages.

"You were saying?"

"Yes — I was reading by the fire, when all of a sudden, three filthy ruffians burst into my house. There was no warning, not even time to react. It happened so fast. They dragged me outside and threw me into a carriage, where I was bound hand and foot. Then two of them went back inside to steal any valuables they could find."

Warrington leaned against the mantel, watching her. He appeared to be taking great pains to restrain himself, keeping his face carefully expressionless. But something in his eyes had turned quite terrifying.

As he listened to her with his arms folded across his chest, his fingers slowly tapped his massive biceps. He nodded at her in encouragement. "Go on."

She swallowed hard. "A few minutes later, the other two returned to the carriage. I heard one of the younger men address the leader as 'O'Banyon.' Do you know a man by that name, Your Grace?"

He shook his head. "No, but I assure you, I will find him. Continue, please. And by the way, between last night and nearly dying together this morning, I'd think we're past the formalities. Call me Rohan."

His invitation surprised her, but she resumed her account, unsure if she wanted to take him up on it. "As soon as the other two men got into the carriage, we drove off at breakneck pace to the smugglers' village. When we got there, they hauled me out of the coach and locked me down in a cellar for, I think, it's been five weeks. *Five weeks,*" she added resentfully. "I spent Christmas in that cellar, in the dark, alone."

She would have been alone on Christmas, anyway, but that was not the point. "It was just a few days ago that the smugglers finally brought me up to a bedchamber in the house above the cellar. I didn't know why at the time, but I see now it was because they had decided to get me ready for you."

The very room throbbed with his brooding silence. "Tell me," he murmured, "would you recognize your kidnappers if you were to see these men again?"

"Absolutely. Why?"

"Because I think it altogether possible that I may already have them locked up in my dungeon."

"Really?" she breathed as an unholy eagerness for revenge took hold of her. "Now, that is a sight I would love to see."

Her fierce reply appeared to please him. He tilted his head slightly, studying her with a searching gaze, just as a knock on the door signaled his servant's return. He gave her a shrewd glance and went to answer it.

"Here are the things you asked for, sir."

Kate turned in her chair as Eldred gave the duke an armload of dry garments.

"Will there be anything else, Your Grace?"

"No, thank you, Eldred. This will do."

The butler bowed and pulled the door shut while Rohan carried the clothes into the room and deposited them on the table.

Kate watched him with veiled admiration as he reached for the fresh shirt his servant had brought him and slipped it on over his head. He pulled the dry coat on, as well, and headed for the door with a look of grim determination.

"Come below when you're ready," he ordered, sending her a nod of encouragement. "You and I are going to get some answers."

Rohan stepped out of the watchmen's chamber and pulled the door shut behind him, leaving Kate to dress in privacy.

He paused, letting out a long exhalation and shaking his head in shock over all she had told him. Then he marched down the dim, narrow stairs to the sparse room below, where a couple of the guards remained on duty.

They rose when he joined them, asking if the young lady was all right. He nodded and continued pacing, as he had upstairs.

In point of fact, he was too furious to stand still. Now that the whole story of her nightmarish ordeal had come out, he could not wait to get his hands on the men who had done this to her.

They were going to pay.

Last night, his anger at the smugglers had been mostly for show. Today, by God, they were going to find out what his rage looked like when it was genuine.

Damn it, he had known Caleb had seemed nervous about something, but he had attributed it to guilt over the shipwreck! Now that he knew there was more to it, he would wring the old man's neck for trying to trick him into deflowering a drugged, abducted virgin.

Why? Why would Caleb have deliberately tried to lure him into unwitting involvement in this? If Kate had not passed out before he could make love to her, he would have been as badly bound up in this perfidy as the smugglers were. To be sure, what had seemed a dashed inconvenience last night had proved a boon.

He shook his head with a black look as he continued pacing. Something here wasn't making sense.

His people were no saints, but he simply could not bring himself to believe they would resort to trafficking in abducted females.

Then again, he had not expected them to

resort to shipwrecking in their desperation, either.

Rohan paused to glare absently out the window, lost in his roiling thoughts, rather sickened to realize that he was partly responsible for this. If he did not spend so much time abroad on his various missions for the Order, the smugglers would not have dared try such a thing.

Yet they had gone beyond trying. They had terrorized this poor, defenseless beauty.

He would make them rue it.

As for Kate, after all she had been through, she had impressed him with her self-possession, to say nothing of her fiery spirit. She had stood there ready to battle him like some spunky little terrier barking at a wolf, aye, and throwing the greater predator into temporary confusion with her unexpected show of ferocity.

Though petite of build, she was large in courage, a little lady of intrepid spirit, he thought, just as the sound of the door opening above heralded her return.

Slowly, he raised his hungry gaze and held his breath. God forgive him, he wanted her still. He throbbed at the mere sound of her hesitant footsteps creeping down the stairs. Who was this woman, that she should have such a deep effect on him?

When she appeared, however, he pressed his lips together and fought the urge to smile. She looked comical, in an adorable sort of way. Something about her made his heart clench. Dressed in the clothes Eldred had found for her, she looked like some sort of angel-faced page boy. But the glance she shot him warned that if he said a word, it might well cost him his head. He dropped his gaze, stifling a chuckle; she cleared her throat and lifted her chin, clearly determined to press on with the business at hand, never mind her ridiculous appearance.

Her businesslike attitude only amused him more. His twinkling gaze traveled up from the black boots on her feet, up to the dark blue breeches that revealed the shapely turn of her legs and a sweetly rounded derriere.

A long livery waistcoat with brass buttons molded her waist and the flare of her lovely hips. The close-fitting sleeves of the livery coat showed off her slender arms, then widened with big, folded cuffs at the sleeves.

All she lacked was a tricorn hat to make her the world's most seductive footman. He swallowed his amusement as she pulled on a pair of borrowed gauntlets like a highborn lady heading out for a drive. This done, she swung the cloak she had been given around her shoulders, apparently eager to hide her male apparel.

"After you," Rohan invited, gesturing toward the door.

"Thank you, Your Grace." She eyed him in red-cheeked hauteur, then marched ahead, pulling up the cloak's large, draping hood to shield her face.

Dryly, Rohan nodded his thanks to the two remaining guards, who were also fighting smiles.

He got the door for his fetching little page girl, and they left the shelter of the gatehouse.

As they stepped outside, a silver burst of sun fought its way out from behind the pewter clouds, and for a moment, the thin layer of ice that still coated everything glittered with extraordinary brilliance.

With the whole courtyard sparkling around them, Rohan turned to Kate. She returned his gaze uncertainly, her creamy cheeks pink with the chill. The wintry sunbeams illuminated the raw vulnerability and the almost painful hope hidden deep in her emerald eyes.

Hope in him.

He looked away, narrowing his eyes against the glare and feeling damned uncomfortable with the knowledge that the softness she no doubt required after her ordeal was in no wise his forte.

Even so, she was gazing at him like she had decided he was some sort of hero. If she only knew the savagery he was capable of when the occasion called. That deadly gift that made the Warrington line so valuable to the Order. He did not want any woman ever to see that side of him — but at the moment, he understood that she needed someone to believe in right now.

Avoiding her stare, he scanned the castle's forbidding exterior for the shortest route to the dungeon. He spotted the door they needed and sent her a military nod.

"Follow me," he ordered, then added gruffly in spite of himself, "Careful on the ice."

CHAPTER 6

Holding the edge of the hood over her face to ward off the wind, Kate followed Rohan back to the castle in wary reluctance.

He forged on ahead like a force of nature himself, the shoulder capes and long skirts of his dark wool greatcoat billowing in the wind, and wrapping around his towering stature.

When he reached the castle, he hauled open a massive door and shepherded her inside, where they both stood for a moment, stamping the melting slush off their boots.

Then he jerked an autocratic nod in her direction: a wordless order to follow. She raised an eyebrow as he marched ahead of her once more.

She was beginning to think the man only knew how to communicate in the imperative; the fact that he was so certain of being obeyed roused the rebel in her blood. But given her situation at the moment, she

curbed her stubborn streak and obliged —
though she nearly had to jog to keep up with
his long, swift strides.

He stopped at the end of the dim stone
corridor and opened a very old-looking
wooden door. A dank draft wafted out of
the darkness beyond, reminding her of the
smugglers' cellar. Peering past him into the
void beyond the door, she grimaced slightly.
"What's down there?"

"The dungeon."

"Oh," she murmured with an involuntary
shudder.

He turned and scanned her face. "Are you
sure you're up to this?"

Glancing at him, she had to decide anew
if she really ought to trust him. If not, his
leading her down there could prove to be
the cruelest trick yet. What if he was luring
her to the dungeon only to lock her up
again?

Shoving the fear away, she nodded bravely.
She was going to have to trust somebody
sometime.

He regarded her in approval. "Good. Then
let's go get some answers."

Laying hold of her courage, Kate followed
as the Beast descended the cobwebbed
stairs into the eerie netherworld beneath
Kilburn Castle. She stayed close to him,

trailing right behind him like his shadow.

At the bottom of the stairs, the three black-clad guards on duty were warming themselves by a small blaze in the fire pit. They stood at attention when they saw the duke. "Your Grace, sir!"

"At ease." Reaching the bottom of the stairs, he greeted his men with a nod, then he turned to hand her down the rest of the way. His chivalrous gesture surprised her.

"We need to have a look at your prisoners," he informed the guards.

"Aye, sir." Asking no questions, they picked up their weapons, lifted torches from old iron sconces on the walls, and hastened to accommodate their lord's request.

Around here, it was obvious his word was law. Kate sent him a suspicious glance as the guards escorted the two of them down a rough-hewn corridor that surely led to some back door of Hell.

"Why do you keep so many guards around here?" she murmured.

He raised an eyebrow, looking askance at her. "I don't know . . . I just like having people to order around."

She couldn't help but smile at his wry nonanswer.

"Come on," he ordered with a low timbre almost of affection in his deep voice.

As they moved deeper into the cavelike labyrinth of the dungeon, the echo of the soldiers' bootheels striking rock rebounded all around them. Various aisles of rusty bars branched off this way and that.

Kate did not envy the soldiers their dark and clammy post, but it did not seem to bother them.

Torchlight flickered over the huge stone blocks that made up the castle's foundations. A faint, foul-smelling draft moved up the inky corridor and blew gently on the shredded gray veils of hanging cobwebs, causing them to float upon the air. She glanced repeatedly over her shoulder. This place raised the hackles on her nape.

As they approached the dank cells housing the prisoners, Rohan leaned closer and murmured in her ear, "They're in the cells ahead. Now, you tell me if any of these men took part in your abduction, all right?"

She nodded, warding off a startling frisson evoked by his nearness.

As they pressed on, desperate male faces began to appear behind the rusted bars of these godforsaken cells.

"Yer Grace!" The first was a tall, lumpy mountain of a young man with a sweaty face. "For the love o' God, let us out of 'ere, sir!"

"The prisoner will not speak unless spoken to," the head guard clipped out, his warning rolling down the dark corridor to the men in the other cells.

The imprisoned smugglers began to stir, leaving the stone slabs that served as their cots and coming to the bars to see what was happening.

Knowing she could come face-to-face with her kidnappers at any second, Kate felt her heart begin to pound. Instinct had her edging closer to Rohan for safety in the dark. He gave her his arm, then laid his hand over hers where she had tucked it in the crook of his elbow.

The man in the next cell was a thick-necked smuggler with a bald head and a small hoop earring. She did not recognize him, but he stared at her in her footman's garb in unwelcome curiosity.

"Eyes down!" Warrington snarled at him. "Don't you look at her. Give me that." He commandeered the torch from one of the guards and, from there, took over her guided tour of this hellish place personally.

Giving Kate his other arm, he raised the flame so she could inspect the man in the next cell.

Her blood ran cold at the sight of a shifty-looking man in his early twenties with greasy black hair and a scruffy jaw. "Him." She held on to his arm more tightly.

"Denny Doyle," he said softly. "I should have known."

The prisoner offered no sign of respect, merely sent them a sullen glance over his shoulder. "What are you lookin' at?"

"I hear you've added more than just shipwrecking to your list of accomplishments, Denny."

"I don't know nothin' about it," he replied with a shrug and a ready sarcasm, both learned, no doubt, at his smuggler mama's knee.

The guards made a disapproving move toward him. Denny Doyle jumped up and whipped around in a fighter's stance with his back to the wall, but Rohan held up his hand, calling off his men.

"In due time," he cautioned them. "You and I will talk soon," he added, pinning the miscreant with a foreboding stare. He glanced at Kate, then nodded toward the pitch-black corridor ahead. "Let's continue, shall we?"

She swallowed hard and managed a nod.

"W-what's going on, sir, please?" pleaded the skinny fellow in the next cell. "Has the Coast Guard come to take us away now?"

Spectacles perched atop his nose, but

beneath it sat a scraggly attempt at a mustache, like a smudge of coal soot dirtying his upper lip. "Your Grace? Will you let me out, sir? I'll cooperate, I promise. I don't want to die!"

"Shut up!" One of the guards banged the bars with the butt of his musket.

The little man jumped back with a yelp, but when Kate shook her head to let Rohan know that this was not one of her kidnappers, the prisoner began to cry, seeing them moving on and leaving him behind.

"God! Let me out of here! There's something down here, I tell you! Somethin' unnatural!"

"Shut it, Fitch, you cockless worm," Denny Doyle ordered from farther down the row in a tone of great disgust.

One of the guards scowled and marched back to tell him to pipe down, in turn, but Rohan merely sent Kate a dubious glance. "How are you holding up?"

"Well enough," she answered grimly.

"Good. Charming fellows, aren't they?"

She mustered a wry smile in answer.

He put his arm around her shoulders gently. "Come, we're almost through. What about this one?" He nodded at the cell ahead.

It held a tall, lanky fellow with long, carrot red hair tied back in a queue. He unfolded his gangly limbs, shot up from his cot with a quick-tempered scowl, and glared at them.

She shook her head. "No."

"One more, then," Rohan murmured. "Another Doyle. This one is a cousin to the other. They're both the old man's nephews."

Kate approached the last cell warily, gazed through the bars while Rohan held up the torch, and confirmed the last man's guilt with a grim nod. "Yes. Him, too."

"Me? What?" The fellow in the cell looked up with a blank air of utter innocence. "What's she talkin' about?"

"What, indeed?" Rohan answered dryly. "Peter Doyle, isn't it?"

"Aye, Your Grace." He stood and approached his overlord with a much humbler attitude than his cousin had shown. Sensible lad.

Rohan glanced at her. "You're sure?" he clarified with a trace of regret in his low voice.

"Certain of it," she replied.

"What do you want with me?" Peter Doyle whimpered.

The duke narrowed his eyes at him. "Oh, I think you know."

"Huh?" He gulped at Rohan's dark look

and began backing away toward the corner of his cell.

Kate glared at the prisoner. "This was the man who held me at gunpoint in the carriage while the other two went in to rob my home, like I told you."

"What the — what is she talking about?" Pete stammered, playacting amazement.

Kate seethed at his denial, but out of her three captors, he was the least intimidating.

Peter Doyle was a large but flabby rectangle of a man, also in his early twenties like his cousin, but with coarse and curly hair an uninteresting blond shade. He had nervous hazel eyes and something of a horse face.

"Is there something that you want to tell me, Pete?" Rohan focused his unnerving stare on the young man.

"Uhm, er, I . . ."

"Something to do with a kidnapping, perhaps, hm?"

"What? Sir!" he exclaimed with great indignation. "I'm sure I don't know what you mean!"

"Don't you dare deny it!" Kate flew at him without warning, gripping the bars.

"Easy, Kate."

"He was there! You dragged me from my home —"

"No, I — sir, the lass is daft. Kidnapped? What? Someone kidnapped you? I'm Caleb Doyle's nephew!" he cried, his face beginning to look quite terrified by the flickering torchlight. "Sir, you've known my family for ages! Surely Your Grace cannot believe this harlot over me? Whatever she says, she's lying!"

"Well, I believe her," he answered softly.

"I am not a harlot," Kate reminded him in a withering tone. "As you well know."

"Aye, you are!" Peter insisted. "You want to become some rich man's ladybird . . . in London! Remember?" His own conviction in his uncle's lie seemed to be dwindling, but his eyes suddenly widened when Rohan took off his coat and handed it off to a guard.

Then he removed his gloves and loudly cracked his knuckles. "Show Miss Madsen upstairs," he instructed his men. "Tell Eldred to see her settled into a guest room."

"What are you doing?" Kate murmured.

"Unlock the cell," he ordered the guard in an almost amiable tone.

"Miss, if you'll come with me." The guard gestured to her to follow.

"I'm not leaving! This is my affair as well as yours!"

"Run along, Kate."

"You won't want to see this, Miss," the guard advised her in a low tone.

"I'm not going anywhere!" she protested, shaking off the guard's light hold and turning to the duke.

He was staring at Peter Doyle like a wolf homing in on the weakest sheep in a flock.

"M-maybe she *should* stay!" Peter said with a gulp as he pressed himself flat against the far wall of his cell. "Like she said, it is her business, too, uh, right?"

"You'd appreciate that, I'm sure," Rohan murmured.

"I thought you didn't know anything, Peter!" Kate reproached him.

"I think . . . I might be remembering." He gulped. "Please, Your Grace . . . can't the lady stay?"

"Oh, now I'm a lady?" She shook her head at Pete in disgusted surprise. Obviously, the only reason he wanted her to remain was in the hope that the Beast would not unleash his full wrath in front of a woman.

Rohan was staring at Pete when she tapped him on his massive shoulder. "May I have a word with you, please, before you sound the trump for Armageddon?"

"Of course, Miss Madsen." He turned to her, looking as unperturbed if he did this sort of thing every day.

138

He took her aside.

"Is this all of the men you've got captive?" Kate whispered.

He nodded, gazing into her eyes. "Why?"

"I don't see O'Banyon, the leader."

"Do you want to look at them again? I can have them brought upstairs into the light."

"He's not here." She shook her head, then shuddered. "There's no mistake. I could never forget that ugly face."

"Maybe the Doyle boys will know where he is. Now, Kate, I really do think you'd better go upstairs."

"What are you going to do?" she asked uneasily.

"Get answers, like I promised you. Don't worry, you just leave it up to me." He gave her a rather charming smile that chilled her, given his murderous intentions. "Run along, now. Eldred will show you to one of the guest chambers. You haven't eaten breakfast yet, as I recall. I'll let you know whatever I find out."

So you say, she thought with a frown, but she was not about to take his word for it.

"Don't make me go, Rohan, please? After all they put me through, I deserve to hear for myself what this blackguard has to say! Besides, I'm the only one who can verify if he's telling the truth," she pointed out.

He took this in with a skeptical look, but as he straightened up, he shrugged to himself. "Very well, but I make no promises that what you see will not offend your sensibilities."

"Sensibilities?" She snorted. "All I care about now is getting justice."

His expression sobered at her fierce-toned words, but he nodded, then walked back to Peter's cell.

Kate followed, masking her amazement that the mighty Beast had granted her request.

Eavesdropping by the bars, Pete began backing away again when he saw them coming. "She's staying, right?" he asked nervously.

"Don't look to me for help," Kate replied in a breezy tone. "For my part, I hope he beats you senseless."

"Now, then, Peter, dear lad." Rohan sounded amused at her taunt.

"I don't want any trouble, sir!"

"Then I suggest you take a seat and start talking."

The guards slid back the door and let them in.

The duke stalked in first, filling up the space.

Kate hung back to watch the interrogation unfold from a safer distance, staying behind Rohan as her giant human shield. Peter didn't sit down, he just kept backing away from the duke, like some poor Christian tossed in with a lion.

"Why was she taken? Did you three mean to sell her? Are there more girls you're hiding down in the village?"

"God, no, Your Grace!" Peter blanched. "I swear, it ain't nothin' like that!"

"Then why did you kidnap her?"

There were several more rounds of denials before Rohan grabbed him by his shirt and threw him up against the rough stone wall. Peter squealed and looked away, squeezing his eyes shut in anticipation of a punch that did not come.

"You'd better start explaining."

"It was O'Banyon's idea!" he cried. "I was only doin' as I was told!"

Kate held her breath.

"Denny said it would be good money! We didn't hurt her, I swear! Nobody touched her! If she said otherwise, she's lying!"

Rohan glanced over his shoulder at her with a piercing look of question; she conceded this point with a nod and a shrug. At least she had not been subjected to the most extreme form of violation.

"O'Banyon wanted her for himself," Peter added hoarsely. "He still does, once she's served her purpose."

"What purpose?" Rohan demanded.

"I swear, sir, I don't know!"

At his words, Kate shivered from more than just the cold, but she rallied her courage. "Tell us about O'Banyon," she ordered Pete. "What do you know about him?"

He glanced fearfully at Rohan.

"Answer the question," the duke commanded.

Pete swallowed hard. "My cousin Denny said O'Banyon used to live just over in Brixham years ago."

Rohan eased his grip on him slightly.

"He went to sea with the navy or something," Pete continued. "He was gone for a decade or more. Then he came back. Showed up at Birty's Tavern down by the pier, looking to find some help for some new scheme. That's the first I heard of him or what he was planning." He shook his head. "I knew right away Denny was gettin' us both in over our heads. It was no good. I wanted to ask my uncle's advice. But Denny said I was yellow. Twenty guineas apiece plus whatever we could carry from her house."

"Not a bad deal," the duke murmured in

biting irony. "Was O'Banyon targeting other girls or just Miss Madsen?"

Pete frowned and looked at him for a moment. "Madsen, sir? No. That ain't her name."

Kate began to scoff. "Don't start that again!"

But Peter was staring at Rohan with a gaze that seemed to plead for forgiveness. "O'Banyon let it slip her name is Fox. Kate Fox. As in . . ." His voice trailed off, but the duke appeared suddenly riveted.

"As in . . . Gerald Fox?" Rohan murmured.

"Aye, Your Grace." Peter nodded slowly, holding his stare. "That is why Uncle Caleb vowed we had to get rid of her."

Kate did not know why Rohan had gone so still. "This is nonsense," she informed him. "I think I would know my own name!"

"Would you, now?" He turned around and pinned her in a stare full of sudden dark suspicion.

CHAPTER 7

Rohan's whole body had tensed. *Gerald Fox.* He knew that name from his boyhood days. The ex-Marine gone bad, a bloody hurricane on two legs — the privateer captain who had got his start with the local smugglers.

Years ago, the bold, brash Captain Fox had served Rohan's father in the same capacity that the tamer Caleb Doyle now served *him.* Delivering messages. Spiriting agents back and forth between England and the Continent, no questions asked.

Unwitting courier to the Order.

An extraordinarily dangerous job, but very well paid. A man could lose his life in it.

Or his soul.

At once, Rohan's mind whirled back to the last case his father had handled for the Order before he died.

The DuMarin affair . . .

Twenty-odd years ago, while the Red Terror had raged in France, the previous duke had hired Captain Fox for the dangerous mission of secretly transporting a beautiful French aristocrat girl to safety in America.

Lady Gabrielle DuMarin — the informant's daughter.

The DuMarins had been a leading family of the Prometheans. Indeed, they were descendents of the very Alchemist who had laid the curse on Rohan's line.

All he knew was that after Lady Gabrielle DuMarin had sailed away with Captain Fox, neither had ever been heard from again.

Now Peter Doyle's claim that Kate's last name was Fox suddenly had Rohan wondering if she might be the product of a forbidden union between the English captain and the young French belle.

"What is the matter?" Kate exclaimed. "You're looking at me as if you've seen a ghost! Who is Gerald Fox, anyway? I don't know anyone by that name."

"How old are you?" he asked abruptly.

"Twenty-two." She shook her head with a mystified frown. "What's that got to do with anything?"

The very ground seemed to toss beneath his feet.

The timing matched.

It was almost too uncanny even for *his*

superstitious brain to accept. He stared at her with a chill in his bones, like someone had just walked across his grave.

God, he had known from the first moment he had seen her in the great hall that somehow their destinies were intertwined.

But if the suspicions now flooding his mind were true, then that meant that Kate . . . *had Promethean blood.*

And he trusted her at his own peril.

Good God, if she was a creature of the enemy, then he saw that she had played him expertly so far. Laudanum? A perfect ruse to make him lower his defenses.

Obviously, no well-trained spy would ever willingly take leave of their senses on the job — and that could be exactly what she wanted him to think.

Perhaps she had even tricked the smugglers into playing an unwitting role in her game.

If Drake, the Order's captured agent, had given up Rohan's identity under torture, then the Prometheans need only look at his rakish mode of life in London to see that, while any man attempting to come at him with a weapon would probably not survive, a woman would have a much easier time getting close to him.

Close enough to sink a knife into his back?

Was Kate the one they had sent to slay him in her own delicate way — to beguile him and perhaps, in time, to lead him to his doom?

Impossible! he thought, unable to believe it as he searched her troubled green eyes, trying to discern the truth.

On the other hand, he had battled the Prometheans long enough to know better than to put any sort of elaborate ruse past them. What lengths would they not go to, especially if they thought they had finally found a way to target one of the Order's most capable assassins?

He had to find out more.

Like who Kate really was, if there was any truth to her kidnapping tale, and, if not, what the hell she was really doing here.

Turning back to Peter Doyle, Rohan was now doubly eager to continue his interrogation, but until he knew the truth about Kate — whether she was an innocent or some enemy spawn — he did not want her made privy to the rest of this conversation.

"Why did you ask me how old I am?" she pursued, while Rohan stared at Pete.

He kept his back to her, so she wouldn't notice any change in his demeanor — and because he suddenly did not want to face the acute temptation of her beauty.

Promethean blood! God, and to think he had almost made love to her last night.

"Naturally, Miss Madsen, if you were underage," he said smoothly, "that would make their crime against you even more abominable."

"Oh. I see." She sounded mollified, but Pete, meanwhile, cringed before his dark stare.

"I'm tellin' ye the truth, m'lord! Her name is Fox, not Madsen!"

"Peter, I don't know sort of game you think you're playing," Rohan replied in a businesslike tone, "but you can quit wasting your breath and my time on these foolish lies. Obviously, the lady would know her own name, just as she said. Go upstairs now, Kate," he ordered. "I'm afraid this conversation is about to get more serious. I warned you to cooperate, Peter."

"But, sir!"

"Rohan, you needn't shield me —"

"Parker! Wilkins!" he barked, ignoring her protest. "Escort Miss Madsen upstairs. Have Eldred show her to one of the guest rooms. And stay with her, in case she needs anything," he added with a sharp glance over his shoulder at his men.

Parker's eyes instantly registered the stern warning behind his communicative look.

"Yes, sir! Miss Madsen, if you'll come with us now."

"I will not! Your Grace, this is as much my business as yours! Besides, as soon as my back is turned, this weasel is going to start lying about me, I know it!"

Her protests sounded a little too emphatic for his peace of mind. "Miss Madsen, you will go, now, of your own accord, or I will have you forcibly removed."

She stopped, looking startled at the rumble of thunder in his command. "Fine," she replied stiffly after another stubborn heartbeat. Pivoting in her borrowed boots, she flounced out of the cell, muttering under her breath, "If that's the way you want to be about it!"

Watch her, he told his men with a hard look as she marched back up the shadowy corridor ahead of them.

Parker nodded to him and followed her. Wilkins also fell into step. At least he could count on his men to obey, whether or not they understood the whys and wherefores.

When Rohan turned back to Peter Doyle, the young man braced for a thrashing. "Please don't kill me, sir! I swear on me granny's grave, I'm tellin' the truth —"

"Be quiet!" he whispered harshly, grabbing him by his grimy lapels. "I believe you!"

149

Peter stopped, his eyes widening. "You do?"

"Peter, our two families have been associated for a very long time. Your people have long been the Warringtons' tenants, and we have always looked out for the Doyles. Now, I don't want to inflict any unpleasantness on you, God knows. With the lady out of the way, perhaps we can speak frankly." He released the lad's coat.

Peter sank against the wall, staring at him in wonder and stunned, newfound hope. "Aye, sir, gladly!"

"Good. Now, listen to me. You can get yourself out of this hellhole and into more comfortable quarters if you will answer my questions with complete and total honesty. Agreed?"

Peter nodded quickly with a gulp. "Aye, sir! Agreed!"

"What makes you think she's Gerald Fox's daughter?"

"O'Banyon mentioned it. He kept callin' her Miss Fox, but I didn't think nothin' of it till I saw Uncle Caleb's reaction to that name."

Rohan narrowed his eyes. "So, your uncle *is* involved?"

"Not like that, sir — Uncle Caleb had nothin' to do with the kidnapping. But afterwards, well, we couldn't keep her hidden from him very long. She's a loud, angry, rowdy lass when she's a mind to fight. Pirate's daughter, plenty."

"Yes, I've noticed."

"When some of the womenfolk found out we had her, they insisted we tell Uncle Caleb about her. They said we must have his permission to hide her in the village, and if *we* wouldn't go to our uncle ourselves, *they* would rat us out. So, we had no choice. We went and told my uncle what we done, and showed the girl to him."

"What did he say?"

"He was furious." Pete gave a morose shrug. "He said we'd brought down ruin on the whole village. He was scared to death that Captain Fox was goin' to come with his whole wicked pirate crew and sack our town when he heard what we done to his daughter. Fear o' Cap'n Fox is why Uncle Caleb planned to pass her off to you," Pete admitted. "Better the devil you know, he said — no disrespect intended."

Rohan quirked an eyebrow and folded his arms across his chest. "Pete, your uncle's well aware that Captain Fox disappeared over twenty years ago. The man's presumed dead, so why would your uncle expect Captain Fox to come with his men and sack the village?"

Pete's eyes slowly grew as round as saucers.

"What is it?" Rohan prodded, waiting. "Come, you can't quit now, Pete. A comfortable room in the tower awaits you. No rats. No foul smells. No phantoms," he added knowingly. "Answer me, or you're staying down here with the others."

The lad glanced about nervously, then screwed up his courage. "My uncle thinks Cap'n Fox is still out there somewhere on the sea, alive and well. And he ain't the only one to say so."

"Really?" Rohan murmured, scrutinizing him.

"O'Banyon claimed he worked for Cap'n Fox aboard his ship just a couple o' years ago. Served as first mate, chasing merchant vessels all across the seas. That's how O'Banyon learned about the daughter and where she was livin' in Devonshire under the false name her father gave her many years ago."

Rohan furrowed his brow.

"See, O'Banyon found out about Miss Kate from working on Fox's ship," Pete explained. "There were letters from the girl's caretaker datin' back for years. He said the daughter was Captain Fox's one Achilles' heel. Take the girl, O'Banyon said, and you can get her father."

"Why would O'Banyon want to 'get' Cap'n Fox?"

"Partly for revenge," Pete admitted. "I don't know the whole story, sir, but there's bad blood between 'em. The two was close for a while — Cap'n Fox and O'Banyon, like father and son. Fox was grooming O'Banyon to take over the ship for him in a few more years."

"Hm."

"But something must've come between 'em, for now they are sworn enemies," Pete continued. "Fox got so fed up with O'Banyon that he tricked him into getting caught by a bounty hunter — that's how O'Banyon ended up in Newgate."

"Newgate?" Rohan echoed.

"Aye, O'Banyon was supposed to be hanged for piracy, Yer Grace, but he got out, and now he wants revenge on Fox for gettin' him thrown into gaol in the first place. That's all I know, but I have a feelin' there's more to it that O'Banyon didn't tell me."

"Hold on." Rohan shook his head. "O'Banyon was in Newgate?" he repeated.

"Aye, sir, he bragged of it constantly, how hard he was, that it didn't break 'im."

"Nobody gets out of Newgate unless it's

in a coffin or a gallows cart."

Pete was looking increasingly frightened.

"Did O'Banyon say how he got out? Well?" He braced his hand against the rough stone wall. "I'm waiting, Peter. Would you rather I ask Denny?"

"No, sir," he forced out, steadying himself with a deep breath. "O'Banyon claimed that some Old Man came down to Newgate and sprung him." He hesitated. "A lord."

"Well, well," Rohan murmured barely audibly. All things considered, his first thought was of James Falkirk, the Promethean magnate believed to be holding their captured agent, Drake. "What is this lord's name?"

"O'Banyon refused to speak it. He just referred to him as the Old Man." Pete's voice dropped to a whisper: "Sir, it was the Old Man who paid for the job."

"The kidnapping?"

"Aye." He nodded grimly. "That's where O'Banyon got the gold that he paid out to Denny and me, and the other sum, too, for the girl's upkeep while we guarded her."

"What was her mode of life when you found her, and where, in Devonshire?" He wanted to compare it with what she had told him to find out if Kate had been lying.

"What was she doing? Was anyone with her?"

He shook his head. "She was alone in a cottage on the edge of Dartmoor, sir. When we broke into her house, she was just sittin' there readin' a book."

"I see." At least this comported with what Kate had described a short while ago in the gatehouse. Rohan stared at Pete as he mulled it over. "So, this lord, the Old Man, somehow arranged to get O'Banyon out of Newgate, then funded the kidnapping of Gerald Fox's daughter, whom you found living alone, quietly, at some remote edge of the Dartmoor wastes."

"Aye, sir. You've got it perfect."

"Sounds to me like the Old Man is out for Gerald Fox's blood, as well, quite apart from O'Banyon's desire for revenge."

"That's the feelin' I got, too. That the girl was just the bait to lure her father in."

"Did O'Banyon give you any indication why the Old Man might be out to get Captain Fox?" Rohan asked noncommittally. He already had a strong notion of the answer, but it involved matters that Pete would never know.

The lad shook his head. "The best I could reckon, sir, any pirate's got lots of enemies. Denny and me thought maybe the Old Man was an investor in one of the merchant ships that Fox attacked at sea."

"Ah."

"As for the Old Man, well, O'Banyon seemed afraid to say too much about him — and the O'Banyon I know ain't afraid o' nothin'!" he added emphatically. "Whoever the Old Man is, I'd say he ain't to be trifled with. Not by the likes o' me and O'Banyon, anyway. We told my Uncle Caleb about the Old Man, and that was another reason why he said we had to give the girl to you. She's in the middle of somethin' bigger'n us. If I had any idea what Denny was getting me into . . ." Pete's words trailed off. He just shook his head in regret.

"Why did your uncle deceive me? Why didn't he simply come and tell me all of this last night?"

Pete lifted his eyebrows but dropped his gaze. "Beggin' yer pardon, sir, that's something you'll have to take up with my uncle. He had his reasons, I warrant, but they ain't for me to say — no disrespect intended."

"None taken," Rohan answered dryly. "Very well. Do you have any idea where I can find O'Banyon at the moment?"

"No, sir. When the job was done, he left the girl with us to mind her for as long as needed. When Denny asked where he was going, O'Banyon said it was none of our damned business. Said when the time came, he'd write to us and tell us where to bring her."

"O'Banyon is literate?" he asked in surprise.

"Enough to get by, like Denny and me."

"Anything else I should know?"

"Not that I can think of, sir. I've told you everything."

Rohan gazed at him assessingly. "You've been most helpful, Peter." As two new guards arrived to take over for Parker and Wilkins, who would now be keeping a close watch on Kate, Rohan beckoned them into the cell. "Have this young man removed to more comfortable quarters," he ordered the men. "You will, of course, keep him under guard."

"Aye, Your Grace." The men came into the cell to shackle Peter's wrists for transport.

As they put the manacles on him, Peter hung his head. "I *am* sorry for my part in this, sir. Would you mind tellin' Miss Kate that I do apologize? Sincerely. I tried not to let the other two abuse her too much. I was just tryin' to make a living," he added in a glum tone.

"I will tell her," Rohan answered. "If you

remember anything else, let your guards know, and we will talk again."

Peter nodded, then the men led him away.

Rohan followed a few paces behind, which was how he heard the other Doyle taunt his cousin as the guards escorted Pete past Denny's cell, on their way out of the dungeon.

"Yellow," Denny accused him in a low and bitter voice.

"Keep quiet!" one of the guards ordered, but Rohan paused in front of Denny's cell.

He stared at him through the bars for a long moment.

"Maybe I know something, too," Denny vaunted, a hint of fear beginning to show beneath his bravado, envy, too, upon seeing that his cousin had found a way out.

"I'm afraid you're too late." Rohan gave him a cold look, then walked on, leaving the sullen bastard and his mates to rot.

Mercy had never been his forte.

When he returned upstairs into the castle proper, at once, he saw his lanky butler striding toward him.

"Sir!"

"What news, Eldred?"

"Caleb Doyle is here, as you ordered. Your carriage just returned from the village with him a few moments ago."

"Good. Where's Kate?"

"Settled in her chamber, eating breakfast. Parker and Wilkins have stationed themselves outside her door," he added with a questioning look.

"Yes, I asked them to. I'm afraid we're going to need to keep an eye on her, Eldred. What's that?" He nodded toward the large leather traveling trunk that two of his footmen were now carrying up the stairs.

"Ah, clothes for Miss Madsen, sir. When you sent the coach down to the village, I took the liberty of telling the men to bring back something more suitable for her to wear than the footman's uniform." Eldred studied him. "Should I be concerned, Your Grace?"

"Ah, not at all. I've got her well in hand."

Pete's revelations had not erased Rohan's suspicions of Kate but had admittedly reduced them.

"Eldred?" He turned back to his butler, suddenly inspired with a way to learn more about the lady.

To be sure, his methods of interrogating a beautiful woman would prove quite different from those he had just used on Peter Doyle, but he would get his answers all the same.

"Yes, sir?"

"Tell Miss Madsen I would like her to join me for dinner tonight. Say, seven in the dining room. Have the kitchens prepare a fine meal. And bring up my best vintage from the wine cellars."

Eldred's eyebrows lifted. "Very good, sir."

Rohan nodded in anticipation. "Now, then. Where is our old Caleb?"

"Waiting for you in the great hall, Your Grace."

He nodded. "Much obliged, Eldred, as always," he said with an idle wave, already striding away.

The butler bowed and withdrew to inform Kate of their dinner appointment, while Rohan headed for the great hall to see what the double-dealing smugglers' chief had to say for himself.

As soon as Rohan stepped into the great hall, Caleb Doyle rose from his chair. He held his hat humbly in his hands, but the pugnacious glower stamped across his weathered face was anything but repentant.

Rohan's shadow fell over the old man as he approached.

"You lied to me."

"Aye," the old trickster grumbled, not bothering to deny it or to attempt any irritating excuses.

"That you deceived me is hardly a shock,

160

Mr. Doyle, but how could you sink so low? You nearly tricked me into taking a young woman's innocence against her will."

"Eh, she wouldn't have minded."

"Of course she would, and so do I! You nearly entrapped me in an act of great dishonor, damn you. Why didn't you simply tell me what the hell was going on?"

"As if you'd care!"

Rohan looked at him quizzically; Caleb eyed him up with a scowl.

"You want a fight?" the smugglers' chief challenged him. "Very well, then! I ain't afraid o' you! No, indeed. I've known you since you was knee-high, my fine lord — and now you'll listen to me!" he declared. "Pshaw, your father would be disappointed. We could've counted on him, but you! It takes a damn catastrophe to drag you away from your pleasures in Town!"

"Pleasures?" Rohan echoed in furious amazement. "Do you actually believe that?"

"How should I know! I had to do something to make sure you'd get involved this time instead of ignorin' our predicament the way you did my letter!"

"So, that's what this is about."

"I wrote to you months ago and asked for your assistance —"

"You came whining to me for another

bloody handout."

"You turned us down — your own people!" he cried. "You turned your back on us in the midst of so much want all over England!"

"Enough!" Rohan thundered. "Good God, how long will you and your followers act like hapless, spoiled children instead of grown men? Will you never take responsibility for your own lives? I warned you to save your money. You made a fortune on the black market during the war, so where is it now? Gone! Already spent! Is it *my* fault you lot choose to squander every penny you make on gin and trinkets? I am sorry, Mr. Doyle, but in my view, it was time that you all learned your lesson."

"Well, beggin' yer pardon, sir, we thought we'd teach you a little lesson, too."

Rohan stared at him in outrage, then turned away, shaking his head. Doyle was lucky in that moment that he was an old man with a long history of loyal service to his family; otherwise, Rohan would have put him through a wall for his insolence.

"If you had been a bit more patient," he said through gritted teeth, "you'd have soon found out I did not so much refuse your request as begin seeking to help you in a different way." He sent Caleb a pointed look. "As it happens, I've been working on getting the proper licensing to turn your smugglers' boats into a legitimate fishing fleet. That way, you'll be able to fend for yourselves in future without turning to crime, though I'm beginning to think you prefer it. Meanwhile, are you aware that the girl you kept a prisoner in your cellar had assumed you were running an abduction ring, supplying kidnapped virgins to the stews of London? And you actually let her believe that I am a top customer!"

"Aren't you? Well, sir, we hear about your exploits all the way in Cornwall."

He threw up his hands in exasperation. "I cannot escape the world's notice, Caleb! It's impossible for any man of my rank not to be constantly watched. Better they think me some soulless libertine than take note of my more serious pursuits — which you already know I cannot discuss, so do not even ask me."

"Believe me, I don't want to know," Caleb grumbled.

Rohan fell silent for a moment. "If I didn't care, I wouldn't be here," he added in a low growl, pacing past him. "Now then, if you are quite through scolding me, tell me why you think Gerald Fox is still alive."

Caleb eyed him warily. "I've heard rumors

over the years." He shrugged. "Now this. O'Banyon's tale confirms it."

"What do you know about O'Banyon?"

"That dirty whoreson," Caleb muttered. "Fox would've trusted him as a fellow West Countryman, I'd reckon. God knows my fool nephews did."

"Did your nephews ever reveal the identity of this 'Old Man' who supposedly got O'Banyon out of Newgate?"

Caleb shook his head. "They don't know. Nor do I."

"And what about Kate?"

He snorted. "Why, she's her father's daughter, ain't she. Put her on deck of a ship and give her a cutlass, and she'd probably cut yer head off."

"She can use a weapon?" he asked swiftly.

Caleb waved his hand. "No, no. I was speakin' metaphorical, but it wouldn't surprise me if the little hellion could, now that you mention it. She nearly gelded Denny with the kick she gave him. Hell, if she wasn't such a spitfire, we wouldn't have had to drug her."

"Well, you're lucky you gave her enough to make her pass out on me last night. Otherwise . . ." He shook his head with a dire stare. "It was very wrong of you, Caleb."

"Aye, well, we haven't got many saints round here," the smugglers' chief said pointedly.

Rohan knew he couldn't argue that. "You'll be happy to hear that Peter has decided to cooperate. Unless he's deceiving me, too, I will see that his life is spared. In the meanwhile, your nephews are to receive a letter from O'Banyon with instructions on what to do next. When it arrives, you are to bring it to me immediately. Understood?"

He nodded.

"Very well, then. You may go."

Caleb lingered, eyeing him in uncertainty.

"What now, Mr. Doyle? Was there another insult you wanted to add before you take leave of me?"

The old curmudgeon scowled. "I didn't like deceivin' ye, sir, but it seemed the only way."

"Is this your way of apologizing, or now do you merely fear some petty retaliation from me, hm?"

When Caleb shifted his weight uncertainly, Rohan let out a large, sardonic sigh. "Nobody around here seems to know me at all!" he remarked to the air. Then he flicked his hand at Caleb. "Go away before I come back to my senses and repay you for your lies as you deserve."

"Harrumph."

"And don't forget to bring me that letter when it comes, or I may do something dreadful to you all. Unleash my hellhounds, or toss one of your babies in my supper pot."

Caleb shot an indignant scowl at him over his shoulder as he trudged out.

Rohan smiled with an assassin's sangfroid. *Why, they really do think I'm a Beast.*

He sat down slowly on the great throne-like chair of his ancestors and began brooding on the past. Combined with his many questions about Kate, Caleb's stinging reproach had him thinking about his father. He rested his head against the chair back, the particulars of his father's final mission for the Order turning in his mind.

The DuMarin affair.

The Count DuMarin had been a member of the Prometheans' elite High Council at the time of the French Revolution, and if Rohan's theory about Kate's true identity was right, that would be her grandfather. And the French aristo blood would explain a lot about her, he thought wryly.

In any case, frightened by the chaos he had seen unfolding in France, DuMarin had secretly reached out to the Order, desiring to turn informant against his sinister coconspirators.

Rohan's father had been the agent assigned to the case. The French count had provided the Order with critical intelligence concerning the Prometheans' future plans, how they were carefully driving the guillotine mobs, intent on using the chaos to spread their vision of tyranny well beyond the borders of France.

Thanks to Rohan's father and his team, along with coordinated action by the Order, uprisings in various German and Italian states had been prevented based on DuMarin's intelligence.

Of course, the count's evil former colleagues had eventually made him pay for his newfound conscience with his life. Within a year of his betrayal, DuMarin had been assassinated in London despite the Order's round-the-clock efforts to protect him.

DuMarin had given his life for what he finally understood was right, and in that sense, Rohan had to admit that Kate's Promethean lineage contained a certain heroism.

On the other hand, one good man out of generations did not quite put his mind at ease.

The one condition that DuMarin had placed on the Order before he would tell them what he knew was that he wanted his daughter, then seventeen-year-old Lady Gabrielle, fresh out of convent school, to be sent off to her kin in New Orleans. Across the ocean in America, DuMarin believed his daughter would be safe from the Prometheans' retaliation.

Rohan's father had, of course, agreed to this condition, and from the pool of sailing talent among the local smugglers, he had selected Captain Gerald Fox to transport the French belle to America.

Fox's well-armed ship was fast. He was a fearless, well-trained fighter, having served in the Royal Marines, and he had performed loyal service to the Order in the past without asking any questions.

Rohan knew all this for, at the time, he had been a ten-year-old boy home from school at the Christmas holiday, spying through the minstrels' gallery on his father's private business in the great hall.

Whenever he had the chance to be anywhere near his idolized father, after all, he had been the great man's shadow. His father usually did not mind his eavesdropping, knowing it would help his son to absorb the nuances of how to conduct the Order's business when it was his turn to be the duke.

Rohan still remembered seeing the veiled

French lady dressed in black mourning, holding a large, leather-bound book in her arms that he had assumed was a Bible.

No doubt she had had need of it, considering that before leaving Paris, she had seen her governess's head go past her window on a pike.

Next, the swashbuckling Captain Gerald Fox had marched in. Given his age at the time, Rohan remembered the sea captain more vividly than the lady, for he had considered the bold privateer second only to his sire in impressive masculine glamour — either one, the sort of man any boy wanted to be like when he grew up.

The captain and his high-value passenger were introduced, and before long, Fox had led the sorrowful mademoiselle out to his ship to make sail for America.

That, however, was the last time anyone had heard from them. It was assumed that something had happened, that the Prometheans must have caught up with them somehow.

But their fate had been forgotten, for, closer to home, his father's days had been numbered from that night on, as well.

Rohan had soon been shipped back to the private, military-style school in Scotland where all members of the Order were educated. But only a few months later, he got word that his mighty sire had fallen.

The previous Duke of Warrington had died a hero's death carrying out a successful raid on the Prometheans along with his team, based on the intelligence provided by the Count DuMarin.

Rohan heaved a sigh, left to wonder if Kate really could be the end result of all this, and if so, how she fit into it now.

If the Prometheans had eventually caught up with Fox, bent on killing the traitor DuMarin's daughter along with her swashbuckling protector, might they have been startled to find the pair caring for a baby?

If the Prometheans had got their hands on Kate as a child, killing her parents, but sparing her, they might have raised her to be molded into one of their own twisted deceivers. A well-trained temptress, specifically sent after one of the Order's most dangerous men.

It seemed plausible, at least to a slightly paranoid assassin like him. The most startling part was that, if he recalled correctly, the DuMarins' medieval ancestor was none other than Valerian the Alchemist — the same dark wizard who had laid the Kilburn Curse upon his family.

This heritage would've made Kate practically royalty among the Prometheans — and could make her all the more dangerous to *him*. For beyond superstition, the girl seemed uniquely suited to enchant him.

But a number of obvious questions still loomed large.

What did it mean if, indeed, Gerald Fox was still alive? Had he survived his Promethean pursuers by turning traitor? Was that why the Order had never heard from him again? And what of Lady Gabrielle? What ever had happened to her? Most importantly, where did Kate fit in?

If she was part of the enemy's organization, then why would James Falkirk need to have her kidnapped? Or was that just an elaborate cover story of some sort?

Might she be as innocent as she seemed?

That sweet vulnerability he had seen in her in the gatehouse . . . was that the real Kate or just another mask? There was no way he could be sure until he learned a great deal more about her. Which was exactly what he intended to do.

Tonight.

CHAPTER 8

Darkness, deep and black, had crept over the castle as evening arrived. Kate glanced at the clock. It was almost time to go down to dinner with the Beast.

She just hoped that when she soon joined him in the dining room, she would not find that *she* was on the menu.

Seated before the mirror in the bed-chamber she had been assigned, she was feeling increasingly nervous about tonight as she finished fixing her hair and fighting the too-low neckline of her borrowed gown.

Her day had been pleasant enough — the first in weeks that had borne any resemblance to normalcy. She had spent the afternoon in quiet rest and recuperation from her long ordeal; had eaten; bathed; had donned a warm, soft dressing gown from the trunk of clothes the footmen had brought her, then had napped — until a nightmare of the smugglers' cellar had jarred her awake.

Upon opening her eyes and realizing anew that she was safe — it was only a dream — she had abruptly burst out in a most uncharacteristic flood of tears.

She had been bewildered by her own reaction, but the pent-up terror and rage from all she had gone through demanded some sort of belated release. Still, her pride could not have borne for the guards posted outside her chamber door to hear — not that they'd care. She had muffled her sobs with a pillow, crying her heart out in secret. To think, she had nearly died today!

For as long as she lived, she would never forget the fateful moment the ground had fallen away beneath her, how Rohan had lunged to save her. In that instant of scrabbling for purchase on the cliff's ledge, half-blind with panic, all she had seen was his face: his clenched jaw and glittering eyes.

Pure fearless ferocity come to save her.

Perhaps that was why she now felt inexplicably bound to him, as by a debt of honor — or a bond of blood. Yet at the same time, she was not entirely sure that Rohan was not evil. Just when she had started to think this morning he wasn't half-bad, he had ordered her out of the dungeon so he could pulverize poor, hapless Peter Doyle.

She shook her head uneasily.

To be sure, Pete probably deserved perhaps a black eye or a bloody nose for his role in her kidnapping. But if Rohan had given him *too much* of a brutal beating, this would cast a most unsettling shadow over his character in her mind — one that did not bode well for *her.* For if the giant, iron-muscled Beast did not scruple over thrashing a smaller, weaker, unarmed man, then that would betray a ruthlessness in her self-appointed protector, a willingness to give in to his baser impulses that made it doubtful he would continue treating *her* honorably for long.

One look at the Duke of Warrington made it clear that he was a man who got what he wanted. He was too strong to fight, and she owed him besides, so if he made the demand that she come to his bed, what could she do but surrender?

Not for a moment did she forget that she had been brought here as a "present" for the duke; and she knew in her bones that that was how he still saw her.

So far, he had behaved like a gentleman, but she was still highly wary of him. What might he expect from her tonight?

What might he still want, or even feel entitled to, because he'd saved her life?

The question made her set her comb down with a flutter of frightened confusion in her belly. She sat there for a long moment, feeling trapped, but eventually, shook her head. *I'll just have to use my wits.* Steadying herself, she gave her own reflection a hard look in the glass.

Perhaps it was ungrateful of her to regard her rescuer with such distrust, but it was important to face this night without any illusions. She was no fool. This intimate dinner with a decadent man of the world raised her suspicions with good cause — especially after what had happened between them last night in his bed.

She was already dressed like somebody's mistress. The beautiful emerald satin gown that she had chosen from the traveling trunk was obviously expensive, but the overall effect was indecent because the thing did not quite fit. It was not merely that the off-the-shoulder sleeves seemed a chilly style for January, or that the skirts were about two inches short, giving an overly generous peek at her ankles.

No, more worrisome by far was the way the too-low, too-tight bodice smashed her breasts upward into a sweeping display of cleavage. Scowling, she tried to pull the neckline up again. *Blast.*

For all she knew of the latest Town fashions, perhaps it was supposed to fit that way. She was merely concerned that her host downstairs might like it a little too much.

Ah, well. When it came to stolen goods, one could hardly complain about imperfect sizing. She hardly had to ask how the smugglers had obtained the fine French clothes in the first place, judging by the saltwater stains that marred the satin skirts. No doubt some fashionable stranger in London was waiting in vain for her delivery from Paris.

Anyway, the gown was a vast improvement over her footman's uniform. It might be too revealing, but after facing death today, an ill-fitting gown was too trivial an issue to worry about overmuch. She'd be going home soon. That was all that mattered.

Surely, the worst was over now, and before long, she'd be back in her cozy, heathside cottage with her books and scribblings and her trusty teapot by her side. She just had to hold on a little while longer, perhaps a few days more, so the aftermath of her abduction could be sorted out, the consequences dealt out to all those who had wronged her.

Rohan had promised her justice, and she needed with all her heart to believe that the duke meant what he said.

If he had to have his way with her before he would let her go home, at least she knew that, if nothing else, he would make sure she enjoyed it.

She shivered at the scandalous thought, but another nervous glance at the clock warned her it was time to go.

He'd be waiting for her. She must not annoy him by arriving late.

She slid a final hairpin into place. Taking a long, deep, calming breath, she gave her reflection one last survey in the mirror. By the soft glow of the candles, she supposed she looked tolerably elegant. It wasn't her fault if the gown was a little too seductive.

Shrugging off her virginal anxiety as best she could, she rose from the vanity and walked across the chamber, the shush of the satin skirts whispering around her. As she reached for the door handle her frisson of fear was laced with anticipation.

Upon stepping out of her room, she was immediately surprised to find the two guards from this morning, Parker and Wilkins, posted by her door. "You're still here?" she exclaimed, but before they could answer, an astonishing thought filled her mind. *Am I prisoner, then?*

But why else would the duke have posted armed guards by her door? She pulled the door shut behind her with a flurry of fresh doubts scattering through her mind. Did he think she'd try to run away again, or had he merely decided that he did not trust her, either?

Whichever the case, it was not a good sign; however, she already knew there was no point in asking these two about it. She had already seen that his henchmen did not make a move without his authorization. She would have to save her questions for the Beast. The two guards watched her every move with cautious deference, standing at attention.

"Could you gentlemen possibly point me in the direction of the dining room?"

Her civilized tone appeared to startle them after witnessing her wild display of suicidal rage this morning, to say nothing of her mindless drugged state the night before.

Parker cleared his throat, dropping his gaze from the region of her chest. "We'll show you there, miss. This way," he replied in a businesslike tone.

Kate eyed them warily as both guards left their stations flanking her chamber door.

They walked her down the long, shadowy corridor, past the closed entrance to the duke's chamber, where they had so unceremoniously tossed her in last night to face her fate.

Stone-hearted cretins.

Buoyed up with indignation to think that she might be as much of a prisoner here as those men in the dungeon — only, one being kept under nicer circumstances — she marched down the stone-carved stairs with her guards trailing her on either side.

The arrival of evening had sunk the stairwell into gloom. Her pulse quickened in anticipation of her imminent encounter with the Beast. She warned herself not to show her cards too soon, at least until she figured out what the rogue was up to.

Eldred met her and her guards at the foot of the stairs. "Miss Madsen." Gliding out of the shadows, he greeted her with a bow. "His Grace awaits you in the dining hall. If you'll follow me."

She inclined her head politely. The butler nodded the guards' dismissal and led on. Kate followed, still in a heightened state of vigilance.

They bypassed the empty soaring cavern of the great hall and proceeded down a moody Gothic hallway. There were several doors to other chambers along the corridor, but most were closed, probably to keep the scant heat in the drafty castle where it was needed.

Eldred sailed ahead of her into a large, red-walled chamber, which turned out to be the dining hall. Once over the threshold, the butler stepped aside to announce her arrival to the room's solitary occupant, but even before he spoke, her gaze homed in on the magnificent man seated alone by the fireplace.

Rohan was staring into the flames and savoring a brandy. The sensual way he cupped the rounded snifter in his palm caused a completely unexpected shudder of wild longing to run the length of her entire body, for his tender hold on that globelike glass brought back hazy memories of his attentions last night to her breasts.

And when he raised the glass to his lips and took a slow, leisurely sip, Kate had to close her eyes for a moment to steady herself. *Dear God.*

His butler announced her in a formal tone. "Your Grace: Miss Madsen."

Kate flicked her eyes open, but her cheeks were already burning when the duke looked over.

He cast her a dangerous smile, and a giddy weakness crept up her body, starting at her knees. She tightened them reflexively and gave her quivering legs the silent order to move, and by all means, to forget the feel of his forbidden caresses running up her thighs.

As he rose smoothly from his leather wing chair, Kate marched into the dining room with her head held high. She tried with all her might to hide her discomfiture. It would have been mortifying in the extreme if he sensed the lustful confusion that he caused in her.

Dangerous, too, for no doubt he would interpret it as an invitation. Which it was not. At least she did not *think* it was . . .

She swallowed hard as he moved toward her, elegantly attired in black trousers and a dark plum tailcoat. His shirt was white, his black neckcloth secured with a gleaming pearl cravat pin. His long raven hair was pulled back into a sleek queue, and his eyes glowed with an appreciative smolder as she joined him by the fireplace.

"Miss Madsen," he welcomed her in a deep purr while his gaze trailed over her. "You look lovely."

"Ahem. Thank you."

"I trust your room was comfortable."

"Yes. Very." Her heart was pounding in the most disturbing fashion.

He studied her. "Did you get to rest?"

"I did. Yes. Thanks," she answered, suspicious of the solicitude in his gaze.

He suddenly frowned. "Your eyes are red."

"No, they're not — er, are they?" With a blanch, she ducked her head, chagrined that he had detected her earlier bout as a watering pot. "I-I suppose nearly dying today shook me up a bit more than I realized," she mumbled.

"Ah. Well. That is understandable," he said with a smile in his deep voice. "But all that is behind you now."

Kate jumped when he collected her hand from her side as though it were some delicate flower and placed a careful kiss on her knuckles.

She stared at him, wide-eyed.

Before he released her hand from his light grasp, she thought to steal a quick glance down at his knuckles, scanning them for any telltale signs of how badly he might have thrashed Peter Doyle.

There was no mark on them. Relief eased her tension by a small degree.

"Now then," he said, giving her back her hand, "having cheated death successfully today, tonight, you and I are going to celebrate life."

Oh, dear. "Are we?" she echoed faintly.

"Yes." He nodded with firm expertise. "I always do that after facing death. There's a certain pleasure in it, I find. Reminds you what it means to be alive. Drink? You look like you could use it." He was already brushing past her, heading for the liquor cabinet.

She turned, watching him in guarded fascination. "You . . . do this often?"

"Celebrate? God, yes." He flashed a wicked smile.

"I meant — face death."

He merely laughed. "What do you say to a brandy?"

"Um, I don't drink strong spirits." She had good reason to keep her head about her tonight, as well.

"A glass of wine, then?"

"Why not," she conceded with a reluctant shrug.

"Excellent." Ignoring her question, he tossed himself a crystal goblet from the lower shelf with an easy motion and reached into the ice bucket, where an open bottle nestled. "But I must warn you, prepare to be dazzled."

She feared she already was.

"This is my favorite wine, and I don't usually share it." His roguish little smile nigh entranced her.

"I am honored," Kate said faintly, watching him with cautious but growing delight.

Locked in that cellar for so long, scared

for her life, no one had been this nice to her in ages.

"Here you are. An exquisite white burgundy, straight from the bosom of France." He inhaled its bouquet as he came back and presented her with the glass. "Indulge."

"Thank you, Your Grace." She accepted the drink with great curiosity, unsure if he was flirting with her or simply trying to put her at ease. Smiling, he watched her raise the glass to her lips — but then she suddenly stopped.

A dart of fear shot through her as she remembered the drugged wine the smugglers had given her last night, which had rendered her so helpless.

Rohan waited expectantly. "Go on, try it."

Kate floundered, trying to hide her distress. She made a show of inhaling the wine's bouquet, buying time as she tried to detect any hint of laudanum he might have poured in it.

He raised an eyebrow. "Something wrong?"

She suddenly recalled her hesitation before the stairs leading down to the dungeon. He hadn't worked any treachery on her then; he had only brought her down there to help her seek justice. Realizing she was being irrational, she laughed rather awkwardly at herself and found the courage at last to take her first exploratory sip.

Slowly, the wine rewarded her with its complex, subtle flavors . . . apricot, pear, a hint of vanilla . . . and some indescribable flavor that made her think of sun-drenched, flowery meadows.

"It's wonderful," she murmured at length, lifting her gaze to his. She felt chastened for her mistrust. "It's as if they've bottled summer."

"Yes. That's very apt." His smile broadened as he held her gaze deeply. "And a welcome change it is from all this ice and snow."

Kate could not look away, even as she felt a blush rise in her cheeks. Surely, one swallow of wine could not have gone so quickly to her head, but all his attention focused on her had a similarly intoxicating effect.

Heavens, it was an overwhelming feeling, having a virile, darkly handsome, six-and-a-half-foot duke apparently engrossed in one's every movement. He gazed at her lips, and for a fleeting instant, Kate held her breath, certain he was going to lean down and kiss her.

If the thought had crossed his mind, however, he refrained, dropping his gaze and pulling back a bit.

He turned away. "Our meal will be arriving any moment. Shall we?" He swept a polite gesture toward the table.

"Uh, yes, of course." Blinking away her bedazzlement, she paused and turned to him. "But Your Grace — there is something I must say to you first."

"Oh?" He turned to her with a keen look. "What is it?"

Kate stared at him. "Thank you. For saving my life. I'm sorry, I should have said it earlier, but with all that was happening —"

"You're welcome."

"I mean it." She took an earnest step toward him. "I can't believe you risked yourself like that for me. You barely even know me!"

"I'm just glad I got to you in time," he answered softly.

"Well — I want you to know I will never forget what you did for me. We both know that I am in your debt."

"Careful, Kate. Don't give a man ideas. Come," he ordered with a rakish half smile. "I'll show you to your seat."

Rather routed, Kate dropped her gaze but went along obediently. His hand came to rest on the small of her back as he escorted her over to the long, formally laid table. His light touch was unmistakably possessive.

She was intensely aware of him as he led her over to her chair and pulled it out for her; she flicked her lashes downward and lowered herself to her seat.

When he pushed her chair in for her, the fleeting brush of his fingers against her bared shoulders made her throb. He slowly walked around the table with a subtle swagger in his movements and sat down across from her.

In the next moment, she could feel him watching her, but she refused to look at him — could not bring herself to chance another gaze into his eyes. Her courage had fled from the potent temptation in his touch. She kept her gaze down stubbornly, silently trying to talk herself out of this feverish attraction.

This was madness! She was not about to make a fool of herself over the man to whom she had been given as a gift. That would have been humiliating in the extreme. He was a libertine who used women as bed warmers and consorted with criminals — a duke, moreover, too highborn to give a fig about wrecking the life of an ordinary girl.

He was dangerous.

Determined to avoid temptation, she occupied herself with studying the china arrayed before her instead, dishes painted with his family crest and edged in gilt. Likewise, a flowery "W" was engraved at the tip of the handle of each piece of silver. Between them, an artistic arrangement of apples and pears in a crystal bowl adorned the table, their sleek red and golden skins burnished by the candles' glow.

The silence stretched, and still he watched her, as though waiting to see what she would do with it, like a scientist carrying out some type of experiment.

She took a deep breath and lifted her head at last with a pointed look. "You are staring at me."

"Your beauty gives me pleasure," he replied.

She drew back with a worried frown.

"Kate, try to relax —"

"How can I when you say that sort of thing?" she cried.

"Would you rather I lie?"

"Well — no." She shifted unhappily in her seat.

"Good. Because I'd much prefer that we be honest with each other."

"As would I! Perhaps you would answer a question for me, in fact."

He shrugged. "Fire at will."

She eyed him guardedly while he watched her with the amused interest of a man familiarizing himself with the workings of some new toy.

"Why were there guards posted by my door?"

"To keep me out, of course."

She did not smile at his quip. "You said we were being honest."

"They're there to protect you, Kate. I assumed after all you've been through, having some protection on hand would have made you feel more secure."

"Ah." She doubted it.

He studied her. "I hope they did not bother you at all?"

"No, they did not bother me at all. It's just, seeing two armed men outside my chamber door . . . I couldn't help wondering if I am some sort of prisoner here?"

"If you were a prisoner, why would I have you for dinner?"

Her brittle smile faded at the wicked way he had worded the question. He was already looking at her like he meant to have her for dessert.

He let out a worldly sigh, noting how she had paled. "Dear, oh, dear, Miss Madsen. Next you'll be worried the food is drugged."

"Is it?" she whispered, her gaze locked on his face.

"Of course not." His expression sobered.

He leaned closer as his stare intensified. "I want you to trust me, Kate."

"Very well. If I'm not a prisoner, then tell me when I can go home."

"Hm." He leaned back in his chair, his eyes gleaming with shrewd speculation. She held his hooded gaze in challenge. He drummed his fingers briefly on the chair arm. "I'm afraid it's not that simple, Kate."

I knew it! Her blood ran cold. "Why not?"

"O'Banyon is still out there," he replied in an oh-so-reasonable tone. "If I send you home now, there's nothing to stop him from simply coming back and capturing you again."

"Is that what Peter Doyle said?"

"Yes. Among other things."

"Like what? What else did he say? Tell me — please! I deserve to know!"

He looked at her for a long moment, then chose his words with care. "O'Banyon is going to contact the Doyle boys with their next instructions. He thinks they still have you. Now, I've ordered Caleb to bring me O'Banyon's letter as soon as it arrives. O'Banyon is to write to Pete and Denny to tell them where they are to bring you. This will reveal O'Banyon's location. Once I know where he is, believe me, I will deal with him personally."

Kate stared at him in wonder.

"In the meanwhile," he added darkly, "I think it's best that you stay here. Where you'll be safe."

She paled. "Here . . . with you?"

He raised an eyebrow at her stricken look. "I'll do my best not to be disagreeable company."

"No, of course, Your Grace. It's not that. It's just — I was so looking forward to going home."

"Well, you can't yet. It's not safe."

"I would not want to impose."

"I promised you justice, Kate. Besides, it's not just for you." He sat back again and picked up his wineglass. "I am these people's lord, and they have committed a very serious crime. Looking after you has now become my responsibility." He paused. "My duty."

"I see." She stared down at her empty plate, hoping that his talk of duty might make it less likely that he would opt to pass the time by subjecting her to some casual seduction. "Do you — have any idea how long this might take?" she ventured, peering warily at him from beneath her lashes.

He shook his head. "There is no way to know." She thought she detected a flash of annoyance in his eyes. "I realize this is a

191

great inconvenience, Miss Madsen, but my staff and I will do all in our power to ensure that your stay here is not too terribly unpleasant for you."

"Please — I didn't mean to sound ungrateful — but after all those weeks in the Doyles' cellar, I have been . . . very homesick." She lowered her gaze, embarrassed to have to make this vulnerable admission, but she could not afford to offend the only ally she currently had in the world. "I am sorry, Your Grace. I meant no rudeness. I am altogether grateful to you for helping me, of course. Thank you — once again."

For a long moment, he said nothing. But she could feel him studying her. "Try to understand, Kate. I know you don't want to be here any more than I do. But at the end of the day, you really have no choice except to trust me."

That's what I was afraid of. She gazed at him in mingled distress and gratitude. "Perhaps you could tell me what else Peter Doyle had to say?"

Before he could reply, Eldred stepped into the dining room and made his formal announcement. "Your Grace, Miss Madsen: Dinner is served."

While the two of them sat there studying each other from across the table in mutually attracted mistrust, a parade of liveried footmen marched into the dining room carrying silver-lidded serving dishes, baskets of bread, assorted gravies, and a lavish selection of wines.

Eldred, with his white-gloved hands clasped behind his back, announced each dish in lugubrious tones: "Scalloped oysters. Fillets of veal, stuffed and roasted, with savoys, carrots, and potatoes. Roasted capons garnished with dilled sausage . . ."

As he droned on, the footmen worked around them, placing the serving dishes on the table with geometrical precision. They no sooner whisked the lids away than others dipped forward like life-sized clockwork automata, pouring the newly arrived wines into their proper glasses and setting in easy reach the bottles that went with each dish.

"Broiled sturgeon with French beans, carrots, and cauliflower. A fricassee of rabbit, oysters, and mushrooms. Squab pigeons with asparagus. And finally —" He bowed to the duke. "Mince pies."

"Excellent," His Grace murmured in approval.

Eldred drew himself up politely. "Will there be anything else, sir?"

"Thank you, Eldred. That will do for now."

The butler bowed and signaled to the

footmen, who then marched out in a line, except for two, who took their places in the shadows of the distant wall, to wait on them as needed.

Rohan turned his attention to the burgeoning table, taking a leisurely survey of the spread, rather like a wolf looking out over a flock of sheep. "Where to begin?"

"I cannot fathom how you are not as stout as the Regent."

"I stay active," he drawled with a wicked gleam in his eyes. "A toast to you, my darling."

"Honestly," she muttered, but, alas, could not resist him as he lifted his glass of now-red wine in her direction.

"To new acquaintances," he said. "And outwitting the Grim Reaper once again. And most of all, to young ladies of remarkable courage. I drink to their health."

When he cast her a teasing wink full of outlandish charm, Kate did not know if she would throttle him or swoon.

"Aren't you going to tell me what else Peter Doyle had to say?" she demanded.

"Not in the presence of good food, my dear. Well, it is English food. All the more reason to eat it before it gets cold. Cheers." He reached over and clinked his glass to hers with a cheeky look that informed her the conversation was closed for now.

"Warrington."

"Come, Kate. No arguing over supper. 'Tisn't civilized."

The Beast was going to critique her etiquette? "At least tell me if Peter explained —"

"Kate! Surely you can enjoy a simple meal," he chided. "Look at all the trouble my poor kitchen staff has gone to for your sake."

"For my sake?" she exclaimed. "I'm just a prisoner!"

"Prisoner, guest, semantics. My servants so want to impress you. Now then." He took up knife and fork in each large hand. "Let's eat, shall we? God knows, there are so few pleasures in life, we might as well enjoy 'em."

She clenched her jaw. She believed she had just been told, more or less, to shut up and eat.

But as the mouthwatering aromas of their feast teased her nose, she had to concede that her questions weren't going anywhere for the moment. At least she was out of that cellar, and had not died today.

Perhaps she ought to let herself enjoy her first night of relative freedom in weeks.

Rohan gave her a coaxing nod toward the

food like a man trying to get a wounded wild animal to eat.

Was that what she had become after her ordeal? At home on the windy moors, alone with the falcons and the wild ponies, she had never been all that tame to start with.

She regarded him a wary look, but slowly, uncertainly, she picked up her fork and proceeded to dine with the duke.

CHAPTER 9

As the evening passed and the candles burned low, and the dining room darkened, but for the fire, Rohan was beginning to wonder if his attraction to this woman could become a problem.

The whole purpose of tonight had been to provide himself with a chance to study her carefully at close range, but he was beginning to think that even if she *had* been sent by the enemy to destroy him, it might not be a bad way to go.

Her reticence intrigued him. He still didn't trust her, but her obvious vulnerability, from embarrassment over her tears to her confession of homesickness, plucked at heartstrings in him that he thought he had ripped out by the roots long ago.

For two hours, he watched and listened to her, trying to determine if her claims about herself were true, if she was being honest or if her seeming innocence was a façade.

Wholly attuned to every idle shift and movement of her luscious body in that jaw-dropping gown, he ignored his growing desire for her as he sought to read each flicker of emotion in her face and eyes. Trying to penetrate her nature through judicious observation, continuously scanning her for signs of deception or ill intent, he monitored every subtle change in her demeanor and listened to her casual conversation with intense absorption.

Indeed, his wariness about her caused him to pay a much deeper attention to her than he normally did to any woman.

But in spite of all his doubts about Kate, by the time the rich and colorful dessert course was unfurled before them, they had somehow fallen together into the natural camaraderie of two people who had shared a brush with death — never mind the fact that their two families had been at each other's throats for hundreds of years.

Her throat interested him greatly, the lovely arc beneath her dainty earlobe, the milky skin, the silken cascade of her perfumed hair . . .

His mind drifted, the wine warming his senses. It had now been three days since he'd had a woman, and he had not forgotten the way she had felt beneath him last night. He still wanted her in spite of himself.

Her lips' dewy roses beguiled him, along with the teasing sparkle in those emerald eyes beneath her black velvet lashes. The candlelight brought out a golden luster in the depths of her light brown hair and danced along the delicate lines of her bare shoulders.

Was it wrong to want to lick the caramel sauce out of her splendid cleavage instead of drizzling it politely on the cheesecake? He did his best to keep a tight rein on his dangerous hunger for her, even as his hands tingled with yearning to caress all her creamy, glowing skin.

As he took another large swallow of port, he contemplated the fact that there was one sure way to find out if she was really as innocent as she would have him believe.

If she was a part of her forebears' sinister conspiracy, it was unlikely that she was a virgin. He was keenly tempted to verify her status for himself by luring her into his bed and finishing what they had started last night.

But even if he sensed that a well-timed advance from him might not be unfavorably received, he refused to set foot down that road.

There were only two possible outcomes,

and he already knew he'd regret it either way. If she was a heartless Promethean agent, he'd hate himself for joining his body with hers. If not, and she was as pure as his instincts felt her to be, well, that was almost as bad.

His father had taught him as a lad that what you broke, you paid for. If he bedded Kate and ended up taking her virginity, then he would be saddled with her in earnest. Which was precisely why he never dallied with virgins. He liked his women worldly and experienced, as coldly able to walk away from their couplings as he was, without a sentimental backward glance.

Nevertheless, he throbbed as he watched the languid motion of her fingertip circling along the brim of her champagne flute.

He had plied her with wine to get her to open up to him, and by now, they were having a rather cozy time of it.

She was chatting about her hobbies, for he had asked her what she liked to do for amusement, part of his subtle effort to draw her out. "As it happens, I have a terrible weakness for books."

"What kinds of books?"

"All kinds." Her white shoulders lifted in a charming little shrug, momentarily fascinating him. "History, science, natural philosophy."

"Really?" Born and bred for action, he had never been much of a scholar himself.

"Oh, yes. The ancients. Traveler's tales. And . . . Gothic novels," she admitted, biting her lip with an impish twinkle in her eyes. "Ghosts and curses and such."

"Oh, Lord."

"Don't groan!" she protested, laughing. "You don't know what you're missing! I'll bet you've never even read one!"

"I'm living one," he muttered under his breath.

"Pardon?"

"Haven't you heard? The castle's haunted. Keep an eye out for the Gray Lady," he said dryly. "You'll find she especially likes the staircase. I am not jesting!" he added mildly as she scoffed.

"Your Grace!" She tilted her head, her green eyes shining as she narrowed them at him. "You don't believe in ghosts."

"Stranger things, Horatio."

"Very well, I'll play along — though I know you're bamming me. Who is this ghost of yours?"

"The first Warrington duchess, Mathilda — supposedly strangled to death by her husband."

She studied him for a moment. "Now that

you mention it, I recall the smugglers trying to scare me with some cock-and-bull tale about your bloodlines being cursed. What's all that about?"

He looked at her for a long moment, drumming his fingers slowly on the table. If she was feigning ignorance, perhaps he could lure her into giving herself away; she should already know the tale, being the descendant of the story's villain.

Frankly, superstitious as he was, Rohan did not like talking about it. It seemed bad luck. But the story of the Kilburn Curse could provide him with a neat side entry into the darker matters they still had to discuss.

He heaved a sigh when he finally started. "A great long time ago, the first Lord Kilburn was a knight in the service of Edward the Black Prince, and one of his boon companions. My ancestors were the Earls of Kilburn before they were given the dukedom," he explained as an aside. "Lord Kilburn was my courtesy title when my father was alive."

"I see."

"At any rate, a conspiracy to kill Prince Edward was unearthed. Justice was swift in those days, and all participants in the plot were sentenced to be hunted down and brought back, dead or alive. My ancestor, Lord Kilburn, volunteered to pursue the one conspirator that no one else dared oppose — Valerian the Alchemist. None of the other knights would do it for fear of the sorcerer's black magic."

She tapped her lip for a moment. "Valerian the Alchemist . . . why does that sound so familiar? I could swear I've heard of him."

"Have you?" Rohan studied her keenly for a moment, but he could find no trace of guile or deception in her eyes.

"What was he? Some kind of court astrologer?"

"Oh, your average medieval sorcerer. A man of some renown."

"I must've come across his name in one of my history books." She nodded, smiled at him, and poured herself a little more champagne. "Go on, please. I like this story."

"When Lord Kilburn finally cornered the Alchemist, there was a great battle. You can believe what you like, but according to legend, there were various demons involved, summoned by the power of the Alchemist's dark spells."

"Demons, too! Are you sure you didn't get all this from Mrs. Radcliffe?"

He sent her a dry look. "Though the

sorcerer's demons were sorely attacking our brave Lord Kilburn, at last, he got one clear shot and picked up his crossbow to put an arrow in the warlock's black heart. Unfortunately, somehow, he hit the Alchemist's bride instead."

"Oh, pity! What was she doing at a battle?"

"It was her home. Kilburn had tracked Valerian to his castle and laid siege. She expired in her husband's arms. Officially, my ancestors have always maintained that Valerian pulled the girl in front of him to use her body as a shield."

"Most ungallant!"

"Quite. So, you see, her death was actually Valerian's own doing — but that only heightened his wrath. Distraught as he was, he failed to defend himself and was struck down a few minutes later. But with his dying breath, he laid the curse on all the Kilburn lords, that they would murder their own wives in revenge for slaying his."

She stared at him, wide-eyed.

"Our Gray Lady, the Duchess Mathilda, was the first, but I fear, not the last Warrington bride to die by her husband's hand."

"Oh, Lord. I'll never fall asleep here now."

Rohan smiled at her, but his eyes were grim. "Every few centuries, somehow, it happens again. Most unfortunate. The Lord

Kilburn who cut down the Alchemist ended up strangling his poor Mathilda — allegedly."

"Allegedly?"

"Some claim it was a disgruntled servant who attacked her. Others say she actually hanged herself after losing a baby, but Kilburn took the blame so she could be buried in the churchyard."

"How sad!"

He shook his head and sighed. "Then there was the third duke, who allegedly pushed his lady off the tower roof."

"Allegedly?"

"Gust of wind. Uneven stones. She might have tripped."

"Let's hope so."

"The seventh duke discovered his wife in flagrante delicto with his best friend and, I'm sorry to say, shot them both. Not allegedly."

"That's terrible!" For a moment's brooding silence, she peered into her champagne. "Well," she said, glancing up again with a mischievous glimmer of deviltry in her eyes, "at least your curse must keep the ton huntresses at bay." She began chuckling merrily. "Honestly, it's brilliant! What a perfect plan to keep all those matchmaking mammas at a safe distance. It's the perfect excuse!"

He looked at her in astonishment. "I beg your pardon?"

"Now I see how you managed to remain a bachelor all this time. Truly, it's ingenious! All I want to know is did you concoct this tale yourself, or was it handed down to you by your forebears? This must be a perennial problem for eligible dukes."

"You think we made this up?" he exclaimed.

"Well, surely, you are not serious!" She laughed harder. "How it must torture them! All of those haughty debutantes who long to set their caps at you — but are they brave enough to risk the Kilburn Curse?" she asked with feigned drama. "Believe me, I don't hold it against you. I'm sure without some sort of device like this to drive them away, you would never have any peace, poor fellow! But it doesn't lose you *too* much," she added with a wicked sparkle in her eyes. "It does not altogether negate your appeal. In fact, to some girls, it might make it all the stronger. Gothic novels are the rage, after all, and curses are completely glamorous."

Rohan scowled and picked up his dessert spoon, nonplussed by her irreverent mirth. "You asked me a question. I answered it.

Nobody's asking you to believe it."

"Good. Because I don't. Because it's nonsense," she added with a grin from ear to ear. "I'm not as gullible as some people."

He could scarcely believe she was sitting there making fun of him — the fearsome, the terrible Beast. She ought to be paling and quaking and running for her life, from the horror of him, the assassin and his curse, but instead, she just sat there looking like the blasted cat who swallowed the canary.

Without another word on the subject, Rohan took a large, resentful bite of cheesecake and washed it down with a swallow of wine.

"What's the matter?"

"Nothing," he grumbled.

She frowned. "You don't really believe all this?"

"Of course I don't," he shot back with a self-conscious scoff.

"You *do*!" she said in amazement. "The ghosts, the curse, and all that! Oh, my goodness." She stared at him, slackjawed. "That is adorable!"

"Do you mind?" He threw down his napkin.

"So, that's why you never come to the castle! I heard the smugglers complaining about that. But you don't look like you'd be afraid to duel with the Devil himself, and some silly ghost —"

"I am not *afraid* of ghosts!" he declared.

But she just smiled at him — and Rohan suddenly found himself laughing. Damn her, she had disarmed him.

"I'm just a little superstitious, that's all! The dead duchesses supposedly want revenge on the current duke. How would you feel?"

"Don't worry, Rohan, I'll protect you from the ghosties."

"Little mockingbird!" He shook his head at her with half a mind to lunge across the table and stop her laughter with a hearty kiss. Instead, he glanced toward the sideboard. "You see that lemon meringue pie over there? You're going to get it in the face if you persist."

"Oh, no! A shot across the bow."

"Fair warning." He eyed her hungrily. "Now, eat your cake or whatever it is and try to be a good girl."

"It's German apple puff, for your information. Have you tried it? It's delicious. Here." She leaned slowly across the table and fed him a bite from her spoon.

He helped himself to a leisurely look at her décolletage as he opened his mouth and accepted. "Mm. That is good."

"Told you so." Her eyes twinkled as she leaned back in her chair in leisurely contentment.

"I thought you said a while ago you had no room left for the sweets."

"I'm pacing myself. Besides —" She took another dainty nibble off her dessert spoon. "There were no corsets in the trunk of goodies your servants brought me, so, you see, I'm wonderfully free to make a glutton of myself."

This little fact arrested his full attention. His stare homed in on her figure — what he could see of it over the table. "You mean . . . ?"

"Indeed, Your Grace. Tonight, I go *au naturel.*" She laughed like she enjoyed teasing him and took another remorseless bite of German apple puff.

Rohan watched her with strange sensations of delight.

God, she was a maddening woman. An unpredictable blend of innocence and passion. Intelligent, mercurial. Her prickly side amused him, but he liked her even better like this, open and relaxed.

Uncorseted.

In her scintillating humor, she threw off light like the candle glow as it played over the cut-crystal facets of their wine goblets.

In short, she enchanted him. Maybe she had inherited some of her ancestor Valerian's magic.

Rohan had a feeling he was doomed.

He could sense a most unforeseen bond growing between them and did not know what to make of it.

"Staring again, Your Grace?"

"I've just decided you are rather naughty. And I like it."

She shrugged. "You said we were celebrating. Anyway, it's your fault. If you wanted me to behave, you shouldn't have made me try so many wines."

"Why on earth would I want that?" he asked softly.

"Hm." She caught a bead of condensation running down the shaft of her narrow champagne flute on her fingertip and brought it to her lips.

Damn, but just watching her got him hard.

"Rohan." The way she purred his name made his blood pound with wild potency.

"Yes, Kate?" he responded barely audibly.

"Can we talk about serious things now?"

He gazed deeply into her eyes, slowly pushing his lust aside along with his dessert plate. "Yes. I think we should."

"I still have many questions."

"As do I."

"You do?"

He nodded, bracing himself for the chess game. "Is there anyone you need to contact? Let them know you're safe?"

"No. There's no one." She shook her head, lowering her gaze, but she held her chin at a proud angle despite this painful answer.

"There must be somebody —"

"There's not," she said sharply. "I want to know what Peter Doyle said." She glanced up again in defiance, as though daring him to pity her.

He saw her prickly side was back, defenses up and ready to shield her pride.

"Was I right?" she persisted. "Are they stealing women to sell to depraved men of means?"

"No."

Her eyes narrowed. "You're sure?"

"Trust me, I'm entirely certain."

She furrowed her brow and slowly looked away. "But then, that would mean that I . . . was the sole target of their scheme."

"Yes."

Her eyes flared with alarm. "But, why?"

"You tell me."

She looked at him in confusion. "What do you mean?"

He paused, then took another tack. "Peter Doyle seems to think that someone is after your father."

"But that's impossible." She shook her head with an incredulous look. "My father is dead. He's been dead for over a decade."

"You're sure of that?"

"Of course I'm sure! What a thing to ask!"

"Do you mind if I ask how he died?"

"At sea. He was a merchant captain. He was making the run from India. His ship hit a terrible storm off the Horn of Africa. Why are you looking at me like that?"

"Like what?" he asked quietly.

"Like you think I am lying!"

He leaned back in his chair, steepling his fingers. "Tell me something." He ignored her feisty scowl. "What do you make of Pete's claim that your last name is Fox?"

The scowl faded slowly; her eyes grew large and soulful.

"Kate?"

The question had clearly upset her. Her face had paled, and she looked a bit shaken.

It did not escape his notice that she made no attempt to conceal her emotions. They were written plainly on her face, and no Promethean agent would ever allow that.

Besides, no one was that good an actress, especially after three glasses of wine. Avoiding his scrutiny, she let her gaze wander off across the table. "All right," she whispered more to herself than to him, then she nodded. "There is something that I-I think I need to tell you."

Stoic down to his bones, he refused to betray any sort of reaction, though her quiet words struck him like a punch in the gut. "I'm listening."

"It makes no sense that I can figure. None that puts my mind at ease. An old childhood memory . . ."

"Yes?" he urged when her words trailed off. "Go on."

"I'm not sure where to start. You don't want to hear my whole life story."

"I'd like that very much, actually." He leaned his elbow on the table and rested his face against his fingertips.

"Well, it's fairly hazy, because I would've only been about five years old," she began in a halting voice. "I had just been sent to live ashore after my mother's death. Wait — let me back up," she amended with a wave of her hand. "As I said, my father was a merchant captain."

"His name?"

"Michael Madsen."

Or Gerald Fox? Rohan wondered. Pete had said that "Madsen" was just the captain's alias.

"I was born at sea," she continued. "In

my earliest years, we lived aboard Papa's frigate. Our floating home. The crew was like our extended family. That boat and everyone on it was my whole world."

"Sounds like a colorful childhood."

"I suppose it was. But that's not the half of it." She offered him a pensive smile. "My parents' story was the most romantic thing you ever heard."

"Really? Do tell." She had his full attention.

She rested her crossed arms on the table before her. "My mother was a French émigrée, the daughter of a count at the time of the French Revolution."

"Do you know his name?" he asked, holding his breath.

"Of course — though I never met him. The Count DuMarin."

He could have sworn he felt the very castle stones groan and shake around him at the name. He hid his astonishment to hear it confirmed.

She certainly had not tried to hide it.

"What's wrong?" She tilted her head with a slight scowl. "You don't like it that I am half-French, is that it?" She snorted. "I know, I'm quite familiar with the prejudice from all you full-blooded English folk. But I assure you, Your Grace, my relatives were no Jacobins. My grandfather was a royalist, I'll have you know, and a personal friend of the King."

That's not all he was. "Believe me, Kate, I have nothing against France or the French people. They have their strengths and weaknesses, as do we, and every other nation on the globe. Have you ever been there?" he added. "To France, I mean. Your mother's homeland."

"I have never been anywhere," she answered crossly. "I have had the dullest life you could possibly imagine." Then she heaved a sigh and idly scratched her eyebrow. "I used to travel about and go on adventures with my parents when I was little — back when I lived aboard Papa's ship. But ever since I moved to the cottage in Dartmoor, my guardian, old Charley, kept me living in the middle of nowhere like a blasted hermit. He wouldn't even take me to London, ever, or anywhere else interesting." She paused. "He died about a year and a half ago, and I thought then that I'd go myself, but —" She shook her head, her words breaking off in frustration.

"But what?"

"I didn't know anyone! I did not know the way. I was — too scared." She gazed at him in dismay. "How or when or why

Charley managed to turn me into such a coward, I hardly know."

"You may be many things, Kate, but a coward isn't one of them." He watched her intently.

"I don't know . . . at least being kidnapped pulled me out of my safe little nest, didn't it? I suppose that sounds odd." She laughed cynically. "But they say everything happens for a reason."

She didn't talk like a Promethean, he thought. She was too honest and made no effort at self-aggrandizement.

"Not that I'm happy to have been kidnapped, mind you," she amended, "but I was . . . so bored and isolated out there. Yet too afraid to leave. It's like I was trapped."

"What were you so afraid of?" he asked in a murmur.

She considered with a shrug, then shook her head. "I don't even know. Charley always drummed it into my head that the world was much too dangerous out there. That people couldn't be trusted. That certainly turned out to be true! Well — except for you," she added very cautiously.

He gave her a guarded half smile, beginning to wonder if the remote Dartmoor cottage, the false name, and her caretaker's efforts to keep her at home were all measures

Gerald Fox might have taken to *hide* his daughter from the Prometheans.

She dropped her gaze. "Anyway, I was telling you about Mama."

"Yes, please, go on."

"When the French Revolution broke out, my mother was still at her convent school, soon to make her debut, and having been so completely sheltered there, she was in no way prepared for all the chaos as France began exploding. Before long, my grandfather, the count, decided it was no longer safe for her to remain in France, so he arranged for her to be taken to safety in America. She was to join some of our relatives in the Vieux Carré, the French Quarter of New Orleans."

It all matched. He was stunned that she was being so open with him. Everything she was saying corresponded with what Rohan knew about the DuMarin affair — which meant she was wasn't lying. At least not yet.

He urged her with a silent nod to continue.

"My grandfather hired Captain Madsen to take his daughter to New Orleans," she said with a nostalgic little smile. "Papa's frigate was known to be very fast. Plus, my father had been in the Marines, so if there was trouble, he knew how to handle a sword."

Rohan knew in his bones then that "Michael Madsen" had to be Gerald Fox. But it wasn't the Count DuMarin who had hired him but Rohan's father.

"What happened once they set sail was something no one could have planned." Her smile turned dreamy. "Along the voyage, the two of them fell in love. The bold English captain and the delicate French miss. They eloped — and I was the result."

Rohan returned her smile cautiously, but was shaken to the core to hear his suspicions so utterly confirmed. It awed him all the more to think that if it weren't for his heroic sire's choice of Gerald Fox to take Lady Gabrielle to America, the beautiful Kate would never have existed.

He shook off his amazement, needing to make sure this was all she had been told about her origins. "You're right," he said mildly, "that is pretty romantic. So, what happened then?"

"Disaster, of course." She gave a decidedly Gallic shrug. "Life at sea is dangerous. It didn't help that my father's brash influence led Mama to attempt a degree of adventurousness that she was not suited for in the least. You see, my parents shared a pastime: hunting for treasure between Papa's cargo runs."

"Treasure?" he echoed in surprise.

"Mm-hmm. It took them all over the world. That was how she died. They went into a cave one day, along with some of the crew. I don't know what horde of hidden gold they thought they were searching for this time — they never found anything. But this was their chief form of amusement, a hobby, their shared passion. I was still too small to participate. I stayed on board with Charley — he was Papa's bo'sun and like a grandfather to me. I remember standing on the rails, watching the longboats row up to those caves."

"Where was this?"

She thought about it. "I don't really know. There were seals. That's all I remember. The rest is a blur. For, you see, they went into those caves to search for some stupid pirate treasure, and when Papa came out, he was carrying my mother's lifeless body in his arms."

"My God . . . what happened?"

"Some kind of accident inside the cave. Part of the rock overhead collapsed and fell on her when it came crashing down. They tried to keep me from seeing her body." Kate stared through her empty wineglass.

"Before the day was out, they buried her at sea wrapped in a shroud and weighted down with a cannonball. I kept screaming like a wild thing because I was convinced she was only sleeping."

"You were how old?" he whispered.

"Five." She looked at him grimly. "Her death changed everything. Especially my father. He didn't want me aboard his ship anymore for fear that something would also happen to me. Within a few months, he bought the cottage and sent me to live in it, with Charley to look after me. The old man was set to retire, anyway, and as for me, it was time to begin my schooling. My mother's dearest wish was for me to have the sort of education usually reserved for a son."

"Why is that?"

She shrugged. "She disliked having been so sheltered at her convent school. The nuns wanted to mold young ladies who were virtuous, not learned, and when France went mad, she resented having been molded into a beautiful, helpless damsel, unprepared to fend for herself in any particular.

"She convinced my father that that must never be allowed to happen to me. That I must be molded with great independence, and raised to be able to care for myself. She wanted to make sure that if the world ever went to hell in a handbasket again in my day, as in hers, that I would be able to survive."

The painful truth of her words, with their edge of bitterness, penetrated his heart. He gazed at her for a long moment. "That would explain your resilience after what you've been through."

She looked gratefully into his eyes, then shook her head. "I'm not as brave as you think."

He gazed tenderly at her in question, but she did not explain the remark, continuing her story instead.

"As soon as we were settled in Dartmoor, Charley began hiring my various nurses and governesses, and later, my tutors. Poor Charley. He's gone, too, now. My last link to my parents. He was not just the bo'sun, you see, but my father's confidant, and part owner of his ship." She smiled nostalgically. "Gruff old thing. He never had much to say, but behind that grizzled exterior was a heart of gold.

"O'Banyon and the Doyle boys were lucky old Charley wasn't on hand to defend me the night they burst in," she added. "He'd have blown them all to smithereens with his shotgun. He was very fond of that shotgun," she mused aloud. "He taught me to use it as part of my boyish education."

"Really?"

She nodded. "Unfortunately, those cretins got to me before I could lay my hands on it."

Rohan raised an eyebrow at the prospect of a little thing like her firing a shotgun. "The recoil must throw you across the room."

"I brace myself. But yes, I do go flying," she admitted with a grin. He laughed softly, trying to picture any of his elegant London paramours having a conversation with him about guns.

Pirate's daughter, plenty, Pete had said, and Rohan had to agree. A consistent picture of who this unique young woman was finally was beginning to come clear in his mind.

"At any rate, Papa went back to sea, leaving Charley to keep watch over me. Charley, in turn, hired a string of nurses and governesses to help take care of me — and that leads me back to what I originally wanted to tell you."

Rohan nodded in encouragement, waiting for her to take it at her own pace.

"There was only one time in my life when Charley ever really yelled at me — I mean, he *bellowed.*"

"At you? The little angel? What ever did

you do?" he asked, quite entertained to think of her as some naughty child in ribboned ringlets.

"The first nanny he hired for me was trying to assess how much I already knew, so that she could determine where to start my education. She asked me if I could write my name. So I did. But she rejected it. I did it again, and she began to scold me." She paused, staring at him. "I had written down my name as Katherine Fox."

He went motionless, completely focused on her.

She shook her head. "I refused to budge on this. The governess thought I was lying. I wanted no part of her, anyway. Charley heard me yelling at the woman, and her scolding me, in turn. He came to see what was the matter, and when the governess showed him my signature, he dismissed her on the spot.

"I'll never forget what happened next. I was so pleased, thinking I'd won, but Charley grabbed me by the arm and stooped down to my level. He stared right into my eyes and told me that my name henceforth was to be Kate Madsen." She paused, looking slightly haunted. "He threatened to leave me if I ever told anyone again that my name was Kate Fox."

He saw her swallow with emotion.

"So, of course, I never did. That was the most terrible threat. He was all I had left." She shook her head. "Time passed. Eventually, I forgot all about it. Kate Madsen was my name — but then, that night, O'Banyon came along calling me Kate Fox, and I remembered that incident again after all these years. It was as if he knows something about me that even I don't know about myself." She looked at him with fear swirling in her eyes. "What does it mean, Rohan? Why is this happening to me?"

Everything in him longed to offer comfort, but he knew he must not give in to that temptation. Not yet.

"What do *you* make of it?" he countered.

"Well . . . there's only one explanation, isn't there?" She was growing paler by the second. "Logically — it sounds as if my father ordered Charley to raise me under a false name. But why? Why else would Charley tell me to lie? Did he and my father know that someone would eventually come after me? My God!" she exclaimed all of a sudden. "My whole life have I been deceived about who I am?"

"Easy," he murmured, reaching across the table to lay his hand on her forearm. "We're going to get to the bottom of it, I promise you." Judiciously, he withdrew his steadying touch. He had a delicate balance to keep here. "Let me ask you this."

She nodded, her fearful eyes focused on him in question.

"Did you ever receive official confirmation of your father's death?"

"What, like a death certificate? No — I don't think so. I don't know for sure, I-I was only ten when we got word of his ship going down," she sputtered. "But we *must* have! Charley would have got it. Besides, I received my inheritance! A sizable sum — I mean, it wouldn't seem much to someone like you, but it was all my father's fortune, enough for me to live in a comfortable independence." She shook her head and looked away. "God, what am I to make of this? Why would my father change my name?"

"Probably to protect you."

"From what? From whom?"

"He must have known he had some serious enemies. Somebody *did* just kidnap you. What does that tell you?"

She looked overwhelmed. "Are you saying that I could have been in hiding from somebody all these years and not even known it? Is that why Charley would never take me beyond the confines of our village?"

"Perhaps. Or —" He hated to do this, but he had no choice. Best to get it over with quickly. "There could be," he murmured, "an altogether different explanation."

She looked up desperately and met his scrutinizing stare.

He knew the time had come to let her see a couple of his cards. If this was an act, then he would take one last chance to jar her out of it with a more aggressive warning.

"What do you mean?" she pursued.

"You could be lying to me right now," he said softly. "And if that's the case, I want to give you this chance to come clean."

"Come clean? What are you talking about? Rohan — you're scaring me."

"It's not my intention. Not if you are innocent. I am willing to take your words at face value. But if you are lying to me, if all this is a masquerade, and you came here thinking to trifle with me, then be warned, you are in far, far over your head."

"What?" she breathed.

He refused to budge, hardening his heart as she paled, looking bewildered, and a little like she might cry. If in the off chance she *was* a Promethean agent, she would know exactly what he was talking about and hear him, that he'd called her bluff.

If not, then she did not need to understand.

"Look around you," he advised. "In six hundred years, my family has never shirked our duty. If you came here with aught against me, take this chance to confess. It will not come again. I promise you, you will find mercy if you speak up now. On the other hand, if you refuse, don't expect me to spare you just because you're beautiful. I am giving you this chance, but if you think you can deceive me, what happens to you, I'm afraid, will be your own fault."

She stared at him, slack-jawed.

He waited patiently. "Well?"

"You are a madman!" she choked out, then abruptly pushed up from the table and began striding away, looking terrified.

He shut his eyes, but it appeared he had his answer. Everything in him longed to go after her, but he remained in his chair, given that his last effort to follow her had resulted in her running out onto a cliff. "Come back, Kate."

"Did you just threaten me to *kill* me?" she demanded, pivoting to face him from a safe distance.

"Nothing to hide, nothing to fear."

"Rohan, I haven't the foggiest notion what you are talking about!" she cried.

He looked over at her for a long moment. "I do hope that's true."

"God, get me out of here — I thought I could trust you!"

"Kate!" he barked. He stood as she started running from him in a swish of whooshing skirts and pattering slippers. "Kate." He checked his tone. "Please come back."

"I want to go home!" she yelled, whirling to face him with an impassioned stare, tears in her eyes.

"In the middle of the night?"

"In the morning, then! Order your soldiers to take me back to my cottage tomorrow!" He could see her shaking.

"Back to your isolation?"

"Oh, you *would* throw my words back in my face! Who are you? Why do you have all these soldiers around here, anyway? Why does a duke need soldiers?" she shouted. *"What is going on around here?"*

"Kate, please." He relented, softening his tone. "I did not mean to scare you. I needed to make sure you were telling the truth. Come back and sit down, I beg you. Don't be afraid. I'm not going to hurt you."

"You just threatened my life!"

"I was only testing you," he insisted calmly. "I would absolutely never hurt a woman."

"Like your ancestors?"

"Please," he said simply.

"Why? What were you testing me for?" she demanded as twin tears spilled from her eyes and rolled down her cheeks. "Why would you do that to me? I thought I could trust you."

"You can." He could not bear her tears. "Kate — I work for the government in certain . . . covert capacities," he said cautiously. It was as close to the truth as he was authorized to tell. "That is why I have the soldiers, and it's also how I can promise to get you justice. But I had to make sure you were being honest with me before I could give you . . . the most important piece of information that came out of my talk with Peter Doyle."

"Well?" she demanded.

"Come back and sit down, please."

"No! I'll stay where I am." Fists clenched at her sides, she made no move to come closer. "Tell me what you know! If I passed your stupid test, I deserve to hear it now!"

"Very well." He watched her with a hooded gaze. "O'Banyon claims your father is alive."

Kate was already reeling, but this news shocked her to the core. She took an unsteady step toward him. "Papa's . . . *alive*?"

"Someone out there seems to think so," he said. "Someone with the rank and wealth to get O'Banyon out of Newgate and send him after you. Though you were the one abducted, I believe it may be your father who is their real target in all of this. It's possible you were taken hostage simply as the bait to lure the captain back to land."

"How can this be?" she whispered, walking back to the table like a person in a trance. She sat down abruptly in her chair, her heart pounded as she tried to absorb it.

She shook her head. "You must be mistaken. I *know* Papa is dead."

"How?"

"Because if he were alive, that would mean he just — left me all those years ago!" She winced at the mere suggestion of it. "It's impossible. He would never do that. He would not just abandon me. What, falsify his own death? Trick me? You don't know what you're talking about. My father loved me!"

Indeed, as a little girl, she had been very close to her doting sire. The whole crew had known that when the hard, weathered captain was in a foul temper, the one person who could always melt his heart was his "wee barnacle."

"Kate," Rohan murmured, staring at her.

Seething, she refused to look at him. What a heartless brute he was. At the moment, she despised him for even daring to suggest that the person who had loved her most in this world had not cared about her.

She shook her head. He would make her feel as if she did not matter at all. "Contrary to what you are suggesting, Your Grace, my father would never abandon me. He would never have just walked away from me without a backward glance."

"Perhaps he had good reason."

"Like *what*?" She shot him a furious look, lifting her head again.

"To lead his enemies away from you."

Her eyes widened. "What enemies?" She felt the blood drain from her face. *Oh, God, this can't be happening.* "Why would someone be after him?"

"Hard to say at present," he answered guardedly. "But I think it's clear that the only way we're going to get answers is to play this thing out."

"How?"

"We wait for O'Banyon's letter and follow his instructions when it comes. The letter should give us our next step. Where we are to rendezvous."

"You mean *go* to him?" She stared at him

231

incredulously. "Walk into a trap?"

"With our eyes open, of course."

She looked at him in dismay, then turned away without answering. God, if there was any chance she could ever see her beloved papa again, she absolutely wasn't leaving Kilburn Castle.

She lowered her head again, mulling it all, then she suddenly looked up. "Could this have something to do with one of those treasures my parents were always chasing? — but they never found anything."

"That you know of," he murmured, then he shrugged. "Anything's possible. At this point, I don't think it's wise to jump to any conclusions. We are at a standstill until we hear from O'Banyon. Once his letter comes, we'll know our next move. Until then, we will just have to be patient."

She realized, like it or not, he was right, but her head was spinning as she let out a rather shaky sigh. *Blast.* A few hours of peace today, and once more, her world was in chaos.

Could her beloved father really be alive?

Rohan approached, regarding her with a slight frown of concern. He crouched down before her chair and laid his hand over hers in reassurance. "Are you all right?"

"Other than not even knowing my own

name — yes, I'm perfectly splendid."

"Kate. You know I'm not going to let anything happen to you, don't you?"

Chastened by his patient tone, she met his steady, blue-gray gaze, and instantly regretted her sarcasm. She nodded in reluctance, then looked down at the simple touch that joined them. His right hand gently covered both of hers where they rested, anxiously clasped, on her lap. His hand was so much larger and more hardened-looking than hers.

In the silence, she relived those horrible seconds on the cliffside when his right hand, so gentle now, had stopped her from falling to her destruction.

"I'm sorry," she forced out. "I'm just — a bit confounded by all this."

"I know. But everything is going to be all right. Come. Let me show you around the castle since you are to be our guest here for a while. You might as well learn your way around your temporary home."

She gazed gratefully at him, but he barely noticed as he rose and leaned toward the table, picking up the candelabra. He nodded to her to follow before stalking out of the dining room ahead of her.

Kate gazed after him.

He's kinder than I ever would have thought.

She shook her head to herself. One moment he was scaring the stuffing out of her, and the next he was playing the perfect host. But she had to admit he seemed genuinely concerned for her well-being.

Warily, she rose and followed him.

The light from his candle branch flickered over the carved stone arches of the dark corridor beyond the dining hall, where he showed her some of the chambers behind the various closed doors: two different sitting rooms; a music room; a morning room for the ladies; a billiards rooms for the gentlemen; a stately formal parlor.

When they reached the last pair of large wooden double doors at the end of the hallway, he cast her a half smile. "This one I think you're really going to like." With that, he opened the door and lifted up the light.

Kate's jaw dropped as she stepped past him into the castle's magnificent library. "Oh . . . my . . ."

She could barely believe her eyes as she scanned the long, shadowy walls lined with tall Gothic bookcases. The dark wood shelves were crammed with tomes collected over several centuries. Her heart soared.

There was a partner desk and a library table with a large globe on a stand beside it, and far away, down at the end, a wonderful reading nook tucked into the bay of mullioned windows. A large grandfather clock could be heard ticking away steadily by the wall. Kate thought it quite possible she had died and gone to heaven.

"This ought to help you pass the time while you are here, don't you think?" he drawled.

She turned breathlessly to Rohan, who leaned in the doorway, watching her in amusement.

"Oh, it's . . . do you mind if I . . . ?" She pointed eagerly at his candle branch. "Um, may I?"

"Be my guest." With a hospitable nod, he handed over the candelabra.

She took it from him and lifted it high. Treading deeper into the library, she looked this way and that in a state of wonder. She had never seen so many books all in one place! Back at home, her entire collection of books, so precious to her, could all have fit easily on about four of these endless shelves.

It was sublime.

"Do you mind if I take a book up to my chamber to read for a while before bed?" she asked hopefully.

He arched a sardonic eyebrow. "Take as

many as you like. No one else is using them."

"Oh, thank you." She turned back to the shelves with a dreamy smile.

"You'd think I was lending you diamonds."

"Who cares about diamonds, I'd rather have these. Don't you like books, Your Grace?"

"I prefer life."

She did not care for his answer, but shrugged, not looking over. "You're a man. That's your prerogative," she answered under her breath.

"Excuses," he replied.

"I beg your pardon?" She turned to him in startled indignation.

"If fear is holding you back in life, you must attack it, Kate. Not make excuses about why you cannot attempt what you wish to do. That you can't because you're a woman. Especially you, given that your parents educated you as a son."

She blinked. "Well, thank you for your opinion, Your Grace," she answered rather primly. She was surprised he had paid that close attention to what she had confessed about her fear of leaving the familiar safety of her cottage after Charley had died.

It was true, she had *wanted* adventures,

but once she found herself alone, she had only seemed to have the nerve for those contained in books.

She was not sure she appreciated him holding her to account for her private flaw and gave a low snort. "At least I'm not afraid of ghosts."

His white grin flashed in the shadows. "You will be, after you've slept a few nights in this haunted old pile."

She sent him a pointed glance, but could not help returning his smile. It was obvious he'd meant no offense. He just seemed very sure of knowing what advice he ought to give her. *Men.*

She shook her head, then stepped up onto the sturdy library stair nearby, examining the contents of the next shelf. "Heron of Alexandria! I've never read his treatise on pneumatics and hydraulics!" she cried in excitement.

"What luck."

She barely heard his droll comment, gasping aloud when she spotted the rarest of tomes. "You have Al-Jazari's *Book of Knowledge of Ingenious Mechanical Devices?*"

"Do I?"

"I don't believe it! Is this the original fourteenth-century Latin translation from the Arabic?"

"Couldn't tell you."

She handled the aged manuscript with awe. "You mean you haven't read it?"

"Alas."

"Oh, Rohan! Sir Isaac Newton wouldn't have been able to formulate the laws of motion if it weren't for writers like this." She turned away as another volume on the shelves caught her eye. "Oh, that looks intriguing. Hullo — *Medieval Mathematicians.* And this one . . ." Taking three, then four books down, she piled them into her left arm, still holding the candle. "Perhaps just one more —"

"Let me help you." He strode toward her.

By the time they left the library, Rohan was carrying the candle branch, as well as a few books for her, while Kate hefted another several in her arms.

"Any sign of the Gray Lady?" she asked, as they climbed the stairs.

"None so far," he answered, his brief smile askance etched with wry, self-deprecating charm.

Cautiously, she smiled back, though she supposed he must think her a thorough quiz and a bluestocking, as well. She supposed she was, but she would never be embarrassed of her brains.

When they reached the bedchamber, he

carried her books into the room and piled them atop the squat bombé chest, also leaving her the candelabra.

"There you are."

Kate was right behind him. When he turned around, she was taken off guard by the power of his nearness. His masculine aura of strength engulfed her; she was suddenly all too aware of the bed nearby. Without warning, the air between them was charged with overwhelming tension.

Her heart slammed in her chest. His hard face was shadowed by the candles' glow as he gazed almost wistfully into her eyes. In spite of all his assurances, his hunger for her was palpable in the room, confusing her. She drew back from him a little, once more doubting his intentions.

He lowered his gaze with a wry look and retreated to the threshold of the hallway, where he paused. "Well, good night, then."

"Good night, Your Grace." She hesitated. "Thank you — for tonight."

He turned back to her, slowly bracing one hand against the doorframe. "You're welcome." He gazed into her eyes. "I, ah, I'm sorry if I frightened you earlier. I had to make sure you were telling the truth. I didn't mean to ruin your night."

"You didn't. I understand." Folding her

arms across her chest, she leaned her shoulder against the frame of the doorway. "I enjoyed this evening." She shrugged. "I want you to know, I appreciate everything. I realize you didn't ask for this."

He nodded. "It's no trouble."

As he stared into her eyes, she went motionless, her skin flushed with heat. She was certain in that moment that he was going to lean down and kiss her.

But for the second time tonight, he apparently decided against it.

Her heart was still pounding as he smiled faintly in the shadows. "Well, good night, then."

"Oh, wait, let me give you back the candelabra —"

"Keep it. You've got a lot of reading to do."

"See you tomorrow!" she called.

Already walking away, he sent her an idle salute.

Still blushing scarlet, Kate closed her chamber door; her heart was racing as she leaned against it. *Hm. I wonder why he didn't kiss me.* She chewed her lip, pleased with the Beast's restraint, but as she moved away from the door and began undressing, she couldn't seem to wipe the silly smile off her face.

Chapter 10

Within a fortnight, the Coast Guard agents arrived and took the smugglers into custody, all but Peter Doyle. Rohan had bargained to spare Caleb's nephew from arrest in exchange for Pete's cooperation when it came time to deal with O'Banyon — from whom there was still no word.

Meanwhile, as the days unfolded, waiting for O'Banyon's letter to arrive, Rohan remained perplexed by his own contradictory reactions to Kate.

He hated to admit it, but her effect on him was not, well, it was not normal.

Perhaps it was merely that he was not at all accustomed to having a young lady constantly in his house, underfoot, especially one whom he forbade himself to touch.

But the strangest part was he did not entirely mind it. His growing hunger for her made him restless, yet he soon got used to having her around every day. Before long, he even began waking up in the mornings looking forward to seeing her smiling face and wondering what bizarre thing she might say today. The chit amused him.

Her influence in his home was undeniable. She brought a sweetness and simplicity, a disarming warmth that made the cold, foreboding stronghold of Kilburn Castle begin to feel like a slightly more welcoming place.

Still, he found his own preoccupation with her slightly disturbing. It would have helped his peace of mind if he could have been sure his fascination with her was strictly physical, if he could have seen her as he usually chose to see women, as little more than a beautiful assemblage of alluring curves to be explored.

But with Kate, this approach proved impossible. He found too many real traits to admire in her character — courage, independence. With all of the needy, clinging ladies waiting for him back in London, he particularly liked her sturdy self-reliance. Gerald Fox's daughter was as sharp as a tack and yet quite down-to-earth.

She did not weary him with mindless prattle; did not simper, grovel, or pry; did not even seem to know how to toady to a man of his consequence. She did not play the coquette, either — a tactic he had enjoyed from women but had never trusted. Instead, she spoke her mind almost as plainly as a man, and as a result, her conversation actually held his interest.

Kate peppered her language with witty observations, occasionally made at his expense. He found her saucy impudence oddly refreshing, and instead of minding it, served it back to her. It was great fun to jest and needle each other in mutual irreverence, as they had that night at dinner; one thing they had in common was a willingness to mock their own foibles. Kate laughed at herself for a bluestocking, while he knew very well he was a superstitious fool.

But even all of this did not get to the heart of her effect on him.

Growing up out there on the moors, isolated from the world, she had an untouched quality about her that made him ache in ways he could not explain.

He was so drawn to her.

It made him rather uncomfortable. But that night at dinner when she had described her solitary mode of life at her cottage, he had realized that, unlike so many others, she, too, understood the degree of loneliness that he knew all too well.

Deep down, he knew his heart had never

been in such jeopardy before, and considering both their bloodlines, this was a very bad state of affairs. His instincts whispered that her arrival here was destiny. It remained to be seen, however, if she was to be his doom or the answer to his curse.

Given his reputation among his brother warriors as the Order's most expert killer, all he knew was that his teammates would have been utterly stunned to see the way he was with Kate.

He was also rather sure they would be horrified to learn that the little "present" who had so captivated him came from Promethean bloodlines. But of course, the Order still knew nothing about Kate, a fact over which he suffered serious pangs of guilt.

He knew bloody well that he should have written to his handler in London about her by now. He had composed the letter to Virgil and had even gone through the tedious process of putting certain parts of it into the necessary code. But he had no sooner written it, than he crumpled it up and tossed it into the fire. He did not want to give Virgil the chance to order him to bring Kate in for questioning.

He had promised to protect her.

An interrogation by his colleagues would

not be a pleasant experience, and by God, the girl had already been through enough. If he handed her over to them, her fragile trust in him would be destroyed. She needed him. Right now, he was all she had. If he did not help her, no one would, and perhaps . . . in a way, he might just need her, too.

He was fiercely committed to protecting her; that she openly appreciated it and trusted him to keep her safe sealed his resolve. Her utter reliance on him for her very survival had somehow renewed his whole sense of meaning.

For once, he had taken up a mission to preserve a life instead of snuffing one out. No wonder everything in him took hold of the mission as if his soul depended on it.

Thus he made up his mind that the Order could wait until he knew more about who exactly was after Kate and what their plans might be. Virgil would be furious — to be sure, it was practically unheard of for any dutiful Warrington to ignore protocol.

But as her protector, he determined that Kate was still too fragile after her kidnapping ordeal to withstand his colleagues' questioning. And this was the same reason why he stuck to his decision not to touch her.

Honor required it, though he burned for her. He had given his word that she would not be made to pay for her safety with her body, so he stifled fantasies of laying her down in his bed for a second interlude.

Perhaps a part of him wanted her to see that, on occasion, he could be more than a Beast.

Still, her tantalizing nearness was exquisite torture, having had a fleeting taste of her that first night, only to be denied the fullness of the feast.

He was not sure if Kate was aware how closely he was watching her. He hoped not. Surely, she sensed his deepening hunger, but she, too, kept a careful, friendly distance, occupying herself with the library books.

In turn, Rohan kept looking for reasons not to trust her, any reason to keep on holding her at arm's length. So far, it had been a losing battle.

One day about a week into her stay at the castle, he decided to bring her into the high medieval family chapel.

He wanted to see if Valerian's enchanting descendant betrayed any flicker of recognition when she viewed the Order's many ancient symbols on display there. They were in plain sight if one knew what to look for, from the white Maltese cross above the altar to the princely marble statue of St. Michael the Archangel, the Order's namesake. Perhaps he was trying to test her again, still hoping to expose her for a fraud.

Perhaps because her innocence was too much of a threat.

Taking her lightly by the hand, he led her into the chapel, where most of the Warrington dukes had wed their brides, and watched her face intensely as she gazed at the towering archangel statue.

The warrior angel, Michael, was portrayed clad in his Roman-style breastplate, a fiery sword in his hand and the writhing Lucifer under his sandaled foot. Though Kate stared at it in wonder, she did not appear to realize it held any particular significance.

She smiled shyly at him, nodding at the statue. "He reminds me of you."

He just looked at her.

She moved on, turning away, soaking in the serene beauty of the chapel. She stared at all the old relics and intricate carvings both in stone and wood, then knelt to say a prayer. Fiercely aware of her, Rohan watched her from the corner of his eye.

The more he felt the power of her innocence, the more it struck him how much he was asking of her, expecting her simply to trust her life to a man she barely knew, a man she had been given to as a plaything — and a Beast, at that.

A few nights later, they were in the library, her favorite room, drinking chocolate by the fire, while flurries fell gently beyond the mullioned windows.

Rohan had propped his feet on the low table across from the leather couch and was perusing the results of the latest prizefights in the sports page of the *Times*.

Kate, meanwhile, for reasons beyond his understanding, was tormenting herself with the cruelest book in his family's entire collection: the Latin volume of time-honored logic puzzles by the ancient scholar, Alcuin.

"Oh, here's a good one! The wolf, the goat, and the cabbage. In what order shall we get all three of them across the bridge without any of them eating the other?"

"You are the strangest girl I've ever met," he remarked idly, turning the page of the paper.

Seated at the other end of the couch, she shot him an indignant look. "Why? Because I enjoy using my brain?"

" 'Enjoy' and Alcuin don't belong in the same sentence, darling."

"I see, but bare-knuckle boxing is vastly amusing," she countered archly, leaning over to flick the back of his newspaper.

"Winning is."

When he cast her a smile, she held his gaze a little too long and began to blush. He did not fail to detect the sparkle of feminine interest in her eyes before she demurely dropped her gaze again to the book.

She turned the page. "Very well, forget the wolf, the goat, and the cabbage. Perhaps I should wrangle the problem of masters and valets, instead. Or the three jealous husbands?"

"You have at it, sweeting. I'll go schedule an appointment for you with the King's mad doctor."

"Ha, *ha,*" she replied.

Laughing softly, he set the paper aside, then, leaning his head back on the couch, he studied her. He had an inkling that her Alcuin puzzles were simply her way of keeping her too-clever mind off the dire threats that waited for her just beyond the safety of the castle walls.

"How are you these days?" he asked.

"Oh — all right." She lowered the book onto her lap and briefly held him in a wistful stare. "Rohan?"

"Yes, Kate?" he murmured in a tone gone slightly husky. He could not explain why this girl made his heart clench.

Restlessly, she turned away, staring for a long moment into the fire. "What if my father really *is* alive?" She looked over at him again. "Doesn't it seem strange that he never tried to contact me to let me know he was all right? What if he just — forgot about me?"

"No one could ever forget about you, Kate."

Her emerald eyes filled up with a soulful longing to believe. But shaking her head, she cast her book aside. "I could never do that. If my child were in danger, I'd stay with her, no matter what."

"Me, too," he answered in a low tone.

Hugging her bent knees, she returned her troubled gaze to the crackling hearth fire. "Did *you* get along with your parents, Rohan? Were you close to them?"

He considered, watching the pale flames licking at the darkness. "I admired them greatly," he replied in guarded tones. "Especially my sire. Hell, I worshipped the man."

"What about your mother?"

"She was a fine lady, but, um . . . rather distant. I don't know. I think she found me somewhat loud and aggravating. I was too rambunctious."

Her eyes twinkled when she glanced at him. "You, Your Grace? Rambunctious?

Surely not."

He arched a brow at her. "As I was saying. They sent me off to school when I was seven. My mother died when I was eight, and my father, well, he was hardly ever home. He had a . . . lot of responsibilities. But you know, my friends at school were my real family."

Which made his unwillingness to reveal her existence to his brother warriors all the more meaningful — but Kate didn't know that.

She studied him in surprise, resting her chin on her forearm. "I'm sorry to hear of your loss. How did your mother die?"

He looked askance at her, saying nothing.

Her eyes flared at his meaningful silence. She lifted her head and stared at him in astonishment. "The Kilburn Curse? You mean your father —"

"No, no, he didn't actually *kill* her. But he certainly held himself responsible for her death, and . . . not without cause."

"What happened?" she asked, wide-eyed.

Having gone that far, Rohan saw no point in stopping now. "My father was sent on a diplomatic mission to North Africa." It was always a "diplomatic mission" when speaking to outsiders.

The Order had charged the previous Duke

of Warrington and his team with the task of rescuing an English dignitary who had been captured by Barbary pirates off the coast of Malta. The ambassador's aide was being held by the fearsome Bey of Tripoli for an exorbitant ransom. Somebody had to get him out without implicating the Crown.

"My father had no sooner completed his task than he fell ill with some unknown North African fever. He spent a couple of days on Malta being bled by the physicians, but he soon had enough of that. Declared he was over it, and proceeded on to London. Tough as nails, my old man. He was never a very good patient. Unfortunately, he was not as much recovered as he wanted to believe, and he brought the fever back with him. My mother rushed to Town to tend him, caught it, and was dead within a fortnight."

"Oh, how dreadful!" she breathed with an unabashed look of compassion that disconcerted him. "Rohan, you poor thing. It must have been terrible for you."

He looked away uneasily. "No, it was worse for my father. He never believed in our 'family curse' until that happened. But from then on, he made a point of warning me it was real." He paused for a long moment, staring into the fire. He tried to comprehend how he would feel if he were ever responsible for hurting Kate. "I'm not sure how he lived with it," he said at length. "He didn't, actually, for very long. He died about three years later."

Killing Prometheans.

But he did not tell her that, either. He just shrugged.

"Father said his only comfort was that I was at school at that time and had not caught the fever, too, and also died." A world-weary sigh escaped him. "But I know it wouldn't have killed me, anyway. Nothing ever does."

She gave him a quizzical look, but leaned closer, bridging the small distance between them; she cupped his face with tender affection. "Well, I, for one, am glad of that."

He stared at her. Her touch was so soft it made him ache. He closed his eyes as his control slipped; tilting his head, he pressed a fervent kiss into her palm.

He heard her breathe his name, then her delicate hand turned his face forward again; without warning, she moved forward onto her knees and pressed an urgent but virginal kiss to his lips.

His heart slammed in his chest.

Wonderstruck by her unexpected move, he sat in trembling stillness, chaining himself back, only returning her kiss gently as his pulse pounded. God knew, he barely dared breathe for fear of scaring her away.

His restraint emboldened her. She moved closer, kissing him again, and again. Her lips stroking his were supple, satin, sweet.

He shuddered with the need to unleash his passion, but still, he held himself back, just as she paused with the air of a woman stopping herself with great effort.

"I'm sorry." Her breathless whisper inflamed his senses as she drew back a small space. "You looked like you — needed that."

"I did. I do." He nodded and drew her back to him.

But before she would let him claim her mouth, she looked into his eyes, then moved higher, pressing a soft kiss to his latest scar. He closed his eyes as her lips lingered above his left eyebrow.

Then he felt her lips glide slowly down the side of his face until they reached his waiting mouth. Passion raced through their hands and lips as they kissed with an intensity that told him she had dreamed of this as much as he had. She clutched at his waistcoat; his hands clasped her waist, in turn, as though with a will of their own. He couldn't fight it anymore.

When he pulled her astride his lap, she

did not protest. His heartbeat slammed as she lifted her arms around his neck and went on kissing him endlessly.

He felt the softness of her lush breasts against his chest and reveled in the intoxicating glide of her sweet tongue caressing his. He could not believe she was doing it, but could not bear for her to stop.

Want raged in his blood, swelling his member to full arousal as she knelt across his lap. He knew the moment she discovered it there, waiting for her, throbbing between her legs; he felt the fiery thrill of her excitement in response. Her fingers dug into his shoulders.

He absorbed in delight her sharp intake of breath when the gentle pressure of his hands on her hips guided her needy core against the hardened ridge of flesh straining the placket of his trousers.

She moaned against his mouth as she began rocking slowly against him. Instinctually, her body knew what to do with him. Rohan began unfastening the back of her dress before he even noticed what he was doing. He didn't care anymore. He could not contain himself. Every atom of his being had to feel her bare, silken back beneath his hands.

A moment later, her loosened bodice

crumpled down about her elbows. He ran his hands hungrily up and down her naked back, then he took her now-exposed breasts in both of his hands. She did not protest but welcomed his touch with a dreamy smile. At the back of his mind, he wondered what the hell he thought he was doing.

She kissed him again, and tugged away the length of black cord binding his hair as she did so. She drove him slightly mad raking her fingers through his hair. Breathing heavily, he dragged his mouth away from hers and lowered his head to taste the milky throat that had tormented him for so long.

She sighed with pleasure as he sucked and kissed her neck. She hugged his head and, beneath her skirts, spread her legs wider to sit more firmly on his lap. He understood better than she did that she wanted fucking, but he was not going to do it.

No, no, he was not. No, indeed. He was not that lost to all decency, surely. That bereft of judgment.

That much of a Beast.

She dragged her fingertips down his chest and began unbuttoning his waistcoat. With the damp heat of her core penetrating through their clothes, warming his deprived cock, his control was hanging by a thread with the sheer, wild unreason of his lust for her.

The next thing he knew, her exquisite hands were on his bare skin. She had bared his chest, exploring him, and when she slipped her fingers down into his shirt, eagerly caressing his stomach, he trembled as her dainty hand inched down toward his waist.

It took all his will, but he found a shred of strength to stop her from going any lower. He knew he would lose his mind if she touched his cock, as she seemed very curious to do. He ended the kiss, pulling back from her in a ragged haze of lust. "Kate — you know this isn't wise," he panted.

"No — I know — yes — you're right." Her chest heaving, she did not remove her hand from inside his clothes.

"You should go to bed. Go on, now, sweet."

Her fingers curled into the light furring of hair on his chest. "Don't you —"

"Please. Go, Kate. *Run,*" he growled at her, removing her hand from inside his shirt as his body throbbed. "Now. Before I change my mind."

She went motionless, holding his gaze, startled confusion warring with feverish arousal in her eyes. Innocent temptation incarnate, she still sat on his lap, her hair mussed by his fingers, her unfastened gown falling around her bared shoulders in an alluring state of tousled sensuality.

Craving her, Rohan closed his eyes. Could she not see he was trying as hard as he could do the right thing for her sake? "Go to bed, Kate."

Hurt, reproach, and confusion at his perceived rejection flickered in her green eyes.

"As you wish," she forced out in a raw whisper, and finally obeyed. Getting up from his lap, still holding her loosened gown to her chest, she fled the room in a rustle of skirts and a chastened patter of running, slippered footfalls.

He stared after her in wicked yearning, the taste of her still lingering on his tongue. He sat for a moment longer, brooding as he gazed into the fire.

Maybe he should send down to the village for a proper whore, he thought as sanity gradually returned.

That was when he realized he was worse off than he thought. For the only one he wanted now was Kate.

The kiss had been a mistake.

Kate was mortified that she had let her

desire for him run away with her like that. To think that, of the two of them, it was the Beast who should prove the better behaved!

Unable to face him the next day, she avoided him, more or less hiding in the library, while Rohan was elsewhere in the castle, doing Lord-knew-what.

Chastened for having made his job of protecting her all the harder, the least she could do, she thought, was to try to make herself useful. All morning, she worked at putting the haphazard, vast collection of books in the Warrington library in some kind of logical order.

Apparently, this was a task no one had bothered with in about a hundred years.

Trying to keep Rohan out of her thoughts, wondering endlessly if she should apologize for throwing herself at him when she saw him, she traveled from shelf to shelf, re-arranging the books by language, by historical period, by size, as was practical, and above all, alphabetically, by the writer's last name.

She had found multiple titles by individual authors scattered willy-nilly through the collection. It made her want to pull her hair out. Obviously! — an individual author's body of work all belonged on one shelf, the works arranged, in turn, by whatever system was most suitable: by volume number, alphabetically by title, or by the year of publication, or, in the case of the playwrights, works grouped by genre — tragedies with tragedies, comedies with comedies, histories with histories, and so on.

All the while, he lurked at the back of her mind, a large, looming shadow of temptation, haunting her, even though she knew her preoccupation with this man was nothing but foolish.

Soon all this would be over. O'Banyon's letter would arrive, bringing an end to her sojourn at the castle. In due time, Rohan and she would surely get to the bottom of why she had been kidnapped and who was out to get her; once these people had been dealt with, the two of them would go their separate ways. And then what?

She would probably never see him again, so why set herself up for unnecessary heartbreak? Logic sounded the alarm that she must quash her budding infatuation with him now. She had to fight it. The intelligent thing to do was to keep her thoughts fixed on her eventual, yearned-for goal of finally going home.

No matter how much she might want him, how secretly giddy she might feel around him these days, it was important to keep it front and center in her mind that she could never truly have him.

Rohan was a duke, too highborn for her. She could never be more to him than a favored mistress . . . though, lately, truth be told, that didn't sound so bad.

She was a grown woman. She could do as she pleased, and who was going to scold her? She had never been much of an active participant in the outer world in the first place to care if anybody out there disapproved.

Instead, after all those lonely years cooped up in her cottage, she finally felt connected to someone.

Someone wonderful. How was she supposed to ignore the kind heart she had discovered beneath the Beast's intimidating exterior?

How was she not to be swayed by a man who had saved her life, who had pledged himself to her protection, talked to her like a true friend, and charmed her daily — a big, beautiful man who had already given her an unforgettable taste of pleasure that first night in his bed?

Did he think her made of stone? God help her, but she wanted more. Last night, she had so needed to taste his mouth again, to caress his splendid chest and arms, desperate to get as close to him as she could.

And when he had opened up to her about losing his mother as a child, she had been overwhelmed with tenderness. Her caring for him had to spill out somehow — she had only kissed him because she thought her heart would burst if she didn't *do something* to show him how much she felt for him.

Well aware of how intensely he watched her every day, she thought he would have liked it. But instead, he had pushed her away. Kate was so confused, unsure if he had been rejecting her or protecting her.

Of course, everything Rohan had done stuck to the single theme of keeping her safe, yet self-doubt plagued her. Maybe he had stopped her because she had not acted like a lady, crawling onto his lap like the little harlot Caleb Doyle had first told him she was. Maybe Rohan had decided that she somehow was not good enough for him.

She knew she was an oddball, too. Only an eccentric bluestocking would take such pleasure in rearranging books.

Kate's jumbled thoughts continued as she sorted through the shelves. Though her mood was morose with her embarrassment over the kiss, the library itself was a comfort despite the dust tickling her nose.

The tick-tock of the nearby grandfather clock was a welcome companion in the quiet, soothing her nerves, along with the steaming cup of tea waiting for her on the nearby table.

"Oh, you don't go here," she murmured to a stray translation of Tacitus on the next shelf.

She pulled it out and carried it across the room, placing the historian with his fellow Romans, but on her way back to the spot where she had been working, her glance happened upon a title that brought a wry look to her face.

Dante's *Inferno.*

She was still highly curious about Rohan's involvement in that Inferno Club. By now, thankfully, she knew firsthand that her initial theory about the club's consumption of kidnapped virgins was naught but a Gothic figment of her overactive imagination.

But then she paused, her faint smile turning to a frown as she noted an unacceptable situation.

"Dante Alighieri, what are you doing all over the place?" she chided, going closer.

The three parts of the Italian's peerless *Divine Comedy* had been shoved in carelessly on different shelves all throughout one bookcase: the *Inferno,* the *Purgatorio,* and the *Paradiso.*

"You should be together!" she mumbled. It did not occur to Kate that she was talking to the books as she busily rolled the library stair over to the fourth tall bookcase on the eastern wall.

She set the brake, stepped up onto the wheeled stair, and reached up to pull out the *Inferno* to put it with its siblings.

But then, the most curious thing occurred.

When she tilted the book's spine toward her and started to slide it out, it stopped — and at the same time, she heard a mysterious click inside the wall somewhere. She gasped and yanked her hand away with a small cry.

It was not a book at all! Egads, it was some kind of lever! She stared at it, open-mouthed, just as Sergeant Parker dashed into the doorway.

"Are you all right, miss?"

"What?" she looked over, quickly trying to appear nonchalant.

"You cried out."

"Oh — I almost tripped off this little library stair, that's all." She managed a self-conscious smile.

"Do you need help getting down?"

"Oh — no. No. Thank you. I'm fine. That

will be all."

"Do be careful, miss."

"Yes, of course — I will. You may go!"

With a terse nod, Parker returned to his card game with Wilkins in the hallway. When he had disappeared, Kate turned back to the *Inferno* in wonder.

She could barely contain her excitement, for she knew all about such things from reading Gothic novels! Dear Lord, she thought Mrs. Radcliffe made all that stuff up, but Rohan was right — he was living in one. A castle complete with a ghost and a curse, and now, surely, some kind of secret passage.

Kate's heart was pounding. From her perch on the library stair, she looked all around the room, trying to find any sign of some hidden passageway opening up.

Nothing so far.

Perhaps she should try the other two parts of Dante's masterpiece. Quickly jumping down from the stair, she tried the same thing with the *Purgatorio.* Cautiously, she pulled on the spine, but again — *click!* — the book would not come out any farther from its spot, attached to the back of the bookcase somehow. It was actually a second lever only disguised as a book.

Her heart pounded as she bent down to

see if the third volume, the *Paradiso,* would be the key to activating whatever mystery the secret levers helped conceal. She pulled it forward. This time, however, there was no click.

She furrowed her brow. *Hm, what did I do wrong? Some kind of puzzle or pattern? Perhaps you have to pull them in a particular order.*

She experimented with possible combinations, hopping up onto the library stair again and again, and jumping back down to pull the levers in all six different orders.

When nothing availed, she thought of one last possible approach. It took a certain gymnastic talent and a spread-eagle stretch, balancing precariously on one foot on the library stair; but when she succeeded in pulling all three levers simultaneously — the lowest one with her right foot — suddenly, a mysterious sequence of muffled mechanical sounds began to whir and slide and creak behind the wall.

Oh, what have I gone and done?

Stunned it had actually worked, she slunk from the stair-stool and backed away from the bookcase, wide-eyed.

Pop!

Far above her, the top shelf of the bookcase suddenly jumped out — just a bit —

but enough to startle her.

Kate stared up at it, her heart in her throat, torn between astonishment and delight. "Hullo," she murmured under her breath.

Ever so cautiously, she tiptoed forward again, creeping back up warily onto the little wheeled stair. As she approached, she discovered that the top shelf of the bookcase concealed some kind of hidden drawer.

One she knew she had no business peeking into.

Oh, but she could not help herself!

I'll bet Rohan doesn't even know it exists, she reasoned. He made no bones about the fact that he was barely interested in the contents of his family's library. He would probably be glad she had found it for him.

With a surge of the same rash boldness that had inspired her to kiss him last night, she reached up into the hidden compartment and blindly felt around, for it was too high to see into, even if she stood on her toes.

Something is . . . up here. Her fingers closed around the leather bindings of a book. *Hmmm.* Heart pounding, she took hold of it and pulled it out.

A cloud of dust promptly rained down on her.

She waved it away with a cough, only glancing at the brittle tome she had liberated before reaching up again to find several more illuminated manuscripts.

What she had discovered appeared to be the oldest pieces in the Kilburn collection. They looked many centuries old; she could smell the cedar lining of the hidden drawer where they had been hidden, safely protected from the ravages of time.

No wonder they had been concealed. They were extremely valuable. Priceless, she thought in scholarly excitement.

Rohan probably had no idea of the kinds of treasures hidden away in the great library that his ancestors had assembled over the centuries. She couldn't wait to show him what she had found.

Her discovery was so exciting that maybe it would make him forget all about her foolish blunder of last night. A splendid change of subject.

With eager reverence, she carried her discoveries over to the large library table.

She stole another sip of tea, then set the cup carefully aside, well away from the precious artifacts. Taking extra care in handling the centuries-old books, she pulled the white fichu out of her neckline — she was wearing, today, a lovely but again ill-fitting French silk walking dress from the fashionable lady's traveling trunk.

Using the delicate cloth like a handkerchief to protect the brittle pages, she opened the first book she had unearthed: *On Dragons.*

"Oh, how wonderful!" she murmured to herself, gazing at the wildly colored illustrations of giant reptiles, winged and breathing fire.

The Chaucerian English was going to take some work to decipher. She would have to see what reference texts she could find in the collection to help her work out the captions, but for now, the pictures fascinated her.

The next page showed a silver-armored knight astride a galloping white steed. Armed with a lance, he was shown charging at a hideous, horned dragon that loomed over him, its black, batlike wings outstretched.

The knight in the picture had a winged ally of his own, however. In the sky above him hovered none other than St. Michael the Archangel again, her old friend from the duke's family chapel.

Come to think of it, she mused, wasn't that white Maltese cross on the little knight's pennant another detail she had noticed in the chapel?

She turned the page and stopped at the next colorful picture of a dragon holding its egg in its claws. Some sort of curious symbol was depicted inside the rounded contours of the egg. Kate furrowed her brow and leaned closer, studying the symbol on the dragon's egg. A tingle of faint recognition ran down her spine.

I've seen this before.

The symbol showed an eight-spoked wagon wheel, with a flaming torch in the center. Beneath the wheel was the Latin motto, *Non serviam.*

Easy enough to translate: *"I will not serve."*

Yet the drawing of that mysterious symbol filled her with an inexplicable sense of dread.

She straightened up again, not sure at first what made the sight of it so unsettling.

Resting her elbows on the table, she stared out the window across the room, but her thoughts drifted off a million miles away, across the sea . . .

Eyes burning from the dust, she rested her face in her hands, idly rubbing her brow and racking her brains about where she had seen that ill-omened symbol before.

Painful thoughts of her late mother, vague, wispy remnants of memory, floated through her mind. For a long moment, Kate sat in stillness, simply listening to the tick-tock of the grandfather clock. Her mind traveled back to her childhood days aboard her father's ship . . .

All of a sudden, she drew in her breath, lifting her head. She stared straight ahead with a stunned, unseeing gaze as it all came flooding back.

I remember.

For a moment, she could hardly breathe for sheer, stunned disbelief. Then she paled.

Oh, God. I have to tell Rohan.

Her embarrassment was suddenly swept aside, irrelevant in the magnitude of what she had remembered. She closed the dragon book with a jerky motion, suddenly loath to touch it. Her heart took up an ominous drumming rhythm, but she jumped up from her chair.

Already in motion, she swiped the book off the table, tucked it under her arm, and strode out swiftly into the corridor, where she found Parker and Wilkins lounging over their casual game of cards.

The two still served as her minders, but lately, they shadowed her at a more permissive distance.

"Where is His Grace?" she asked at once, marching toward them.

"Practicing, Miss. In the Hall of Arms. But you can't go in there —"

"I must see him."

"He is not to be disturbed."

"It is extremely important!"

"What's wrong?" Parker asked.

"You look like you seen the ghost," Wilkins offered with a grin.

She glanced grimly at him. "Something like that."

The ghost — of another key childhood memory. Who she really was was finally starting to come back.

Wilkins's jaunty smile faded at her somber look. The two men exchanged a guarded glance.

"Please. I have to see him." She swallowed hard. "He will understand. If he doesn't, I'll take the blame."

"Very well, then. This way." Parker beckoned grimly, starting down the hallway.

Hugging the dragon book to her chest, Kate followed, shaken to the core.

CHAPTER 11

Kate's guards led her into a wing of the castle she had not seen before. After a short walk down the corridor, they ushered her into the Hall of Arms, a vast stone chamber, cathedral-like, with a high vaulted ceiling and a row of tall, narrow, pointed windows down one wall.

"He'll be down there, through that archway, miss." Parker pointed. She nodded her thanks.

Still holding the dragon book, Kate uneasily crossed the empty Hall of Arms, glancing around at all the odd equipment for physical training arranged throughout the chamber. There was some sort of elaborate and hazardous-looking obstacle course, and one wall covered in scaffolding with various platforms to be climbed. The opposite, windowless wall was covered in straw-stuffed targets of all shapes and sizes, some on wires and other mechanical devices to provide moving targets for practice.

Iron dumbbells, leather punching bags. Knotted ropes here and there suspended high over the stone floor. A ten-foot wall for men to scale standing by itself in the middle of the room.

In the far corner was a rack laden with classical sporting pieces — javelins and discuses. A fight pit was cordoned off with ropes and filled a few inches deep with sand, to make the footing even more difficult, she gathered, as she passed.

Approaching the archway Parker had indicated, Kate braced herself for whatever she might find in the shadowed space ahead. Upon stepping through the arched doorway, she found herself in a narrow cloistered passage overlooking a square stone chamber, dimly lit by a couple of torches.

Crossing slowly to the waist-high wall of the arcade, she peered down into the room below and held her breath, staring in mingled dread and desire when she saw him.

Rohan was battling invisible foes, wielding the large, lancelike weapon she had seen in his hand that first night in the great hall. His long hair flowed around his shoulders, wetted with the sweat that streamed from him and made his body gleam with rippling, raw power. He was bare-chested, wearing only loose black trousers that draped his compact buttocks and muscled thighs gracefully.

His bare feet were silent on the flagstones as he lunged, leaped, and spun about, the torchlight flashing crimson on his long, wicked blade.

Kate watched, riveted by the play of shadows and gold torchlight that slid over his sweat-slicked body, gliding across the sleekly muscled contours of his back and massive shoulders, his powerful chest and chiseled abdomen as he thrust, swung, jabbed, then spiraled up to parry an imaginary blow, only to gouge again with precision perfectly balanced with killing force.

His blade sliced through the air with naught but a deadly whisper, each slashing arc of his weapon, like his honed body, under his exquisite control.

In constant motion, he wove through the changing patterns of his regime with a beautiful — an almost otherworldly — prowess, a creature of elegant savagery.

He attacked again with a low war cry, but then suddenly went motionless, standing in a sure-footed stance below her, his chest heaving.

Slowly, he looked up, as though he had

felt her there.

Kate found herself looking into the eyes of a predator; she held absolutely still.

"What are you doing here?" he demanded in a low tone, breathing hard. He lowered his weapon.

"I-I did not mean to intrude . . ."

The brooding, skeptical look he sent her brought back her sheepishness over last night all in a rush.

"I-I wouldn't have bothered you if it weren't important."

It had better be, his wary glance replied. He brought his weapon back up and rested it over his shoulder. "Very well. What is the matter?" He turned away and walked toward the small table in the corner of the chamber, stretching his neck from side to side and loosening his taut shoulders with a large shrug.

His unenthusiastic reception rather worried her, but Kate hurried along the cloistered arcade, heading for the few stairs that led down into the sunken stone chamber.

After that display of devastating capability, he was decidedly intimidating at the moment. She wondered if this rigorous practice was his way of burning off the frustration of their wanting each other.

She wished she had not done that last

night, but looking at him now, she doubted any woman alive would blame her. Nevertheless, she could see he was annoyed at the interruption. As a result, the prospect of admitting to the rude way she had snooped in his family's library suddenly did not sound as easy as she had first anticipated.

It did not help matters that his glorious display of warrior prowess had scrambled her wits with wild longing. Her heart pounded, but she reminded herself she had come here with a purpose. She dropped her hungry stare from his mouthwatering physique, for she did not get the feeling right now that he would appreciate her gawking.

Pull yourself together.

With a stern mental effort, she kicked herself back onto the task that had brought her here in the first place.

Fortunately, she somewhat managed to clear the haze of lust out of her brain before she reached the bottom of the shallow stairs and strode across the chamber, carrying the dragon book.

He was standing at the small table in the corner, and as she approached, he smoothly closed the lid of the mahogany case resting there — but not before she glimpsed the array of cunning weapons and razor-sharp tools cradled in the box's velvet-lined interior.

She blanched, then looked up quickly at him, but his closed expression did not invite questions.

She held her tongue as he locked the case and set it on the floor. "What did you want to talk to me about?" He picked up a small towel lying on the table and wiped the sweat off his face and throat, then his chest, which was still heaving from his exertions.

He turned to her as she neared with new-found caution, stopping a short distance away. "I have to show you something."

He tossed her an inquiring nod. "What is it?" The darkness had receded from his eyes, but it was not gone entirely.

Bravely, Kate went closer, joining him beside the table. "Here." She set the dragon book on it while Rohan dragged his fingers through his hair, shoving his long, sable locks back from his face. Tendrils of his hair still clung to his hot, damp skin.

The heat radiating from his big, hard body and the musky male scent of him had a maddening effect on her senses, which she strove to ignore.

"I think I know why someone might be after my father, if he's still alive."

"Really?" He glanced sharply at her.

"And," she added, "I finally remembered where I first heard about Valerian the Alchemist."

His fierce stare homed in on her.

"This symbol." Flipping through the pages until she found the illustration with the dragon egg, she tapped it with her fingertip. "I've seen it before. Do you know what it means?"

Before glancing down to see the picture she was pointing to, Rohan decided to thrash Parker for letting her in here.

He did not want any female to see this side of him, yet, somehow, Kate appeared undaunted by her first true glimpse of his . . . hidden talents.

Then he looked down and saw her pointing to the hated symbol inside the dragon's egg; he looked at her keenly and felt everything inside of him go cold.

"Do you know what it means?" she repeated urgently.

"No," he replied in a dull tone, but of course, he knew it well. It was called the Initiate's Brand. The central symbol of the Promethean Council.

It stood for everything he hated, everything he had joined the Order to help destroy.

It stood for her kin.

And it brought back a measure of the mistrust he had managed to overcome when he had convinced himself that she was innocent.

He looked at her shrewdly from the corner of his eye. "Where did you get this?" he inquired.

"Um — well — I was in the library and, er, . . . I found this little compartment."

"You found it?" He turned slowly and stared at her, folding his arms across his chest. He refused to think about last night, the aching sweetness of her kiss. "What compartment?"

Wide-eyed, she shrank back slightly from his dark stare. "I was putting your books into order," she said. "And I came across the Dante — the three parts of the *Divine Comedy.* They weren't together, and that didn't make any sense, so I went to pull them out — but they were levers, Rohan! False books!"

"You don't say."

Her head bobbed in an eager nod. "I pulled all three of them at once, and the top shelf popped open!"

"I see. So, you looked inside."

"How could I not?" she retorted with a nervous smile and a defensive little shrug.

"I didn't think you'd mind! There was a treasure trove of the most amazing illuminated manuscripts hiding in there! Did you know your library had a secret compartment?"

He eyed her warily. "No."

"I didn't think so! It looked like it hadn't been opened in ages! Do you want me to show it to you? I mean, I really am sorry — I know it was rude of me to snoop, but I was only trying to help." She furrowed her brow prettily. "Please say you are not angry at me? I meant no harm."

He dropped his gaze and gave an incoherent grumble that was neither yes nor no. Damn it, why hadn't he written to Virgil about her when he should have?

Here she stood with Promethean blood in her veins, cheerfully informing him that she had discovered his family's collection of secret, coded works relating to the Order's history. He knew exactly what the Highlander was going to say. *You let this woman lead you around by your cock.* He shut his handler's burred accent out of his head.

"So, what are *your* thoughts about this symbol, Kate?" he asked mildly.

"Well, you see, the picture jarred my memory. Actually, I can't believe that I forgot — but, then again, I was just a wee

281

thing at the time."

"Forgot about what?" he asked impatiently.

"My mother's book!"

He eyed her warily, recalling at once the book he had seen the Count DuMarin's veiled daughter, Lady Gabrielle, holding tightly to her chest on the night she had been handed over into the watchful care of Captain Fox.

Rohan had assumed it was a Bible.

"My mother brought a book with her from France containing this same symbol!" Kate explained. "It was a big thick tome, with all kinds of strange symbols and diagrams and writings. It had little maps and puzzles of different sorts to figure out. Back when I was a little girl on my father's ship, my parents were constantly poring over it."

He frowned.

"Rohan, it was all about Valerian the Alchemist!" she exclaimed. "I don't know if the book was *by* him or simply written *about* him, but it contained clues to the secret location of his tomb. They were on a treasure hunt!"

He narrowed his eyes. *The Alchemist's Tomb?* But it had passed into legend long ago.

"Alchemy — you know!" Kate was saying

excitedly. "Changing base metals into gold? There was supposed to be a horde of hidden treasure buried with him." Her expression sobered. "That's what my parents were looking for when my mother was killed."

Rohan lowered his gaze, doing his best to veil his awe. The Alchemist's Tomb was one of the enemy's great lost mysteries. It had been hidden so well that, over the ages, especially during England's civil war, its location had been forgotten; Valerian had taken his occult secrets to the grave.

No doubt, the Prometheans would go to any lengths to get their hands on it, not for the sake of any gold but for the scrolls containing his black-magic spells.

If Gerald Fox had found the Tomb and knew where it was, then that explained why James Falkirk would want to reel the pirate captain back to land.

Then an unbidden thought intruded.

If it really existed, the Tomb might also hold the secret of how to break the Kilburn Curse.

He eyed Kate dubiously. "So, you just remembered about all this now?"

"Yes, when I saw this symbol in this dragon book. Only now, I'm beginning to wonder if it's really about dragons at all," she murmured, marveling at it. "What if it's all symbolic?"

It was, actually.

The "dragons" depicted in the book represented the various Promethean families that the Order had been battling for centuries.

Like hers.

"Wouldn't that be something," he answered softly, scrutinizing her.

"I'll bet you this symbol has something to do with the Alchemist," she remarked, pointing at the Initiate's Brand. "Since he cursed your family, that must be why your ancestors have this book. That's the connection, I wager."

Her theory was close, not entirely right, but far be it from him to reveal the Order's secrets.

Kate shook her head, glancing at him in wonder. "It's remarkable, isn't it? What are the chances that you and I should meet, and both of us would have ties to some bizarre medieval warlock?"

It was not as big a coincidence as she believed.

"Hm, yes, amazing," he agreed, feigning ignorance. "Tell me, do you still have it? Your mother's book."

"I should," she said eagerly. "I have all her things in storage back at home."

His heart pounded at the prospect of snaring such a prize for the Order. Lady Gabrielle must have inherited the book since Valerian was her ancestor. It had probably been passed down through the DuMarin family . . . until it had been bequeathed to Kate.

"Can we go and get it?" she prodded in an urgent tone. "I really think we must," she added before he could reply. "If my mother's book points the way to a treasure in gold, that could be the reason someone out there could be after my father! If he's alive. Maybe that's why they had me kidnapped! To force Papa to tell them where the Tomb is so they could get to the treasure! But they must not know about the book," she added, "because if they did, they would not have needed my father. Or me."

He mulled this for a second. "You said the night you were kidnapped, O'Banyon and Denny Doyle went back into your cottage looking for valuables. Did either of them return to the carriage carrying the book?"

"No! It wasn't in the cottage, anyway. It was hidden out in the storage loft that Charley built above his work shed in one of the outbuildings. It should still be there, along with the rest of my mother's possessions, all she originally brought with her from France. Well — minus the more expensive things. My parents pawned most of her jewelry when they fell on hard times."

Rohan frowned. "Did they? Maybe that's the reason they went to the Alchemist's Tomb in the first place. If they thought there was gold inside . . ."

Kate shrugged, then folded her arms across her chest. "Charley did tell me once that my father found it difficult in some ways being married to an aristocrat. He was just a sea captain, and my mother was from a very wealthy family, used to nothing but the best."

"Frenchwomen usually are a force to be reckoned with, in my experience —" He snapped his mouth shut as Kate lifted her eyebrow at him. "Never mind."

She glanced back down at the dragon book on the table. "My mother didn't care about having fine things. She loved Papa, and that was all that mattered. But my father, well — typical male pride." She looked askance at him. "The point is, we need to go and get Mama's book before whoever's after me finds out about it first. After all, if they get their hands on the book, they'll be able to find their way to the Tomb themselves, and they won't need my father. Which means O'Banyon can shoot my father on sight in revenge for getting him thrown into Newgate. I'm *not* going to let them kill Papa — if he is alive."

Rohan studied her, impressed by her deductions and rather amused at her ferocious vow to protect the iron ex-Marine, Gerald Fox.

But he nodded. "You're right," he murmured. "We can't let your mother's book fall into the wrong hands."

He could well imagine why the Prometheans would want now, more than ever, to uncover the secrets hidden away inside the Alchemist's Tomb.

The Order had decimated their ranks simultaneously with Wellington's defeat of Napoleon. The Prometheans had infiltrated Bonaparte's empire, seeking subtly and gradually to commandeer it as their vehicle for eventual control of the entire Continent.

So much for their plans.

Last summer, while Welly's army dueled in the Belgian field with the Little Emperor, the Knights of the Order had hunted down Promethean agents embedded within every court in Europe. Their blood had flowed.

Afterwards, for about one hour, Rohan had been foolish enough to hope it was all finally done.

But it was never done. The evil bastards

never actually went away. They merely retreated, like fat, bloody spiders hiding in the woodpile.

On and on through the centuries, they never stopped trying to fulfill their twisted dream of one world united under their soulless tyranny. Perfectly willing to dabble in occult mysteries to attain their goals, the Prometheans could use the discovery of their revered Alchemist's Tomb as a rallying point to gather back all their scattered believers, the few who had survived the Order's last, devastating onslaught against them.

No doubt, the High Council was eager for any new advantage they could gain to help them regroup and formulate their next strategy.

"So, what do you think?" Kate prompted.

"I agree with you," he replied. "We should go and get your mother's book before they find out about it."

"Oh, can we really go? Will you finally take me to my cottage?" She lit up, clapping her hands in girlish anticipation, while the radiant joy on her face nearly stole his breath. "Oh, Rohan, it would mean the world to me to be back in my own house again, even if it's only for a visit! You *will* let me come with you? I must — I'll know where to look for it! Besides, this will give me the chance to pick up a few of my own things . . ." She chattered on, but his thoughts drifted.

He nodded absently, only half listening, for now he saw that if, in fact, he had been deceived by her sweet face, if somehow, his worst fears about Kate were true, then she could be leading him into a trap.

For all he knew, an ambush could be waiting for him at her cottage. *Bloody hell.*

Well, if that was the case, he was not about to hide from it. He would simply take a capable contingent of his men and play this out for good or ill.

Wryly, he put Parker's thrashing on hold for now, as he'd need the sergeant's services.

In the meanwhile, he masked his roiling suspicion of Kate and her seeming innocence, unsure himself if it was his survival instincts warning him or classic Warrington male paranoia.

"Dress warmly," he advised, veiling his mistrust. "We're going to be outdoors all day, and probably won't be back until tonight. Can you ride a horse?"

She nodded. "As long as it's not overly spirited."

"Good. I'm sure we can find you a suitable mount."

"Rohan?" She searched his face in what at

least appeared to be guileless concern. "I am — sorry if I overstepped my bounds with the library, and, also, um — last night. I want to apologize for my — inappropriate . . ."

Her words trailed off when he lifted his eyebrow at her.

"If I offended you," she started again.

"No. Of course not," he clipped out. "Don't be absurd."

"Then why did you push me away?" she asked softly.

He dropped his gaze, fighting a fiery surge of renewed craving for her. He warned himself to fight it — now more than ever. "It's for your own good, Kate."

"I'm not afraid."

"You don't really know me."

"But I want to," she whispered.

"No, you don't. Trust me." He turned away and coolly unlocked the pieces of his lancelike weapon with a twist of the handle. "Go and get dressed for the ride, please. We mustn't waste the light. Darkness comes early this time of year, and it's better for the horses if we're back by nightfall."

She made no move to go, still studying him, looking crestfallen and confused. He ignored her until she gave up after a moment. She shook her head, shrugged off his uncommunicative demeanor, and walked away, leaving the dragon book behind for him to examine.

As he listened to her soft footfalls echoing in the stone chamber, he closed his eyes. *Please, God, don't let her betray me.* If Kate was plotting treachery, he did not even want to think about what he might have to do to her.

CHAPTER 12

Snow crunched under the horses' hooves as the six riders from Kilburn Castle cantered across the countryside.

They had passed two of the three hours that the journey ought to take, but Kate still didn't feel like talking even to pass the time.

She could not believe that, once more, Rohan had pushed her away. The man was impossible.

Her attempt to apologize had merely left her feeling all the more foolish, while he, no doubt, was wishing that when they reached her cottage, he could have left her there. Then she could not bother him anymore.

Little did he know that, as they pressed on northward, Kate was having a silent argument with him in her head.

You could hardly argue aloud with someone when your life depended on him, after all. Honestly, her dependency on him was really beginning to chafe. But she kept her comments to herself, stewing in confused resentment.

You don't really know me, nor do you want to, he had said.

Oh, really? Why not? How do you know what I want? It's not as if you've ever asked, she retorted mentally.

But a part of her thought that maybe she should listen. Maybe he had good cause to warn her away.

Obviously, he was not the buyer of abducted virgins that she had originally feared, but perhaps there were still dark things about him that she did not know.

Well, I never took him for a choirboy, she thought crossly. But on the other hand, it took little imagination to surmise that he had secrets which might well make her back away from him of her own accord if she were to learn them. She heaved a sigh that puffed a cloud of steam in the biting cold of the winter afternoon.

All she knew was that he had called her apology absurd, which was very rude — and maybe it was, but at least *she* was trying to be honest about the attraction that she knew they both felt. His Grace, on the other hand, seemed determined to ignore it, to pretend this was all business, and to shut her out.

She was losing patience with it. Why were

his answers always so cryptic? She gathered, insultingly, that he did not trust her, but why? For snooping in his library? Or was it bigger than that? Did he think she was after his money, somehow, scheming to snare him for his title? Laughable. She did not care in the least about either.

She just wanted . . . to be close to him. She wanted him to acknowledge that what she felt for him was not entirely one-sided.

Unless, of course, it was.

In which case, he was doing the right thing, she admitted, trying to discourage her growing attachment to him. Maybe he saw her as nothing but a burden.

Her thoughts churned as they traversed the snow-covered countryside. She found herself longing for the freedom of her old life before she had ever heard of Rohan Kilburn or his silly curse. She missed the independence of not having to answer to a single soul, especially not some large, brooding, overprotective aristocrat, whose every word held a maddening undertone of terse command.

He was not good for her peace of mind.

Shoving aside her frustration, she did her best to ignore him, though he rode beside her, sitting tall astride his sable horse, looking every inch the warrior.

In truth, she was acutely aware of him, but she refused to indulge herself in savoring the memory of his magnificent, gleaming body, the way she had happened upon him at the castle earlier today, in the Hall of Arms.

It was nice to know that at least he had to work for all those muscles. He had been born with his towering height, but honing that demigod's physique clearly took some effort . . .

Blast it, why was she thinking again about his body? He wasn't that good-looking. Was he? She sneaked a sideward glance, only to repress a wistful sigh. *Afraid so.*

His black hair hung unbound around his shoulders, blowing slightly with the motion of his horse. His caped greatcoat was unfastened; beneath it she could see the array of weapons he had donned for the journey.

After witnessing his practice earlier, she had no doubt he was a master of each one.

The cold had ruddied his complexion, but his expression was hard and closed; with somber vigilance, his piercing gaze restlessly swept the snowy desolation of the landscape, scanning for any signs of trouble.

Before leaving the castle, he had warned her that O'Banyon and possibly more of his henchmen might still be lurking around her house, which was why the four guards had joined them. Presently, two of the men rode ahead of them, and two behind.

Parker and Wilkins, her usual guards, were to get Kate out of there and to speed her off to safety if, indeed, they encountered her kidnappers; Rohan, meanwhile, planned to stay and fight if it came to it.

That was the plan, anyway. She didn't think it likely, but she had long since realized that her friend the duke, somewhat gloomily, was a man who liked to plot out exactly how he'd respond if the worst possible outcome in any given situation were to occur.

Just in case he was right, she had donned her borrowed footman's livery. It was not only warmer and more convenient, allowing her to ride astride for their three-hour journey. It would also help to disguise her identity in case the shiftless O'Banyon really had made himself comfortable at her cottage.

Appalling thought. It infuriated her too much to dwell on it. She had to believe the much-more-likely scenario, that she would find her home much as she had left it. She couldn't wait to get there. Not even Rohan's dark and distant attitude could quell the anticipation bubbling up in her with every yard of ground the horses covered.

After all that she had been through, she was desperate to be surrounded once more by all the familiar sights and sounds and smells of home. Practically speaking, as well, the brief visit home would give her the chance to collect some of her own clothes, so she could finally quit wearing those too-tight, stolen gowns from the traveling trunk.

She wondered what Rohan would think of her humble home when they arrived. To be sure, she had never thought she would entertain a duke there. But although His Grace was used to grandeur, there was nothing pretentious about him, she mused, slanting him another sideways glance.

He caught her eye. "Everything all right?" he clipped out absently.

Far be it from her to complain. "Of course."

"Ground seem familiar to you yet?"

"Not really."

He nodded warily. "Think I'll go have a look over that rise." He clucked to his horse and cantered ahead to scout out the territory over the next rolling ridge.

Kate watched him speed away with a pang of vexation. Truly, it had seemed easier for him when he had assumed her to be some drunk, degraded whore from the smugglers' village. She shook her head. Well, this would all be over soon, then he'd be rid of her.

Almost home, she assured herself as they pressed on toward Dartmoor. But in spite of herself, she couldn't help wondering if her cottage would still feel like home once the Beast was no longer in her life.

Another hour passed.

When they finally arrived at the edge of the heath and spotted her home a few hundred yards away, Rohan was astonished by its desolate location.

Perhaps Gerald Fox knew what he was doing, he thought, for this remote outpost looked like just the sort of place that Rohan also would have chosen as a safe house, if he had been charged with hiding some high-value target.

The cottage sat atop a gentle rise in a clearing ringed by tall pines painted with snow. He saw no tracks or footprints in the layer of virgin snow everywhere, but he felt a familiar eerie prickle on his nape, a sixth sense that usually alerted him when something was wrong.

He'd know more soon, once he got inside her house and had a careful look around. First, he had to make sure that nobody else was already there.

With a lifted fist, he signaled to his men to halt.

They gathered near the stand of trees, where he gave them their orders in hushed tones. "Findlay, Mercer, you're with me. Parker, Wilkins, stay with Kate. We'll sweep the perimeter and call for you once it's clear. If there's trouble, take evasive action while we hold them off. Get her out of here. If we're separated, take her back to the castle, and we'll see you there. Otherwise, if it's quiet, we shall be back shortly."

"Yes, sir."

"It looks fine to me," Kate murmured, anxiously scanning her property.

Rohan paused to study her. The moment of truth was at hand. If this was an ambush, they were about to find out. "Anything you want to tell me before we go?"

She furrowed her brow. "Like what?"

"Never mind. Stay silent," he warned her. "And don't worry," he added, begrudgingly giving her the benefit of the doubt, just in case. "You'll be safe with these two. Follow their instructions, and all will be well."

Kate nodded. "I will."

"Good." He nodded to Findlay and Mercer as he drew his pistol and cocked it, then took out his knife. "Let's go."

He could feel her watching him as he

walked away.

A few early stars winked to life in the winter's early twilight as he and his men approached her house. He could see its simple outline through the trees, a blacker shade against the pearlescent snow and the gray midafternoon.

Silent as shadows, they advanced, keeping abreast of each other as they pressed on in their sweep of the premises.

Constantly scanning the area, peering into every pool of shadow amid the trees, Rohan soon concluded they were alone.

No enemies, no ambush.

Kate had been telling the truth. The place was quiet, her small house as still as a tomb. No voices could be heard. No light shone through branches. And as they slowly crossed the clearing, it became evident why.

All three men stopped. Findlay and Mercer glanced uneasily at Rohan. But he stared straight ahead with a sinking feeling in his chest.

There was nothing to threaten them here. The damage was already done. Now he had to go back and tell her . . .

Her cottage had been put to the torch.

All that remained was a charred, empty shell, like a shipwreck's hull broken open on the rocks. The gutted ruin slumbered under a thick white coating of Devon snow. He cursed in a whisper and slid his knife back into the sheath at his waist.

In that moment, he hated himself for doubting her. He could no longer believe that she was anything but innocent. The realization finally sank in that she had been telling the truth from the start. She was completely innocent.

And now she had nowhere to live.

His mind churned with self-directed rage as he thought of sweet little Kate that first night in the great hall. Drugged. Terrified. Ripped from her home.

Given to him as a gift.

And what had he done? Why, the soul of gallantry, he had put the girl under surveillance.

Beast.

"What do you think happened, sir?" Mercer asked, staring at the wreckage of a young woman's life.

"Hard to say," he forced out.

The Prometheans might have done this, or it could have been as simple as a hearth fire left unattended after she had been dragged out of her home.

The point was, her only real place in this world had been destroyed. She was going to be devastated. *How much more is she sup-*

posed to take?

He drew a deep breath and glanced at the stars for guidance. He exhaled slowly, steadying himself to break the news to her. "Have a look round," he said to his men. "See if you can find anything useful. Be careful going in there, though. Those charred beams are likely quite unstable."

"Aye, sir." His men holstered their weapons and went to do as he had said.

Rohan turned away from the burned ruin of her home and faced the direction where she waited with her two minders.

He braced himself for the painful task, marching back grimly through the snow. *God, for once in my life, let me do something gently.*

"At ease," he said to Parker and Wilkins as he approached. "There's no one here but us."

"See? I knew you were just being overly cautious — as usual," she teased with a return to her usual cheeky cheer.

Her words pained him more than she could guess as she jumped down off her horse at once and grabbed his hand in hers. "Come on! I'll make some tea to warm us up!"

"Sweeting — wait." He tightened his hold on her hand and drew her back to him

before she could go dashing off in her eagerness.

"What is it?"

"Kate — I have bad news." Haltingly, he
said: "There was a fire."

"Fire? What do you . . . ?" Her words
trailed off. Reading his bleak countenance
with a searching gaze, she drew in her
breath in horror and suddenly pulled her
hand free of his light hold, running toward
the cottage.

Rohan flinched at the blow she was about
to receive, but he let her go. No point delay-
ing the inevitable. He strode after her, the
snow crunching under his boots.

She ran ahead, her borrowed cloak flowing out behind her like some dark phantom
chasing her. He saw her reach the clearing
and stop cold. Her back was to him as he
approached, her posture ramrod-straight.

When he stepped up beside her and
looked at her in profile, he saw stunned
dread written all over her beautiful face.

Her mouth was agape, her eyes slightly
glazed as her shocked stare traveled over
the burned-out husk of her home.

"Kate?" he whispered.

She did not even seem to hear him as she
took a dazed step forward. She did not say
a word; he did not hear her breathe, as

though the air had been knocked out of her lungs.

He reached out to steady her, but his hand barely grazed her when she sprinted toward the ruin without warning.

"Kate, no! The whole thing could collapse!"

He was behind her in the blink of an eye, grasping onto her arms, stopping her as she tried to pull forward, panic breaking through her shock.

"Let go of me!"

"You can't go in there! It's not safe!"

"Oh, God, I'm ruined," she gasped out. "What am I to do?" Straining in his arms in wild-eyed confusion, she suddenly stopped trying to escape and sagged against him as a low, keening moan escaped her. "It's gone. It's all gone. My home!"

Rohan's throat tightened as she hung her head. Her delicate shoulders began to shudder with her quiet, soul-deep sobs.

He wound his arms around her and held her up, otherwise she would have crumpled to the ground. "I will help you," he said fiercely as she wept.

She wasn't even listening. "It isn't fair!" she sobbed. "Why is this happening to me? You think you're cursed? I'm the one who's cursed — I lost my mother, my father. I lost

Charley, and now this! Why?" she wrenched out, tears pouring from her eyes. "Rohan, why, why did they have to come back and do this, vicious thing — for no reason!"

"Shh," he soothed as her sobs climbed toward hysteria. "We don't yet know how this happened —"

"I don't bother anyone," she charged on, trying to push him away. "I keep to myself. What did I ever do to deserve this? Let go of me," she said abruptly, shoving against him with a sudden angry sniffle. "I want to go and see if I can find anything worth saving."

"Leave it, Kate." He held on to her. "It's too dangerous. At least you're safe. I'm not going to let you go in there and risk the whole thing caving in on you. Come, it'll be dark soon. There's no point staying here much longer. Where's Charley's work shed? We've come this far. We might as well just get the book and go."

"Go, where? I have nowhere to go," she uttered mournfully.

"Of course you do." He grasped her shoulders and stared into her face, trying to bring her back from despair. "You will come back to the castle with me."

"I don't belong there. I don't belong any-place."

"You belong with me," he replied without the slightest hesitation.

Her chin trembled as she held his gaze. "I-I'm not your responsibility."

"Yes, you are. You are mine. They gave you to me, remember? And I want to keep you. Come here," he ordered softly.

She lifted her arms and stepped into his embrace without another word.

He hugged her close, his heart pounding. "Listen to me. I don't want you to worry for one instant what will become of you, all right? I'll look after you. Whatever you need. You have my word, Kate. You're not alone, do you understand?" he whispered as he held her.

After a moment, he felt her nod against his chest.

"There's my brave girl," he murmured, brushing a kiss to her forehead.

It was at that moment that it dawned on him what he was going to do when they returned to the castle. The thought shocked him as it struck, igniting his heart, even as it filled him with an odd relief.

Of course.

She was already under his protection. By now, anyone outside the castle no doubt assumed she was already his mistress. They already wanted each other so badly. He saw no reason now not to offer her his carte blanche.

Yes. She must become more securely his.

It was not his way to keep any one particular mistress to service his needs. But if Kate were his, then he would not have to worry about her, even beyond all this business with O'Banyon. He would know exactly where she was, that she was fed, clothed, protected, and provided for.

Admittedly, it might come across as utterly ruthless of him to make such an offer at a time like this — as though he were coldly taking advantage of her at the moment of her greatest vulnerability. But he was not motivated by lust.

At least not entirely.

Obviously, he could not marry her — not with his curse, and her Promethean blood. But if Kate was his mistress, then he could watch over her, and if anyone ever tried to hurt her again, they would have to deal with him first.

Besides, he knew by now how her mind worked. If he were simply to make her a promise of financial help, she wouldn't take it. She was too proud. Hell, with her independent spirit, she would abhor any offer that she interpreted as charity. So, let her work for it.

God, he had dreamed of making love to her since that first night when Caleb Doyle had brought her to the castle for that very purpose.

Even now, she felt like heaven in his arms. If she was willing, he knew one sure way to comfort her when they got her back to the castle. He could make all her tears and sorrow melt away. . . .

Cradling her in his embrace, Rohan pressed another possessive kiss to her brow. "Come now, tell me, where is Charley's work shed?" he asked in a voice gone husky with anticipation.

"Over there. At the back of the garden." With a sniffle, she pointed to a modest outbuilding set back at some distance from the house. "It should be locked. Unless whoever did this got in there, as well. Oh, God, I can't look — what if they've taken all my mother's things?"

"Do you know where Charley kept the key?"

She shook her head. "It would have been in the cottage. Somewhere in the rubble . . ."

Rohan nodded, then called out to Findlay and Mercer: "Check that building there!" He pointed to the outbuilding Kate had indicated.

The men strode off across the snow-covered garden, then tried the door with a few loud jiggles of the latch.

"Locked, sir!"

Rohan glanced at Kate. "That's good news," he pointed out. "It probably means the fire was an accident. If intruders had set it, chances are, they'd have broken into the shed, too."

She looked at him uncertainly.

"I'm sorry, but I'm going to have to have the lads break down the door," he added.

She shrugged with a weary shake of her head. "It doesn't matter anymore."

Her defeated tone worried him a great deal. "Let's get that shed open!" he called to his men. "Once you're in, I'll need some light, as well. Call me when you've got it."

"Yes, sir."

At once, the first cracking, crunching bangs filled the stillness of the snowy garden as Mercer and Findlay began working to kick the door in. Wood splintered, and the metal locks groaned on their hinges under their violent bashes.

"This won't take long," Rohan murmured, pained to see the way Kate jumped with each resounding blow. "Do you want to come and help me find the book?"

She shook her head vehemently and turned away, pressing her lips together. "I can't face it right now."

"I understand. Don't worry, we'll find it
—"

"*You* do it, Rohan," she pleaded in a shaky
tone, turning back to him. "She was my
mother. I don't want strangers going
through her things —"

"All right. I will do it. It's no problem,"
he soothed. She was trembling visibly in the
cold. "Come with me, let's get you warmed
up."

She managed a nod, but sent one last,
tearful stare over her shoulder at her ruined
home. Then he put his arm around her
shoulders and walked her back out to the
stand of trees where they had left the horses.

When they rejoined the animals, who were
pawing away the thin snow for a bit of grazing, Kate went over to the placid gelding he
had given her to ride and leaned her head
against the animal's warm, fuzzy neck.

As she stood hugging the horse, Rohan
saw another tear run down her cheek; he
clenched his jaw, saving up his fury for all
those who had done her harm.

He could hardly wait to make them pay.
Marching over to his tall, powerful hunter,
he greeted the animal with a pat, then
opened the laces of the saddlebag, and
pulled out a small flask of whiskey he had

brought along to help ward off the cold.

Slipping it into his greatcoat pocket, he then unfastened the rolled blanket attached to the back of his saddle. He had thought she might need it. He carried both items back to her, unfurled the blanket and draped it around her shoulders just as he had on the morning he had saved her from the crumbling cliff. Next he presented her with the flask and nodded at her to take a drink.

"Go on, it'll help."

She did not argue.

As he watched her lift it to her lips and take a tentative sip, he rested his hands casually atop the weapons attached to the leather belt slung around his waist: the butt of his pistol beneath his right hand, the handle of his sword below his left.

He gazed at her, wondering if she had any idea of how dear to him she had become. At least now he could finally discard his efforts to hold her at arm's length.

"Sir!"

The guard's distant holler reached them from beyond the ruined cottage. "We've got it open!"

Rohan turned his head and yelled back absently, "I'll be right there!" When he looked again at Kate, he found her soulful stare fixed on him.

He reached out and caught a stray tear from her cheek on his knuckle. "I'll be right back, all right?"

She nodded bravely, but the vulnerability behind her feminine resolve turned him inside out. He tried nevertheless to lighten the somber mood with a mild jest. "Now, you take care of her for me," he ordered, pointing at the horse.

At this, the faintest trace of a grateful smile shone through her teary eyes.

Pivoting, he marched off toward the work shed. "Parker! Mind your post here," he called, gesturing at Kate as he stalked across the grounds.

"And me, sir?" Wilkins asked from over by the simple country post-and-rail fence that hemmed the garden.

"Keep looking for any sign of how this fire started. Just in case it *was* arson, whoever started the blaze might've left behind a trace."

"Aye, sir," Wilkins said with a willing but skeptical salute.

Rohan shrugged at him in answer. It was impossible to say for certain without a thorough investigation, but his instincts told him the fire had been accidental.

Thatched-roof cottages like those throughout the countryside burnt down all the time — and that was *with* someone at home minding the candles and the fireplace.

The hard truth of it was, though, they might never know. He dared not say it to Kate at the moment, but the chance to figure out how this fire had started was probably long past.

He glanced back at her once more as Parker marched toward her. He knew the men had grown fond of her. Parker patted her on the shoulder as he joined her. She was still standing near the horse, with the blanket wrapped around her.

Satisfied that she'd be all right for the moment, he arrived at the work shed, from which a lantern's light now beamed.

"Poor little mite," Findlay remarked as Rohan stepped into Charley's work shed. "How is she, sir?"

"Ah, she's tougher than you'd think. Wait here," he added, glancing at them. "I'll see to this."

He held up the whale-oil lantern and scanned the dusty space with its clutter of carpentry tools and garden implements, until he spotted the ladder that led up to the storage loft that Kate had mentioned.

Crossing to it, he carried the lantern in one hand as he climbed the ladder. When he reached the top, stepping into the loft, he had to duck his head to fit under the slanted ceiling.

Ahead, a large rectangular pile draped in burlap seemed to be stacked crates or something of the sort. He hung the lantern on a hook that he noticed sunk into a thick cobwebbed beam overhead. Then, dusting off his hands, he approached the pile and whisked the burlap covering away.

He narrowed his eyes against the cloud of dust that puffed up from the mound of battered, but once-elegant leather luggage he had uncovered. The pink stitching and dainty proportions of the various portmanteaux and sea chests he had discovered certainly seemed to suggest the luggage had once belonged to a lady.

Rohan flipped open the silver hasps on the first trunk atop the pile, then he lifted its barrel-topped lid and proceeded to search it. The contents had a musty smell: gowns, slippers, hair combs, gloves. An empty perfume bottle. An ivory-handled hairbrush and a matching hand mirror.

He felt very strange sifting through the belongings of the Count DuMarin's daughter. Never had anyone related to the Promethean Council seemed to him so much like an ordinary person.

This realization only sharpened the guilt he carried with him at all times though all he had done was his duty.

Nevertheless, it pained him to brood again on all the women and children in the periphery of this struggle who had been bereaved because of his excellent skill as an assassin.

Beast.

By God, the book he sought now might hold the answer to how he might break the Kilburn Curse, but when he thought of all the things he had done, he was not sure he deserved to break it. To be freed.

Free to love.

After all the blood he'd spilled, what made him think that he would ever deserve *that*? He wavered, anger and confusion pulsing through him. Taking a deep breath, he put all of Lady Gabrielle's possessions back into the trunk and moved on to the next. This process was repeated several times until he reached the final piece of luggage at the bottom of the pile.

He emptied its contents, piece by piece, then examined the base of the portmanteau with a frown. He pulled on a small strap he discovered tucked into the corner of the frame, and at once, a false bottom lifted away.

Wrapped in a swaddling of unobtrusive

brown cloth sat the same large book he had seen Lady Gabrielle DuMarin clutching to her all those years ago.

His heart pounded as he moved the cloth away and stared at the strange symbols engraved on the aged leather cover, along with the title: *Le Journal de L'Alchimiste.*

The Alchemist's Journal.

Wonder filled him as he opened the book and saw the writings of the very man who had cursed his family line. This was it, all right.

He closed the book with a superstitious shudder. Anxious to get back to Kate, he did not linger. Quickly returning the rest of her mother's things into the trunk, he closed it, then rebuilt the pile of luggage, hefting each piece back into place and covering the whole pile once more with the tarp.

Carrying the book securely under one arm, he took the lantern off the hook, then climbed back down, rejoining his men below.

The whole search had only taken him about twenty minutes. Given his line of work, after all, he was used to this sort of errand.

Handing the lantern back to Mercer and Findlay, he ordered them to nail the broken door closed using the tools and extra boards near Charley's workbench. He didn't want anyone coming in and fooling with Lady Gabrielle's possessions before he could send a wagon to come back and collect them all for Kate to keep somewhere.

"When you're through here, follow me. I want to get her back to the castle."

"Aye, Your Grace."

He left them to their work. As he marched back across the garden, he spotted Wilkins. "Did you find anything?"

"No, sir." The guard shook his head glumly.

"Very well, you and Parker can wait for those two. I'll get started home with Kate."

"You found it!" she murmured warily, staring at the book under his arm as he strode toward her.

He nodded. "Let's look at it later." He went past her and stored it safely in his saddlebag. "Feeling warmer?"

"I suppose." She shrugged. "I think I could develop a taste for whiskey."

Rohan and Parker exchanged a wry glance at her half-hearted attempt at a jest.

"Come on. Up you go." He lifted Kate up onto his hunter, then told Parker to stay behind with the others.

"Aye, sir," the sergeant replied. "Be careful goin' back, sir."

"You do the same."

Parker saluted him, then marched off to see if Findlay and Mercer needed help.

Rohan took hold of her horse's reins and tethered the docile gelding to the back of his hunter's saddle. Finally, he mounted up behind her, gathering her onto his lap.

"Come, sweeting," he whispered. "Let's get you back to the castle."

"I missed you," she mumbled, letting herself lean against him a bit.

"I'm here now." As he took up the reins, he could still feel her shivering, probably due as much to the shock she had received as to the cold. His own body heat would help to warm her now. Nevertheless, he was determined to get her back to his home, where he could care for her.

Scanning the moonlit countryside, he saw no source of threat, but with Kate and *The Alchemist's Journal* both in his possession, he knew he must stay on his guard now more than ever.

No matter. He had been born for this.

With fierce determination stamped across his countenance and one arm wrapped around Kate's waist, securing her before him, he squeezed his horse's sides with his calves and clucked to her gelding trailing behind them. They set out for Kilburn

Castle with daylight already fading in the east.

CHAPTER 13

The ride back was cold and long and silent.

The distance seemed so much farther now that her world at one end of the journey had ceased to exist. Life as she knew it was over. The only solid thing left for her was the man guiding the horse they shared.

She closed her eyes and allowed herself to lean back against him, accepting the sturdy shelter Rohan offered, the warm, hard comfort of his body.

Though she was touched by his promise of protection, she did not want to be a burden. At least her enemies hadn't taken her pride. Still, her mood was bleak. Loss and wintry cold had seeped into her blood, making her numb and weary and indifferent.

After another three hours, they rode into the courtyard in front of Kilburn Castle.

The weary horses clattered to a halt before the same portcullis entrance where the smugglers had brought her the first night.

Little could she have known then that, within a fortnight, she would be glad to be arriving here, that the forbidding stone castle would come to seem like the closest thing she had left to a home.

Rohan dismounted, got the book out of the saddlebag, and returned to help her down. She took it from him, and in turn, he lifted her easily out of the saddle. But instead of setting her on her cold-numbed feet, he carried her tenderly toward the door.

It opened before they reached it.

Warm orange light spilled out onto the flagstones as Eldred let them in, while a groom rushed out from the stable to tend to the horses.

"Is she hurt?" the butler asked in alarm, looking at Kate.

"Not physically," the duke murmured, carrying her past him.

"Where are the others? Was there trouble?"

"Everything's under control. They'll be along by morning."

Eldred hurried after them, clearly unsettled by her air of defeat. "Is there anything I can do, Your Grace? Miss Madsen? Some warm negus? Or there's soup —"

"I don't want anything," she rallied herself to mumble. "Thank you, Eldred."

"Give him the book," Rohan murmured to Kate. "Eldred, hide this away in the safe. We'll look at it tomorrow," he added with a glance at her.

Kate shrugged.

Eldred took the book without a word, then Rohan gave his wiry-haired butler a taut nod. Eldred dropped back as Rohan marched on, carrying her through the dark corridors.

Still draped in her snow-dampened cloak, Kate laid her head on Rohan's muscled shoulder, her gloved hands clasped behind his neck.

In her despondency, she was past the point of arguing about anything, nor did she bother to object as he climbed the dimly lit stairs, moving with relentless strength, the dark woolen skirts of his greatcoat flowing out behind him.

She merely stared at his jawline and breathed in the smell of him as he carried her up the stairs; somehow his natural, masculine scent had become so familiar.

The castle had become familiar, too. It made her feel better to be back here, where she knew she was safe — but for how long? And then what?

It was so strange knowing she could never go back to the way things had been before. She wished she could have had at least had a little time to say good-bye to her old life before she had been kidnapped. It was too late now.

When they reached the upper hallway, Rohan stopped at the door to the solar instead of taking her to the guest room. Her heart skipped a beat, but she did not protest as he stepped into the master chamber and nudged the door shut behind him.

He crossed the room toward the crackling fire in the hearth, still carrying her, until at last, he deposited her gently in the toasty leather armchair before the fireplace.

"Now then," he whispered, assessing her condition with a deep and probing stare.

Kate gazed back at him in dull, despondent silence.

"Right." He measured out a worried exhalation and drew off his riding gauntlets. He walked away to lock the door, took off his greatcoat, and returned.

He crouched down slowly before her, searching her face in concern. "Is there anything at all that I can do for you?"

He said that a lot, she mused, staring wistfully at him. A lump rose in her throat at his goodness, but she shook her head.

"Look at you," he murmured. "You're frozen, poor babe. Do you want a blanket, some tea?"

"Thanks, no."

"Surely you can think of something I can do for you. Give me a task, Kate. Or I may go quite mad."

A wan smile lifted one corner of her mouth.

"It's not a far jaunt for me," he added in soft coaxing. "What, with believing in ghosts and curses and such, I'm already halfway there."

The other corner of her lips turned up slightly.

"There's that pretty smile," he whispered, gazing at her, but when he cupped her cheek, her eyes misted with pensive appreciation for his kindness. He frowned. "Don't cry, sweet. You're safe now. That's what matters, isn't it? I know it hurts, but everything you've lost — it's all just *things.* Things can be replaced. Not so, when it comes to life and limb."

"I know, of course, you're right." She lowered her head, but she could feel him watching her. "Stop worrying about me. I'm sure I'll be fine."

He furrowed his brow, studying her with a dubious look for a moment. "Let me take your cloak."

It was wet from the snow. She hadn't even bothered to lower the large, draping hood but had sagged down in the chair, an exhausted traveler. He lowered the hood for her, pushing it back tenderly from her face. He unfastened the thick, wooden button-latch at the neck and pulled the cloak away; her borrowed livery costume was revealed.

He smiled faintly. "My little page girl. You make a charming footman, you know."

"Except that I don't like being told what to do," she mumbled.

"So I've noticed. Actually, I find it an oddly endearing quality." He reached up behind her head, untying the ribbon that had bound her hair neatly beneath the hood.

His gentle fingers brought her tresses tumbling down about her shoulders. "There, now you're a girl again." He gave her a rueful half smile, but when she began untying the damp neckcloth that had been keeping her throat warm, the helpful fellow took it upon himself to assist.

"Perhaps someday I'll teach you how to tie a proper cravat," he remarked, as his deft fingers plucked at the knot at her throat, then slid the length of cloth away.

With the makeshift cravat removed, the deep V of the white shirt went slack against her skin and fell open to the middle of her chest, where the waistcoat hugged her bosom. Rohan's gaze slid down her chest, but then, he averted his eyes with a look of determination.

As the fire crackled, he sat back slowly on the ottoman across from her chair.

"Come, Kate. I need you to rally. We are going to get through this, but we've still got a fight ahead. You can't quit now."

"I don't intend to quit," she forced out. "It's just — now what? What am I supposed to do?"

"I told you that I would take care of you."

"Rohan, bless you, but I can't live off your charity."

"I wasn't offering charity," he answered in a low tone.

She looked at him in question.

He held her gaze for a long moment, then leaned forward, resting his elbows on his knees, loosely clasping his hands. "I was thinking about something you said to me that night at our celebratory dinner when you first got here."

She lifted her eyebrows. "Was this something I said before or after all those different wines?"

He just smiled.

"What was it?"

"You weren't happy out there, Kate. All alone at the edge of the moors. You said you felt trapped."

"That is true," she admitted, dragging a hand wearily through her hair. "I suppose I'll just have to figure out what to do next." She shrugged. "I have some money left in the bank, though it's not enough to live on if I have to buy a house and furniture. Dishes, drapes. The basics of everyday life. And clothes. I don't have a stitch of my own clothing left."

He studied her as she shook her head and let out a cynical sigh.

"Ah, well. I think my only choice now is to find someone to marry. That is what women usually do, isn't it?"

"Yes, usually."

"Unfortunately, most men don't want a bluestocking for a wife."

"No, they don't," he agreed. "Or a wife who's more intelligent than himself. I'm afraid, Miss Madsen, you are too clever for most men out there."

"I'm not ashamed of who I am!" she replied, bemused that he was not telling her what she wanted to hear — that she could easily find a groom.

He smiled faintly at her in roguish approval.

Settling deeper into the armchair, she was beginning to feel much better as she reviewed her options. Something about him made everything seem like it would be all right.

She stared absently into the fire. "Maybe I could start some sort of little shop in London."

"You don't want to do that," he said mildly.

"I don't?"

"No. Good to see some color coming back in your cheeks, by the way."

"I'm finally starting to warm up. So, why don't I want to own a shop?"

"You don't want to deal with nagging customers all day. Be at everybody's beck and call? The wealthy don't pay their bills for years at a time these days, you know."

"Really?" she exclaimed.

"Oh, yes. Everything's on credit now. When the shopkeepers finally turn to the sponging houses to help them collect, even the bailiffs are afraid of offending the upper class. Thus, the aristocracy is filled with the worst deadbeats."

"I had no idea!"

"Besides, if it turns out the threat against you goes beyond just O'Banyon," he added, "I don't want you in a situation where any stranger can walk in off the street and get to you."

Her expression instantly sobered. "I hadn't thought of that."

He shrugged. "Anyway, starting a business, especially in London, takes a huge amount of capital at the outset, which I'm afraid you do not have."

"Hmm." By the way he described it, it did not sound the shopkeeper's life was the choice for her. She brightened. "Perhaps I could teach somebody's children! Become a governess."

"Children . . . hm."

"What?" she prodded, seeing his guarded look.

"Oh, nothing."

"You obviously have an opinion."

"Well, they're noisy little vermin, aren't they?" he drawled. "Hard to concentrate on your books with them thundering about — and then there are the parents. Constantly criticizing the nanny's efforts to raise their little darlings for them — even while they're too lazy to do it themselves."

"Oh, you're awful!" she gasped, laughing at his irreverent observations.

He shook his head. "It's true."

"Do you intend to shoot down every option I have to save myself? Or perhaps you have a better idea?"

"Actually, I do."

"Aha. What is it, oh, wise one?"

"I thought you'd never ask. I already told you, Kate. You should just let me take care of you." He held her gaze with a seductive frankness in the gray depths of his eyes, and ever so slowly, his meaning began to dawn on her.

"You mean — even after we've dealt with O'Banyon?" she asked gingerly.

"Yes. Even after." His stare was locked on her. "Do you understand, Kate, what I am offering you?"

"I think so," she said faintly. It was certainly not marriage. Not that she expected that. Not from a duke, especially one who believed he was doomed by some old family curse to slay his future wife.

It was a surreal moment as she realized he was offering her his carte blanche.

She dropped her gaze, blushing fiercely, shocked by the offer, and by him.

It was only because of all that he had done so far to protect her that she immediately knew that, in reality, he was throwing her a lifeline. But it was breathtakingly ruthless of him to lay this devil's bargain at her feet just when she had come to the end of her rope.

"You'll want for nothing," he murmured in a low, velvety voice. "Do not mourn the loss of your cottage too much. It was a cage for you. But now you are free. No tiresome husband, no nagging customers, no screaming brats. I can give you a very good life, Kate. London, Paris. Anywhere. All you need to do is fulfill the desire that I think you already feel. We both do."

Her heart was pounding, her cheeks flaming crimson.

Never in all her life did she think she, Kate Madsen, would receive an indecent proposition from a worldly, gorgeous, and fabulously wealthy duke.

At first, she was so embarrassed and confused she could not even look at him. She did not want him to see in her eyes that he already had her half-seduced, and had since the night of her arrival.

She swallowed hard. "Your Grace — I am a virgin."

"I realize that," he purred, "and it pleases me. You do not doubt that I can be gentle with you?"

"No — it's not that." She couldn't believe he was doing this to her, putting her in this position — and worse, that she didn't mind that much. Indeed, nothing sounded sweeter than for him to lay her down tonight and make all her problems go away in a luxurious night of pleasure.

But he was offering her far more than just one night.

The chance to keep him in her life for some period of time into the foreseeable future was a thrilling prospect. It was the proof she had been seeking that this hard, unyielding man did care for her, in his own way.

"What are your thoughts?" he asked.

Kate peeked at him shyly from under her lashes.

It wasn't marriage, which she believed she could probably find without too much trouble. Safe, boring, biddable men were easy enough to come by — but Rohan?

A fierce, wild creature like a wolf?

"Belong to me," he whispered, staring into her eyes.

She stood up quickly from her chair and moved away, dizzied by the potency in his stare.

Think.

His magnetism was nigh irresistible.

Of course, if she went the decent route, she was still going to have to sleep with some man anyway. At least like this, she'd keep her treasured independence.

Having lived with Rohan for a fortnight,

she had seen that, aside from being slightly paranoid about her safety, he placed no real demands on her.

He respected her studies. They got on well.

Then belatedly, she realized she was fooling herself if she imagined that any nice, biddable husband was ever going to overlook the fact that she had stayed at Kilburn Castle for a fortnight as the personal guest of the Beast.

Certain assumptions would be made.

Blazes, I forgot. I'm already ruined.

The fact that it was not her fault that she was here and that he had hardly touched her would not matter.

It all meant that her choices now were more limited than she had assumed. Henceforth, the only respect she could probably hope to command from the world was the shady sort that could come to her as an extension of the respect due him on account of his rank.

Truly, her fate was in his hands. It sank in that Rohan already knew this. Therefore, as shocking as his offer sounded, the protection he was offering was more than physical. He was offering her a place inside an exclusive little niche that she had heard existed in society but which she knew little about.

The world of rich men's ladybirds.

Dear God, Caleb Doyle is a prophet.

Her heart was pounding, and Rohan was waiting for an answer. Gathering her courage, Kate decided to press for information. Having paced across the solar, she turned around to face him, leaning her hips back against the chest of drawers. "Forgive me, Your Grace, but I must be pragmatic."

"Yes?"

She swallowed hard. "Well . . . in short, what are you willing to pay for it?"

The question brought a glimmer of sardonic approval into his eyes. "Hm." Drumming his steepled fingertips together, he looked her over in a slow, cheeky appraisal. "Oh, say, fifteen hundred pounds per annum."

Kate's eyes widened, but she quickly masked her astonishment. It was a staggering fortune — but only a fool accepted any first offer. "Two thousand."

He flashed a wolfish grin. "Done."

"What if there is a child? Or several?"

"Five hundred a year for each until the age of maturity."

She raised an eyebrow. He certainly had a speedy answer. Perhaps the world was littered with illegitimate baby Warringtons.

"It's what the Regent pays, Kate. At least

that's what I've heard."

"You sound like you've done this before," she murmured, folding her arms across his chest and searching his face sharply.

"Actually, I haven't. But of course, I am familiar with the workings of the world."

"You've never had a mistress before?" she asked skeptically. "Healthy strapping fellow like you?"

He shrugged. "I don't usually hold with getting attached to any one particular woman."

"And yet you see fit to make an exception for me."

"You were given to me as a gift. I merely believe in taking good care of my possessions."

She narrowed her eyes. Obviously, he did not care to explain himself, nor was he accustomed to doing so, but, for her part, she was not content to let him sidestep the issue. "The stakes could not be higher for me, Rohan. Please understand. I am not fishing for flowery compliments, I just need to know if you are serious about this. If I am going to depend on you —"

"Of course I'm serious," he cut her off with a mild scowl. "Very well, if you must know, you impress me, Kate. You are, perhaps, I think, in some ways . . . good for me," he conceded haltingly. Then he quickly returned to his usual brusque manner, sending her a lustful look askance. "Besides, I think you know how badly I have long wanted you."

His aggressive male sexuality intimidated her, but then it occurred to her that perhaps it was supposed to.

By leering at her, he could succeed in driving her off the path of asking about his feelings. Little did he know she was beginning to figure out all of his tricks.

She decided to try a rather brazen experiment, refusing to be rattled by his hungry stare. "Believe me, Your Grace, the feeling is mutual," she replied. "But I confess, I'm a little confused by this about-face, considering how you pushed me away last night."

The flicker of curiosity in his eyes told her that her new tactic intrigued him. One corner of his mouth lifted wryly. "At least one of us was trying to behave."

"You did not want to get involved with me at all, did you?" she murmured, studying him in fascination.

"No." He shrugged, holding her stare. "But after tonight, frankly, I give up."

"It does seem inevitable," she agreed in a quiet tone.

He nodded. "The ideal solution for us both."

They stared at each other for a long moment.

Kate held her deep breath. "Very well, then. I accept."

"Good! Then come over here and give us a kiss," he ordered in sudden, rugged cheer. When he slapped his muscled thigh, inviting her to sit there, she refused to smile.

"Write up the agreement first," she chided archly, perhaps just to buy a wee bit more time. "And I'll want your ducal seal beside your signature, to make it doubly official."

He laughed, low and hearty, like a pirate. "Katy girl, don't you trust me?"

"If I'm going to sell you my body, Your Grace, at least I want a legally binding receipt."

"Quelle femme," he murmured, rising from the ottoman. But he eyed her admiringly. "As you wish."

A small corner of her soul was panicking, but Kate refused to let fear run amuck. This was her best option.

And look at him, she thought. That magnificent warrior physique was about to become her playground.

She let her stare roam boldly over his tall, broad-shouldered frame as Rohan lifted a portable desk down from atop the armoire. He took out a quill and ink and scrawled the particulars of their agreement on a sheet of foolscap; he finished their contract a few minutes later by pressing his bronze seal into the melted wax medallion at the bottom of the page.

"Here you are. Signed, sealed, and legally binding."

With the ink still drying, he brought the paper over to her. She accepted it, glancing it over by the glow of the hearth fire.

"Satisfied?" he murmured with a hint of worldly amusement in his deep voice.

She nodded. "I believe so."

"Then I'd like to seduce you now, unless there are any more questions?"

"Only one."

"Yes?"

"You know I'm not as experienced as you are, Rohan." Blushing at his nearness, she kept her gaze down. "I might not be as able as you to separate my feelings from the things we do."

"And?"

"What if I fall in love with you? What then?"

He laughed idly as he collected her hand from her side. "I consider that highly unlikely."

"Would it irritate you?"

"I don't think so. Not too badly. As long as you don't make a spectacle of us like Caro Lamb. Other than that —" He shrugged. "It's your prerogative."

"Who's Caro Lamb?"

"Oh, some Society woman who fell for Lord Byron a couple of Seasons ago. Daft chit smashed the punch bowl at a ball and threatened to slit her wrists with the shards of glass if he continued to ignore her. You wouldn't do anything silly like that, now, would you?"

"Over you?" she retorted. "No. For Lord Byron, maybe. Not for you."

"Well, you've already threatened to throw yourself off a cliff in the short time I've known you," he teased in return, laying his hands gently on her shoulders. "Now, my little present, be quiet and let me unwrap you."

She stared at him, his jest reminding her of how he had saved her life that day on the cliffs. "We're really going to do this?" she ventured softly. "You're serious, you want *me* for your mistress? You could have anyone."

His gaze strayed to her lips. "Kate, my sweet enchantress, I've dreamed of you from the moment you walked through my door."

He leaned down and kissed her with a tenderness that amazed her as he gathered her into his arms. "Don't be nervous," he whispered, ending the kiss. "Trust me."

She nodded, lifting her face to offer her lips again.

He claimed her mouth, his expert kiss dizzying her senses. Her heart hammered as she lifted her arms around his neck; crossing her wrists behind his head, she stood in his embrace. As she leaned against him, the feel of his body pressed to hers ignited long-suppressed fires in her blood.

It would not do to think about this too much. But as he caressed her gently, skillfully, kissing her again and again, her ability to reason began dissolving, anyway, into sheer pleasure. The problems that had loomed so insolubly a short while ago now seemed to belong to someone else.

Sensuality stole over her, awakening her senses. He was everything. She loved the taste of his mouth, his soft lips stroking hers, his hard body under her hands. The scent of winter clung to his long, sable hair, and the soothing way he touched her made her toes curl, his large, warm hand cupping the back of her neck beneath the cascade of her hair.

He continued kissing her, laving her

tongue with his own, but she grew breathless when his fingertips left her nape and skimmed over her collarbone, then began trailing down her heaving chest.

The male-styled shirt that was part of her footman's uniform still hung open in a deep V to where the top of her vest started. Kissing her all the while, his simple touch kept her temperature rising as he began patiently unfastening each brass button on her waistcoat.

An offhand realization occurred.

Though at first it had seemed cold-blooded of him, seizing the very low point of her life to make his scandalous offer of taking her for his mistress, Kate now understood that at least he had given her a choice.

Now that she was in his arms, already becoming intoxicated by his kiss, she saw how easy it would have been for him to seduce her first and impose the same arrangement on her afterwards. He could have dictated the terms, and she'd have been none the wiser.

But instead, he had been open with her about his intentions, giving her a thorough opportunity to think it through and decide for herself.

The truth was, he was right. She wanted this as badly as he did.

"There," he breathed as he undid the last button.

"Y-you make a good valet," she praised him shyly. Then she caught her breath as his fingers grazed the valley between her breasts.

"Your coat, sir," he teased in a whisper as he turned his attention to the frock coat that was part of her borrowed livery. Taking hold of the bottom of one long, cuffed sleeve, he helped her ease free of it, first her right arm, then her left.

He tossed her jacket aside and took off his own, then led her over by her hands to the armchair by the fire. Without a word, he made her sit down. Kate held his stare, her heart pounding as he reached down and removed her borrowed boots, freeing her feet from their cold leather casings. With the firelight from the hearth behind him casting a ruddy halo over his black hair, he paused and cupped his warm hands around her stockinged feet.

As he did so, Kate slid the waistcoat off her shoulders, increasingly eager to be rid of her clothing. Then Rohan trailed his hands up her legs and hips until he reached her waist; he discreetly unbuttoned the placket of her livery breeches while she lay back in the leather wing chair, watching him in avid fascination.

"Lift your hips for me," he whispered.

She bit her lower lip and reached above her head, hooking her hands over the top of the chair's back to brace herself; when she followed his instructions, arching up from her seat, he slid the breeches off her slowly.

There was nothing underneath.

Her skin was hot now, though all that remained on her body was the long, white shirt and her thick wool stockings. He stripped her of the latter, one by one, then bent his head and pressed a worshipful kiss to her bare knee. He stayed like that for a long moment, his head bowed before her, his lips against her skin.

She petted his head, hesitantly at first, running her palm over his snow-dampened hair, as black as the night.

Then, gently, she molded her fingers against his roughened cheek and rugged jaw. He lifted his head and gazed at her with a passionate near adoration that took her breath away.

Without warning, she sat up and lifted the shirt off over her head, offering herself to him in virginal, tongue-tied silence.

Surely he knew she'd have done this for free.

Just like she knew he'd have protected her,

expecting nothing in return. He breathed her name, heartily accepting her gift of herself. He rose to claim her lips once more, enfolding her in his arms.

She gloried in his mouth on hers and the smooth warmth of his hands caressing her bare back, her arms, her sides. She returned his kisses in wild, reckless abandon, burning for him now, touching him everywhere, relishing the sleek iron hardness of his broad shoulders, massive arms.

There was no one left to disapprove, no claims of respectability left to salvage. Besides, if her aristocratic French mama had ditched respectability for passion, then why should she not follow in her footsteps?

Deepest hunger was driving her to become one with him tonight as she returned his kisses in fevered desperation. She began undressing him, too, her hands shaking, her skin burning after all the cold outside. Cravat first. When she had bared his throat, she stroked his neck, eagerly exploring. His skin was rough like the scruff on his jaw after their long day.

Sitting on the chair before the fire, she wrapped her arms around him as he knelt between her legs. His tongue was in her mouth; her breasts were in his hands. She gently loosed his wild hair, unwinding the length of cord that bound his queue. As it fell to his shoulders, she twined her fingers through his sable mane, reveling in his virility.

Never had she found any man so utterly thrilling, especially like this; Rohan was more hungrily lustful for her and less civilized every moment. She urged him on, loving the fiery, untamed force of him, the hard, unyielding potency of the warrior. Losing herself in her want of him, she slipped her fingers inside the V of his loose white shirt, yearning for the chance to finally touch the gorgeous body she had so long craved.

She ran her palms over him, exploring. His muscled shoulders seemed carved of stone, but his smooth skin had the luxurious feel of kid leather. She moaned softly at the marvel of his heaving, sculpted chest.

He groaned in answer. "You're driving me mad. I want you now," he panted against her lips.

"*Yes.*" Greedily, she peeled his shirt off him. But when he paused to lift it off over his head, she stared in dazed awe at his chiseled abdomen. Oh, *my.*

Delights never ceased.

"Come here," he whispered in a low, raw, husky tone.

The order excited her terribly. At the moment, she did not at all mind him telling her what to do.

With a burning passion in his eyes that would brook no denial, he scooped her up, lifting her to him with his hands under her derriere. She wrapped her arms and legs around him, feasting on his kisses as he brought her to his bed and laid her down.

He moved atop her. Surely he could feel her heart slamming in her chest, she thought, but he cupped her face and leaned down hungrily to kiss her once again.

"God, Kate," he breathed as he paused above her only briefly, unfastening his breeches. "You tempt me beyond bearing."

"Give in, then," she whispered, for surely, he must know by now that, in truth, she had belonged to him from the start.

Rohan was shaking with his desperation to claim her for his own. She ravished his senses to the point of madness; he could not stand another moment of the life he had always lived before her, so alone. God forgive him, he did not mean to take advantage of her after what she had been through tonight, but there was no holding back now, not for either of them.

He wanted to be in her.

To tear down the final walls between them. Indeed, he vowed that once he saw the proof of her virgin blood, and knew she was finally and indelibly his, then he would tell her everything. As much as he could. The shadow war between the Order and the Prometheans was as much a part of her heritage as it was his. She had a right to know the truth. Who she was. What she came from.

He could give her that.

But right now, all he wanted to give her was pleasure unlike any she had ever known. He could hardly comprehend than the wild, irrational hunger she spurred on, racing through his blood. A hunger not merely to satisfy his lust, but to bind her to him somehow — this woman and no other. To close the circle of what had begun between them even before she was born. He knew down to the marrow, aye, from the first, that she belonged to him. His to protect, to heal, to reassure after all she had suffered. She needed him like no one ever had, and he would comfort her in the most physical way he knew how.

Maybe this was just their destiny. *Superstitious*. Perhaps. He struggled to find a rational cause for his crazed longing for her, some logical explanation why her hurts should hurt him, too, and why her arrival in a room could clear the darkness out, at least for him.

The answers danced away from him, dissolving in the pleasure of her kiss. Kate cradled his face between her hands, drinking him in with her mouth while her beauty and her sheer, sweet innocence enveloped him in an almost holy fire.

As his hands began to wander over all the soft enticements of her body, she undulated under his palms in seductive invitation. Her breasts swelled beneath his roaming touch. He chafed her erect nipples with his thumbs, but soon could not resist their tautened allure. He dragged his lips away from hers and moved lower to pay homage.

He sampled each with a deep, slow, savoring kiss. Her chest heaved as she lay back on her elbows, watching him, and enjoying his attentions. With her breast in his mouth, his hand was free to discover and to claim new territory.

And he had a very clear idea of where he wanted to go. His hand inched down her stomach, teasing her as he neared her mound of Venus. His fingers drew playful circles at the bottom of her belly; he made sure she was dying for his touch before he deigned to give it to her. When she groaned with kittenish frustration, her hips rising impatiently to meet his cupped hand, he introduced himself to her mound with a deft caress.

Ah, but when his fingertips pressed deeper, he nearly lost his mind. She was dripping for him, anointing his hand with her yearning nectar. She let out an urgent sigh of pleasure and dropped her head back as he began to finger her. His pulse slammed in his arteries, for she was as ready for love as any woman he had ever bedded, her breathless motions urging on his explorations. *So wet.* It was at about that moment that her unexpected wantonness enslaved him, heart and mind, body and soul.

Her silken moans transported him to a throbbing frenzy. He had never wanted anyone with such a deep and elemental need. He freed his raging member, then captured her hand by her delicate pinky, and led her fingers to his feverish shaft, clasping her hand around it.

A small sound of wonder escaped her. He didn't know whether to laugh or to wince with frustration, but she delighted him. Then he quivered violently as her delicate fingers wrapped around him with an endearing enthusiasm for this new task. He fantasized about her mouth, but there was a time and a place for everything.

He had his work cut out for him tonight to conduct her initiation without causing her too much pain.

He pushed his breeches lower down his hips but tensed with a groan of pleasure as her hand's tight grasp began stroking him harder, faster. She had moved onto her side to get a better hold of him. She was amazing.

"Does that feel good?" she ventured, sounding eager to work him into a lather.

"Very. But —" he whispered as he stopped her, "I know something that feels . . . even better." Goaded on by climbing lust, he laid her on her back again and maneuvered himself gently atop her, taking care not to crush her with his weight. He slid his arm around her, cradled her lovely head in his hands, and gazed at her for a heartbeat. "I'm going to take you now."

"Mm, yes, Rohan, please." She writhed beneath him. He lowered his head and consumed her mouth with kisses as he entered her. Inch by inch, pressing in, he gave her what they both so desperately yearned for. She welcomed him, though he could feel her feverish uncertainty.

He moved slowly, throbbing inside her. He was only about halfway in, pleasuring

350

her with small motions, caressing her tight inner walls. Her breasts heaved against his chest as she grew accustomed to his incursion, warily accepting it; he sensed the moment she had need of more.

He gave it to her, riding in more deeply, resolute in his taking. She licked her lips, opening to him, but still he held himself back. He moved slowly until her head thrashed back and forth on his pillow and her body squirmed beneath him in quivering frustration.

He drove in harder, quickened his pace. She arched, clawing at his trembling hips, a whispered curse torn wildly from her. He could bear no more self-denial. As she lay trembling beneath him, he braced himself on his hands above her, gazed fiercely into her eyes, and thrust again, taking her completely.

This time he drove in to the hilt, and a small cry of pain escaped her; he instantly regretted it. But when he started to pull back, she clung to him, her arms around his sweat-dampened waist.

He swallowed hard, for a quick glance down at the juncture of their joined bodies had revealed a scarlet streak of her blood.

Dear God. He had not expected the rush of emotion he now felt as it truly struck him that he had just deflowered her. She was the most beautiful, most astonishing creature he had ever met. And she had willingly given him her virginity.

All of a sudden, Rohan did not know what to do next; he was lost, just for a heartbeat. Should he stop? Should he continue? Had he just committed a terrible sin, taking her innocence, when he had only darkness to give her in return?

Kate made the choice for him, curving her body up to kiss his chest over and over so sweetly he was sure he'd lose his mind.

He cupped her head against him reverently and closed his eyes. Without a word, she told him it was worth it to her, and though it might have hurt, she wanted him like this, all the way inside her. That he was her choice. But the angel had no idea what she was getting into.

Rohan shuddered, stroking her hair with a hand that shook slightly under the violence of his passion. Never before had any lover moved him so deeply.

After a moment, slowly, they eased down together onto the mattress. Taking pity on her inexperience in light of his notorious size, he lay beside her; they stared at each other, their bodies still joined.

With her left thigh draped over his right

hip, he pleasured her at a more leisurely pace. She closed her eyes and let him love her.

Before long, however, he had stoked her fire until it blazed again. She pressed him onto his back and, looking intrigued with the possibilities, sat astride him; he never left her body. Victorious atop him, she appeared to savor this position — and her newfound power over him.

There was no denying it. At the moment, he was hers, body and soul, whether she knew it or not. Whether he was quite ready for that or not. *He* was sure as hell not ready to admit it.

"Rohan," she murmured, "why haven't we been doing this all the time that I've been here?"

He gave her a licentious half smile. "I was trying to convince you that I was a gentleman," he replied, his low tone roughened by desire.

She smiled at his irreverent answer and dragged her dainty fingers down his chest. "What would I want with a gentleman when I could have a Beast?"

"I beg your pardon," he protested in mock indignation. Then he tumbled the saucy wench onto her back. "I'll have to teach you a lesson about calling me that."

"Please do." She smiled into his eyes as he moved back into position between her legs. God's truth, it was like coming home.

"Now, then, my little present. If you don't mind, I am going to give you an orgasm. I trust you are familiar with the term."

"How exciting! Of course I am," she answered breathlessly. "I'm not a prude, I'll have you know."

He lifted an eyebrow.

"Orgasm," she said matter-of-factly. "From the Greek: *orgasmos.* To be ripe. To be lustful. 'The little death.' "

He laughed softly. "Book learning, my little scholar. That's all . . . just . . . book learning," he whispered wickedly between kisses on her neck.

Then he began to tutor her so his little scholar might learn from experience.

Their bodies glided together in trembling harmony. Heated skin, rhythmic panting, slamming heartbeats. They made love as if their lives depended on it.

"*Oh, God* — Rohan!"

"Yes, Kate," he whispered raggedly in smitten agreement.

"Oh . . . my . . ."

"Surrender to me," he breathed against her lips.

She pulled him closer, held him tightly,

and obeyed him; her high, wrenching moans intoxicated him, a frantic, soft soprano by his ear. He buried his face in her silky hair, battling himself to hold off just a moment longer until she had taken her full pleasure of him.

Spasms of profound climax racked her lithe body, and the sweet convulsions of her core drove him entirely mad.

She overcame him. How he had the presence of mind to withdraw from her body, he had no idea, for he was already falling into ecstasy, but he refused to risk getting her with child in the midst of all the danger she already had to deal with.

Waves of pleasure rocked him. His explosive release drenched her quivering stomach and her spread thighs with his seed.

He did not care. He had never been one to bother with tedious inhibitions. He let his growls and groans of pleasure fill the searing space between them. All the while, he gripped her hips, only wishing to God he could have filled her body instead.

Indeed, the thought of her carrying his child made such an impression on his member that even after a climax of such fierce magnitude, his ol' fellow showed no sign of slackening.

"Oh . . . *Rohan,*" Kate purred after a

dazzled silence.

He dragged his glazed eyes open and looked at her glowing face by the flickering illumination from the distant fireplace. He reassured her of his affections with a dazed smile and a gentle kiss. A breathless laugh escaped her while his lips still lingered over hers.

When he looked at her again in question, she bit her lower lip, as though to keep herself from saying something she feared might sound silly.

"What is it?" he teased barely audibly, cuddling her nose against his own, while his long hair hung down and veiled the private space where they stared into each other's eyes. He never wanted this moment to end.

But he knew it would.

Even now, it was hard to shake the world-weary pessimism, the grim sense of doom, that lurked in the depths, he supposed, of every assassin's heart.

"You're wonderful," she whispered shyly.

"The hell I am," he answered with a rueful smile on his lips, and satisfaction in his heavy-lidded eyes. *You don't even know me. Not really. Yet.*

But you will soon, my sweet.

As he rested his head on her silken chest and stared up at the dark velvet canopy over them, a faint shadow of uneasiness passed across his brow. *We'll see if you still think so when you hear the truth.*

CHAPTER 14

The next morning was the second time Kate awoke in Rohan's bed since her arrival at the castle. But unlike that first bewildering day, this time, when she opened her eyes to the morning sunlight flooding his chamber, he was the first lovely thing she saw, right there beside her.

In no hurry to arise, they stayed peacefully abed together. She passed a dreamy spell stroking her drowsing lover's bare back in tender affection.

What a long, majestic line it was that flowed from the bulky ridge of his shoulder down to the sleek, lean curve of his lower back. Of course, he had more scars on him than one body ought to bear, she thought, but he was not inclined to answer her mild inquiries about them.

"What happened here?" she murmured, tracing what appeared to be a saber scar along his rib cage.

Lying on his stomach, his face resting on his folded arms, he feigned an in-between state of sleepy inattention, though he was clearly enjoying her touch. "Hm?"

She saw through his evasion but forgave him with a knowing smile. Whatever trouble he had been in, it hadn't killed him. That was all that mattered. She leaned closer and kissed all his old hurts.

Her light kisses soon followed the same path her admiring hands had taken, until at length, he rolled onto his back and showed her the regal evidence of her effect on him. He drew her closer, wanting to make love again, but she was still sore from her first time and softly pleaded his forbearance.

With a husky chuckle at her reluctant denial, he stole a kiss, gave her a ruefully doting look, then arose in all his magnificent naked glory to order a bath drawn for both of them.

After washing and refreshing himself, Rohan dressed for the day and went downstairs to look in on his men. He wanted to make sure Parker and the others had returned without incident, and to retrieve the book from the safe where he had ordered Eldred to hide it last night.

He promised to bring back breakfast.

Kate remained in his chamber to finish

freshening up, herself, and to work the tangles out of her hair. Wrapped in her protector's giant banyan robe, she sat in the cozy window nook, gazing out at the deep blue sea beyond the castle walls and cliffs, and the azure span of sky beyond the window mullions on this clear winter morning.

Her spirits were as bright as the new day, her heart aglow with serene fulfillment. Rohan's absence gave her a few minutes alone to reflect on her new existence and the bold step she had taken last night with him.

Well, there was no going home now. Her house was burned down, and she was no longer a maiden. *Book learning,* she mused, suppressing a giggle of savored remembrance.

Of course, it was ironic that old Caleb Doyle would have the last laugh, considering he had brought her here in the first place for this very function. A "fine young bed warmer" for His Grace. How could she have known then that she would soon embrace this role?

But she had no regrets. Finally, she was not alone.

At the quick staccato of a knock at the door, she lit up and looked over from her perch in the window nook. "Who is it?" she called in a mischievous singsong voice.

The door opened. Rohan poked his head in. "Are you decent?"

"Depends who you ask."

"You are not naked. I'm crushed."

"It's chilly in here!"

"I could stoke the fire."

"Believe me," she purred, "you do."

He grinned at her jest, but Kate refused to blush and sent him a sultry, sparkling look. Mistresses, after all, could say that sort of thing.

Then he swept into the room, bringing her breakfast on a tray like her very own cavaliere servente. "Hungry?"

"For what?" she shot back.

"My goodness," he drawled, "I've created a monster. I'm so pleased."

She laughed as he set the large tray on the bed, then sauntered over to her at the window nook. At once, he leaned down, captured her face between his hands, and gave her a long, luscious kiss after their short separation.

Though he had only been gone about twenty minutes, Kate had missed him desperately. She sighed with pleasure, caressing his arms, as Rohan slowly ended the kiss.

"Done being sore yet, by chance?" he

whispered with a wicked gleam in his pale eyes.

"Almost."

"Very well, replenish your strength." Straightening up from kissing her, he gestured toward the large and heavily laden tray. "Your breakfast, madame."

"Thank you, I'm starved!" She jumped up from the window nook, brushed past him with a caress, and hungrily examined the meal.

They both sat down on his huge bed with the breakfast tray between them. Kate's mouth watered at what was on offer: a pot of tea and pastries drizzled with white glaze, toast with butter and jam; when she lifted the lid keeping the center plate warm, she discovered eggs and sausages.

They helped themselves and proceeded to eat, but eventually, while nibbling on a piece of toast, Kate pointed with her pinky finger at the largest lidded serving platter, which remained unopened.

"What's under there?"

"Voilà," he answered softly, lifting the lid.

Kate went motionless, stopped chewing, then swallowed her mouthful with a gulp. "My mother's book!"

The weathered, leather-bound tome lay heavily on the platter, freed from the rough cloth swaddling in which Rohan had found it last night. She read the title engraved into the cover, probably an addition by a later owner helping to preserve it: *Le Journal de L'Alchimiste.*

"Lord," she murmured, "I had nearly forgotten about it in all of the, ah, excitement." She shot him a flirtatious look, then gazed at it but decided on the spot there was something about it that she did not like.

She glanced warily at him. "Have you looked at it?"

"I started to. Then this fell out of it, and I thought I'd better wait for you." He reached over to the book, lifted the leather cover, and pulled out an old, yellowed, folded letter, which had been tucked inside. "I think you'd better read it. When you're ready."

Kate took it from him, intrigued. "Did my mother write it?"

"No, I think your grandfather, the Count DuMarin, wrote it to her. Forgive me for looking at it before you, but I wanted to make sure there was nothing in there that was going to hurt you."

"Ohh." With an adoring smile, she kissed her fingers and reached across the tray to press them to his lips. When he had bestowed a dutiful kiss on them in answer, she moved on with a smile, unfolding the letter.

"I suppose I am as ready as I'll ever be."

She began scanning the neat lines. "God," she murmured, "it looks like my grandfather wrote this to Mama on the occasion of their parting."

"Are you sure you're up to this?"

Rohan was watching her with a frown. Kate nodded in answer, mentally switching over into French, the language in which the letter was written. As Rohan took another sip of tea, she delved in:

My Dearest Gabrielle,
We will not meet again upon this earth. I wish that I had years or even months to explain what I must do, but I have neither time nor heart to confess to you the Pandora's box that I have helped to open. Perhaps one day, the Duke of Warrington can tell you.

Kate looked up abruptly. "The Duke of Warrington?" She glancing from Rohan to the letter in confusion. "My grandsire . . . knew your father?"

He nodded slowly.

She stared at him in shock. "You didn't tell me!"

"Read on," he murmured. "You will soon see why."

Her heart began pounding inexplicably as she looked at the letter again. "What is my grandfather referring to — this 'Pandora's box' he says he helped to open? Do you know?"

"Just read it, Kate."

She eyed him warily. Something strange was going on here. Consumed with curiosity, she read on:

My only hope now is to assist those I had always deemed my enemies. Whatever the cost, we must stop what has been put into motion before the chaos spreads.

She was baffled and could feel herself becoming slightly upset. What did it all mean?

At least the next line made some sense.

In America, you will be far away from all of this, and there, I must believe, you will be safe.

That much comported with what little she knew of her mother's past.

Trust in these good men under whose protection I commend you. How could I have known it was our enemies who were right all this time, and we who were in the wrong? May you never be led into such folly as I was. Everything that I believed was backwards. I go to my death repenting everything — my entire life, blinded by the Council's deceptions and my own greed — but most of all, regretting what I allowed to be done to you in the name of the creed that I now know was naught but lies and wickedness.

"Good God, what is he talking about?" she breathed, glancing up at Rohan as she paled. "I thought Grandpère stayed behind in France to fight the Jacobins!"

"Not exactly."

"You know about this?"

"I do."

"How?"

"Because my family's involved in it, too."

"These 'good men' he's referring to — does he mean your father?"

Rohan nodded stoically.

Kate realized he was waiting for her to finish reading the letter before he intended to answer her questions.

She felt slightly dizzy with the sudden uncertainty of realizing he had known things about her and her family without ever saying a word about it till now.

He must have his reasons, but good God, she had entrusted him with her virginity last night.

She could not help feeling a tiny bit betrayed by his secrecy. Shaken by these sudden feelings of distrust for the man on whom her life depended, she forced herself to focus again on the letter.

My daughter, henceforth, you must beware the Council's wrath. There are those who will seek to punish you for what your father is about to do. You know their names; they have dined with us on many an evening. They have been like uncles to you. But in your pure child's heart, I believe you sensed the truth: Their souls are dark. Know now that I go to reveal their secrets to our rivals. I have no choice. The Order of St. Michael is Europe's last remaining hope.

"St. Michael," Kate echoed, recalling the magnificent marble statue of the archangel in the duke's family chapel.

Rohan's face was impassive; she read on.

As for you, my dear, this volume that I

entrust into your care is to be used as your last line of protection. If you are ever threatened by my former colleagues, use <u>The Alchemist's Journal</u> to bargain for your safety. The Council will not harm you so long as you keep it out of their clutches. But handle it as little as possible, lest you, too, become infected by the evil it contains. Breathe nothing of it to outsiders, and trust no one who would demand it of you. It must stay in our family since Valerian was of our own blood.

Kate's jaw dropped. She looked at Rohan in astonishment. "My ancestor — ?" she cried. "Valerian the Alchemist? That's why Mama had this book? T-the sorcerer who cursed your line? I am his descendant?"

"Good thing you don't believe in curses," he murmured with a pointed look.

She could barely speak, and did not know what she could possibly say, in any case. Her head was reeling.

And yet there was more. She lifted the letter again and rushed on through to reach the end, only praying there were no further mind-boggling revelations.

And so, now, my precious child, we must

part. May you and whatever God exists behind the firmament forgive me for the mistakes I made as your father. I shall spend the rest of my life trying to make amends — however short a time fate allows before the Council learns of my betrayal.

But do not weep for me. The information that I can provide to the Order shall be my penance for my part in the hell that has been unleashed in our beloved France. Tyranny is coming, Gabi. That is why you must move to America. I fear bloody days ahead for all of Europe.

Her grandfather had been right about that. The letter was dated 1792, and nearly twenty-five years of bloody battles had followed. Napoleon's ambitions had spread the upheaval across the Continent, from the French seaside, across the fertile Rhine Valley of the German principalities, over the Alps, blasting past the Habsburg stronghold of Vienna, into the cold reaches of Russia itself, and south, too, to the Spanish plains and the boot of Italy. Even the Ottomans, she understood, had not remained untouched.

The only place that had been safe was England, though, to be sure, up until the great Admiral Lord Nelson had crushed Napoleon's navy at Trafalgar, the sentries had watched every night from their coastal towers for a possible invasion from the sea.

Rohan was watching her intently, waiting with an almost predatory patience. It sank in then that he was somehow involved in all this. What had he said that night at their celebratory dinner?

"I work for the government in certain . . . covert capacities."

She swallowed hard and read on, rushing to reach the end. She was beginning to get the feeling she had stumbled into something far beyond her ken.

One by one, the crowns of Europe will fall until all are conquered and brought under the Prometheans' one rule. But all is not yet lost. The Council's aims cannot be allowed to proceed un-checked, and I can provide the Order with crucial information of their future plans.

Remember, as I have often told you, do not believe anything you see. The tumult of this world is naught but spec-tacle and illusion, a magician's trick to distract your eyes away from the real sleight of hand — the unseen hand behind all the thrones and powers of this world.

I should know. I helped to craft it.

Adieu, my darling. It is for you and for your children that I have made this choice. You are the one product of my days that I can look back on in pride. May you lead a long life in peace, with whatever joy you are able to discover in this dark world, my darling child. If not for you, I should have been swallowed by the darkness long ago.

With love and tears,
Ever your Papa

Kate sat for a long moment in utterly stunned silence.

When she finally looked at Rohan through a sea of confusion, he returned her bewildered glance with a calm, steady gaze.

"So — my grandfather," she said haltingly, "was some kind of — informant?"

"Correct. And my father was the agent put in charge of his case."

"What is this Council he mentions, and the other thing — the Order?"

"Kate . . . what I'm about to tell you, you must never repeat. To anyone. I am only prepared to discuss it with you because it concerns you directly, especially now that you have been targeted. But also because you deserve to know the truth about your bloodlines. I must have your word that you will never share the following information with anyone. Many lives are at stake, including yours and mine. Can you make me this promise? If not, I've already said too much."

"Of course I promise," she murmured, wide-eyed.

"Good." Still sitting on the edge of the bed, Rohan leaned forward and rested his elbows on his knees, loosely clasping his hands. He was quiet for a moment, considering how to begin. Then he looked askance at her. "Remember that dragon book you found?"

She nodded quickly.

"You were right," he said. "It wasn't really about dragons. It's about a struggle between good and evil that's been going on for hundreds of years. A secret war played out in the shadows." He rose and began to pace. "My ancestors have been in it from the start, all the way back to the Middle Ages.

"Likewise, your French kin, the DuMarin family, had a part in it for many generations, from Valerian the Alchemist, all the way down until your grandfather had his change of heart."

"Had a part in what?" she murmured, paling.

He studied her for a second. "A very dark, very dangerous organization of conspirators known as the Promethean Council. We estimate there are fewer than a thousand of them, all told —"

"We?" she interrupted.

He sent her a sharp glance that bade her to be patient. "The leaders of the Protheans are highborn, very wealthy, and strategically situated in high places in every court in Europe. Some wear crowns, but most of our royal houses are merely their lapdogs, puppets." He shrugged. "These men give an outward appearance of serving their various rulers, but in actuality, they are secretly following their own well-coordinated agenda."

"What agenda?"

"They insinuate themselves into the halls of power. It can be in any capacity, from generals to advisors, treasurers, high court judges, royal physicians, priests, trusted members of the aristocracy — even favorite artists. But behind their masks, their loyalties lie elsewhere. That sketch you saw in the dragon book. The dragon's egg. Remember?"

She nodded, mute with shock.

"It's called the Initiate's Brand. Every convert to the Promethean cult receives the mark of the *Non Serviam* on his or her body. For you see, more than mere political ambition drives these devils. Their roots are in the occult. That is why they have such a reverence for the likes of Valerian and his black magic."

"My ancestors were on the evil side?" she cried, stricken. "But you will never convince me that Mama was evil!"

"No, no, Lady Gabrielle had nothing to do with it. She was an innocent, as far as I know." He hesitated. "Would you prefer that I stop? After all you've been through, perhaps this is too much —"

"No, I want to hear it! You've told me more about my own origins within the past few minutes than I have known about myself my entire life. I need this information, Rohan. I need to know who I am. Please, go on."

He nodded, giving her a tender look. "The Prometheans do not consider themselves evil, which honestly makes them all the more deadly. In their own view, they are beneficent, only employing darker powers to bring about the 'universal good' of their own supposedly enlightened rule. Yet the proof of who they are is there, in all that they believe. To them, the ends justify any sort of brutal means."

"What do they believe?" she asked in a hushed tone.

"They do not acknowledge the worth of any human life, no human dignity. Anyone is expendable, anybody can be sacrificed for what they like to call the greater good. Of course, the real motive behind all their high-minded philosophy is nothing more than the naked lust for power." He studied her for a second through narrowed eyes, then paced back across the room in the other direction.

"Mankind, to them, consists of no more than pawns on their chessboard, about equal in value to a herd of sheep, or a plague to be eradicated over time. No matter how pretty their speeches, they are driven by an arrogant conviction of their own superiority. Fortunately, however, they do not stand unopposed."

He paused and drifted over to the mullioned windows.

Kate watched him, wide-eyed.

Rohan looked out for a long moment, then he turned to her. "I belong to a secret hereditary Order sworn to rooting out the Prometheans and destroying them before they can become entrenched in power. It is called the Order of St. Michael the Archangel."

"The statue in the chapel."

"Yes." He nodded with a gleam of hardened family pride in his eyes. "My line has been a part of it going back to when it all started during the Third Crusade under Richard the Lionheart. My father was one of the Order's greatest warriors. As for me, from the moment of my birth, I've been trained and shaped and molded to follow in his footsteps."

She thought of the Hall of Arms and his ferocious practice with his unusual, lance-like weapon.

At last, it was all beginning to make sense.

"I was a boy at the time of the French Revolution. The whole world was shocked by the storming of the Bastille and the arrest of the French royal family. But soon, the leaders of the Order began seeing signs of the Promethean puppet-masters' hands behind the growing chaos.

"My father's team tracked down a few Promethean agents provocateurs that had been dispatched to spur on the guillotine mobs. You see, the more blood and chaos they could cause in the streets, the more desperately the people would begin to cast about for some seemingly benign authority to restore order. Their plan was that the people themselves would clamor for a new form of rule that would soon grow into inescapable oppression.

"The Prometheans did not care in the least about liberty, equality, fraternity — the ideals of the Revolution. I can assure you, the liberty of the people is the farthest thing from their minds. But they are very skilled at turning the political passions and philosophies of the moment to their use. It doesn't matter to them.

"Religious fervor, prejudice. Persecution of the Jews or other races — whatever comes along will suit, as long as they can sink their claws into a group of biddable zealots with some fury they can point in a useful direction."

"Vile."

"Yes. They've been using this same old strategy for hundreds of years. In this case, the result was the wholesale slaughter of the upper classes in France and anyone close to them. Not that corrections weren't needed, but surely the women and children didn't also have to be snuffed out in public executions."

She shook her head with a shudder.

"When your grandfather saw the excesses of the Red Terror, he knew things had got completely out of hand. That was when he reached out to the Order."

"To your father."

"Yes. You see, the Dukes of Warrington have had this long association with the local smugglers' ring. They're very useful to us. Count DuMarin needed a ship to take his daughter to America. My father offered to get him the smartest, boldest captain he knew who could get her into New Orleans without anyone taking note of her arrival. He selected Gerald Fox."

Her jaw dropped. "My father . . . was one of Caleb Doyle's smugglers?"

"I wouldn't put it quite that strongly, but, yes, they were acquainted in the early days. That was why Caleb was so keen to get rid of you. If Captain Fox is alive, as we now believe, Caleb did not want to cross him. He gave you to me because he was afraid to send you home or to keep you. He didn't know what else to do."

"But I was always told my father's name was Madsen . . . How are you so sure this Gerald Fox was the one who took my mother off to sea?"

"I was there the night your parents were introduced."

"What?"

"Count DuMarin remained in London,

protected at the Order's headquarters, but your mother was brought here to Kilburn Castle, for her departure to America. I was about ten years old, spying from the minstrels' gallery on my father's affairs in the great hall when I saw her."

"You saw my mother?" The room was spinning as she stared at him in stunned disbelief. "She was here? Right here — in Kilburn Castle?"

He nodded, leaning against the bedpost, arms folded across his chest. "She was veiled and dressed in black mourning — I suppose, since nearly everyone she knew had gone to the guillotine, poor thing. So, I didn't really get to see her face. But she had that book in her arms." He nodded at the tome they had collected from the loft above Charley's work shed. "That was the night my father introduced her to Captain Gerald Fox. Her future husband, and your sire."

"Papa . . ."

"Yes. They were only here a short while. Fox escorted Lady Gabrielle off to his ship, and that, I'm afraid, was the last the Order ever saw of them. Their fate remained a mystery to us. Shortly after that, I was carted off to school to begin my training. You see, when the Order realized it was all starting again with the Prometheans, they saw that future warriors would be needed. So, the Seeker went out seeking, and I was one of the boys selected. Meanwhile, my sire went tearing off with his team to wreak havoc on the Prometheans based on the information your *grandpère* had provided."

Kate stared at him in awe, while his expression turned somber, lost in thought.

"My father died on that mission," he said. "It only doubled my desire to be the best hunter the Order had ever seen."

"Hunter? What do you mean?" she pursued. "What is your specific role in all this, Rohan?"

He stared at her for a long moment. "I hunt down Prometheans and kill them."

"Kill them?" she whispered.

He nodded calmly, without a trace of remorse in his eyes.

Kate looked away, chilled by his silence and unable to bear the intensity of his gaze. "So, that's where you got the scars." A moment later, she let out a shaky exhalation. "I have Promethean blood. Does that make me your enemy?"

"No. I know now you are innocent. Like your mother was."

She narrowed her eyes, observing him. "You weren't sure for a while there, were you?"

He held her in a stormy stare. "I could never hurt you, Kate. Curse or no."

"I see." She pondered his revelations a moment longer, then looked askance at him. "How do you kill them? Your enemies, I mean."

He flinched. "You don't want to know that."

"I do."

"Efficiently," he retorted.

"Ah." Perhaps he was right. Maybe she was better off not knowing the gory details. "Do you . . . ever wonder if some of them don't deserve it?"

"They all deserve it," he replied with a forcefulness that let her understand this was not a question he could permit himself to entertain. "They are evil. Killing one of them can mean saving thousands of innocent people. Besides, it's not my role to ask questions. Others specialize in gathering the intelligence. I do some of that, but my specialty is eliminating the targets."

"You mean killing them."

"Yes. The decisions come down from the top. When the Order gives me a name, I carry out my objective." He shrugged.

"I see."

"Do you?" he inquired, staring keenly into her eyes.

"I think so." She swallowed hard. "You're telling me you're kind of an assassin."

"Not 'kind of.' "

"Ah." It was fortunate she was not the fainting sort. Sweet God in heaven, she had just become the mistress of a professional government killer.

Her head was swimming, but although she was shocked, somehow, she was not surprised. Things that had seemed out of place before were beginning to make sense.

Still, she could not believe Rohan had let her give herself to him without first admitting something this monumental. He must have known it might have changed her answer, and he had wanted his way.

She was beginning to think there was a side of her duke that could be a bit of a bastard. Of course, considering his profession, there would have to be, wouldn't there?

He was staring at her rather formidably, arms folded across his chest as he waited for her to respond.

Kate was not sure what to say. She was not angry at him, per se, but what *else* did she not know about this man?

She knew he had not meant to hurt her, but a part of her felt as though she had been tricked into sleeping with him under somewhat false pretenses.

Even so, he was not the kind of man any sensible person should anger. In all, it was too late now for regrets.

"Say something," he growled.

"Well — now I see why the smugglers were so terrified of upsetting you," she forced out with a guarded attempt at humor.

"They don't know about this."

"Nevertheless — it explains a lot about you."

He frowned as though he wasn't quite sure how to take that.

"Why would the Order choose a duke for such dangerous work?" she asked. "Aren't you too valuable?"

"To protect my country?" he countered. "No. Besides, it's a matter of access. Most doors in the world are open to a man of my rank. It's easy for me to get close to the ruling idiots who don't even realize they're in danger."

"Ah." She dropped her gaze, trying to wrap her mind around it. She recalled that first night when he had hosted the grand dinner party for two, how he had made some cynical jest about eluding the Grim Reaper.

Now the joke sent a chill down her spine.

She could feel him watching her intensely.

"You regret last night."

"No." She looked up swiftly at him. "But God, Rohan, you really should have told me."

"I'm telling you now. It was not possible until I was sure that I could trust you."

"Is that why you made love to me? To find out if I was a virgin?" She stood up with a sudden flush of anger. "Were you testing me again? Like you did that night at dinner when you scared me half out of my wits?"

He just looked at her.

"Oh, my God."

"Kate — try to understand the risk that I'm taking, telling you these things. Only a handful of ministers in the cabinet and a few of the royals even know the Order exists. Everyone else believes it's just a legend. The secrecy is part of what allows us to be effective. We answer directly to the Crown, but Prinny himself didn't know the truth until the King's illness grew severe. What my colleagues back in London are going to say when they find out I've brought you in on all this, I am not eager to imagine, especially with your Promethean blood."

"What could they do to you?" she murmured warily.

He shrugged and shook his head. "Never mind that. The point is, I did not *have* to tell you any of this. I wanted to *because* I care, so don't accuse me of indifference. I know how unsettling it's been for you, not even being sure of your own name. I realize these answers are hard to hear, but I hoped that at least you could reach some sense of peace from finally hearing the truth. As for last night, well — damn it, I'm sorry if I'm not Lord Byron. I don't write love poems. But I tell you on my honor last night meant more to me than you will ever know."

She stared at him for a long moment. "I don't care about love poems," she said softly.

"Good," he mumbled. "Because I'm afraid there are none forthcoming."

Oh, Rohan. My Beast. His disclosures were difficult to accept, but she had to admit that at least his explanation made sense. It also showed her why he had been pushing her away, despite the attraction between them. Until last night, he had not been entirely sure she was not his enemy.

His mistrust of her hurt, but at least he was being open with her now.

He cleared his throat, returning to a businesslike demeanor. "Now. One final point you need to understand."

"Oh, Lord." She braced herself. "What now?"

"There is a high probability that O'Banyon

is working for the Prometheans. One of the cult's top leaders, James Falkirk, was spotted in London a while back, and it's possible he could be the 'Old Man' that O'Banyon mentioned to the Doyle boys."

She furrowed her brow, recalling the bits they had pieced together so far. "Ah, right — the unnamed lord who got O'Banyon out of Newgate and paid him to kidnap me?"

"Yes."

"So this James Falkirk could be the one who wants to lure my father back to land?" She tried to sound calm, but her heart was pounding.

He nodded. "According to our information, Falkirk is a true believer in all that occult hocus-pocus. He's just the sort to become obsessed with unearthing the Alchemist's Tomb. We've already discussed how your father may be the only man alive who knows where it is."

"Right," she murmured. "That's why they kidnapped me, you said. To make Papa come back to England and show them where the Tomb is."

"Well, to make things slightly more complicated, the Prometheans also captured one of our agents a few months ago. We believe James Falkirk is the one holding Drake, likely torturing him to try to turn him against us."

"Dreadful," she breathed.

"Indeed, but all this could work to our advantage. If O'Banyon answers to Falkirk, and Falkirk is holding Drake, then our expected rendezvous with your kidnapper might just help us track down our missing agent. From what our sources tell us, the only reason Drake hasn't broken yet is because they've abused him to the point where he's lost his memory. Whatever they did to him, the poor bastard's mind somehow just shut down."

Kate stared at him, paling. "I couldn't bear it if something like that ever happened to you."

"Don't worry, it won't. Drake should have never let himself be taken alive, and he knew that, but for whatever reason, he disregarded protocol." His words came to an abrupt halt, and he lowered his gaze.

"You mean he should have taken his own life? Is that what you would do?"

He ignored the question. "You have nothing to fear, Kate. If they even try to come near you, I will tear them limb from limb."

"I know you will," she murmured. "It's not for myself that I worry, but for Papa — if he really is alive."

Rohan shook his head at her. "You just

can't let yourself believe it, can you?"

She gave him a pained look in answer. "Can you keep him safe, too?"

"Your old man?"

"I'm just the hostage, like you said. He's the real target. Now that you've told me what these Prometheans are like, I'm terrified of what they might to do him."

"Kate, he's Gerald Fox. Your 'Papa' eats rusty grappling hooks for breakfast. The mere mention of his name had Caleb and his boys shaking in their boots. The Sea Fox, as they call him, he's a bloody terror of the seas."

She succumbed to a nostalgic smile. "That's not how I remember him."

"What do you remember about him?"

"To me, he was the kindest, tenderhearted, big old bear."

"Well, you're his little girl. No doubt you knew a side of him few others got to see."

"Will you help him, Rohan?"

"Of course I will. For your sake."

"Thank you," she whispered.

Just then, a hasty knock pounded at his chamber door.

"Your Grace!" It was Eldred; his tone sounded urgent. "Caleb Doyle has just brought the letter — the one you've been waiting for!"

Kate drew in her breath. Her gaze flew to Rohan's. "From O'Banyon?"

He stalked over and opened the door, plucking a small, folded note off the butler's tray. "Thank you, Eldred."

"Any further instructions for Mr. Doyle? He is waiting below."

"No. Tell him he can go up to the tower room and visit his nephew if he wishes, as a reward for both their cooperation."

"Very good, sir."

Rohan nodded and closed the door, glancing at the front of the envelope as he sauntered back toward her. "Well, this should be interesting. It's addressed to Denny Doyle." He sent her a sardonic glance, then broke the seal, a dingy blob of dirty white wax.

She curled her lip in disgust, recalling O'Banyon's leering face. "He hit me, you know," she announced abruptly.

Rohan turned and stared at her with sudden, great stillness. "What?"

"Oops," she said mildly. "I wasn't going to tell you that."

"O'Banyon. Hit. You."

She shrugged.

"In the face?" he demanded.

"He slapped me because I was fighting him."

"I see." Rohan stared straight ahead, every muscle tensed. He suddenly looked very much like an expert assassin. "Well, he won't do that again."

"What are you going to do?"

One lifted eyebrow said it all.

"Oh, it didn't hurt that much! I'm fine. There's no need for anything excessive."

"Stay out of it, Kate," he said politely, then he shook open the note with cool and steady hands.

She looked askance at him in curious satisfaction.

She could almost taste the justice that she had hungered for constantly since her abduction. But now that she knew it was all but guaranteed, somehow, it didn't matter so much anymore. Just knowing that Rohan was willing to champion her was enough.

"What does the blackguard write?" she asked, as he quickly scanned the three scrawled lines.

He handed it to her. "Looks like we're going to London."

"Are we?" she exclaimed, sitting up swiftly. "I've always wanted to go there! Though perhaps not under these circumstances."

"Don't you worry," he said, tugging a length of her hair affectionately. "It'll all be over soon, then I'll give you a tour of the

London I know."

"I'd enjoy that," she murmured, as he rose and walked off across the room. For a moment, she was distracted in spite of herself by his powerful male frame.

Her gaze swept up from his shiny boots, over the casual elegance of his day clothes, up the magnificent length of the man, to his black hair, then, when he turned around, his handsome face.

"What is it?"

"Nothing." She stifled a dreamy sigh. Even now that she knew the truth about him — that he was some sort of spy for the Crown, frankly, a killer, and a bit of a liar and a hardened bastard by necessity, as well — her attraction to him was every bit as strong as it had been last night.

Lord, she must be in bad shape, to have become his willing thrall. But truly, if she had a dozen virginities to get rid of, she'd have gladly given them all to him.

It was useless. To her, he was completely irresistible.

Uneasily, she tore her stare away from her protector and glanced down at the letter. She didn't even like touching the paper O'Banyon's grimy paws had handled.

Denny,

Bring the package to London. Be careful to keep it concealed, especially in Town. When you get here, pay a call after dark to the rat-catcher's shop in Shadwell. The man there knows where to find me. Have the package with you. Send for me, and I'll meet you there. All's ready on this end, get here quick. The Old Man don't like being kept waiting.

O.

"Package?" Kate tossed the note aside with an indignant snort. "How dare he call me that? And a rat-catcher's shop, of all places? How very apropos."

Rohan did not answer. He was all business now, collecting various items he intended to take with him, including the weapons case he'd had with him in the Hall of Arms.

"When do we leave?" she asked in trepidation.

"Tomorrow, dawn. We'll get our preparations done today. With the weather this time of year, the journey takes at least three days. Much delay beyond that could raise their suspicions."

She heaved a sigh, wistfully watching him

392

take out more of his personal effects. "Do we have to go?" she asked idly. "I don't want to leave."

"Oh, really?" He cast her a smile. "I seem to recall a time not too long ago when this castle was the last place in the world you wanted to be. Aren't you the girl who threatened to hurl herself into the sea to escape my wicked clutches?"

She gave him an arch look, but just in time, she bit back the answer that came to the tip of her tongue. *That was before I fell in love with you.*

Good God.

She dropped her gaze at once. Fortunately, Rohan did not notice her astonishment at this realization but merely continued packing.

Oh, dear. She feared it was true. The real reason she had allowed last night to happen. It was also why she had specifically asked if he would be annoyed if she fell in love with him. She just hadn't wanted to admit it to herself because until his scandalous offer last night, she had thought there was no way she could ever have him.

She drew his warm, oversized robe closer around her body, suddenly feeling lost, not knowing how to act.

"Well, go get dressed," he ordered with a

lordly little smile as he noticed her wavering. "How's a man to think with a luscious naked woman lying around? You, my dear, are far too distracting."

His smoldering gaze, so full of desire for her, thrilled Kate to the marrow. His glance alone could warm her blood on this cold winter's day.

Her heart soared in spite of her better sense telling her to be extraordinarily careful with him. Oh, to have snared such a man.

She suddenly thought she would die if she could not keep him.

That in itself was reason enough to go.

After all, she was only his mistress — and should act accordingly.

She rose from his bed, playfully letting his robe slip a little from her shoulders as she strolled, barefooted, toward the door. "As you wish, Your Grace."

He tracked her progress with a glazed stare, looking tempted to throw her back down on the mattress and have his way with her again.

But she did not give him time to act on the notion, blowing him a kiss by the door before shrugging his dressing gown back up into place. She stepped out into the drafty hallway, heading back to the guest chamber to pack her few, ill-fitting, stolen clothes.

On the way, she paused to glance down into the Gothic stairwell, letting her gaze travel over all the ancient carved stone. Strangely enough, she would miss this place.

She wondered if she'd ever be back again.

Good-bye, Gray Lady, wherever you are. For what it's worth, I'm betting your Lord Kilburn was not the one who murdered you.

Kate had stayed at the castle long enough to have formed an opinion on the so-called Kilburn Curse. Her official ruling as a bona fide descendant of the Alchemist was that the whole thing was hogwash. Just like in Mrs. Radcliffe's novels, in the end, there *had* to be some logical explanation for what only appeared supernatural at first.

The Warrington men could not be cursed; there was too much honor in their blood. If the rest of them were like Rohan, they were surely incapable of harming any woman. Everything he had done, after all, had been centered around keeping her safe. It was all just a tale.

Convincing Rohan of this would probably prove impossible — but then again, as long as he believed it, he would never take a wife. She would never have to share him.

Hmm. Now there was a thought worthy of a courtesan. She moved on, sauntering back to her room.

CHAPTER 15

The journey to London took four rather than the three days Rohan had predicted, due to the inclement weather of waning January. Their party traveled in two carriages: Rohan and Kate in his long, luxurious traveling chariot, Eldred and Parker minding Peter Doyle in another closed black coach. A few more of the castle's black-clad guards accompanied them, now transformed into liveried footmen, drivers, and grooms.

Occasionally, their caravan had to stop for a snowdrift blocking some lonely country road. The men would jump down, grab their shovels, and clear the way for the horses and carriage wheels to pass.

Kate did not mind these delays. The chariot lacked for no comfort, and she savored all those hours alone with Rohan in the coach. It felt more like they were going off on holiday than traveling to confront people who were out for her blood. True, her trust in him had suffered a bit of a blow after all his revelations, but she had made up her mind to take it all in stride.

They spent the journey talking, enjoying each other's company, and trying together to decipher some of the mysteries of *The Alchemist's Journal.*

It was a most eye-opening volume. The book had entries written by several different generations of DuMarins, giving a glimpse into some of the activities of the Prometheans over the last few centuries.

Some pages were written in code, but from the parts in plain French, they learned that the religious and political clashes of the sixteenth and seventeenth centuries had given the Prometheans many opportunities for advancement. There were even a few stunning details about their hand in the Great Fire of London of 1666, apparently a key year for their occult beliefs. But by the early 1700s, it became necessary for the Prometheans to move the Alchemist's burial place, which was about to be discovered by the Order.

The book said that when the new site was chosen to hold their revered warlock's remains, the location was determined to be ideal for the establishment of a large and elaborate underground compound where the Prometheans could conduct training, initiations, and various other rituals.

The complex, which they simply called the Alchemist's Tomb, had taken nearly thirty years to build and employed all the genius of those men of the Enlightenment.

Valerian's coffin and secret scrolls were now sealed in a hidden chamber within the subterranean compound. The book was evasive about its location, but she managed to learn why the mysterious facility had fallen out of use.

During Bonnie Prince Charlie's exile in France, the Prometheans had taken an interest in the Scottish prince's claim to the English throne. In other words, they had smelled their own advantage. The Council — the leaders of the Prometheans — had decided to back the Stuart prince in his goal to seize power from the Hanoverian King George II. Then their meddling had begun, much as Rohan had described their activities during the more recent French Revolution.

But after the disastrous Battle of Culloden in 1746, the Order had come hunting for the various Prometheans whose soulless machinations had brought such devastating ruin on the great Scottish clans. One by one, the Order had cut them down, until the Tomb complex was abandoned; the few Prometheans who knew about it had been killed. Over time, it was forgotten.

Despite this sobering tale, there was still much to decipher. Kate was especially intrigued by entries in the book showing scientific notations for chemical compounds.

The long, complicated sequences of elements left her wondering what sort of substances these ingredients produced. Had her ancestors managed to preserve some of Valerian's ancient formulas for alchemy potions?

She did not know. She turned the puzzles over constantly in her mind, but as they drew closer to London, she tried not to let it get in the way of the precious time she had alone with Rohan.

The best part of the trip were the warm, wanton nights they spent together in the cozy rooms of various galleried coaching inns along the way. They passed the ruddy, firelit hours enrapt in delectable exploration, deepening their knowledge of each other in body and soul.

Alas, they arrived in London before she knew it, suddenly thrust among the throng of carriages whirring and clattering past, this way and that, weaving through an endless maze of slushy streets lined with shops and crowded houses.

The windswept austerity of Dartmoor and the lulling quiet of the Cornish castle by the sea seemed a world away. Kate peered eagerly out the window, her gloved hand linked with Rohan's. She had never seen so many people in one place.

Vendors loudly hawked their wares, boys sold newspapers on every corner, hackneys picked up passengers, while wagons made their rounds with all their various deliveries. Mail coaches trundled into the city, while stages gusted away from their depots, loaded with travelers bound for the far-flung shires.

Then the bell towers of countless churches throughout the great metropolis began to toll the hour of noon all at once, from all directions. She glanced at Rohan, delighted by the glorious clamor; he smiled back, but when she looked out again, she shook her head, for the hurried people in the streets paid no mind to the joyful noise.

Soon they passed through the hurly-burly of the mercantile City and proceeded into the refined environs of the West End. Grubby shops gave way to graceful park squares, bounded on all sides by giant stately houses.

Instead of delivery wagons, now fashionable phaetons clipped by, pulled by high-stepping blood horses. They passed gleaming mahogany barouches and elegant Town coaches with liveried footmen on the back and aristocratic coats of arms emblazoned on the doors, not unlike the chariot in which they rode.

As they swept along a stylish avenue dotted with lavish boutiques catering to the wealthy, a pair of ladies emerging from a shop spotted Rohan's carriage passing by.

Though Kate caught only a glimpse of them, their wild reaction was difficult to miss.

"Oh, look! It's Warrington!"

The first pointed feverishly at their already-retreating chariot, while her companion waved her handkerchief in the air, as though tempted to try running after them.

"Your Grace! Yoo-hoo! Dear Warrington! Come back, darling!"

"Shite," he whispered, glancing back, his epithet fogging the window glass.

Kate glanced in surprise from the expensively clad Society ladies to the duke, who had flattened himself back from the carriage window, keeping out of view.

She began laughing. "Who are they?"

"I have no idea."

"Right." She regarded him in chiding amusement, but when she glanced through the back window, she saw the first two ladies flutter over to speak with more women on the street. The whole, fashionable tribe of perfectly coiffed beauties turned and stared eagerly after the chariot until it turned the corner.

Rohan cleared his throat and gestured to the road ahead. "We're almost there. Just a few blocks more."

Kate looked at him matter-of-factly, but he refused to comment; she suddenly had a better sense of why Caleb Doyle had thought it fitting to give His Grace a female for a gift. Jealousy plucked a discordant note on her heartstrings, but she wryly decided to shrug it off. That unpleasant emotion would not do either of them any good.

Linking her fingers through his, she thrust his crowd of admirers out of her mind, and a moment later, his chariot pulled up in front of a sprawling Town mansion.

"Here we are."

"Oh, my," Kate murmured.

Behind an elaborate, wrought-iron gate it sat, a great gray block of Portland stone, with tall rectangular windows trimmed in white, and stone urns with matching topiaries flanking the front door.

The carriages stopped at the gate, but Parker got out with the key and opened the way before them. Halting only briefly, the chariot rolled up under the white portico on the side of the house, where it stopped.

Kate rejoiced to be freed from the confines of the carriage, while Parker and Wilkins hurried Peter Doyle into the house before he was seen.

As she stood glancing around, feeling the excitement of London in the air, and taking in the beauty of the sculpted grounds, Rohan captured her elbow and quickly guided her inside, as well.

"Don't forget the little rules that we discussed," he chided in a low voice.

"Yes, I know. Stay out of sight. Don't talk to anyone besides Parker and Eldred. Don't worry, I'm not even here," she assured him, parroting back the guidelines he had laid down for her own safety before they had left Cornwall.

"Good girl," he answered as he got the door for her. "I appreciate your patience. I know it's a bore for you to be caged like this, but just you wait and see. I'm going to spoil you as you deserve when all this is over."

"Are you really?"

"Every woman in London is going to hate you," he replied with a smile, but she frowned.

"I'm not sure that's actually necessary."

"Don't worry, they'd never dare say it to your face. They'll all be too busy groveling."

"Who grovels to a mistress?" she asked dryly.

Rohan laughed and put his arm around her. "My little Dartmoor darling, you are so adorably naïve."

"Why? What do you mean?" she exclaimed.

"Ah, you'll learn soon enough how this place works." He got the door for her with a worldly look. "Inside with you now, before the neighbors start their snooping. And welcome . . . to my humble abode."

"Humble?" she murmured, staring all around as she stepped inside. Egads, she had never been in so opulent a building in all her life. It was nothing like the stark medieval castle. Here, luxury was piled atop luxury, every room a statement of the owner's wealth and rank.

She followed in a daze as he led her through the ground level, with its black-and-white-marble floors and reception rooms of deep blue and stately red with touches of cream and gold and formal black. Twenty-foot ceilings. Soaring Corinthian columns with gilt-touched capitals, ornate chimneypieces carved from alabaster.

The pomp of the ducal residence stretched from the luxurious carpeted floors to the magnificent painted ceilings. The walls between were hung with fine wood paneling and pieces of great art.

The whole place bespoke proud strength and noble service to the Realm, but everything was in a state of such perfection that she barely dared sit down on the furniture. For heaven's sake, the satin-brocaded armchair beside a rosewood table inlaid with mother-of-pearl, along with the oil lamp on it, dripping with cut crystal — that little grouping alone probably cost more than her entire cottage.

She was afraid to touch anything and was beginning to feel entirely out of her league.

Those Society ladies in Bond Street would probably have felt perfectly at ease. Kate suddenly wondered how many of them had been inside his house, especially upstairs, where the bedchambers were . . .

"Now, then. Make yourself at home," he said, when they reached the entrance hall.

"Hm?" She had been staring with some trepidation at the impressive marble staircase that swept up to the next floor.

"Feel free to relax. Pick a room and take a nap if you like, or if you're hungry, just tell the staff, and they'll fix you a meal. I need to go check in with the Order."

"Will you be gone long?"

"A couple of hours. I also want to have a look at this rat-catcher's shop where we are to meet O'Banyon. Get the lay of the land."

She winced slightly at his mention of the coming confrontation. "Be careful out there, all right?"

"Don't worry, I'll be back before you miss me."

"I doubt that," she murmured with a doting smile, then he leaned down and kissed her good-bye.

Kate slid her arms around his neck and made sure to give him a kiss intended to bring him home soon. Neither of them paid any mind to the guards and servants passing here and there; Rohan wrapped his arms around her waist and claimed her lips with unabashed passion, his warm, clever mouth slanting over hers.

She was breathless when he slowly ended it.

"Hurry back," she whispered. "I'll be waiting for you."

"Mmm." He ran his hands down the sides

of her waist as he held her in a smoldering gaze.

Kate gave him a knowing half smile.

As he reluctantly released her from his embrace, she trailed a mischievous fingertip down his chest as he pulled away. "Perhaps I'll go exploring and see if I can't find my way to your bedchamber."

"Damn, you make it hard to leave." With a lusty glance at her wetted lips, he gave her a wink, then turned away to leave his men with a few final instructions.

She overheard him telling Eldred to make sure no one came in. He got confirmation from Parker that Peter Doyle had been locked up in the strong room. Then he left the house. A few minutes later, he rode away on horseback.

Kate watched him through the window until she remembered she had orders to stay out of sight. With a dutiful sigh, she pulled away from the sparkling glass panes and decided to have a look around the upper floors of his home.

Lifting the hem of her gown, she ventured up the pristine staircase, one hand resting on the sculpted banister. A gallery on the upper floor overlooked the entrance hall below, but beyond it, the layout of the rooms flowed with formal grace.

As she wandered from the princely drawing room to the handsome music room beside it, she suddenly heard the clatter of carriage wheels outside, followed by the sound of female voices.

Oh, you must be joking, she thought, instantly recalling the women they had passed.

Though Rohan had told her to stay out of sight, she stole across the music room and sneaked over to the window, peeking out from behind the drapes.

To her astonishment, she saw not one but *two* carriages in the drive, with equally beautiful ladies alighting from each. They wore fabulous hats and gorgeous, fur-lined coats, had perfect skin, and were dressed in the first stare of fashion. They hurried with dainty, mincing steps racing each other playfully to the door.

Kate watched, agog, as one woman pulled her long coat open and stopped to adjust her bodice, tugging down her décolleté slightly, thrusting out her chest. Others fluffed their curls hanging from beneath their bonnets as they fought to reach the front door first.

She shook her head, staring down at them, his rule of staying out of sight be damned. She saw them talking, but simply *had* to hear their words.

She reached up to the window latch, unlocked it, and discreetly opened it a crack, listening in on their exchange.

"Why, Lucinda! Imagine finding you here."

They exchanged the most artificial pecks on the cheek she'd ever seen.

"Pauline," another woman greeted a new arrival with a haughty sniff. "Shouldn't you be at home helping your dear old husband find his teeth?"

Lucinda let out a trill of brittle laughter. "At least my husband *is* at home, not passed out under a table in some bordello. Not that it's any of your affair, darling, but Warrington wished me to come and see him." She preened. "I have a standing invitation."

"Oh, really?" the other drawled with a skepticism equal to Kate's own at this assertion.

"Oh, yes! Didn't you know? Warrington and I have always got on *famously.*"

"Then I suppose you know where he's been these past few weeks, hm?"

"Well, no, not exactly. You?"

"Wouldn't tell you if I did," she shot back lightly.

Several of them laughed.

"Oh, come," another of their fair rivals interjected as they all strolled toward the door. "You both know he dashed off and never said a word to any of us."

"Well, yes — but I'm sure it's nothing."

"I'm just glad he's back!"

"Some lark must have come into his head. You know how wild he is."

A lady in light blue sighed. "I love that about him. You never know what he's going to do."

"Or whom," another drawled.

The others gasped; their tittering filled the air.

Kate scowled.

A total of eight women had descended on the house like so many queen bees drawn by some potent, irresistible flower. Kate in part wanted to laugh, but mainly, she seethed with indignation.

When the doorbell clanged, she abandoned her post by the window and rushed to the gallery above the entrance hall to eavesdrop on whatever Eldred was going to say to stave them off.

Bravely, he kept them outside. "I am very sorry, ladies, His Grace is not at home," the butler announced, his back to Kate.

To her surprise, his claim was rejected.

"Look here, my good fellow, we just saw

his carriage!"

"Yes, madam, His Grace has returned to Town, but regretfully, he had to rush off again straightaway."

"Where did he go?" demanded one pampered, petulant princess.

"When's he coming back?" Lucinda asked hopefully.

"Er, I am not sure, on either point, ladies, but if you'd care to leave your cards —"

Crestfallen moans of disgruntlement floated up through the entrance hall.

Then, all of a sudden, one of the nosier ladies craned her neck past Eldred's lanky frame and gasped. "Who's that?" she cried, pointing past him at Kate, who was standing on the gallery.

Uh-oh. Her cheeks flushed, but Kate drew herself up as Eldred looked over his shoulder with a wince.

One of the women shoved the door open the rest of the way, and they all stared at her, looking utterly indignant that another female had beaten them to the punch.

"Why, that blue-eyed devil! He's *with* someone already!"

"Warrington, you Beast! Oh, let us in, old man. We know he's in there!"

"Mesdames!" Kate flung out sharply, unable to stand another moment of their intru-

sion. One hand on her hip, she lifted her chin and summoned up every ounce of elegant French hauteur that she had inherited from her mama. "His Grace is not at home," she clipped out. "Leave your cards, please, and I will make sure he receives your — well-wishes," she finished cynically.

None of the ladies moved.

No one made a sound.

They stared at her in shock, and Kate stared back, giving no ground whatsoever, though her heart was pounding.

She could not believe she had just given them an order. Clearly, she was spending too much time with Rohan. She was even starting to talk like him.

Even less could she believe her eyes when the women actually started to obey.

A nervous incredulity had descended over the coddled company. The ladies glanced uncertainly at each other; whispers were exchanged.

They kept staring at her.

"Well," Lucinda said, gathering herself and smoothing her little reticule over her forearm. "W-we are very sorry to have disturbed you, I am sure."

Kate bowed her head, accepting the apology.

Eldred held up his silver tray for them to

leave their cards. Most of them seemed to decide against it on second thought, but they took pains to get a look at Kate before retreating from the doorway.

She, in turn, refused to budge. Rohan was going to be furious, for she had broken both rules — stay out of sight, don't talk to anyone — but her pride simply would not let her flee the scene. Not when she, unlike they, had every right to be there!

Then Lucinda curtsied to her, and the others began doing the same before filing away from the door, and all of a sudden, it dawned on Kate the conclusion they had drawn. She nearly choked. *Oh, my God. They think I am his duchess!*

With newfound respect, the haughty Society ladies retreated from the house. They got in their fancy little carriages and trotted away, chagrined faces glancing out again from the carriage windows.

Eldred closed the door, turned around slowly, and shot Kate a look of disapproval. "Well, you've done it now, haven't you?"

She pursed her lips together for a moment, as stunned by their orderly exit as she had been by their arrival, but she forced a smile, still playing the duchess. "That will be all, Eldred. Carry on!"

He raised an eyebrow at her. "Do you

want to tell His Grace about this, Miss Madsen, or shall I?"

A sudden angry pout flashed over her face. "I don't care what he says!" she exclaimed, but a terrible thought now gripped her, a cold, deflating weight that brought her back to earth after the pipe dream of the past few days.

She sat down slowly on the stairs as it shook her to the core. How could she be so thick?

If Rohan had sported with all those beautiful women and eventually cast them aside, then she was a fool to think it would end any differently with her.

CHAPTER 16

Never in his life did Rohan imagine he would withhold information from the Order to protect a Promethean descendent, but as he rode to Dante House, he knew what he was doing.

With O'Banyon waiting, he could not waste time trying to convince the others that despite her Promethean blood, Kate was not a threat. He'd explain his actions later when there was time to go through all the details. For now, he trusted his own judgment, and really, given his record, so should they.

Urging his tall, steady hunter on, he weaved through the traffic at a nimble canter, the reins taut in his gauntleted hands at the horse's withers, the brim of his hat pulled low over his eyes, his greatcoat billowing slightly with the horse's motion.

All the while, he pondered the past few days with Kate. He still could not figure out her accepting reaction to his having told her point-blank precisely what he was.

Why had she not fled from him in horror?

Obviously, she had not yet grasped the full, dark reality of it. How could she? Kate was an innocent. She hadn't seen the blood.

But she soon would. And then what? She would probably never let him touch her again, he thought grimly.

Arriving at the club, he swung down off his horse, tied the animal to a hitching post, and entered the tall, black, wrought-iron gate, striding up the short front path to Dante House.

To the outer world, the sinister-looking, deliberately ill-kempt Tudor mansion on the Thames was the gathering place of the scandalous Inferno Club. In actuality, Dante House was a compact, heavily fortified stronghold that concealed the secret headquarters of the Order of St. Michael the Archangel.

With the glass-domed observatory bulging from the roof, flanked by twin black spires rising like horns, as though some giant devil were hiding in the house, too big to fit, it was no wonder that Londoners called it "the Town residence of Satan." The menacing façade was meant to keep the curious away; it also added to the lurid tales about the dastardly, highborn libertines and diabolical rakehells who supposedly frequented the place.

To be sure, the Prometheans were so conscientious about maintaining a respectable appearance that they would never have dared come near such a nefarious landmark.

The ruse of Dante House had worked for several decades now, though the Order had owned the building for much longer than that. No doubt, it would be closed up eventually and some new location chosen for the Order to continue its secret work.

The door knocker, shaped like a medieval scholar's head, seemed to smirk as Rohan let himself in. At once, he was surrounded by the joyful clamor of the dogs.

He had always been a great favorite with the fierce guard dogs of Dante House. They understood each other.

He took off his hat as Mr. Gray, the gaunt butler, hurried into the foyer to attend him. "Welcome, Your Grace. May I take your coat?" he asked loudly over all the barking.

With a nod, Rohan handed him his hat, shrugged off his greatcoat, and let the butler hang it on the coat-tree.

As the solid-bodied guard dogs danced around Rohan in shameless adoration, he bent down and greeted them. "Is Virgil here?"

"Pardon, sir?"

"Quiet!" he ordered the dogs in German.

At once, the pack fell silent.

"Where is Virgil, Gray?"

"In the parlor with Lords Rotherstone and Falconridge, Your Grace."

"Excellent." Good timing, he thought, pausing to scratch one of the massive, black-and-tan dogs affectionately under the chin, then he gave another rugged beast a fond pat on the head.

He straightened up again, and when he left the entrance hall, the pack trotted tamely after him.

Stalking down the hallway, he ignored the club's oppressively florid décor. The crimson rococo style was modeled after a whore-house; the cloying atmosphere oozed decadence and excess. It helped to further the charade.

"Look who's back from Cornwall!" Max, his team leader greeted him when Rohan stepped into the room. "Heard the commotion. Thought it might be you."

"What are you doing here?" he countered as he sauntered into their midst. "Wife kick you out already?"

"I'm only here for the food," drawled the

newlywed marquess, still looking as absurdly happy as he had the last time Rohan had seen him.

"Midas" Max St. Albans, the Marquess of Rotherstone, dark-haired and sardonic, was sitting on the couch, cleaning a fine pair of Manton pistols, the disassembled parts neatly splayed before him on the low table.

In addition to being the Link, or leader, of their three-man team, Max was something of a financial wizard, who was excellent at tracking the Prometheans' mischief through their bank transactions. He had also helped to fill the Order's coffers for future operations for many years to come through his shrewd investments.

Rohan also nodded to the other member of their team, Jordan Lennox, the Earl of Falconridge. "Jord."

Another highly accomplished agent, Jordan was their code expert, a quiet, clean-cut man of understated elegance and cool capability. He looked up from the newspaper advertisements that he was perusing for any disguised messages, a daily discipline.

"Have a nice visit with your ghosts?"

Rohan answered with a wry smile and a rude gesture in the Italian style. Jordan laughed under his breath and turned the page of the *Times.*

Virgil snorted at their exchange, but his gruff demeanor fooled no one. He loved them as if they were his own sons.

At present, the head of the Order in London was leaning by the window, slicing off pieces of an apple with a penknife and eating them off the blade. The tough old Highland warrior had wild reddish hair shot through with gray.

He had handpicked and recruited them as lads out of the ranks of the aristocracy, had directed their training at the Order's ancient castle in Scotland, and had coordinated their various missions ever since.

Rohan nodded to him. "Sir."

"Did you secure the smugglers' ring?" Virgil asked with his usual taciturnity as he flicked a piece of apple to the dogs.

"Of course. All's well." Rohan nodded, setting his hands loosely on his waist. "The Coast Guard's satisfied. I handed over the fools who carried out the shipwreck. The rest have seen the light. They won't be doing that again."

"Good. Those smugglers are no use to us dead," the Highlander said gruffly.

Rohan nodded, dropping his gaze, besieged by the first wave of guilt at his staunch decision to say nothing about a certain "gift" the smugglers' chief had given him in Cornwall. "So, what did I miss?"

He quickly learned that there was little news.

He had been gone less than a month, and during that time, the Promethean assassin, Dresden Bloodwell, had not surfaced again. Jordan had been assigned to watch for him in Society, then to go after him when he reappeared.

"No sign of him yet," Jordan reported.

Max, meanwhile, had been keeping an eye on Albert Carew, the new Duke of Holyfield, whom they suspected of possible involvement with the Prometheans, ever since Carew's elder brother had died under highly suspicious circumstances, leaving second-born Albert with the dukedom.

Of course, Albert had had a solid alibi, and nobody wanted to question the word of the former dandy who had suddenly become one of the richest men in the House of Lords.

"Now that Carew has been elevated into such a high place," Max explained, "he's been toadying to the Regent even more than usual. He seems to be slowly insinuating himself into the Carlton House set. One cannot be surprised the Council would try to get someone else in close to Prinny again after we killed their last spy. Believe me, I am keeping Carew under close scrutiny."

Rohan looked askance at him. "I trust he is staying away from your wife these days?"

"Damned right he is," Max snorted, for Carew had courted the golden-haired Daphne before Max had made the choosy belle his own — and Lord, she'd made him work for it.

In light of his own new acquaintance with Kate, Rohan suddenly did not find Max's romantic agonies several months ago quite so droll as he had at the time.

But he chased Kate fiercely out of his mind once again, determined that they should detect no change in his demeanor. And she *had* changed him. He knew it down to the core of his barbaric soul. She made him . . . what was that foreign word — ? Oh, yes.

Happy.

"What about Drake?" he asked, ignoring the pleasurable memory of her sighs when he had taken her from behind last night. "Any more sightings of him or of James Falkirk?"

"Neither." Virgil lowered his head with a brooding air.

Rohan leaned his elbow on the back of an empty wing chair nearby. "Well, then, what

about that other team that you've been waiting for?"

"Beauchamp's team," Jordan reminded
him.

"Right. Are they back from the Continent
yet?"

"Beau and his men are on their way," Virgil answered. "They should be here any day
now. In the meantime, they sent me some
interesting news. They managed to track
down Tavistock."

"The Prometheans' banking fellow, right?"
Rohan clarified. "That thieving blackguard
in the Stock Exchange?"

"Exactly," Max replied as he continued
polishing the barrel of his pistol. "Sir Richard Tavistock was the one who scooped up
millions for the Prometheans when they
caused the market crash right after Waterloo."

"So, what did they find out?"

"Tavistock's dead," Virgil clipped out.
"They tracked him as far as the Loire Valley, where some villagers led them to a shallow grave. Tavistock was in it. He had been
garroted."

"It wasn't me," Rohan said in an offhand
jest.

Max sent him a sardonic look.

Then Rohan frowned. "Isn't the Loire Valley the same place Carew's elder brother was murdered?"

"Indeed, it was. Right in Malcolm's back garden."

They all glanced at Virgil, for Malcolm Banks was not only the head of the Prometheans' elite High Council; he also happened to be Virgil's younger brother.

The brawny Scotsman lowered his gaze, bristling as always at the mention of the traitor.

Jordan spoke up to explain. "We believe Malcolm called a meeting of the Council at his chateau in France after Waterloo. According to Beauchamp, Tavistock did not make it out of that meeting alive."

"Curious," Rohan answered quietly, furrowing his brow. "After he had done so well for them, sweeping so many millions into their coffers?"

Jordan shrugged. "Maybe he'd served his purpose, or maybe they wanted to cover their tracks. Either way, they got rid of him. Whatever the reason, it does raise the interesting prospect that a power struggle has begun inside the Council. Malcolm likely feels his position as the head of the Prometheans is in jeopardy."

"Which would make sense — considering he has presided over their greatest defeat,"

Max interjected.

"If you ask me, Malcolm would've had Tavistock murdered to prove a point, that he won't tolerate dissension in the ranks," Virgil opined.

"Hm." Rohan considered all this for a moment. "Any idea who would want to overthrow him?"

The other three exchanged grim glances.

Rohan realized why. "You think it's James Falkirk?" he asked swiftly.

"The two never got along, according to our sources," Max replied. "And Falkirk is extremely influential in their circles."

They all fell silent, brooding on the matter.

Folding his arms across his chest, Rohan drummed his fingers on his arm in thought for a moment.

This new information presented a very specific, possible motive for why James Falkirk could be trying to get to the Alchemist's Tomb.

If, indeed, Falkirk was the one conspiring to challenge Malcolm to become the head of the Prometheans, he could use the legendary occult scrolls from Valerian's tomb to win followers away from Malcolm to himself.

Staring at the floor, Rohan realized that if

he could somehow get to the scrolls first, perhaps Falkirk would be willing to trade them for Drake.

All he had to do was make sure that Gerald Fox did not fall into Promethean hands in the meantime. His mind whirled, but none of the theories taking shape in his mind could be confirmed until he confronted O'Banyon.

Suddenly, he was extremely anxious to get to Shadwell and survey the ground around this rat-catcher's shop. *Best get on with it.* "So, I really haven't missed anything, then," he concluded.

"Actually, no," Jordan said with a shrug. "Damned frustrating."

"I, for one, do not mind the quiet." Max rammed the pieces of his pistol back together.

"Nothing interesting in here today, either." Jordan closed his newspaper and cast it aside.

"I should go," Rohan murmured, turning toward the door.

Max was studying him now with a peculiar intensity. "Are you all right?" he asked abruptly.

Rohan glanced over his shoulder in surprise. "What?"

"You seem — odd."

"Odd?" he echoed, praying he did not look too suspicious. He hated deceiving them, but he shook his head and kept his face a mask. "No, I'm fine."

"Just asking," Max answered with a shrug. "You're invited to supper tonight, by the way. Jordan's coming. Virgil refuses, as always, but you are welcome."

"Thanks, but I have some errands that came up in my absence," Rohan said.

"Join us after, then? We're all going out to a soiree afterwards to watch for Dresden Bloodwell and Carew."

"Can't, sorry. Unless you need my help?"

"No, we've got it. You're sure you're all right?"

"Of course. Give Daphne my best." Rohan took leave of his all-too-perceptive friends with an evasive nod.

Shrugging off his uneasy conscience, next, he rode to Shadwell, where he spent some time taking a discreet survey of the ground. He made a few strategic decisions about how to handle the night's confrontation, then left to assemble the supplies he would need from a variety of sources.

He rented a room for the next few nights in a lodging house in Shadwell to serve as their temporary safe house, stocking it with weapons and ammunition, water and basic medical supplies. Eldred would be stationed here, and Kate and Peter Doyle could retreat there on his orders, if necessary. In the unlikely event that he fell, he'd tell Eldred and Parker to take them to Jordan. He did not want to bother Max now that their team leader was a married man.

Having made all his preparations, he went to the Bank of England to set up the account for Kate, as promised.

Finally, he returned home, eager to see her again. Her reaction to the ugly disguise she'd have to wear tonight was sure to be amusing, though, in truth, he doubted it was possible to make his green-eyed goddess look the least bit homely.

"Oh, Katherine?" he called in wry affection as he jogged up the stairs. "Where are you?"

After calling for her several more times, he finally received an absent-sounding answer coming from the direction of the music room: "In here."

When he reached the music room, he leaned in the open doorway for a moment and smiled as he studied the alluring arrangement of his darling mistress reclining on the light green settee.

Dressed in a pink gown with striped satin skirts, Kate was idly thumbing through her mother's book, open on her lap. She had loosed her soft brown hair; it flowed over her shoulders in crimped waves from her earlier chignon.

"There you are," he greeted her with a glow of appreciation in his eyes. "And don't you look as pretty as a picture."

Kate slanted him a guarded look.

In his absence, she had done a lot of thinking. Similar to her reaction when Rohan had told her he was an assassin, the arrival of the ladies today had shocked but not surprised her. After all, from the first night she had been dragged to Kilburn Castle to serve as his bed warmer, Caleb Doyle had made it plain that His Grace saw females as objects of pleasure.

Thus, she could not say she had not known what she was getting into. But confronting the reality of it, meeting his past conquests face-to-face — Pauline, Lucinda, and the rest — had whipped her emotions up into a storm.

Her first reaction had been anger, waves of anger, to glimpse what a selfish, callous libertine he had been in his past exploits. Hopeless disappointment followed, that she had what it took to make him change.

Mostly, fear had ruled her, that this passion between them could only end in crushing hurt for her. With a sense of doom, she had brooded on her certainty that, sooner or later, she would end up just like them, another fool left in his wake. But she was an even greater fool, for she had made the fatal mistake of falling in love with him.

Fortunately, Rohan's errands that afternoon kept him away long enough for her to get hold of her wild emotions.

His absence gave her time for her temper to cool and her courage to begin regrouping. Finally able to step back and consider in a calmer way how to respond, she was able to look more closely at what all these meaningless affairs actually *told* her about Rohan and his needs.

And it was at that moment that her whole view of the situation had changed. It was as if the scales had suddenly fallen from her eyes. *Of course.*

The tempest of her initial fear and anger had given way to unexpected sorrow at the loneliness that had been revealed in him, grief to see at last how starved he was for love.

He had to be. How could he get close to anyone, with his profession? Even if he wanted to, how could he let them in?

No wonder all he knew was using women

and being used in turn. Sad, sordid mocker-
ies of love.

Kate was chastened by this insight, and
she vowed to let him taste real love for once
in his brave, gallant life.

Jealousy was a stupid reaction when she
had already got farther with him emotion-
ally than any of them ever would. Those
other women from his past were no threat
to her.

Nevertheless, her encounter with them
brought up a troubling question: If she was
going to take his money for making love
with him, didn't that make her an even
worse harlot than those highborn Society
hussies?

At some point or other, didn't he deserve
to deal with someone who would treat him
as a real lady ought to? With grace and
compassion for the needs he was too proud
ever to give voice to? A real lady would
never take advantage of a man where he was
most vulnerable, and for Rohan, Kate now
knew this was in the area of love.

Love was clearly the warrior duke's Achilles' heel. Pondering all she had come to
know about him, she sensed that he was terrified of it, partly because, to him, it was
the unknown, and partly because of that
blasted superstitious curse.

She had to show him what was real.

She had to stand for something higher.

She had to find the courage now to love him even more. Love, not *because of* all that he could give her. Anyone could do that. But love *in spite of* the darkness in him and the chilling threat that he might never love her in return, might not even be capable of it.

What a terrifying chance.

But as hope pierced the gloom of fear like the pinprick patterns of a tin lantern-cover, she knew she had to try. *Love him. Don't judge him. Forget about those women in his past.*

I'm his present. I'm his future.

He walked into the music room, smiling, and leaned down to kiss her on the cheek. "Hullo."

She tensed. Though she was absolutely sure of the right thing to do, what love demanded scared her half to death.

For Rohan's own good, she would have to leave the place of comfort and security she had finally found. Otherwise, he would never see her as any different from all those women who had used him. If she simply abided by their contract, he would never know that he was truly loved.

By offering it so generously to her in her

darkest hour, he had helped her through her deepest fears. It was her turn now to help him conquer his.

But she had a feeling he wasn't going to like it.

"I brought you something," he murmured, dropping the leather knapsack off his shoulder. "A few things, actually."

That low, velvet voice alone was enough to stir her desire. He smelled of horse and leather and his own subtle musk that she had become as addicted to as opium-eaters to the smell of their pipe smoke. As he bent closer and gave her an affectionate little cuddle, she bit her lip with a vague pang of want. "Miss me?" he breathed in a seductive tone by her ear.

She did not answer. *Courage, Kate,* she warned herself, then regarded him cautiously at close range. "What did you bring?"

"Were you crying?" he asked abruptly, frowning as he noted the redness around her eyes.

"Studying the book, that's all." She dropped her gaze at once. "It's dusty."

He studied her, his brow furrowed. "Find anything?"

She tapped her fingertip on the open page. "These strings of elements — they're codes. Each element corresponds to a letter."

"I'll be damned. Well done, my girl!" He pressed a casually possessive kiss to her temple. "So, what does it say?"

"I don't know yet. I'm still working on it." She closed the book, trying to seem nonchalant. "What's in the bag?"

He smiled and straightened up again. "All sorts of goodies for my girl." He picked up the leather knapsack again, reaching into it. "First, this." He handed her a little folio of papers whose cover was stamped with the insignia of the Bank of England. "Your account has been set up. It's fully funded now, whenever you want to draw on it. This, too, so you'll have it." He pulled out a neatly rolled wad of crisp paper cash and offered it to her.

"Rohan —"

"Wait, there's more," he warned with a devilish smile.

Kate looked down at the bank papers, but handling them uneasily, she set them aside along with the roll of cash.

"For you!" He held up a large, drab gown with wicked amusement dancing in his eyes.

She tilted her head, studying the coarse gray gown skeptically. "What on earth . . . ?"

"You are to be transformed, my dear."

"You expect me to wear that?" she exclaimed.

"Sorry, it can't be avoided. Tonight we must disguise your lovely self."

She snorted. "It's a bit big! I would think you'd know my body's dimensions better than that by now, Your Grace. Or perhaps you had me confused with somebody else?"

"It's a larger size on purpose. This goes with it." He reached into the bag once more and pulled out the next piece of her disguise, some sort of theatrical padding. "And . . . voilà."

"I am *not* wearing that ratty old wig."

"Oh, yes, you are. And this hideous mob cap, too." He grinned. "And wait, don't forget your spectacles."

"I'm going to look like a toad," she said in dismay.

"That's the whole idea. Presenting — Gerald Fox's poor old spinster daughter."

She gave him a long-suffering look. "Is this really necessary?"

"I wouldn't put you through it if were not," he replied with a glint of rakish humor in his gray eyes.

"O'Banyon already knows what I look like," she reminded him.

"Yes, but James Falkirk doesn't. And if we happen to run into him and his charming one-eyed bodyguard, let's just say this costume is better than having to look over your shoulder for the rest of your life."

She sobered. "Oh."

"If it's any consolation, I shall also be going incognito. I will be the other smuggler, replacing Denny Doyle. On that note, I must go and give Pete his instructions about his role tonight." He headed for the door. "Try to get some rest. It's likely to be a late night."

"Rohan — wait." She swung her legs down off the side of the settee and swept to her feet. The time had come. "We had a bit of an, er, incident while you were gone."

Instantly, he stopped and turned around. "What happened?"

"I'm afraid you're not going to like it."

His eyes narrowed in question.

"You know those rules you gave me?"

"Yes."

"I broke them," she said flatly, lifting her chin. "I was seen."

"By whom?" he demanded, taking a step closer. "The neighbors?"

"No, by the great crowd of ladies who came here looking for you."

At least he had the decency to blanch. "Ladies?"

She folded her arms across her waist. "Lucinda. Pauline. I don't know the others' names."

"Kate," he murmured sternly, eyeing her in question.

"It's really not my fault," she declared. "They were practically going to break down the door. Eldred needed help! I was standing at the top of the stairs, and that's when they saw me."

"Damn it, Kate, I gave you those rules for a reason!" he blustered, glowering at her. "Did you speak to them?"

"Mainly I listened." She primly averted her gaze. "And overheard some mention of their husbands."

"What did you say to them?" he demanded.

She gave an innocent shrug. "I simply told them you were not at home, and that they could leave their cards if they wished. They didn't. They left . . . rather quickly after I spoke to them."

"Kate, I can't believe you did this. I gave you those rules for your own safety!"

"You amaze me! Half a dozen of your past conquests show up at the doorstep, and that's all you have to say for yourself?"

"What of it?" He stared menacingly at her. "I suppose this is the part where you let loose some petulant fit of hysteria and start lobbing pieces of china at my head?"

"Do I look like I'm having a fit?" she

asked coolly, holding his gaze, refusing to cower though he loomed over her.

He stared at her for a long moment, not entirely successful at hiding his confusion. "No."

She acknowledged his admission with a crisp nod.

"So, what then? You hate me now?" he asked with an air of growing suspicion.

"No, Rohan." Kate was beginning to enjoy confounding him. She reached up and cupped his cheek gently in her hand. "I'm just glad to see the vast improvement in your taste."

He removed her hand. "You don't know what you've done."

She frowned.

"Kate, these were Society women!"

"Obviously!"

"Which means that by tonight the talk is going to be all over Town about the luscious young beauty hidden away in Warrington's house — right when we're in the middle of a highly dangerous operation!"

She heaved a sigh. "Thanks for the compliment, but I'm afraid it's worse than that."

"Worse?"

"Perhaps my tone was a little sharp when I addressed your paramours —"

"Former paramours," he growled.

"Whatever the reason, they began curtsying to me before they scurried away."

He stared at her. "Curtsying to you," he echoed.

"Yes."

"Lucinda is a countess. Pauline is a baroness."

"Well." She shrugged. "They seemed to draw their own conclusions about my presence in Your Grace's home."

He stood stock-still for a moment. *"They thought you were my wife?"*

"It would seem so," she replied, coloring a bit. "It's not my fault! Ask Eldred! It all happened exactly as I've told you."

Well, this is damned awkward.

Rohan was torn between sardonic humor at the thought of his haughty ex-lovers bowing down to Kate and the exasperated urge to throttle her.

He just shook his head, muttering, "I leave the house for two hours, and it all turns into a comedy of errors."

Kate set her hands on her hips and tilted her head. "Are you angry?" she asked in her usual forthright way.

He looked into those emerald eyes — and how could he be? "No," he admitted guardedly. "Are you?"

"I was, for a while." She shrugged. "But I got over it."

He stared at her, amazed and all the more smitten, seeing her calm reaction. "Bless you," he said at length, acknowledging her forbearance with a nod of grateful relief. If the roles had been reversed, and Kate had shown up while he was with Lucinda or one of the others, he'd have been subjected to a show of fury worthy of Caro Lamb. "You have no idea how many times I've been screamed at," he muttered.

"I can imagine," she replied. Then her shrewd gaze narrowed on him. "But don't mistake my serenity for approval. Speaking as one who was given to you as a plaything, your behavior toward women has been beastly. I know for a fact that you're better than this."

He studied her, immediately on his guard. "My, my, now you are starting to sound like a wife. Too bad I'm not in the market for one of those."

"No, why should you be? You're too busy sleeping with other men's wives to bother finding your own." She smiled.

"Everyone does it around here," he replied, stung, but refusing to let her see him wince. "Besides, they pursued me."

"All the same, you know it's wrong. No

wonder you're such a lone wolf."

"What's that supposed to mean?" Furrowing his brow with deepening annoyance, he folded his arms across his chest.

"Simply that you can't expect to be a part of the civilized world when you go about ravaging other people's families. Honestly, Rohan! I can't believe you're thirty-four years old and still behaving like a boy of seventeen."

"I can't believe I'm standing here being lectured by my mistress," he replied crisply.

"Er, yes. About that." She walked back to the settee, picked up the bank booklet and the roll of cash. With her back to him, he saw her take a deep breath before she turned around; then she marched back to him, carrying both.

"I can't accept this. Here. Take it back."

"What are you talking about? Why?"

"Take it, please."

He let out a low expletive. "I knew you were angry!"

"I'm not."

"Well, you should be, damn it!" His cheeks flushed in angry confusion as she raised an eyebrow at him. "Take it, Kate. It's yours. Don't worry," he said, "I can afford it."

"That's just it," she answered softly. "I'm

afraid I can't."

"What is that supposed to mean? You're not making any sense. What do you want? More money?"

"No! I don't want *any.* Please, just take it."

"I will not. Kate, we have been lovers. I have to give you something."

"You already have," she answered with a tender gaze that increased his bafflement by tenfold. "Do you understand what I am telling you?"

"No bloody idea."

"Well . . . you'll figure it out eventually."

A dreadful explanation rose up like a dark phantom in his mind as she turned away and set the items on the nearby table. His heart began to pound. "Are you leaving me? Is that what this means? Why? Because of these stupid women? I don't give a damn about them! You're punishing me —"

"No! Rohan, I forgave you before you even came home."

"What is this, then? I don't understand! Did I do something wrong?"

"No, darling!" she soothed. "This arrangement is what's wrong, and we both know it. I don't want your money. I'd rather have your respect."

"Oh, please."

She ignored his impatient scoff. "I'd rather have you know deep down, that for me, it was never about the gold."

"Kate, this is completely daft. How the hell do you intend to live?"

"My father will help me — if he is alive."

"So, you *do* want to get away from me."

"No!"

"What *do* you want, then?" he nearly exploded.

"I don't want to end up like those women in your past! I-I don't want to lose you."

He dropped his head back with a guttural sound of exasperation. He searched the ceiling, as if some skyward clue could help a man make sense of a woman's logic.

Then he looked at her again. "You don't want to lose me, so you're pushing me away."

"I'm trying to help you, Rohan."

"How?" He was stymied. "You're throwing everything off-kilter! We had an agreement, Kate!"

"Well, we need a different one!"

"I don't understand."

"You don't understand, or you don't want to?"

He fell silent, studying her.

She was getting at something, but for some reason, she wouldn't just come out and say it. This was very unlike her. Scrutinizing her, he began to see the light.

"Why, you brassy little hoyden," he murmured, narrowing his eyes. "You're making a play for marriage, aren't you? You want to be a duchess. Those women put the notion in your head."

"No!" she exclaimed, looking startled at his accusation. "How dare you?"

"I'm sorry to disappoint you, Kate, but that's never going to happen. And I don't appreciate your trying to manipulate me."

"I am not trying to manipulate you, I am being as honest with you as I know how! I'm just trying to do it in a way that will not scare you!"

"You, scare me? Why, you impertinent little thing! Pray tell, whatever do you mean, scare *me*?"

"What I have to say, you don't want to hear."

"No, speak, please! By all means."

She eyed him, clearly losing patience. "Never mind. It's not a play for marriage. I know I'm not highborn enough for you."

"That's not why I said that," he corrected her at once. "Frankly, my refusal has nothing to do with you."

She stared at him for a long moment. "The curse."

He nodded darkly.

"Rohan." She shifted her weight from one foot to the other and folded her arms across her chest. "I'm not sure how to tell you this. But the curse is just a tale."

"Kate —"

"If you don't stop using it as an excuse to keep love out of your life, you are going to end up a very lonely man."

"So, you accuse me of lying?"

"Only to yourself, my love."

"Right. Was it a lie that killed my mother?" He checked his growing ire. "The curse is no 'excuse,' Kate. It's real, and so is my ability to carry it out. Which is why I would rather see my line die out than ever marry, or even fall in love. Understand that now."

"You don't mean that," she reproached softly while his cold, stony words still hung in the room. "You're just scared, Rohan."

"Damn it, I am not the one who's scared!" he fairly roared at her. "*I'm* the one who scares others! You have no idea what I am capable of! But I do. I know what I am, and how far I can go — which is why I made you the offer I did. So, take it or leave it, Kate. It's either my mistress or nothing. That's the best that I can do."

He instantly saw this had been the wrong thing to say. The green eyes narrowed, defiance blazing in their depths; those pretty shoulders he had so often covered in kisses slowly squared; her dainty chin came up a notch.

Damn it, hadn't he learned by now that she could be nearly as stubborn as he?

"Very well." She went to the settee and picked up the pieces of the costume he had brought for her.

Rohan watched her, knowing he was in the wrong, but too full of three types of pride to give an inch: the pride of the duke, the pride of the soldier, the pride of the male. He was choking on all three. "Would you do me the honor of answering, please?"

"You want an answer? Certainly, Your Grace. Here's your answer!" She swept the wad of cash off the table nearby and whipped it at his head.

It bounced off his shoulder, and she stalked to the door. *That's my girl.* "So, it's nothing, then," he drawled.

She kept walking.

"Kate. Come back."

"You'll have plenty of company soon enough. Enjoy your harlots, Duke, but I will not be one of them." She paused in the doorway, glancing back. "You're going to regret losing me for the rest of your life, Warrington."

"If I had a penny for every time I heard that."

She shook her head in wonder. "Why are you being so heartless?"

"Because I have no heart, Miss Madsen!" he exclaimed in a razor-sharp, casual tone. "Haven't you figured that out by now? Just ask the last chap I killed in Naples."

At these words, she paled and came back into the room; he stared harshly into her eyes as she approached with hesitant steps.

Rohan swallowed hard, but he could no longer hold back the bitterest of his secrets. She had to know the perfidy of the man she was dealing with. "The target I was sent to. He had had three little tots and a wife inside the house. So I took him in the garden. He grabbed my gun. They heard the shot. Then I heard the screams when they came out and found him dead. Of course, by then, I was already gone. Now, you tell me," he ground out, "that someone like that deserves what you call love. Don't make me want what I can't have."

"But you can."

He stared at her in longing, but in that moment, he was like a caged animal. He longed for freedom, but if she came too close, he feared he'd bite.

"Don't you understand that's what I've

447

been saying all this time?" she asked softly, coming closer with a gaze full of the most exquisite tenderness. "Love is all you need, my dear, and I can give it to you." Tears filled her eyes as she reached for him. "I love you, Rohan —"

"Stop this — foolishness!" He brushed her aside, roughly turning away. His heart pounded. He tried very hard not to let her see that he was shaken. "You don't know what you're saying."

"Yes, I do. I love you. You already know I do."

"It's a delusion, Kate. I am not fit for *love*. Do not speak of it to me again, I pray you," he finished in a pained whisper.

"Rohan." From the corner of his eye, he saw her gazing at him in tearful bewilderment.

"Kate. If you weaken me, you're the one who's going to end up hurt." He stared straight ahead, refusing to look at the tears that had filled her eyes. He shook his head. "I'd rather die than hurt you."

"What do you think you're doing now?"

"Leave me," he breathed, shutting her out. "I can't give you what you want."

She studied him for a moment longer, then shook her head, pivoted, and strode back toward the door. His heart continued pounding as he shut his eyes.

When he opened them again, she had gone.

And his rage exploded into swirling despair. *Damn it!* He suddenly punched the nearest wall, smashing a splintered dent into the plaster.

He couldn't believe he had just hurt her, but that's all he seemed to have been born and built to do.

As he stood there, chest heaving, blood collecting on his knuckles, he fixed his fiery stare on the ground and struggled to hold his anger in check — for now.

He would save it up, use it for fuel tonight when it came time for him to do what he did best. Then, perhaps, she'd finally see the truth about her "love."

Chapter 17

It hurt. Badly. To tell someone you loved him, only to have it thrown back in your face. But Kate refused to give up hope. Drawing on a great reserve of tenacity she'd hardly known she possessed, she dried her tears and vowed to keep trying until she found a way to reach him.

Rohan needed her whether he knew it or not.

True, some of the things he had said to her had been hurtful and heartlessly cold, but she knew he didn't mean it. It was just defensive bluster. He was merely rattled that she had given him back his money because that meant he was no longer in control.

He wanted to be able to dictate the terms of "how far he could go" in letting himself get close to her, as he had said, but half measures would not suffice for her, when she had given him everything.

Mentally, she stood her ground, determined to gentle him eventually. To tame the wild Beast. She had developed a certain knack, after all, of persuading him to trust her, bit by bit.

He thought he could chase her away with his stormy roars, like a great lion with a thorn in its paw, or that he could scare her off with his terrible tale of murder in Naples. But all this had only revealed to her that he needed her love even more than she had thought.

No matter what dire warnings he invoked, she knew he was incapable of ever hurting her, as he so feared.

How could he think he was not fit for love? He was generous, unselfish, and brave. Yet he could not seem to see that, indeed, he was entirely worthy of her devotion. She wished he would stop fighting it, but no matter. She was at least as patient as he was stubborn.

At any rate, their row had not altered their plans for the evening. They were both adult enough to put it aside in order to deal with the problem at hand.

That night, as scheduled, they set out for the rat-catcher's shop in Shadwell, riding in a plain, shabby carriage used by the servants.

Parker was driving with Wilkins riding,

armed, on top of the coach.

Eldred was stationed in the room at the lodging house that Rohan had prepared as a fallback position if anything went wrong.

The darkness was deep, the January cold relentless.

Rohan sat beside her, remote and brooding as the Cornish cliffs. Kate, meanwhile, was feeling rather silly and self-conscious in her costume. How Papa was supposed to recognize her like this, she had no idea.

Her hair was hidden under the nasty old wig. The ruffled white spinster's cap was tied under her chin. Spectacles with plain glass lenses were perched on her nose, the better to mask her face. The size of her figure had doubled with all the padding stuffed into the scratchy, gray, wool gown. At least it kept her warm.

Sitting across from them in the carriage was Peter Doyle. She hoped that he really could be trusted. If he betrayed them, Rohan would surely kill him on the spot. The rumpled young smuggler looked highly nervous, with good cause. What if O'Banyon refused to accept the tall stranger in Denny Doyle's place?

Kate looked askance at the duke beside her transformed into a smuggler. He certainly looked the part of the cutthroat ruffian. Indeed, he fit the role a little too well. In his outlaw garb, he resembled the worst highwayman in England.

But there must be something wrong with her, Kate thought wearily, for even though he looked like an escapee from the gallows, she still found him wildly appealing. He made the kind of outlaw that left a girl wishing to be kid napped.

He had rubbed a bronze-tinted stage makeup into his face, darkening his complexion to a swarthy suntan like that of a proper seaside ruffian. He had worked some olive oil and a handful of dust into his long black mane; it looked dirty and wild, and so did he, unshaved, a loose red neckcloth tied around his throat, a mass of weapons slung around his waist.

He wore a grubby, natural shirt, a black vest, and loose matelots held up with a rope belt. These ended at his shins, and below them, slouchy boots that concealed an extra pistol in an ankle holster and an extra knife.

Over it all, he had donned a shapeless coat that somewhat concealed the countless sheaths and scabbards for blades, shoulder holsters, and bandoliers of ammunition strapped across his chest. The man was a walking armament, with an evil gleam tonight in his pale eyes.

Looking at him now, she marveled that she had deemed it wise to chastise him a few hours ago. Provoking him looked like a good way to get a swift appointment with Saint Peter.

"Almost there," he reported, watching out the window as the coach rumbled through the darkness toward ever-more-treacherous parts of Town. "Any questions?" He sounded much too calm. "Pete, you remember what you are to say?"

"Aye, sir."

"And do you remember the price you'll have to pay if you betray us?" he added in softer tone.

Pete stared at him. "I won't, sir. I gave you my word."

"Perfect," Kate muttered. "Our lives depend on a criminal's word of honor."

"Stand firm, Miss Madsen. There's no way out but through now. Just be mindful not to let on that you know anything about who they are and what they're really after."

"I'd feel better if I had old Charley's shotgun."

"Trust me, you won't need it with me around," he answered grimly.

They pressed on all the way through the City proper and into the densely packed East End. Heading for the wild-and-woolly docklands, they turned south into the dark and rugged Thames-side warrens of Shad-well.

Though the narrow cobbled streets were dark, Parker did not miss the turn into the oddly named Labor-In-Vain Street, where they had been directed to present themselves to the rat-catcher.

Kate looked out the window in trepidation as they rolled past a noisy, crowded tavern, where a glow of lanternlights and bumptious music spilled out into the otherwise pitch-dark street.

She saw a table where tattooed sailors arm-wrestled, surrounded by their mates, who held pewter tankards filled with foamy stout, loudly cheering for the contestant on whom they'd laid their wager. Meanwhile, a number of garishly painted women were entertaining the men with their drunken dancing on the tables.

Kate sent Rohan a pointed look but refrained from making a sarcastic comment. She had wanted to see the world beyond her little cottage, and to be sure, she was in the thick of it now.

At the end of the street, the carriage slowed to a halt. She glanced out the window and saw a wooden sign hanging above the shop with the cartoonlike picture of a rat in a cage. *Vermin removed. Since 1784. Inquire within.*

Pete looked at them, pale and wide-eyed. "I'd best go in and let 'im know we've come."

Rohan nodded. "Steady, lad. Take a drink. You can do this." He handed Pete his flask.

"Thank ye, sir." The lad helped himself to a swallow and gulped some down, then gave it back to him. Taking a deep breath, Pete nodded and got out of the coach.

He glanced up at the sign of the rat, then went into the small, unlit walking space between buildings. It was as dark as the tomb in there, a perfect place for a murder, Kate supposed. Best not to ponder that while sitting beside an assassin.

Through the darkness, they could just make out Pete's movements as he climbed the rickety, exterior stairs and banged on the rat-catcher's door.

Meanwhile, in the carriage, the silence between them grew more tense by the second. Unable to stand it anymore, Kate broke it with a halfhearted question that she already knew the answer to. "So, someone's supposed to let us in here?" she whispered.

He nodded. "They'll send for O'Banyon to come and meet us."

"I can hardly wait." She shivered, pulling the ugly shawl closer around her shoulders. Another minute ticked past. "I don't think I've ever been inside a rat-catcher's shop before."

"Nor I," he murmured. "But I'll wager there's more to the fellow's business than trapping vermin."

"How so?"

He stared out the window, watching as the door at the top of the stairs opened. A hunched figure holding up a lantern inspected Pete, who, in turn, spoke his piece, gesturing toward the carriage.

"The old fellow rows out to the arriving cargo ships to see if there's any need aboard for his services," he explained in a low tone. "The merchant captains hire him to clear out a few rats, so he heads straight for the cargo holds, where most of the vermin lurk. There, he's able to assess what sort of goods the vessel's carrying. Makes a show of snaring some rats, then goes back ashore and tells the river thieves which ships are worth raiding. How many men are guarding it and so forth."

"Diabolical," she breathed.

"Welcome to the world, Miss Madsen. Let's go," he ordered, ignoring her frown at his cynical remark.

Rohan got out of the coach as Pete came back down the stairs. The old rat-catcher remained on the landing above, holding up a lantern for a wiry young boy, perhaps his apprentice, who darted down the steps, then dashed off into the night, presumably to tell O'Banyon they were there.

"He says to come and wait inside," Pete informed them as he neared the carriage.

Rohan turned to help Kate out of the coach. She faltered, suddenly worried that no one was going to believe her disguise. He bolstered her flagging courage with a forceful stare into her eyes, as if he could read her mind.

She steadied herself, stepping down from the shabby coach. At once, he grasped her arm none too gently, reminding her of her role as prisoner.

The evil-looking child eyed them both as he slipped past, but he did not seem to question the veracity of either one's appearance.

Then they went up while Parker drove away, moving off to take up his next position. He and Wilkins were to give cover from the crowded rooftops if it was needed, but Rohan had been adamant that they stay out of sight.

The stairs creaked as they mounted to the

rat-catcher's dank hovel above. Kate moved gingerly, her scratchy gown stuffed with the padding of her costume.

Pete went ahead of her, and Rohan walked behind, but the old, bearded rat-catcher avoided eye contact with all of them as he let them in the front door and led them through his dingy office, grumbling at them to wait in the tiny back room.

Rohan glanced around; Kate read in his face his instant dislike of the cramped claustrophobic room, little more than a broom closet.

"He told me O'Banyon's at an inn a few blocks away," Pete murmured after the door had shut. "It's called the Fox and Goose."

Rohan nodded. "I saw the place when I came by earlier. Considering we're expected, I doubt we'll have long to wait." He glanced at Kate. "How are you holding up?"

She nodded tautly. "I'm all right. Except for the stench in here." She gathered that the pisspot in the corner had not been emptied in some time. "Revolting."

"You remember where you're to go if I give the order?"

She nodded. He had drawn her a little map to the safe house in case she panicked and forgot his verbal directions. It was tucked in her bodice.

"Now, remember, when O'Banyon gets here," he said very quietly, "you've been locked down in that cellar in Cornwall all this time."

"I remember." She looked around. "What is all this junk?"

"Rat traps. Pitch," said Pete, also looking around at the piled cages and the large, lidded barrels of tar. "You burn a torch with pitch to smoke the rats out o' the cargo holds, y'see. Then you herd 'em into traps and club the little bleeders that slip past."

"How do you know all this?" she asked, grimacing at the rat-catcher's tools of the trade.

"I've been around boats all me life, miss, and most of 'em have rats. You can't shoot the vermin, o' course. Don't want to fire a gun into the wooden hull of a ship. Risk springing a leak."

Pete fell silent.

The air throbbed with nervousness, but Rohan was a rock. Kate padded to the back of the room and stood on her tiptoes, peering through the high, filthy window. Through the film of soil and soot, she saw a forest of masts along the river. Countless ships rode at anchor. To think that right now, Papa could be on one of those vessels . . .

Excruciating tension was building in her, but Rohan remained perfectly calm, cool, and collected. Murderous light glowed in his eyes as he waited in predatory patience.

She paced a bit in the small back room.

He took out a flask and offered it to her. "Draught for your nerves?"

"Lord, no," she whispered. "I'll want my wits about me."

"It's going to be fine, Kate."

She looked over as he glanced at his fob watch and put it away again. "What if O'Banyon wasn't there when the boy went to fetch him —"

Just then, they heard footsteps pounding up the shaky wooden stairs outside.

"It's him," Rohan murmured.

Pete nodded. "Those footsteps are too heavy for the boy."

Indeed, lighter footsteps followed the heavy ones. A moment later, they heard the rat-catcher's front door open.

"Where are they?"

Kate froze, riveted with unexpected terror at the rough sound of her main kidnapper's voice.

Rohan stood up slowly from where he had been sitting on a crate. He and Pete both moved closer to her, resuming their façade as her guards.

She took a deep breath and steadied herself, standing between them. His nearness reassured her. Rohan gave Pete a bolstering nod, and in the next instant, the back room's door banged open.

"Took you long enough." O'Banyon swaggered in, a compact, greasy-haired ex-convict. Upon entering the back room, he took one look at Rohan and instantly drew the pistol from his belt, aiming it at him.

Kate gasped.

Rohan stood stone-cold, but Pete let out a startled yelp. "Ho, now! There's no need —"

"What the hell are you up to, Pete?" O'Banyon demanded. "Who's she? And who the hell is this?"

"Sir, this is Kate Fox! We put her in disguise!"

"Disguise?" Still pointing his gun at Rohan, O'Banyon glanced briefly at her. "Why?"

"There's people lookin' for her, man — Bow Street types!" Pete cried. "Her neighbors reported her missing. We didn't want her to be seen. But it's still her under there."

O'Banyon slid Pete a wary glance, then nodded at Rohan. "What about 'im?"

"He's a different cousin of mine, sir. He's fillin' in for Denny."

"I didn't authorize that."

"Denny got stabbed in a tavern brawl — in the leg — he can hardly walk. He's useless at the moment. This is my other cousin, Curtis Doyle. He's a good man in a fight, sir. You can tell by the size of 'im."

O'Banyon's posture eased a bit. He looked Rohan up and down suspiciously. "Curtis Doyle, eh?"

"That's right," Rohan growled back. "And I expect to be paid in gold."

"Do you, now?"

"Put your gun away, please!" Kate implored O'Banyon.

He eyed her mistrustfully, but after a moment, he did so with a nod. "Very well, then. If you say he can be trusted, Pete, I'll take your word for it. After all, you know better than to cross me. Still, you should'a told me o' this change and not sprung it on me, like."

"There wasn't time, and I had no way to reach you."

O'Banyon snorted, then he leaned close to Kate, scrutinizing her in amusement. "As for you, poppet — is that still you under there?"

"It is," she answered coldly. If he doubted her changed appearance, Kate's withering tone assured him she was still the same unruly prisoner he remembered.

"It's just as well your pretty body's hidden for now." His grin was full of lechery as he straightened up again, letting his crude stare travel over her disguise. "Not a bad idea, dressing her up to hide her face. But I'll tell you, boys. I'm going to enjoy unwrappin' this plump little package later tonight. Nothing like a spell in Newgate to make a man enjoy the finer pleasures."

Kate glared at him in disgust. O'Banyon laughed derisively. Pete followed suit with a show of nervous humor, but Rohan's soft laugh, joining theirs, held a distinctly sinister undertone.

"Come on," O'Banyon ordered. "Time to go."

"Where are you taking me?" Kate demanded, as they grasped her arms again, not as roughly as their hold on her appeared.

"You'll see. Keep your mouth shut, wench." He walked ahead, and Rohan slanted Kate a look that said it all. O'Banyon's fate was sealed.

They left the back room, crossed the dingy office, and returned outside, where she spotted the rat-catcher up on the driver's box of an old, battered coach.

"Get in," O'Banyon ordered.

They all piled into the carriage.

O'Banyon stared at her the whole time.

They traveled a short distance through the docklands' maze of lightless streets, weaving their way down toward the river. Rohan remained stoic, but Kate was terrified, and Pete looked scared, as well. The carriage halted when they were in sight of the River Thames. They all got out.

"Good. They're here." O'Banyon glanced into the darkness in the direction of the river. "Come on, girly. You're the guest of honor."

"Let me go!"

"Quit your fussin'!" Pete retorted, keeping up his role as one of her heavy-handed guards.

"Don't you lot say nothin' in front o' the old nob. He's a deep one," O'Banyon warned with a meaningful nod toward the quay. "When we're done here, take her back to the rat-man's shop. I'll meet you there. See that you ain't followed."

"Aye, sir," Pete murmured.

"Bring her," he ordered her captors.

They obeyed. With Pete on her right and Rohan on her left, each of them holding one of her arms, they all followed O'Banyon toward the quay.

There were inky figures moving in the

darkness at the river's edge, a cluster of men standing around casually with rifles on their shoulders. She glanced at Rohan and saw him counting them with his narrowed stare.

The frigid wind blew stronger as they walked toward the Thames, leaving the shelter of the drab brick buildings that lined the narrow street. The long, sweeping line of the quay stretched out empty in both directions.

Kate noticed that as they advanced toward it, Rohan pulled up the neckerchief that hung around his throat, using it to conceal the lower half of his face. He nodded at Pete to do the same, then tugged the brim of his hat a bit lower over his eyes.

O'Banyon scowled at his helpers. "What are you doing that for?"

"There's no point in lettin' 'em see our faces," Rohan answered, his pale eyes blazing above his makeshift mask.

As distant church bells began to toll the hour, three silhouettes emerged from between the nearby buildings.

"Right on time," O'Banyon murmured under his breath. "Remember, keep quiet, like I told you."

Ten loud, slow bongs reverberated over London as the three new arrivals approached.

Kate was acutely aware of Rohan's taut vigilance. Her heart pounded as she wondered if she was about to meet some real Prometheans. It must be so, she thought, sensing the predatory tension that thrummed through his muscled frame as he stood beside her, holding on to her arm in his role as her guard.

"Mr. O'Banyon," a wry, patrician voice greeted the ex-convict. "Always a pleasure." The owner of the voice emerged out of the shadows, an elegant older gentleman with a slim build and a shock of pewter hair.

He had two others with him, each about age thirty. The first man, husky of build, with dirty blond hair and rugged features, wore an eye patch. His good eye regarded O'Banyon with utter contempt, but he kept watching everything, scrutinizing Kate and her two guards, gesturing some unspoken order to the armed men prowling back and forth down by the water and waiting by the river stairs.

She gathered these were under his control, apparently a contingent of Promethean foot soldiers.

The second man accompanying the older fellow had a wounded air and an introverted posture, though he was strikingly good-looking; his black hair was cropped short, revealing a beautiful, chiseled face. His hands were thrust down into the pockets of his greatcoat, shoulders hunched against the cold. He kept his eyes down but stayed close to the older fellow, perhaps specifically assigned to protect him.

Kate sensed Rohan staring at this brooding, silent man as though he recognized him, and it suddenly dawned on her that this might be their missing agent he had mentioned.

Drake.

"You have the daughter?" the distinguished older gentleman inquired as they approached.

If this was the Promethean magnate, James Falkirk, the "Old Man" that O'Banyon had mentioned to Pete, contrary to the nickname, he could not be described as elderly. He was elegantly fit and appeared to be in his early sixties.

"She's right here," O'Banyon answered, nodding at Kate.

"Hm," Falkirk mused, looking her over with a degree of pity at her unfortunate appearance of this night.

"Who are you?" Kate demanded.

"Be quiet!" O'Banyon ordered, but Falkirk lifted an eyebrow in amusement at her show of spirit.

"I knew your grandfather, Miss Fox. Such a shame, what a wrong path he took in life. I regret to say the last Count DuMarin brought great dishonor to his otherwise-distinguished line."

"You have the wrong person, as I've told these cretins a hundred times. My name is not Fox, it's Madsen," she retorted, just to see what he'd say.

"No, my dear. Your mongrel of a father merely dubbed you with an alias to protect you." He smiled. "I daresay, in the hopes we'd never find you — but, alas."

"My father is dead."

"Really?" he answered in a pleasant tone. "Then, tell me, who is that?" Falkirk turned with an urbane gesture toward the river stairs, where the lone figure of a man was now getting out of a rowboat.

Kate stared, riveted by something familiar in the way the brawny figure moved.

O'Banyon let out a low snort of disgusted laughter, staring. "Well, well. The Sea Fox has arrived."

Papa?

Time seemed to slow. Her heart was thudding in her throat. She barely felt Rohan's hand steadying her with a subtle press of her elbow. She was riveted by the large, rugged silhouette striding slowly up the docking stairs.

"You're sure it's 'im?" The eye-patch man glanced over.

O'Banyon nodded. "Aye, that's him, all right. The illustrious Captain Fox."

Kate let out a small cry as the men with rifles surrounded her father; it dawned on her that they had been waiting down there for him.

It hit her then. Truly hit her.

Not only was Papa alive. He had walked into this fully prepared to sacrifice himself so she could go free.

"Come along," Falkirk instructed in a most polite tone. "Let him see we have her. Then we can proceed without delay to more important matters." He walked ahead of them toward the river's edge. His two younger associates followed, flanking him.

Rohan nudged her gently into motion; they all walked slowly toward the others.

"Captain Fox!" Falkirk greeted him. "It was wise of you to come alone, as we requested. You can no doubt guess why you are here, but suffice to say, I learned from your former shipmate that you are in possession of rare and wondrous information — namely, the whereabouts of the Alchemist's Tomb. All you need to do to ensure your daughter's safety is to lead us to it. We will do the rest." ,

"You claim you have my daughter," the newcomer spoke out boldly. "Let me see her first."

At the familiar sound of that gravelly, defiant voice, Kate's mind reeled.

"Bring the young lady forward."

"Come on," Rohan whispered, tugging her into motion.

Kate walked in an amazed trance toward the burly outline of Captain Gerald Fox. He stood tall, still looking hearty and hale enough to thrash any unruly crewman.

As she went closer, she saw that his square, rough-hewn face was lined now and even more weathered than she remembered. His once-thick hair was gone, now a bald pate shining in the moonlight. The same rectangular goatee beard that he had always worn surrounded his mouth, still shaved neatly to cover just his chin, only now, it was white.

But when she stood before him, it was his eyes, as green as her own, that left no doubt of who he was. They still blazed with the same fiery spirit that she remembered from those days so long ago when she had stood at the helm of his frigate pretending to steer the great vessel, though the wheel had towered over her.

Papa stared back uncertainly, squinting in the darkness. "That's not my daughter," he said gruffly.

"Yes, Papa, it is," she choked out.

"Well, I certainly hope so," Falkirk said sardonically. "Otherwise, I'm afraid we should have no use for her."

Cautiously, Kate lowered the spectacles, letting her father see her eyes. "Don't you recognize me, Papa?"

Profound amazement overtook his manly features. "Katy, me wee barnacle," he whispered. "It is you."

She stepped forward suddenly and hugged him hard, squeezing her eyes shut against the threat of tears. When she felt his arms encircle her artificially plumped-up waist, she somehow managed to put aside the storm of her emotions. She had to let him know there was help at hand that he was not aware of.

Still hugging him, she breathed the message in his ear only loud enough for him alone: *"Warrington is here."*

She felt her father pause, absorbing the news.

"Well, this reunion is all very touching, I'm sure," Falkirk interrupted dryly, "but we have a schedule to keep, if you don't mind."

Shrewd as he was, Captain Fox did not so much as glance at the tall "smuggler" standing next to her, but instead, kept his fond gaze fixed on Kate as she released him from her embrace and stepped back between her guards.

Her father glanced grimly at Falkirk. "Very well, I'll do what you want. You've got me now. You don't need her anymore. Let my daughter go."

"Oh, we'll be holdin' on to her until you've kept your end of the bargain, Cap'n Fox," O'Banyon spoke up, gloating at his former employer.

Papa glowered at him. "I should've killed you when I had the chance."

"Aye, you should've. Because when all this is over, I've got a score to settle with you concerning Newgate."

"That is exactly where you belong, you gallows rat!"

O'Banyon merely smirked at the insult, then he glanced at Pete and Rohan. "Go on. Take her away, like I told ye."

"Not so fast," the eye-patch man spoke up. He beckoned to his rifle-toting henchmen to come and take hold of Kate. "My men will take over from here."

O'Banyon turned to him indignantly. "What do you mean by this? That's not our agreement! My men are to keep watch on the girl!"

"Our agreement?" the ruthless, one-eyed Promethean replied. "You're the one who broke it. Nobody told you to bring outsiders into this. I'm afraid your men's services are no longer required — and frankly, you piece of dung, now that we have the good captain, neither are yours."

Without another word, the eye-patch man pulled out a pistol and matter-of-factly shot O'Banyon dead.

Kate's jaw dropped, but even as her kidnapper's body crumpled to the ground, the man turned with a second pistol to do the same to O'Banyon's "smuggler" assistants.

Rohan was already shoving Kate behind him; reaching with both hands under his coat, he withdrew two pistols, took aim, and almost gaily blew a hole in the eye-patch man's forehead, dropping him to the ground; he almost simultaneously leveled his left arm and shot the first Promethean henchman taking aim at him.

Everything happened in the blink of an eye.

Shots flashed everywhere, blinding bursts of gunfire, sharp reports bounding off the brick box of crowded buildings at the river's edge.

Rohan had already drawn a third pistol, aiming at Falkirk. But when Drake stepped in front of the old man and blocked the shot, Rohan held his fire with a low curse.

Drake immediately hustled Falkirk to safety, taking cover behind a wall off to their right, while a surge of yells erupted from the direction of the river.

Half a dozen of her father's sailors rushed up from unseen hiding places, barreling into the fray against the Promethean henchmen.

As the two groups began to battle each other, Kate peeked out from hiding behind Rohan to see what was happening. She spotted Papa through the mayhem as he pulled out a gun and shot a Promethean foot soldier in the back. The man had taken aim at Pete, who was crouching low to the ground, covering his head.

Another shot flashed at once from off to the right; Gerald Fox let out a curse.

"Papa!" she cried in horror as he fell, shot in the leg by Falkirk to stop him from getting away.

The Prometheans had not come this far only to fail to get the information Captain Fox possessed.

Rohan spun around to Kate, his eyes

gleaming cold above his folded cloth mask. He grabbed Pete by the arm, as well. "Get out of here, both of you! Go!"

"Rohan, save my father! I can't lose him now!"

"I will. Now, go!" As several more Promethean henchmen advanced on him, he turned back to them, positioning himself to cover their retreat. He drew that long, lancelike sword to hold the enemies off while Kate and Pete started running away.

As soon as they ducked behind the corner of the nearest building, Kate looked back in terror. *God, please keep him safe.*

But in the next instant, she realized that she needn't have worried. Indeed, it was not until that moment that she understood Rohan truly.

He attacked with overwhelming force, an onslaught of sudden, wild aggression from which any normal man would cower.

He destroyed them.

She watched, riveted, unable to look away as her lover ran a man through with his lance, yanked the blade out covered in gore, and swung to face the next, lunging at the second man with his left-hand dagger. The bloodcurdling scream was still fading from the first dying man when the second Promethean dropped to his knees, clutching his throat, blood pouring out between his fingers.

Rohan kicked the second man to the ground, and strode toward the fray, seeking a third, who tried to back away. Terror flashed across the third man's face as Rohan swiftly advanced and mowed him down.

Pete pulled on her arm. "Come on!"

"Wait," she forced out. She felt nauseated, but she could not stop staring at Rohan. He was fighting his way through the melee of clashing sailors and Promethean henchmen toward her injured father.

Papa was down on one knee, using his sword to hold at bay the Prometheans who were trying to capture him. As Rohan approached, one Promethean after another turned to face him; again he was hotly engaged, fending off three enemies at once. But when he reached her father and began helping him to his feet, Pete tugged more insistently on her elbow.

"Come on, we've got to go!" Pete pulled her away from the corner, and this time, she willingly followed.

The next thing she knew, they were running through the labyrinth of the narrow docklands streets, looking for the safe house. Through a lightless passage between two buildings, they raced across a cobbled courtyard, where their trespass awoke a huge guard dog.

It let out a burst of vicious barking, but they pressed their backs against the opposite wall and passed out of the reach of the animal at the end of his chain.

When they dodged out the other end of the courtyard, Pete glanced around, then pointed to the right. "There it is! Hurry!"

The galleried inn sat at the end of the block. They sprinted the rest of the way and went barreling up the outdoor stairs, running across the long wooden balcony until they reached the door of the room.

Eldred must have heard them coming. He opened the door and hurried them into the room, shutting the door and locking it behind them.

"They should be along any moment now," Pete told him, panting.

"Miss Madsen, are you all right?" Eldred asked gravely.

"Papa's alive!"

"Yes, and you look rather green."

"Do I?" She sat down heavily on the nearby chair, staring straight ahead, diverse bloody images stamped upon her mind. *God, it's true,* she thought, still shaking. *He really is a killer.*

Pete was peeking out from behind the

ratty curtains, watching for them. "I see them!"

"My father was shot in the leg. I doubt he'll be able to climb those stairs."

"Then let's go down to him," Pete replied at once.

"Let me ask first what His Grace wants us to do. You two stay out of sight," Eldred murmured, going to the door.

Eldred stepped out onto the gallery as Rohan came into view, helping her father limp along down the dark street. He returned in a heartbeat. "He's signaled for us to come down."

"Bring the medical bag!" Kate said.

Eldred picked it up as Pete helped himself to an extra pistol. Kate ran out first, rushing down the stairs.

"Are you hurt?" she asked Rohan as she strode toward them. To her relief, he shook his head. "Papa, how are you holding up?"

"Eh, never better," he said with a wince just as Parker brought the carriage clattering into their midst.

"Get in." Rohan opened the door, waved Kate in, then helped her father climb into the coach. Eldred followed a moment later, bringing the medical bag.

Rohan ordered Pete up onto the top of the carriage with Wilkins and finally vaulted in himself with an agile spring. He had barely shut the door before the carriage was in motion once again.

"I am so glad to see you two," Kate uttered. "Were you followed?"

"No," Rohan murmured.

"The bleeders ran away — from him!" her father said with a hearty laugh and an approving glance at Rohan. "Your father would be proud, lad."

"Where are we going?" Kate asked in a shaky voice.

"Back to my house to get the book," Rohan answered. They had not dared bring *The Alchemist's Journal* anywhere near the battle to avoid the least chance of the Prometheans getting their hands on it.

"As soon as we have it," Rohan added, "we shall put out to sea."

"You mean . . . to the Alchemist's Tomb?" she asked, with an uneasy glance from him to her father. "So quickly?"

"No choice. They got Tewkes," Papa muttered, grimacing as Eldred tried to begin bandaging his leg. "I can do that my bloody self! Give it 'ere."

"Who's Tewkes, Papa?"

"You don't remember him? My old bo'sun, after Charley. Spectacles. White hair sticks straight up like a little downy chick's."

"Ohh! Old Tewkes! Lord, is he still with you?" she exclaimed, remembering him vaguely. "He must be eighty by now! How did he get captured?"

"Not so quick as he used to be. Damned fools, I told them all to stay on the ship. But m'crew feared for my life. When they heard the shots, they came running. Trouble is, old Tewkes knows as well as I do where we found the Tomb." He shook his head. "O'Banyon must have told those blackguards that some of my old-timers were there when we found that cursed place."

"Yes, we'll have to be under way as quickly as possible," Rohan confirmed. "The last thing we saw was the Prometheans boarding their ship. They dragged Mr. Tewkes away with them. Considering they've already embarked, they've got a lead on us. So I'm afraid it's a race now. We've got to beat them to the Tomb."

"Yes, well," her father added, "even if they force Tewkes to show them where it is, they'll not survive the traps inside that wicked place without your mother's book."

"Traps?" Kate murmured.

"Aye, the whole place is rigged with cunning snares and mechanical devices — like the one that killed your mother. *The Alchemist's Journal* contains the clues that Warrington will need to make it in and out of there alive. Even so, you be careful," her father warned the duke. "Those cruel puzzles are all too easy to get wrong."

Kate turned to Rohan in alarm, but he was silent.

Then her father grunted with pain when the carriage hit a bump.

"Are you hurt badly, Papa? Tell me the truth," she demanded, peering worriedly at his progress with the bandages in the dark.

"Just a flesh wound. Believe me, I've had worse. Glad to see these London streets are still the same as I remember — full of holes."

She smiled at his grumbling, then hugged him, mindful of his wound. "I can't believe you're alive," she whispered, then she gazed at Rohan. "Thank you."

He seemed emotionless, staring back at her, his gleaming eyes cold and otherworldly, his angular face expressionless. He said nothing. Her gaze fell slowly to the dark streaks and stains that marred his clothes. She held her breath, realizing he had blood all over him.

He looked out the window.

The carriage rolled on through the night. A gulf as wide as the Thames seemed to separate them while Eldred tried to help her irked father tend his wound.

When they arrived at Rohan's mansion, again, all was speed, efficiency, and action.

Rohan forbade Kate to change out of her costume until they were safely aboard her father's ship and well away from London.

Then he went to change his clothes, while she ran upstairs to the bedchamber and retrieved her mother's book from the bottom of her borrowed traveling chest.

When she caught a glimpse of herself in the bedchamber mirror, she sighed at her dowdy appearance and continued packing, throwing the few items of warm clothing back into the trunk.

But as she handled the same, ill-fitting, stolen garments that she had been wearing since they gave them to her, tears suddenly pricked her eyes without warning.

She did not know why such an inconsequential thing as clothes should hit her so hard at the moment, only that she had not seen her father in how many years, and she did not even have a decent gown left to meet him in.

The stranger's wardrobe seemed a reminder of all she had lost — and she feared what she had lost tonight was Rohan.

Maybe he really could not love her.

After what she had seen . . . maybe his

darkness was greater than her light.

He had claimed he was not fit for love. At least now she finally understood what he was talking about.

"Are you all right?"

Quickly blinking back her tears, she turned in surprise and found him leaning in the doorway. She did not know how long he had been watching her. She had not heard him arrive.

She cleared her throat and nodded, smoothing her skirts. "Yes, of course." He had changed into fresh clothes, and indeed, looked more intimidating than ever, dressed entirely in black.

The fractured look in his pale eyes worried her, however, and she also noticed he had a bandage wrapped around the palm of his right hand. "You're hurt."

"Cut myself a bit. It's nothing. I barely feel it." He walked into the bedchamber and picked up her traveling trunk.

Kate struggled for something to say to try to bridge the gulf between them. She had seen him like this before. Bleak, remote, formidable. She remembered the day she had discovered him practicing his combat skills in the Hall of Arms at Kilburn Castle.

He had not liked her seeing that, and had definitely withdrawn from her when she had shown him the dragon book with the Initiate's Brand. But even when he had escorted her to her cottage, barely speaking to her along the way, even then, he had not been as completely shut down as he was now. It was as if he was slipping away from her, into the night.

She touched his arm, trying to bring him back. "Thank you for saving my father."

He just nodded, then he pulled away and carried the trunk out, mumbling as he brushed past her. "Best hurry."

She frowned as he stalked out, but she followed a moment later. As she walked down the stairs, she could hear Papa cursing with seaworthy vigor as he stood in the entrance hall, gingerly putting some weight on his bandaged leg. Without a word, Eldred handed him a wooden crutch to lean on, apparently keeping a supply of various medical items on hand, given his master's occupation.

"Anything I can do to help?" Kate offered as she joined them.

"Good as new," Papa vaunted, sending her a grin.

"We need to go," Rohan urged them from the doorway, before disappearing again.

"And we're off," Papa replied. He nodded

his thanks to the butler, at whom Kate also smiled.

"Good-bye for now, Eldred."

"Safe journey, miss." Eldred followed them to the door.

Parker was waiting with the coach under the portico as they walked outside. "All aboard," the sergeant said ruefully, opening the carriage door.

Kate let her father go ahead of her and waited to assist if he needed help. But her attention was on Rohan, who was standing restlessly at the edge of the portico, his back to them as he smoked a cheroot.

She could not recall seeing him smoking before.

All of a sudden, she heard running foot-steps coming from behind her. "Wait for me!"

Rohan and she both turned around to look as Peter Doyle came rushing out of the house, clutching his pack of supplies.

"I'm coming with you!" he declared.

"You kept your end of the bargain, Pete. You're free to go back to Cornwall," Rohan said with a distant hint of wry amusement.

"But I've come this far, haven't I, sir?"

"Hm. I fear we've made an adventurer of you, Peter. It's up to Captain Fox. It's his ship."

"Cap'n?" Peter asked her father hopefully.

"Caleb's boy, are you?" Papa tossed back.

"He's my uncle, sir."

"Good enough. Get in, then."

"Thank you, Cap'n!" Pete grinned and bounded into the carriage.

Kate hesitated, waiting uncertainly for Rohan. As he dropped his cheroot on the ground and stepped on it, putting out the spark, all of a sudden, a stately black Town coach drawn by a team of four black horses rolled to a halt in front of Rohan's home.

He glanced at it, while Kate's heart sank.

Oh, no, she thought, dreading the return of one of his persistent lady conquests. Of all the bad timing.

But then, to her surprise, the door opened, and a handsome dark-haired gentleman jumped out of the coach.

"Rohan Kilburn, Duke of Warrington! A word with you, sir! No, I must insist. Immediately!"

"As do I!" shouted a second man, lean and fair-haired, who also emerged from the carriage.

"Max, Jordan," Rohan said uncomfortably.

"There he is, the villain!" a golden-haired lady taunted from inside the coach.

"Daphne?" Rohan mumbled, hands on his hips.

Kate worried that maybe these were two of the countless men he had cuckolded. Angry husbands to contend with.

"Don't blame me, Your Grace!" a dainty red-haired woman chimed in from the carriage, waving to Rohan. "I told them you would tell us when you're ready! They wouldn't listen —"

"You nefarious bastard!" the dark-haired man greeted him in a tone of jovial indignation.

Kate exhaled slightly at the jubilant undertone of humor in his voice.

"What's afoot?" Rohan asked them.

"Oh-ho, don't play innocent with us!" the sandy-haired man warned.

"I *knew* you were acting odd when we saw you earlier today!"

Kate let out a furtive gasp. Agents of the Order!

"*How* could you look us in the eyes and not breathe a word of what's been going on?"

"Ignore my husband, Warrington. We're very happy for you — and your lady! Hullo! I'm Lady Rotherstone and this is my friend, Miss Portland! We're very eager to meet you!"

The two lovely women were now waving at Kate.

Who wanted to crawl under a rock, in her hideous disguise.

But his two friends were not done scolding him. "To think that we, who knew you since we were boys — the closest thing you've got left to family! — had to hear this news secondhand at some bloody soiree!"

"We didn't even need Miss Portland to tell us the gossip this time. It's all over Society — that you're married!" the two exclaimed nearly in unison and quite matched in their fond outrage.

"Bloody hell," Kate murmured, borrowing a favorite from Rohan's idiom.

"Is this the lucky lass?" The light-haired gentleman sketched an elegant bow toward Kate.

"Bride of the Beast. Heaven help you, poor thing," the dark-haired one drawled.

She began gingerly backing away. "Um, actually — I'm afraid there has been a bit of a, er, misunderstanding."

The one he'd called Max lifted one eyebrow, while his friend, Jordan, frowned, studying her. "How's that?"

Rohan cut this charming conversation short. "I have to go. Get in the carriage, Kate."

"Ah, so Kate's her name!" Max taunted, sending his friend an aside. "Did you know he had a Kate?"

"No. Last I heard, it was — never mind that." Jordan smiled innocently at them.

"Aren't you at least going to introduce us?" Max demanded.

"Some other time. Come on." Rohan propelled her firmly toward the carriage.

Kate offered the two handsome noblemen a hapless half smile, mortified in the extreme by her frumpy costume; the padding complicated her efforts to get into the stupid carriage.

"Where are you rushing off to, anyway?" Max persisted. "You know, you're being damnably rude."

"Max, it's Warrington. You know it's just his way," Jordan drawled.

Kate finally wedged her chubby, padded figure into the carriage. They all seemed friendly enough, but this glamorous foursome in ball gowns and velvet coats made her feel even more awkward in her silly mob cap, funny spectacles, and dowdy dress.

Jordan had been studying her costumed appearance in amusement, but now glanced quizzically at Rohan, as if to say, *Not your usual fare, eh?*

"Sorry, we have to go," he mumbled to

his friends as he followed her into the coach. "I'll call on you when I get back."

"When will that be, damn it?" Max demanded.

"I don't know!" he bit back as he banged the carriage door shut. "Parker, for God's sake, drive!"

"Yes, sir!"

"Was it something we said?" Max taunted, stepping out of the way as his carriage rolled into motion. "Ma'am."

"Good-bye, Kate!" Jordan sent her a roguish salute.

She nodded to them, feeling like a fool.

The ladies still sitting in the coach had not heard the particulars of their exchange, but they waved at her, calling invitations that she should come for tea.

She waved back haplessly just to avoid being rude.

"Married?" Her father raised an eyebrow, glancing suspiciously from her to Rohan, but he said nothing.

"No, Papa," Kate answering for them with a blush. Suddenly realizing that perhaps she ought to worry what her formidable sire might have to say about their arrangement, now that he suddenly reappeared in her life, she cast about for a speedy change of subject. She turned to Rohan. "How nice to

491

meet your friends."

"Mm." He folded his arms across his chest, but it was clear he wanted no questions. Once more, he was lost in his brooding, staring out the window while the coach rolled on toward the river, where her father's moored frigate waited to take them out to sea.

Chapter 18

The Prometheans' schooner rode at anchor a few miles out to sea beyond the Thames estuary. Until the prisoner could be made to talk, they could go no farther.

An ugly mood hung over the decks after the death of Talon and several of his men.

Drake knew that Prometheans did not exactly care about each other, but they had respected Talon, and they certainly hated defeat. It was now past midnight. Above them, pillow clouds tried to suffocate the moon.

Leaning against the mainmast with his hands in his pockets, merely trying to stay out of everyone's way, Drake hid his secret jubilation that his oppressor, Talon, the hated eye-patch man, was dead.

Of course, James was saddened by the loss, and Drake could not be too happy about anything that upset his revered benefactor. After all, if it were not for James, he would still be rotting away in that Bavarian dungeon, only waiting for his daily visit from the torturers.

Still, he felt liberated. For a moment, he gazed in concern at James, who stood at the rails, brooding over the demise of his long-time assistant. Then he looked over at the sound of a large splash off the stern.

The surviving Promethean foot soldiers were getting rid of the bodies. One unceremonious watery plunk followed another as they dumped their slain mates into the sea.

Others were busy in the lanternlit stateroom, taking out their anger on the elderly bo'sun they had captured.

Drake was careful not to look in that direction. He could not bear it. The sounds of their taunting and mocking and striking their captive made him cringe, triggering terrible memories of his own ordeals in Germany.

But there was nowhere to go on the sleek, compact schooner where he could escape, and as much as he tried to pretend he heard nothing, he still could not avoid their display of brutality. The flickering lamplight in the stateroom where they were abusing the old man cast the moving shadows of the Promethean foot soldiers in large over the deck.

Everything in Drake told him to go help that poor old fellow. But he would not listen, already sick to his stomach with the nearness of their deliberate cruelty.

Instead, he stared at the dark sea, taking large draughts of the clear, bracing wind. And he distracted himself with the churning questions about the events of this night. If only he could remember more of his old life!

Why didn't he shoot me? That big fellow, that savage, he could've killed me if he wanted to. Were we friends once? He had not looked familiar. Not like the other one had: Max.

Drake still had not told James that in London he had recognized the Marquess of Rotherstone. He was not sure why he kept this secret, but after the debacle of tonight, James had said that that menacing giant who had killed Talon and five of their men in under a quarter hour could only be an agent of the Order. The same organization that Drake had once belonged to, or so he had been told.

Surely he had never done anything like that.

But then again, how had he wound up in that horrible dark dungeon in the first place? There must have been a fight. One he had obviously lost. But why? If only he could remember. He closed his eyes and banged his head back lightly against the solid mast, wishing he could knock his tangled mind into cooperating. So little made sense.

Especially the haunting remnant of a memory of deep violet eyes and a girl's nymphlike laughter, teasing, enchanting him, trailing ahead of him through some familiar forest . . .

He shoved the image away. Of all the scattered fragments in his mind, it was the one that hurt the worst, and yet, the one he treasured most. He had no idea who she was or if she was even real. Maybe he was quite as mad as Talon's henchmen believed.

He could not even say any more what was good or bad.

If the Order is really evil like James says, and the Prometheans are good, then why didn't that tall blackguard shoot me? He had a clear shot. Why did he hold his fire?

It was too threatening to contemplate that James might be lying to him. James was his only hope in this world. The only person since his capture who had been kind to him.

The Germans would have killed him if it were not for James. James Falkirk was powerful among the Prometheans: The

Germans had been afraid of him. James had ordered Drake removed from the dungeon — not unlike the way in which he had arranged for that lowlife O'Banyon to be smuggled out of Newgate by a prison guard in the Prometheans' pay. The similarities ended there, for O'Banyon was merely hired to do a job, whereas Drake was far more valuable to James, though he was not sure how.

His aged savior had taken him under his wing, nursed him back to relative health after his countless beatings, and promised with paternal tenderness that he would help him get his memory back.

Frustration rose anew with his addled mind's inability to give James the information he wanted, but by now, Drake was all too used to living in a state of distressing confusion. He was doing better than before, he reminded himself, refusing to despair.

True, he had not yet remembered everything, but vague phantoms of his past had begun to return when he was calm. He could almost glimpse them from the corner of his eye. Who he was, where he came from, what he used to be. Unfortunately, the answers still fled when he tried to look at them directly. Almost as if his mind had tricked itself into forgetting everything for some reason, as if he had secrets to protect at all costs, even from himself . . .

He clenched his jaw, remembering how Talon had never quite believed that Drake had lost his memory. God, they had hated each other, both jealous for James's favor, like rival brothers.

When a thud and another cry of pain flew out of the stateroom, Drake's heart pounded faster, but he could no longer ignore the henchmen abusing the elderly sailor.

Trembling, he pushed away from the mast and stood staring into the stateroom. The door was open. He could see they had knocked old Tewkes off the chair and were laughing at him.

Drake's eyes narrowed to blue slashes in the darkness. His heart pounded, and his palms sweated at the terrifying prospect of confronting them. But perhaps he was still infected with a trace of his earlier, perplexing reaction to the scene of battle. To his own astonishment, he had wanted to fight, had felt the surge of crimson impulse rushing through him, an ingrained capacity for violence, but he was so taken off guard by it that he had refused it. Besides, he knew his body was weakened, and his chief concern had been protecting James.

But now, perhaps there was just enough

fight in him to be able to show those animals a more civilized approach to getting the information they required.

Like James would do. Through kindness.

He glanced uncertainly over his shoulder at his savior, but James remained at the rails. Drake squared his shoulders and walked into the stateroom, ignoring the cold lump of fear in the pit of his stomach.

"Why, if it isn't the master's pet."

"Look, the lunatic has joined us."

"What do you want, lunatic?"

Drake ignored their mockery, brushing past the Promethean henchmen as if he knew what he was doing.

They all were well aware that James had said he was not to be touched. Drake moved past the ruffians and bent down, gently helping the old fellow back up into his chair.

Tewkes righted his crooked spectacles. Drake felt an unutterable sadness seeing how his bony hands were shaking.

He sat down slowly on the stool across from their white-haired captive. "Mr. Tewkes, is it?" he offered in a low tone.

The guards scoffed at his intrusion. "Get out of here, you lunatic!"

"I want to talk to him," Drake insisted. "Mr. Tewkes, I implore you, tell them what they want to know. You don't know what they're capable of," he whispered, and gazed grimly into the old man's eyes. *I do.* "Please. Where is the Alchemist's Tomb? Don't you see? When Captain Fox's ship appears, they are simply going to follow it, and they won't need you anymore. If you haven't given them anything useful by then, they will certainly kill you."

Tewkes stared at him for a long moment, wide-eyed.

Perhaps he read the haunted sincerity in the depths of Drake's eyes, but after a moment, the aged bo'sun nodded wearily. "Very well." He gulped, then whispered: "It's in the Orkney Isles."

Drake nodded slowly. He murmured to the nearest guard to tell James, and very soon, they were under way.

Not far behind them, Captain Fox maneuvered his heavily armed frigate out of the Thames estuary into the North Sea. Rohan was intrigued to learn their voyage would take them to the Orkneys, a smattering of dramatic, mysterious islands off the northeastern coast of Scotland.

It would be a few days' sail to reach those difficult, frigid waters — plenty of time to overtake the Prometheans, who had a brief head start on them.

That night, they stayed up talking into the wee hours inside the captain's snug chartroom on the quarterdeck. Gerald had wanted to be near enough to assist his crew if they needed him, so they had remained abovedecks in the little navigational office rather than convening in the captain's genteel stateroom at the stern.

But while father and daughter sat at the built-in table underneath the lantern, Rohan kept his distance, leaning in the shadowed corner.

On such a coal black winter's night, the ruddy sphere of illumination that the lantern spread through the low-ceilinged chamber could not reach him where he sat. He preferred the darkness at the moment; as the lantern swung slowly with the rocking of the ship, he watched the shadows sliding up and down the walls like wraiths.

Kate had been amazed upon entering the little room again, now that they were back on the very ship that had been her floating childhood home. Gerald had been equally charmed to behold his beautiful daughter no longer in her homely disguise. She was clad once more in the striped pink dress that she had worn in the music room when she had inexplicably thrown his money back at him.

Gerald had produced a stack of letters from Kate's late caretaker, Charley. These, too, sat on the table now.

Tears had misted Kate's green eyes when she saw the proof that her father had been keeping watch on her from afar these many years.

"Poor old Charley," her father was saying. "I figured something must've happened to him when so many months passed and there was no word from him."

"It was his heart, Papa. He went quickly. About eighteen months ago, he just dropped dead in the middle of his chores. I guess that's why he didn't get a chance to, er, explain certain things about all this."

Gerald nodded, chewing on the mouthpiece of his long-handled tobacco pipe. Fragrant smoke curled out of the bell. "After his letters stopped, I wasn't sure how to check up on you. Given that you had been told I was dead, I was still trying to figure out how to communicate with you, and even questioning if I should, or if it was better just to let you live your life."

"Papa!"

"It seemed cruel to do it through a letter, but if I came to England to see you in person, I could have been arrested for piracy and hanged. Which, by the way, was only a temporary profession for me, and not at all how I preferred to do business," he added.

She sent him a questioning smile.

"Eh, 'twas a dispute with a government bureaucrat in charge of granting the letters of marque," he growled past his pipe between his teeth. "I'd been raiding enemy ships for years, but he wouldn't renew my papers. Wanted a bribe. I told him to go to the devil."

"Of course you did." Kate smiled in fond amusement.

"I just continued on as usual, only this time, for lack of a silly piece of paper, 'twas deemed piracy instead of privateering." He harrumphed. "But then, a couple of months ago —" His tone darkened. "I got the message from O'Banyon claiming he had kidnapped you. I left immediately to come to London, as they instructed me to. I could not let them hurt you."

Kate made a sympathetic noise and reached across the table to take her father's hand.

Rohan supposed he should probably leave them alone to catch up on old times, but as they chatted on, neither seemed to mind his silent, brooding presence nearby.

With the aftermath of violence still burning in his veins, in truth, he did not want to be alone. Though he gave no sign of the turmoil churning inside him, every battle instinct in his blood remained on high alert.

It was hard to come down from it.

He'd had a smoke, and it had helped, but he was still in dire need, bluntly, of somebody to fuck him, drain the aftermath of fury from him, and drown out his senses with lavish, mind-numbing pleasure until he could no longer feel the horror of it all.

If he could just have that, he would be fine.

He stared at Kate, but his terrible hunger for her tonight only partly explained why he could not tear himself away from her. He had to be near her, even though he knew she must despise him now.

He had never wanted her to see the savage things that he was capable of — and that, on top of her finding out firsthand that, yes, indeed, he had long been a profligate seducer of other men's wives, a sinner to the core.

What had ever made him think he could be worthy of her sweetness?

Yet, like a moth to a flame, his gaze returned continually to Kate. He'd been with her for weeks, but he was still fascinated by her loveliness. He never tired of her.

Pink-cheeked with the ocean's chill, her emerald eyes shone with lingering wonder as she listened to her father's tales in rapt attention, her elbow on the table, her cheek resting in her hand.

Rohan wanted her so badly, but all he could do was brace for her rejection. She must find him revolting, now that she had seen the Beast in action.

Of course, he was not sorry for killing those men. He hadn't had much choice. His only regret was that Talon, Falkirk's right-hand man, had killed O'Banyon before *he* had had a chance to pay back Kate's lowlife kidnapper as he deserved.

A clean single bullet had been too good for the man who had dared to slap her beautiful face and to look with lust on a woman Rohan still considered his.

Which he realized was absurd.

Just because Caleb Doyle had given Kate to him as a gift did not mean he really owned her.

Yet some barbaric part of him insisted that, oh, yes, he did. And that she knew it, too.

Ah, well. His instinctual side was in for a rude awakening fairly soon, he mused, for he had a sickening feeling that once they reached Orkney, she was going to announce that they'd be parting ways, that she'd be sailing off with her dear Papa.

He resolved to accept her choice with stoic equanimity. He was not sure how he would say good-bye to her, but now that she knew the sort of heartless, violent brute she was dealing with, he could hardly blame her. She'd be better off. Besides, he doubted he would survive the Alchemist's Tomb, anyway.

Of all the places to have to go, that was worse than anything his deepest fears could have conjured; he must venture in to face the very source of the Kilburn Curse.

God only knew what cunning, formless evil waited for him there — but he shook off his superstitions.

Even if his visit to the Alchemist's Tomb revealed a way to break the Kilburn Curse, he knew Kate still wouldn't want him. Not anymore.

Gerald noticed him staring at his daughter, pausing to take another serene puff on his pipe; Rohan dropped his gaze, ashamed of his searing need for the girl.

He couldn't help it. He hungered for her terribly tonight. He craved the release after his battle. His body was still wound up as tight as a bowstring, and his soul ached. But her father would probably kill him, and he knew Kate wasn't going to let him touch her. Why should she?

There was a remote chance, perhaps, that she needed a bit of physical comfort, too — for he knew she had been stunned by the news her father had casually let slip about an hour ago, when he informed them that he had another family.

Kate's face had drained of color, but she had somehow kept her brittle smile in place as Gerald explained that he had married a second time to "a good woman" in Australia. He had fathered six more children in the ensuing years: four sons, two daughters.

"Really?" Kate had choked out, her tone polite.

Rohan could feel her struggling to absorb it.

Her pained shock was one of the reasons he had stayed with her in the chartroom, even though he was sure he was the last person she would have wanted to lean on. By now it had become habit to be there for her. Watching her inner argument play out across her guileless face, he could almost hear her trying to reason with her stung heart.

Of course, Papa had the right to remarry. He lost his wife. He was still a young man for a widower. It's only right that he should have wanted to wed again and have more children. No one wants to be alone.

What Gerald did not seem to realize, damn him, was how alone *Kate* had been all those years, growing up on the moors with no companions but the falcons and the wild ponies — and of course, her books. In silent empathy, Rohan yearned to hold her though she had quickly masked her pain.

She seemed all right now; she really was the most resilient, brave, unselfish, and remarkable woman he had ever met. But if she was still hurting, she might not rebuff the offer of his body, the consolation of his lovemaking.

Oh, leave her alone. You've already done enough damage.

His mind drifted back to the throng of women he had known, all his past instruments of pleasure.

Kate was right. He had only used them and let himself be used. Lucinda, Pauline, and the rest, names he had long since forgotten, if he had ever bothered to learn them in the first place. He'd never let them close enough to care. But Kate was unique. Only she had opened a hidden door inside the darkness of his heart and showed him another way out, a new path toward the distant light.

Love.

It seemed a bit late to be finding his courage for that now, but he was fairly sure that if he did not move, at least budge, in some direction soon, he was truly going to lose her.

"So, Papa," she was saying, "what made you finally decide to try to find the Alchemist's Tomb? Was it the lure of gold?"

Gerald nodded. "Worst decision of my life. We had no idea what we were doing." He snuffed out his pipe and set it aside. "Your mother soon tired of living at sea, Kate, and I couldn't blame her. We had you, and she wanted more children, a proper home. Settle down somewhere on dry land." He gazed into his cup of brandy. "I'm not blaming her for what happened, mind you. No. I blame myself entirely for her death."

Rohan absorbed this comment, eerily reminded of the Kilburn Curse. It seemed to be catching.

"We had always stayed away from that book due to her father's warnings in the letter. Count DuMarin wrote that that place is evil, and he was bloody right. But we got desperate. We thought that if we followed the clues in *The Alchemist's Journal* and could get into the Tomb, we might find some simple loot in there we could sell. I had hunted a few treasures before — for my own amusement, really — but I'd never seen anything like that. And of course," he added hesitantly, "there was another reason Gabrielle needed to confront that place."

"Why?"

"Ah, Katy. There are questions I never wanted to answer. But you have a right to know. And so do you, Warrington," he added, glancing at him. "It might be useful to the Order."

They had already learned that Kate's mother had told Gerald years ago all she knew about the Prometheans and the Order. The rest he had pieced together himself, after his dealings with the previous Duke of Warrington.

"What is it, Papa?" Kate murmured.

"Your mother was . . . such a fragile beauty, Kate. Like an angel, not of this world, or a delicate wounded bird. I did my best to shield her from every threat against her. But I could not save her from her own anger. God knows she had cause."

"What do you mean?"

He was silent for a long moment, avoiding their eyes. "Your mother told me that, as a child, she had been forced to take part in two terrifying Promethean rituals."

"Rituals?" she breathed.

"Black magic ceremonies of some kind. Satanic things no child should ever be exposed to," he said with difficulty. "Apparently this is what all the high-ranking Prometheans do to their children. It's how they warp their minds from an early age. She told me she was only six years old the first time she was made to participate in these unspeakable rites."

"Good God," Kate breathed, while Rohan's eyes narrowed with fury.

Six years old? The Order was aware of the enemy's bizarre cultic practices, but he'd had no idea the Prometheans subjected their own children to it. And at so young an age?

"How horrible," she breathed.

"You see, Kate," Gerald continued, "that was why it was imperative for me to hide you away as I did. I swore that what these fiends had done to my wife, they would never do to my daughter. So I changed your name and sent you off to the middle of nowhere, though close enough to turn to the Dukes of Warrington for help, if ever you should be threatened. I didn't know your sire would end up dying so soon after I set sail with Gabrielle," Gerald added, turning to Rohan.

"Nor did I," he murmured.

511

"You mean Rohan and I might have met years ago if things were different?" Kate whispered.

Gerald nodded. "Charley knew to take you to His Grace if anything happened, and you would be protected by the entire Order."

They both stared at him in amazement. He had not known of this, either. A pact apparently made by his father.

Gerald reached for her hand. "Katy, you must believe me. I never wanted to give you up. It was the hardest thing I've ever done. But you see, the Prometheans had found out about me. I was in constant danger, for years, until they finally lost interest and forgot about me. I stayed on the move, and thank God, they never learned of your existence . . . until O'Banyon betrayed me."

"Oh, Papa."

"During the time he worked for me, O'Banyon continually urged me to go back to the Tomb so we could get the gold. He had heard about it from the crew. When I continued to refuse, he decided to take matters into his own hands. He started murmuring of mutiny. That was why I had no choice but to hand him over to the hangman. I had no idea the Prometheans had the wherewithal to locate him in the bowels of Newgate. If I had known, I would have killed him myself. I refrained because for a time, he had been like a son to me. When I heard he went after you —"

"Don't, Papa. Don't berate yourself. I am all right," she assured him in a soft, determined tone. "I am not as fragile as Mama. Besides —" She glanced over at Rohan. "Somehow, my destined protector ended up guarding me, anyway, just like you originally intended."

"How did that happen, anyway?" the captain asked with a curious furrow of his brow. "I don't suppose you're goin' to tell me it was Fate?"

Rohan hardly knew where to begin in answering that one, but fortunately, Kate stepped in with a deft response. "Caleb Doyle was instrumental in it," she said vaguely, then changed the subject. "Did Mama say that *all* Promethean children have to go through these, er, dark ceremonies?"

"Yes. They were marked for life there, their future spouses chosen for them."

"I see." Kate turned and looked meaningfully at Rohan.

He understood her pointed glance at once: She meant to refer him to what he had confessed yesterday, about the children he had orphaned in his role of assassin. Like those in Naples.

The ones whose screams upon finding their father dead in the garden still haunted his troubled dreams.

Until this moment, he had never contemplated the kind of ritual nightmare he had spared those innocents from having to endure. Because of what he'd done, now they might be free . . .

The sudden shift disoriented him. His heart was pounding, his wits rather routed. Suddenly needing to be alone, he stood and nodded good night to them. "Miss Fox. Captain. I believe I shall retire."

"Good night," Kate said softly, studying him with tender concern.

He did not understand. Why was she not looking at him with horror and revulsion after seeing him slaughter half a dozen men?

"Fine work this evening, Your Grace," her father remarked with a nod good night.

"Born to it," Rohan answered under his breath. With a slight bow, he left the chartroom and went below to his cabin.

As he made his way down the dark, narrow passage of the lower deck, he preferred to blame his unsteady zigzagging on the motion of the ship, but the truth was he was shaken by this jarring rearrangement of the facts. He could almost feel the ropes that bound the guilt he carried like an anvil on his back beginning to fray . . .

Finding the tiny cabin he had been afforded as a guest on Gerald's ship, he sat down slowly on the narrow berth where he was to sleep.

He let out a long, slightly shaky exhalation and leaned forward, resting his elbows on his knees. He put his head in his hands and stared at nothing, then he shut his eyes. *What the hell is wrong with me?* In the silence, he felt like he was coming apart at the seams.

How ably he had ignored all of his emotions until Kate. It was *her* fault he had to feel these things. Before she came along, he had done quite well never thinking about it, never caring. Why did she have to make him *feel*?

The change she'd wrought in him was now putting him through Hell, for what? She was soon going to leave him, he knew it.

After all I've done for her.

His hands propping up his head clenched slowly into fists. *Damn her.* As his pulse pounded, he thought surely the least she owed him for his pains was one more night of bliss between her legs.

515

■ ■ ■ ■

Kate's emotions were in turmoil, too. Exhausted after the long night's wild events, she bade her father a weary good night with a long hug and a kiss on the cheek.

She still could not quite believe that he was right there before her, real and tangible, alive and well, as familiar as ever. After seventeen years' separation, she was astonished at how easily they got along, as if they had never been apart. Meanwhile, she refused to heed her startled hurt at his announcement about his second family. Finding him alive was reward enough.

As for his revelation about what her mother had been made to suffer as a daughter of the Prometheans, she was sickened, angry, and deeply disturbed by the news. Being on the ship again made her miss Mama even more. She kept expecting to see her everywhere. Her mother was as much a part of her memories of her former floating home as the creaking of the hull, the rocking motion of the waves, the crew's chanteys, and the familiar smells of salt and polished teakwood.

It was strange, being back again.

Pulling her shawl around her shoulders,

she left the chartroom and smiled at the sailors on the night shift who bade her good night as she crossed to the hatch.

Climbing down the ladder into the greater darkness belowdecks, she was still worried about Rohan.

She hoped what he had heard tonight from Papa gave him some peace from the guilt that haunted him. She did not envy him the great responsibility he bore. Hopefully, after a good night's rest, he would not be so coldly closed down tomorrow.

Reaching the bottom of the ladder, she turned around, but had only taken a few steps down the swaying passageway when her path was blocked by a large, formidable silhouette: Rohan stepped out of his cabin and stood waiting for her.

He loomed in the darkness ahead as she approached, his angular face cast in shadow, his black shirt hanging open down his sculpted chest.

Kate felt an instantaneous awareness of him in her most primal core, but she hesitated before the fevered intensity in his stare. "I-I thought you went to bed."

"Can't sleep."

She did not need to ask why. Who could sleep after the night he'd had? She stopped in front of him, wondering what to say. His

517

hungry gaze stayed fixed on her, and something in his silvery eyes made her heart begin to pound. "What did you think of what my father said?"

"I don't want to talk." As he reached out and cupped her cheek, Kate swallowed hard, but she hardly had to ask what he wanted to do. She could feel the heat of his need coming off him in waves.

She drew in her breath as he ran his hand down from her cheek along the side of her neck. He threaded his fingers into her hair, moving closer as he drew her toward him. He bent his head and claimed her mouth, his lips, burning, silken, against hers; she quivered with temptation as he consumed her tongue. The fierce demand in his kiss threatened to overwhelm her.

"I want you," he whispered, breathing heavily.

His bold advance jarred her somewhat back to her senses. "You must be joking," she uttered, yanking away from him and trying to hide her mad desire behind a mask of self-possession. "I'm not your harlot anymore."

"You said you love me. Prove it," he murmured. He captured her hand and brought her palm to his loins, making her feel the massive evidence of his sincerity.

She bit her lower lip, striving to reason against passion. Letting her palm linger on his rigid shaft a heartbeat too long, she withdrew her touch, determined to get around him. "Rohan."

"Sleep with me," he ordered in a whisper, too proud to beg, but then again, he'd never have to.

She looked into his glittering eyes and saw the need in his taut face. She sensed his desperation and knew that he was hard and wild enough to take it if it was not offered freely. The part of her that was still furious at him for shutting her out along with any possibility of love shouted angry protests in her mind, but it was no use.

He might not love her, but for her part, she was lost to him. If she could not win his heart, at least she could satisfy his desire. She knew he was in need tonight.

Slowly, Kate ran her hand up his bare chest and felt the thunder of his heart. He closed his eyes, visibly savoring her touch.

Her mesmerized gaze followed her hand as she inched a caress over the muscled swells of his chest, and lower, to his chiseled abdomen.

She heard his ragged exhalation. Then he gripped her forearm with a touch that would brook no denial and drew her silently into his cabin.

She thought again of refusing as he closed the door, but when she saw his thoroughly determined stare, she knew there was no point. She knew that look. The warrior. He was going to have her, and heaven help her, she wanted wholeheartedly to give in.

God, had she no pride? She was wet for him before he even touched her, lifting her chin softly with his fingertips. She closed her eyes, parted her lips, and surrendered to his feverish seduction.

The next thing she knew, she was in his arms, pinned against the wall. They were kissing roughly. She raked him with her nails, he nipped her with his teeth. She clutched his hair as he left her lips to ravish the curve of her neck, his hands working feverishly to wrench aside the bodice of her gown.

He dropped to his knees with an animal moan and proceeded to suck on her nipples like he would pleasure her for an eternity. Kate thrust the tip of her pinky between her teeth to keep from crying out.

Rohan was shaking as he rose again, freeing his rigid member from the placket of his black trousers. She skimmed her fingertips along his silken length, but his need overtook him. In no mood to play, he lifted her striped satin skirts. His breath was harsh and rasping by her ear, panting in the darkness.

He picked her up and leaned her back against the wall; she wrapped her arms and legs around him and buried her blushing face against his neck as he penetrated her.

The soft groan of sheer relief that escaped him once he was buried to the hilt inside her was the stuff of a harlot's dreams. Oh, to have the power to make him moan like that. It was beyond intoxicating. Perhaps he could corrupt her so she would just take his gold and his body and be content without his love. She caressed his powerful arms, and whispered, *"Yes, I know what you need."*

There was barely room to move, but the cabin was just large enough for what they had to accomplish. His athletic body grew damp with sweat as he made glorious use of her, heaving her up and down as if she weighed nothing, impaling her fast and vigorously on his mighty shaft.

The second she whimpered in pain when he went too deep and hurt her, he instantly slowed and withdrew a little, letting her set her feet on the wooden rail of the cot built into the opposite bulkhead.

Kate shivered, poised between pleasure and pain.

"Better?"

She nodded, her eyes closed, all of her awareness absorbed in him completely.

"Kate — I'm sorry," he whispered. At first, she thought he was only apologizing for her momentary discomfort due to his great size. But his kisses turned soulful as he began making love to her again, whispering to her with haunting desperation. "I am so sorry, Kate. Forgive me. For everything. I couldn't keep my hands off you. I still can't. All I want is to be fucking you, constantly." He closed his eyes as if he could retreat from her, even though they were one. He went motionless, still deep inside her body. "Help me, Kate. I'm drowning."

"Oh, darling, I know." She encircled his broad shoulders in her arms and held him. "I'm here. It's all right."

"No, it's not. The last thing I ever wanted was to hurt you, but I know I did. I can't — I *am* the curse."

"That isn't true!" she whispered, cupping his cheek in tender chiding. "Look at me. Sweeting, you must fight this darkness. Don't despair," she cajoled him in the most intimate whisper. "There is hope for you."

"I doubt it."

"You always doubt, but I believe. That's

why you need me, whether you can see it or not."

"I'm beginning to."

"Look at me," she ordered softly as she leaned her head against the wall behind her.

Slowly, he obeyed. Lifting his lashes, he gazed into her eyes. "Keep looking at me, Rohan." She held his stare as he continued making love to her. "I love you. God, I love you, past all reason." She felt him trembling with emotion, but she needed him to know here and now that this was not a liaison with just anyone.

This time, he was with someone who loved him beyond the point of all reckoning. A woman who'd fight for him, who, she feared, would even die for him, gladly, if it came down to it. "Yes," she breathed as she petted him, soothing away his grief. "Give it all to me, darling. I can take it. I know who you are."

She saw the torment and the heavy haze of pleasure in his eyes, still holding his stormy gaze as he reached his climax.

He held her in a crushing embrace, looking helplessly into her eyes as he filled her body with the life-giving liquid of his seed. His massive thrusts in release caressed her core so deeply that she, too, achieved her climax, succumbing to the mind-melting wonder of their total union.

Moments later, she took him into her arms and held him as they rested against the wall, panting in mutual relief.

Rohan laid his head on her shoulder, burying his face in her hair and into the crook of her neck, as though, just for a moment, he wanted to hide from the world.

She gave him the shelter he sought, not asking any questions, unable to think of any good advice to help him carry the countless burdens that he bore. All she had left to give him in the silence was her love, even though he had claimed he didn't want it. She stroked his hair and comforted him with her touch as best she could.

He lifted his head at length, gazed into her eyes, then pressed the sweetest of kisses to her lips.

She captured his face between her hands and gave him one just like it in return. He withdrew slowly from her body and steadied her as he helped her step back down onto the floor.

He fastened his trousers as Kate righted her dress, but without a word, he drew her into his arms again and held her for the longest time, just hugging her, lost in his thoughts, tenderly stroking her hair. She sighed in contentment with her head against his chest.

"Am I evil, Kate?" he asked at length. "You must decide it for me. I can no longer tell."

"No, of course not. You are not evil, and you are not cursed. But I suppose . . . I do fear for you, if you continue to ignore your heart."

"My alleged heart," he drawled in a low, world-weary tone. "If you must know, it's all but broken by the darkness of this world."

"Then let me mend it."

"I've been trained since I was just a small boy to fight this evil your father speaks of. But I have not been untouched by it."

"I know, darling."

"Do you?" He stopped her from embracing him again, looking somberly into her eyes. "What you saw tonight was not unusual for me."

"I realize that. I'm not naïve. You're a warrior, Rohan. You come from a long line of them. It's in your blood. That doesn't scare me."

"It should. I'm a killer, Kate."

"No. If men like you did not exist, who would oppose the wicked? Besides, I have firsthand knowledge of your true honor."

"You still find me honorable even after I

lured you into a devil's bargain so I could justify seducing you?" he murmured, studying her.

"Oh, Rohan, silly duke." She laughed softly at him and cupped his face in her hand. "I know full well you did it to protect me." She shook her head at him. "I have to go." She turned around and crossed the tiny room in two steps, reaching for the door.

"Kate," he whispered.

She paused, but did not look back. With her hand on the door, listening to him with every fiber of her being, willing him now to, please, God, let him say he loved her.

"Those other women, they never even knew me. Not like you do."

She glanced back at him with a guarded smile that hid her disappointment. He stared at her, his expression somber. Struggling for patience, she gazed at his fierce pale eyes, and the scar above his eyebrow, and his irresistible lips. He was so amazingly good at some things and a walking disaster at others.

But she must find the strength to be gentle with him. It wasn't entirely his fault he was like this. He'd been taught from an early age to keep the world at bay. At least he was trying. "I'm glad you let me know the real you," she finally answered.

He slid his hands into his pockets like a rueful schoolboy and shrugged. "I can't believe you didn't run."

"Perhaps I should have." She cast him a wan half smile. "But, unfortunately, we were stuck in that castle together. And before I knew it, I found out you weren't half-bad. Good night, my love. I daresay you should be able to sleep now."

His smile flashed white in the darkness. "Like a babe." When she turned to go, he ran his finger down her back, sending dangerous shivers through her that could almost tempt her to stay. "Good night, sweetheart."

She sent him a heated glance over her shoulder, but gathered her resolve, and stepped out into the passageway.

Where the first thing she saw was her father waiting for her to come out.

Kate froze. She felt the blood drain from her face and her stomach plummet all the way down to her feet.

Gerald Fox was leaning across from Rohan's door with an ominous scowl on his face, arms folded across his chest.

Kate began stammering, but he ignored her.

"Warrington," her ex-Marine, ex-pirate father growled.

"Er, Captain."

Rohan stood behind her with his shirt hanging open and his long hair as tousled as her own, and it could not have been more obvious what they had been doing.

"How dare you?" her father uttered, glaring past her at him. *"You blackguard!"*

She planted herself in the doorway of Rohan's cabin, fearing violence. "Papa —"

"Debauch my daughter under my very nose?" His green eyes blazed by the distant lantern's flicker of light. "You should be ashamed, sir! It will not stand, do you hear me? This is unacceptable!"

"Papa, please. We are both adults. Let's not overreact —"

"Be quiet!" he roared at her. "Your mother would be appalled at you, acting like a hussy!"

Kate blinked, but Papa returned his furious attention to her seducer.

"For shame, Warrington! You're supposed to be protecting the girl, not using her for your harlot!"

"I beg your pardon!" Kate's cheeks flamed as embarrassment flooded her at his words, but her sire wasn't finished.

He pointed a threatening finger at Rohan. "Your father ruined my life; you will not ruin my daughter's! I don't give a damn for your rank. You will marry her, do you understand me?"

"Papa!"

"Stay out of this, girl —"

"No, *you* stay out of it!" she shouted without warning.

He looked her up and down in outrage, but Kate's temper snapped. "Leave him alone! I've managed just fine these past many years without a father, so don't think you can come barging into my life and immediately tell me whom to marry!"

"Oho, so you do reproach me?" he exclaimed. "I knew it!"

"You sailed off and forgot about me!" she cried.

"I did not!"

"You went on with your life! Your new family. Well, I went on with mine, too," she flung out as the anger burst from her more sharply than she had intended. "Warrington is my lover. So what? Welcome to the world."

Incredulous at her cynical words — words she had borrowed from Rohan — her father turned to him. "What have you done to her?"

He was staring at her as he murmured, "I'm not entirely sure."

"Ugh! I'm going to bed." Abandoning the doorway she had been blocking, Kate dropped her arms to her sides and slipped past her father, then began marching away.

"Kate — maybe your father's right."

She stopped, closing her eyes, for the stoic resignation in his tone caused a great pang in her heart. She turned around slowly.

Rohan had come out into the passageway, and when she saw his face, her fleeting hope sank even lower. His expression was as grim as a man's who had just been sentenced to a hanging at dawn. He swallowed hard. "Maybe it's better we wed."

"You cannot be serious," she uttered in quiet, flabbergasted rage. "*This* is your proposal? *Now* you would agree to it, just because he says so? Do you think I don't know how you really feel? No, thank you — Your Grace! Not like this! Never!"

"Kate —"

"No! Do you hear me? Absolutely, unequivocally — *no!* God, I can't take any more." Shaking with fury, she started to stride away, but blinded by tears, and not having gained her sea legs yet, she bumped into the passageway, accidentally knocking a life ring off the wall.

With a sound of exasperation, she caught the durable white ring as it fell on her.

"Kate — don't go storming off." Rohan had started toward her.

"Stay away from me!" She hurled the life ring at him. "Just — leave me alone! Both of you! I'm not interested in your charity, Duke! Remember yesterday?"

The dolt had surely had not forgotten her hurling his money at his head.

"As for you, Papa, you forfeited the right to pick my husband when you had Charley lie to me and tell me you were dead. So, kill each other if you like. You're both fools, as far as I'm concerned!"

With a furious sob, she ran the rest of the way to her cabin, leaving the two oddly similar men behind in awkward, stymied silence.

CHAPTER 19

What have you done to her? Days later, the question still haunted Rohan as he readied himself to face the Alchemist's Tomb, but the answer, he feared, was unavoidable. He had turned his wild Dartmoor darling into a woman of the world.

He knew his dutiful offer of marriage had been unsatisfactory in terms of sentiment, yet he was stunned by the vehemence of her furious refusal.

She had hardly spoken to him since, and the fact was, he really couldn't blame her. He barely knew what to do with himself with Kate not talking to him. If this was a taste of what life would be like without her, he wanted no part of it. Something had to be done.

For good or ill, Rohan knew his course was clear. He had to get into that Tomb, find a way to break the Kilburn Curse, win Kate back if she had not lost all respect for him by now, and only then, make her *safely* his — forever.

Resolved to tread this precarious path, though he had railed against ever marrying just a few days ago in the music room — more bullheaded than the bloody Minotaur — he ignored the inner howling of his superstitious fears, armed himself with the full complement of guns and knives that he had taken to the docklands, then threw a warm scarf around his neck and slipped on the long, heavy sealskin coat that Gerald had lent him.

It was nearly waterproof, as well as being the warmest choice available. The Orkney archipelago lay only six degrees below the Arctic Circle, after all. Daylight lasted but a few short hours this time of year.

Collecting a few more supplies, Rohan threw them into a sturdy knapsack, anything he could think of that he might possibly need, but what did you take to a battle against a dead sorcerer and his horde of conjured demons?

Ballocks. Stop it. He scowled at his own idiotic imaginings. This was most unlike him. But God's truth, he was ever so slightly rattled. He feared if he did not get his irrational notions under control, he was going to make a stupid mistake and get himself killed.

Knowing he still had to get *The Alchemist's Journal* with all the clues in it from Kate, he glanced at his fob watch and saw it would soon be dawn.

Almost time to disembark.

Thanks to Fox's masterful sailing and more square footage of canvas on the frigate than on the enemy's schooner, they had passed the Prometheans two days ago, but their lead was not great.

He had to act fast. Though doing this in the predawn darkness posed added challenges, Rohan wished to avoid being spotted going into the Alchemist's Tomb, just in case Mr. Tewkes had forgotten which of the many caves in the area was the actual entrance. There was no need to let Falkirk see which one it was.

"I am not looking forward to this," Rohan grumbled to the air with a disgruntled look as he pulled on a black knit hat, followed by thick, heavy, leather gloves. Tossing the knapsack over his shoulder, he trudged up on deck.

He lifted his fur-lined hood against the bone-chilling wind whistling through the yardarms.

He spotted Kate at the rails with her

father. She, too, was dressed in a long sealskin coat, with the hood pulled up to block the bitter breeze from her face. Using her father's telescope, she was looking out to sea.

The moment he clamped his gaze on her, Rohan felt relief spread through his entire body, warming him. He knew she had come up on deck to see him off, and he was utterly grateful. How he would find the strength to say good-bye to her, he did not know. He had a sick feeling in the pit of his stomach that he might never see her again.

If they were ever going to be able to be together, though, first he had to do this.

Stalking toward her through the crisp, chilled darkness, he glanced at the rugged grandeur of the sentinel cliffs looming nearby. The rocky crags were covered in hardy northern seafowl sending up a clamor while others dove for their breakfast of fish. There were no penguins at this latitude, but thousands of puffins and terns, along with gulls and cormorants.

The moon had sunk low over the ocean, but its silver glitter played across the dark water and gleamed on floating platforms of ice that seals rode over the waves before flopping back into the water.

Kate laughed softly at the creatures'

antics; he could feel her merry mood and thought it odd under the circumstances as he joined her and her father at the rails.

He nodded to Gerald, who was clad in a bearskin coat, then he noticed that Kate had her boots on, and realized she must have donned her old footman costume again. No doubt the breeches and livery coat were warmer than the satin gown that he feared was her only other option. The poor girl still had no decent wardrobe of her own.

He heaved a sigh, wistful for the chance to spoil her as he had earlier planned.

"So glum this morning, Your Grace?" she inquired, still peering through the telescope.

She must've heard his sigh. He just looked at her, leaning his elbow on the rail. As long as he lived, he would never get used to her cheeky humor. Or find another like her.

"I thought facing certain doom was your idea of fun," she said, turning to him.

"Right," he murmured, masking his joy that at least she was speaking to him this morning. "Thanks for the reminder. You're up early."

"Look. Whales." She pointed past the seals, then offered her telescope.

He shook his head. "I'm more concerned about the Promethean ship. Where are they?"

"They've just entered visual range," Gerald said.

"Then I'd best be going."

"The small-boat's ready whenever you are, Warrington."

"Did you know Orkney was a favorite stop of Viking ships along their voyages?"

"She's been at the almanac again," her sire said dryly.

Rohan succumbed to a fond grin. "Our little bluestocking."

"There's your marker. The Dragon Ring." Gerald pointed to the hilltop, where a circle of giant standing stones dusted in snow rose against the starry sky, ancient, enigmatic, and foreboding. "The entrance to the cave is just across that cove, aligned with the tallest stone. Under that stone arch, you see?"

Rohan nodded, staring at the dramatic rock formation. The stone arch at the base of the towering rocky outcropping was very low, barely visible, except between the white-capped waves that crashed against it.

"Mind you, there are boulders all over the place, and with all these seals, likely sharks in the water, so be careful. When you approach the cave entrance, you won't have much room to slip under that arch," Gerald warned. "You'll have to row in on the trough of a wave. If you hit it on the crest, it'll capsize you. The water calms once inside the cave, but have your lanterns ready. It's pitch-dark. You remember what I told you about that Shark's Mouth contraption?"

Rohan nodded.

"Good. Once you're in, I'll sail out to meet those blackguards and engage them. It'll give me great pleasure to blow them out o' the water," Gerald added heartily.

Rohan had every confidence in the hardened captain's ability to sink the Promethean ship. "What about your bo'sun?"

"I'll be sending my men in the small-boats to retrieve Tewkes once I've demasted her."

Rohan nodded. "Fox, they've taken one of our agents. A man called Drake. He was the one guarding Falkirk at the docks. Did you see him?"

"Aye."

"If your men are able to pick him up when they rescue Tewkes, I'd be obliged."

"Take him captive?"

"It would be helpful. Be sure and keep him in your brig if you do manage to grab him. Be careful of him — truly. He is as highly trained to make mischief as I am," he said dryly. "If anything happens to me, send word to my manservant in London, Eldred.

He'll contact the appropriate people to come and collect Drake from you."

"I'll do as you ask if I can, but I'm not making any promises."

Rohan nodded. *So be it.* Part of him thought it might be just as well for Drake to die. From what he had seen of him in the docklands, serving as James Falkirk's human shield, it would certainly appear that their agent had switched sides. If Drake had turned against them, the hard fact was he was going to have to be eliminated along with their enemies.

Rohan hoped he would not regret sparing him.

"I can't believe I'm here," Kate murmured, shaking her head at the bleak, timeless landscape before her. "It's as if we've gone to the far end of the earth."

He glanced at her with a pang, knowing the moment of their parting had arrived. "Well, you wanted adventure, didn't you?"

"I certainly did," she murmured as she handed the telescope back to her father. "That's why I've decided to go with you."

"What?"

"I'm going with you," she repeated.

"No, you're not!" he and Fox answered in unison.

"Of course, I am," she said reasonably,

lifting the knapsack by her feet and throwing it onto her shoulder. "I've come this far, haven't I?"

"Kate, you are not going in there."

Her stubborn gaze met his. "You need me in there with you, and we both know it."

"Out of the question! You listen to me, young lady," her father blustered. "That evil place took your mother from me. I'll not lose you, as well!"

"Papa, you know I have to do this. You can't stop me. This is my decision."

"It's madness!" Gerald cried, paling. "What are you trying to prove? It won't bring her back!"

"I know that, but at least then I will have some answers. This is the reason you made sure to have me educated like a son, remember? I can do this, Papa. Rohan, I'll be waiting in the boat."

"You are staying here," he replied.

Anger flashed across her face. "Haven't you two realized yet that you don't run my life? That place killed my mother! Besides, I have a right — the Alchemist is my ancestor, not yours — and also, I'm the only one who has figured out the clues."

"Kate, I don't know what sort of deviltry I may face in there. I'm sorry, but this time, considering I have no idea what I'm getting into, I don't want to be responsible for having to protect you."

"With all due respect, Your Grace, I'm the one who'll be protecting you on this occasion. You're a warrior, not a scholar, Rohan. I've been studying this book, and I've already decoded the clues. You don't stand a chance without me."

"Just give them to me."

"No! I'm going in with you. Now, if you prefer to survive the fiendish obstacle course that lies beyond that cave, quit wasting time arguing with me, because my mind will not be changed. For that matter, the Prometheans will be here soon. So, let's *go*!" With that, she pivoted on her heel and marched off toward the small-boat.

Once more, she had left him and her father stymied, not sure what to say.

"She's very determined," Rohan finally muttered.

"Wish I could say she takes after her mother, but I'm afraid she's a bit too much like me."

"You think?" Rohan drawled, eyeing him askance.

Gerald turned to him and stared sternly into his eyes. "Warrington, you keep her alive."

"I will," he vowed.

"Be careful." Gerald offered him his hand.

Rohan shook it, then took leave of him with a grave nod, heading for the boat. This, he thought, was a bad idea. But there was no denying the fact that his heart secretly rejoiced. He could not believe she had opted to come with him into the jaws of death rather than sailing off with her father.

Gerald followed him over to the chain-suspended rowboat where she already waited. The captain leaned toward her, gave his daughter a quick hug and a kiss on the forehead. "God keep you, darlin'."

"Don't worry, Papa. The Beast and I will do just fine as long as we stick together. Now go fire up those cannons," she added, flashing a pirate grin while Rohan settled himself across from her in the little vessel.

Seeing that they were securely seated, Gerald signaled to his crew to begin lowering the boat.

"Hold on, stay still," Rohan warned her, as they waited for the chains to start lowering them into the cold and treacherous North Sea. He looked into her eyes. "I know why you're doing this."

She merely raised an eyebrow. "Did you think I would desert you?"

Then the boat was dropping, dropping, the cranks turning, the chains grinding, the winches lowering them to the waves. He already had the oars in his hands and was instantly fighting the swirling waters.

The waves jostled them up and down, side to side. Kate held on tightly while he got the rowboat under control. He put his back into it and immediately began rowing toward the cave.

Seals watched them pass, but were more interested in barking at each other and enjoying the spray of the white-caps that broke against the boulders where they lounged.

The boat tilted as a taller wave passed under them.

Kate blanched and kept her balance, while Rohan glanced over his shoulder to keep them on course.

"Did you see that?" she cried suddenly, pointing to the water. He glanced over just in time to see a tall fin slicing through the brine before it disappeared, passing beneath the boat — and rather dwarfing it.

"Bloody hell," he whispered. Even a seasoned assassin had to bow to the killing expertise of the average shark.

Kate's eyes were saucerlike. "Oh God, don't let us capsize, Rohan."

"Don't worry, they're more interested in the seals than in us," he assured her with a bit more conviction than he felt. No doubt the Tomb's builders had selected this remote spot knowing the sharks, silent guardians gliding through the waves, would serve as another deterrent for keeping intruders away.

The stone arch was fast approaching, but getting into position took considerable finesse on the oars. Maneuvering the boat closer, he brought them about ten feet from the archway, but it was impossible to hold the boat still with the water bucking under them. The complex arrangement of boulders outside the cave's mouth divided the waves and brought in currents from many directions. The frigid air stung his lungs, and the morning twilight made it even trickier to gauge the timing.

"Duck down into the boat when I tell you!" he shouted to her over the loud surf and the barking of the seals and the shrill cacophony of the water birds. "As soon as we're in, be ready to open the lantern!"

"I will!"

"Hold on!"

Kate looked into his eyes and nodded with a look of faith in him that gave him the final jolt of strength he needed to time the trough of the wave and throw all he had into the oars.

"Get down!"

They both ducked low as the boat glided under the sandstone arch, already beginning to rise as another wave followed ceaselessly.

It was pitch-dark inside the echoing cave. Rohan's heart was still pounding from his exertions as Kate opened the little metal shutters on the oil lamp.

Like her father had said, the waves were tamed inside the shelter of the cave. The interior of the cavern was extremely tall and tapered toward the top. As the boat drifted over to a smooth, man-made landing, they looked at each other in wary relief.

"Well," Kate said with forced cheer, "so far, so good."

"Kate?" He locked the oars into place and gave her a rueful smile. "I am glad you are with me," he admitted.

She grinned. "I know. So, was that the ordeal my father meant by the Shark's Mouth?"

"No, that is." He lifted up his lantern, showing her the giant head of a shark statue carved into the rock.

"Ohhh . . ."

They climbed out of the boat. While Kate stood marveling at the sculpture, Rohan went over to a large wooden handle that angled up out of the floor.

"Your father told me a little about how this thing works. You'd better stand back. Farther," he warned. He waited until she had backed away before he pushed the handle forward into the opposite position.

Instantly, the cavern was filled with a low rumbling sound of stone grinding against stone. The solid wall inside the shark's mouth rolled aside, revealing a dark tunnel about twenty feet long, with a second stone portal on the far end, which had also opened.

But while throwing the handle opened the doors, it also activated the swordlike rows of blades that began slamming out of their housings, grinding up and down in the Shark's Mouth like giant teeth.

Kate stared while Rohan edged closer, holding up his lantern to examine the task before him. Gerald had sworn there was just enough room to catch one's balance after getting past each row of blades.

The first row of "teeth" had an up-and-down chomping motion, while the second row thrust in horizontally from both sides. Beyond that, the third and final layer, certainly the least appealing, was made up of two large circular blades, which were fitted too neatly into the width of the passage to allow a would-be intruder to slip past on either side.

He was going to have to dive between them.

"Please tell me this isn't what killed my mother."

"No. They made it into the chamber beyond this, but no farther." He had to speak loudly over the metallic churning clamor of the wickedly ingenious mechanism.

Its unseen gears and weights still worked as efficiently as a fine Swiss watch or one of those gilded dining-table automata that the Regent so adored.

Virgil, with his fancy for all sorts of mechanical tinkering, would have loved it, Rohan thought. His Scots mind was very keen on all sorts of engineering.

"I'll go through first and turn it off. There's a second handle on the other end of the tunnel that shuts off the blades. Then you'll be able to follow. But you're going to have to move quickly," he warned. "The doors close in thirty seconds after the blades are stopped. Got that?"

She nodded with a wary frown.

He put down his knapsack, slipped off his coat, then discarded his scarf, as well. He turned again, watching the timing of the noisy, rhythmic blades.

"Quite a welcome, isn't it?" Kate took his hand — a touch he would never forget. "Be careful, all right?"

"Don't worry." He lifted hers and kissed her knuckles in spite of her heavy gloves, then gave her a reassuring smile. He had no intention of getting killed today.

Especially when he knew that if anything happened to him, she would not be strong enough to handle the rowboat in those wild waters in order to get herself out of here and back to her father's ship.

"Don't touch anything. Just hold up the light so I can see what I'm doing."

She nodded and quickly lifted both their lanterns high. Rohan moved closer and studied the obstacle course of gleaming blades a moment longer. As with getting into the cave, it was a question of timing.

Most of the length of the chomping blades withdrew into the ceiling and floor between every "bite" of the shark. He took a deep breath, rubbed his hands together, gathered himself, then leaped through the first row of blades; he landed and froze, avoiding any pitch forward into the next set of teeth. They were less than a foot ahead of him, stabbing in from the right and the left simultaneously.

This one was easier. Once more, he chose his instant, dodging past the thrusting blades. They clanged behind him.

"Are you all right?" Kate called frantically.

"Fine!" *Though this last one could take my leg off. Or worse.* Pausing to catch his breath, he eyed the rotary blades whirling before him like serrated wheels laid flat on their sides. They were set at about the level of his chest and knees. It would every ounce of his physical prowess to dive through the space between them without being chopped into a fricassee.

"How does it look?" Kate called.

"Charming!" With a mental prayer, he crouched down and stared past the two lower blades into the small stone chamber on the other side. He could see that the passage continued beyond it, but Gerald had told him this was the last of the blades.

His heart pounded faster, the seconds slowing down: With a sudden blast of power that started in his legs, he stretched his arms out ahead of him and arrowed his body in between the blades. He felt the breeze of them flutter against his face as he sailed through, landing on his hands in the far chamber, curling into a smooth roll.

"Rohan?" Kate shouted.

"I'm through!" he called back.

"Yes!" she cheered, as he got to his feet, his chest heaving. He glanced around, spotted the second handle, and pulled it; immediately, the blades stopped and withdrew back into their housings.

"Hurry, Kate! Thirty seconds!"

She ran through, scrambling to bring along his coat and the other items he had left behind. To his relief, she was safely through the tunnel when the great stone doors began grinding closed again.

Handing him his knapsack of supplies, Kate glanced toward the passage ahead. "Ready?"

He nodded and put his coat back on. They exchanged a look of relief, then pressed on. The tunnel continued for a few more yards, but Kate stopped, glancing to the right.

"There's light coming in over there. It must be daybreak." She pointed. "And a mirror?"

"Hm. Shutter your lamp for a second."

They both turned down their lanterns, allowing them to better see the single, delicate beam of dawn sunlight glowing down a narrow shaft in the rock overhead.

The feeble ray of sunlight was captured on a large, round, concave mirror on a stand, and the angle of it bounced the light toward a little waterfall ahead.

"Hold on . . . this reminds me of one of the clues in the *Journal*. I think we're meant to go through there."

He glanced at her uncertainly, then they followed the beam of light to the shimmering cascade's edge. They lifted the hoods of their sealskin coats and stepped through the fine sheen of icy water spilling through the rock.

The small stone chamber behind the waterfall had nothing remarkable in it except a brass plaque set into the wall with a dial in the center. Peering at it, Rohan turned up his lantern again and saw that the dial was surrounded by Greek letters. "It's some sort of combination lock."

"Am I off-kilter, or does the floor slope in here?" Kate murmured, then she glanced at the pile of rocks at the bottom of the incline.

"It slopes," he said, but she had suddenly gone very quiet.

"This is where my mother died. Those rocks . . ."

"I'm sorry," he offered, then he pointed to the stone ceiling above the plaque. "Your father said if you enter the wrong answer on this dial, a chute opens briefly and rains down rocks on your head. Enough to kill you."

Kate stared at the pile of rocks that had

taken her mother's life. Her face hardened with anger as she lowered her head. "Then I'd better not make a mistake." She took *The Alchemist's Journal* out of her knapsack and opened it.

Rohan held the lantern so she could find the page she was looking for. He searched her face in concern while he waited, but her grief for her mother had hardened into resolve.

She still did not look at him, searching the book, as she murmured, "How did my father and his men get out of here, especially if they had to carry my mother's body?"

"He told me they used some ropes and pulleys from the ship and got out through that shaft where we saw the beam of light coming in. But he said the gap is extremely narrow and the approach is even more difficult than the cave."

"I see." She swallowed hard. "Ah, here it is." She read the clue aloud to him: " 'Once through the silver veil you pass, speak your vows into the looking glass.' "

"Hm." Rohan pushed back his coat to rest his hand loosely on the butt of a pistol at his hip. "We've already passed the mirror. The silver veil must be the waterfall. So, now what?"

"Speak your vow . . . the vow of the

Prometheans, surely," she said. " 'I will not serve.' *Non serviam.* But we've only got Greek letters on this dial, so, translated to Greek, that would be . . ."

"Wait! 'Into the looking glass,' " he repeated. "You have to do it —"

"Backwards," she finished with him in a thoughtful tone. "Right." Kate took off her right glove and lifted her hand to the dial.

"You, er, did well in Greek, did you?"

She sent him a wry look askance. "Trust me."

He stood by, watching her every move as she turned the dial back and forth between the Greek letters, talking to herself under her breath a bit. He also kept an ear cocked for any worrisome sounds from the man-made rockslide above them. If he heard any hint of an untoward rumble overhead, he was ready to throw Kate out of the way in a trice.

"Almost . . . there," she murmured, engrossed in her work. "Theta, nu, epsilon . . ."

"What's supposed to happen?"

"Not sure, but I think we're about to find about. Here — delta." She turned the dial to the last Greek letter, and they both jumped out of the way as a mighty reverberation began to shake the little chamber.

From inside the mountain came a new mechanical churning noise like that of the shark's mouth blades, but much more forceful. He could feel the echo of it pounding in his chest.

"Uh-oh," Kate whispered.

Instead of rocks falling from above, the solid stone wall of the cave split before them and began rolling apart, opening up a large, hidden doorway.

A gust of stale air poured out of the pitch-black space beyond. The mechanical rumbling grew louder.

"What the devil's in there?" Kate cried.

"I have no idea. Let's go take a look." Rohan braced himself, put a protective arm around her, and led her forward.

All he could see at first were broad, shallow steps carved into the stone, but he had an impression of a vast, cavernous hall, large enough to swallow up the dim illumination from their lanterns.

They were barely through the door and starting cautiously up the stone steps when the cave wall began closing behind them. It shut again, sealing them into the pitch-darkness of the Alchemist's Tomb, alone with a sharp pungent odor and the loud, churning sound, the source of which he could not begin to guess. It sounded like some sort of waterwheel like those that powered riverside mills and factories.

"It's choking in here!" she exclaimed. "What is that acrid smell?"

"Turpentine, maybe? Oil?" Opening up his lantern all the way, Rohan held it high and caught a tantalizing glimpse of tall statues in the darkness.

"I wish we could see what we're doing."

"Stay here for a second. I think I understand . . ."

He found his way over to a waist-high wall with a low channel built into the top of it, inside which sat few sluggish inches of liquid. Rohan dipped his finger into the liquid and felt the greasy texture of it. "Just as I thought. I need a piece of paper. Any pages of that book you can spare?"

"From the book, are you mad? Here. Take a page from my notes. Why?"

"I need it for a match." He quickly rolled the piece of paper into a little scroll, opened his lantern, and put the end of the paper into the flame; when it caught, he brought it over to the waist-high wall and lowered it into the channel.

At once, the oil in the channel ignited.

Flames burst into life all along the wall, following the channel's rectangular course around the vast room. The flames continued around the rest of the room, until the great torch over the archway burst into flames.

The torch formed the apex of an arch where two great statues were joined. Carved from black marble, the two figures framed the hall's entrance like great columns. On the left was a giant Prometheus, whose facial features looked suspiciously demonic. He was depicted handing the torch to a smaller, but still Herculean statue of a man.

Both figures grasped the handle of the torch, which continued to burn overhead as Kate and Rohan advanced slowly into the great chamber.

"I think we've found the Hall of Fire," she murmured.

"It would appear so," he agreed with a sardonic nod.

"This was mentioned in the *Journal*. Lord, look at all this loot! O'Banyon was right."

Treasure abounded in the now-fully-illuminated Hall of Fire. Walking deeper into the chamber, they were surrounded by dazzling riches, mounds of gold, open chests full of glittering coins from bygone eras, jewels, crowns, scepters, swords of power, gold and silver cloth, a throne, ancient vases and jeweled cups, classical statues no doubt worth a fortune. There was even a chariot that looked like it might have belonged to the likes of Alexander the Great.

"Don't. Touch. Anything," Rohan warned. "I'm sure it's all rigged in a most disagreeable way."

"What is that thing?" Kate pointed straight ahead to the source of the churning noise. "Some sort of giant astronomical clock?"

"The Wheel of Time," Rohan murmured, staring grimly at it. "Like you saw in the symbol of the Initiate's Brand."

At the far end of the hall, the giant astronomical clock kept on revolving like a millwheel ducking between two pools of fire.

Beside him, Kate studied it through narrowed eyes. "What do we do with it?"

"I'm not sure. Come on. We'll figure it out."

As they neared it, he saw that the Wheel was covered in a metal casing engraved with Roman numerals, astrological symbols, a display of lunar phases, and more odd figures.

Following its turning with his gaze, he noticed a narrow footbridge suspended above the Wheel and realized what they had to do. "I believe we're to catch hold of the bar and let the Wheel carry us each up to that walkway up there." He pointed at it.

"Oh." She nodded, then glanced at him. "Isn't that whole thing made out of metal?

It must be getting hotter with every pass through the fire. Of course, if you let go, you fall into those pools of flame."

"I'm more concerned about that next set of giant gears the Wheel runs into. You see, at about the two o'clock position?"

"Hm, yes. I wonder which of these devices they operate." She folded her arms across her chest as she studied it. "So, if we let go too soon, we'll be roasted, and if we hold on too long, we'll be ground up into mincemeat."

"Sounds about right."

"Not to mention that flimsy little walkway up there looks treacherous at best. It's suspended in midair, and I don't see a railing."

"I'll go first," he said grimly. "Maybe somewhere up there is a way to shut this thing off, like the last one."

"But if you shut it off, I'll be stuck down here. I can do this, Rohan. You don't have to be so madly protective of me all the time, you know."

"Haven't you noticed protecting you is the whole reason for my existence these days?" he drawled. "You mean the world to me, Kate. No matter what you might think."

She smiled uncertainly at him. "Go on, then. I'll be all right down here. I promise."

He glanced toward the approach to the Wheel, down a short walkway flanked on both sides by shallow rectangular pools of burning oil.

"I'll see you up there in a moment," he assured her as he turned away. But separating from her in this strange place even for a moment was the most difficult thing he had done in a very long time.

"Go on. Impress me," she teased, seeing his hesitation.

He turned around and stared at her, and when she sent him a roguish wink, he was lost. *I adore you.*

He shook his head at her in amusement, then steeled himself, and turned to face the Wheel. He eyed the handle, getting into position like a runner before a race.

Go!

Taking a few running steps, he leaped up on it. The bar was hot, though not yet too hot to touch. He held on to it firmly as it rose toward the walkway overhead. He did not look down, but gathered himself to leap onto the walkway above.

At exactly the right moment, he swung himself onto the narrow footbridge above and let go of the handle. The Wheel churned on as Rohan stopped the impetus of his forceful motion, rolling onto the walkway.

The high, suspended footbridge was unstable; it swayed a bit under his weight, and to make matter worse, it caught a strong cross-draft from somewhere that shook the whole thing and added to the dizzying effect.

He let out a low exhalation finding himself poised above a great hollow pit that dropped away into the mountain. There were more odd devices in the darkness beyond, but he paid them little mind for now, more concerned about getting Kate safely next to him again.

"Bravo!" she called from below in a rather shaky tone, seeing that it was her turn.

"Don't dally," he warned. "That handle's getting hot. Your impulse will be to let go, but don't."

"Maybe I should leave my gloves on?"

"I'd take them off," he called back. "It might be too slippery. Hurry up, I'm getting lonely up here!"

"Coming!" He watched her put the *Journal* back into her knapsack. She took off her gloves and threw them in, too, then she closed her lantern and attached it to her knapsack.

His heart pounded. "You can do this, Kate." He crouched down, positioning himself to grab her off the Wheel.

With his heart in his throat, Rohan watched her suddenly bolt down the walkway just as he had, her knapsack and lantern banging against her back. She grabbed the handle and let out a small cry of pain at the growing heat of the metal bar, but she held on, and in the next instant, the Wheel was carrying her up, up, toward the walkway, toward him.

"Hang on!" he shouted. "Don't look down!" He stared wildly as she neared. "That's good. Not yet. A little more." He reached out to help her. "Let go! I've got you!"

She leaped onto the walkway with a small cry. He guided her with his right hand, then threw his weight atop her to stop her from rolling off the other side.

He could not save her lantern, however. It flew free and went hurtling down into the blackness of the pit. They both stared at the tiny light until it disappeared.

"Thanks!" she panted, then she glanced past him, her eyes widening. "So that's what the other gears operate!"

He turned to see what she was staring at, and as much as he despised the Prometheans, even he was impressed. A giant clockwork orrery whirled through the great, black, empty pit before them. Planets and their moons mounted on octopus-like metal arms revolved speedily around a replica of the sun, but the workings of the complex metal structure were shrouded in the darkness below.

A few small chinks in the mountain let in narrow slivers of sunbeams that gave a better view of the whole bizarre contraption. Strandy bits of thin black gauze trailed from the ceiling like disintegrating banners and wafted in the draft.

Past the solar system model across the pit, on the far end of the cavern, sat a replica of an Egyptian pyramid, about the size of a three-story building.

Rohan stared as an incredulous realization began flooding every atom of his being.

Kate happened to glance at him and noticed his stricken stare into the pit. "What's the matter?" she asked quickly.

He stared at the orrery and blankly shook his head. "It's . . . all mechanical. It's all just clever gadgetry. There's nothing super-natural about — any of this!" he burst out with an angry gesture at the orrery.

Kate tilted her head with a quizzical look. "I know."

He scoffed in amazement, but his eyes were finally opened to the truth, now that he had seen the Alchemist's Tomb for himself. The phantoms and demons he had feared did not exist; they were just the shapes with which his own superstitious mind had animated his guilt, that false condemnation he had carried for so long, which Gerald's revelation about the Promethean children had already begun to reverse.

The insight left him astounded. "You were right," he murmured as he stared into the pit. "It was all just an excuse . . . There is no truth to the Kilburn Curse. Is there? There never was. I hid behind it." He swallowed hard. "Because I didn't think that anyone could ever really love me."

"Well, you were wrong about that," she told him softly, bringing him back to the moment at hand.

When he turned to her, at a loss, she touched his arm in reassurance and shook her head with a tender half smile.

"I feel like such a fool!" he murmured, running his hand through his hair. "You saw it all along."

"Don't worry about that now," she soothed. "Let's just figure out how to get across here, all right?"

Her gentle redirection in that moment was the final evidence that convinced him, if there was any doubt left in his suspicious brain, that Kate's love was real. She shouldn't even be here, risking her life for him, but she had stood beside him, knowing that if she was here, he would be forced to act fearless even if he was quaking in his superstitious boots. Now that her understanding of him had been verified, there was no hint of gloating in her sincere gaze, no I-told-you-so.

She waited, looking at him expectantly, ready as always to put her faith in him. Still willing to see him as a hero, not a Beast. He was humbled, and he wanted with all his soul to show her he could be worthy of that love.

Shaking off his daze, he kissed her on the forehead, rose, dusted off his hands, and got back to work with a vengeance. "Stay put," he ordered.

Then he prowled to the other side of the quivering footbridge, where he quickly found a chest full of grappling hooks and several loops of strong hemp rope.

Given his occupation, he was well versed in the use of this tool, and quickly threaded the rope through the metal eye. He returned to Kate, who watched him search out a target. Spotting a long, black bar running above the solar system model, he drew back his arm and cast the grappling hook with a mighty throw.

It flew over the bar and looped around it twice, locking into place when he pulled the rope to tighten it. Judging the distance with a sniper's eye, he measured out the length of rope they would need and tied the other end into a foot loop for them to stand on.

He got into position, setting his foot through the loop, then held out his hand to Kate. "We've got to time this right so we don't collide with one of these blasted planets." He drew her to him. "Put your foot through the loop on top of mine and stand in front of me. Hold on tight to the rope. Don't worry, I won't let you fall."

She obeyed, blanching as she peeked down at the dark, canyonlike space before them. Keeping her between his arms, Rohan grasped the rope, then began watching for his moment, visually timing the whirling paths of the planets.

"Ready . . . *now!*" He shoved off with one foot, and they instantly swept away from their perch on the high end of the cavern.

Kate shrieked as they flew across the empty space, barreling through the darkness. They swooshed in between Venus and Mars, holding on for dear life, their hair and their coats blowing in the breeze.

Jaw clenched, Rohan kept his stare fixed

on their destination as he held Kate to him. In the next moment, they were tumbling off the rope at the base of the pyramid, rolling onto solid ground.

"Whew! You all right?" Rohan stopped himself and looked over at Kate, his chest heaving. He jumped up, exhilarated by their crossing.

"Am I alive?" she mumbled with her face buried against the furry sleeve of her coat.

He picked her up and set her on her feet again. "You'd better be."

"Ugh, I'm so dizzy my knees are wobbly. I need to sit down for a second." She stumbled over to the first layer of the pyramid and sat down as if on a bench, but as soon as she put her weight on it, the whole row of blocks tilted, spilling her onto the ground. "Hey!"

She got up, dusting herself off, and scowled at the pyramid indignantly. "That wasn't very hospitable!"

"I guess this thing's not as solid as it appears. And look — the row you sat on didn't flip back." He furrowed his brow. The first row of blocks were no longer stepped out like a bench but tilted on a smooth angle. "Curious."

"What do you think we're meant to do, climb to the top of it?" ·

"Yes, then go down inside. There's an opening at the top. Thirteen layers high," he counted. "Did you notice all the blocks are numbered?"

She nodded. "There must be some sort of pattern or number sequence marking out a path to the top."

"Looks pretty random to me." The numbers on the blocks ranged from single digits into the thousands.

They spent a few moments walking around the pyramid, trying to discern a pattern. Meanwhile, behind them, the celestial model kept on revolving, backlit by the distant glow from the Hall of Fire.

"Can you make out any number on the capstone?" Kate inquired.

He squinted in the darkness. "It has a number one on it." The capstone was separate from the rest of the pyramid, suspended over the top of it.

"Hm. Does the top row have a one, also?" she asked.

"Yes, actually."

"What about the second layer — is there a two?"

Rohan scanned horizontally across the second layer in the darkness. "Yes, and there's a three on the third row, but I hardly think it's as simple as merely counting —"

"No, of course not. If you can see a number five on the fourth row, then I think I know the pattern."

He scanned the fourth row. "There it is, number five. Is this some sort of puzzle from your old friend, Alcuin?"

"No, one of his contemporaries — Fibonacci. Thirteen layers, the one's at the top, which means we're working backwards again."

Rohan watched her, impressed, as she began mumbling under her breath and counting briefly on her fingers.

"Three hundred seventy-seven! No, wait that's the one I sat on. You're on the second row up now . . . look for two hundred thirty-three."

Rohan walked down the line of the pyramid and found it, to his surprise. "Got it!"

"Do you want to try stepping on it?"

"Might as well." Carefully, he took a long-legged stride up onto the second row, standing on the block. "Solid! What's next?"

"Um — a hundred and forty-four!"

He glanced at the blocks and spotted it. "You'd better come with me in case you need a hand. Some of these blocks are fairly far apart." She hurried after him, and he gave her his hand, steadying her as she stepped up onto the block with him.

"What's next?"

"Eighty-nine."

He pointed. "There it is!"

They found it and proceeded in the same manner, scaling blocks labeled fifty-five, thirty-four, twenty-one, occasionally having to stretch quite far to make it onto the appropriate blocks without setting off the mechanism.

As the sound of distant thunder reverberated through the hollow of the mountain, however, knocking a light trickle of rock dust down on them, they paused, glancing at each other.

"What was that?" Kate murmured.

"Cannon fire," Rohan answered grimly.

"Papa's engaged the Promethean ship!"

He nodded. "He said he'd sink it."

Kate gave him a look of determination. "Then let's finish doing our part, too."

"We're halfway there. What's the next number? Should be thirteen, right? Over there. Big stretch. Steady . . ."

The echo of cannon fire rumbled in the distance as they pressed on, finishing the Fibonacci sequence, until they came to the opening at the top of the pyramid.

They had to slide down a pole wrapped in scaly, brownish green snakeskin leather to reach the bottom of the pyramid, which contained nothing but a fine layer of sand and four arched doorways, one on each wall. These led into four unmarked, lightless, narrow passages that would take them farther into the base of the mountain.

"Eerie," Kate remarked.

"Looks like we have to choose a path."

"Yes, but choose based on what? They're all identical."

He nodded, gazing into the nearest pitch-dark tunnel. "And all equally deadly, I wager."

"Maybe. Do you have a compass?"

"You know me, ready for anything."

She raised an eyebrow at the roguish innuendo in his voice. He reached into his knapsack and pulled out his compass, tossing it to her with a quick, flirtatious smile.

She blushed a bit and flipped the compass open. "As I was saying. We already know they used the table of elements to devise the clues. Now, the four cardinal directions each corresponds to one of the original four elements of the ancients. We've already gone through water — the waterfall, fire — the Hall of Fire, then we had to swing through the air. That only leaves the element of earth. Which corresponds to . . . north." She looked up from the compass to the door ahead of them.

He stared at her in admiration. "You're good."

"Maybe it's just my Promethean blood." Wryly, she handed the compass back to him.

He returned it to his knapsack. "Better let me go first again." He stalked toward the north tunnel. "I'll make sure it's safe, then come back for you."

"Please don't."

He turned to her. "What's wrong?"

She moved closer. "I don't think we should separate. What if something happens, and we are cut off from each other? Whatever we have to face, I think our chances are better if we stay together."

He gazed into her eyes, flooded with tenderness for her. He gave her a reluctant nod. "Of course. Stay close," he ordered softly.

She joined him with a grateful smile, then they set off into the darkness with only their one remaining lantern to light the way. The passage took a winding route, first dipping low under the seabed, then ascending through the recesses of the mountain.

The climb was steep, but Rohan was just happy that nothing sharp swung out of the darkness to lop off their heads. After they had walked for about a mile, the tunnel began widening ahead.

He held the lamp up higher as they approached a square anteroom with a large iron door. Beside it, he spotted a brass plaque with a dial like the previous one outside the Hall of Fire.

"Lord, I'm glad to be out of that tunnel. Looks like we've got another clue to solve —"

"Careful!" He put out his hand to stop Kate from stepping over the threshold into the anteroom until he had examined it more closely, but she had already put her weight onto her leading foot — and at once, a grinding noise confirmed that she had tripped another mechanism.

"Sorry!"

Rohan looked up and immediately saw the square panel of the ceiling begin slowly descending.

It was covered in long spikes.

"Kate!" To his horror, she dashed ahead of him to reach the brass plaque.

"We have to get this door open! I have the clue right here. Come on, Rohan!"

"Bloody hell." He darted across the room, more for the purpose of pulling her out of there if it came down to it.

The ceiling was now about twelve feet above them, but descending inexorably as Kate flipped open the book, rushing through the pages. "Oh, where the blazes is it?"

"Kate!" He fitted himself between the spikes and put his arms over his head. The instant the base came down to his hands, he began applying counterpressure to slow its descent. "Get out of here!"

"No, I have it now! Here: 'Of wisdom, wealth, and power, he owned the lion's share, but he lost all in losing her, and embraced despair.' "

"Kate!"

"The bride of the Alchemist, Rohan! The one your ancestor, Lord Kilburn, shot by accident when he was aiming at Valerian! What was her name?"

"Her name?" he retorted, pushing with all his strength against the weight. "I have no idea!"

"Rohan! This is central to your family's story, you must know, come now, try!"

"Oh, God, what was it? Her name was, um —"

"Quickly!"

"Mary — no, Maria. No. It was longer than that. Margaret!"

Her back to him, Kate immediately began dialing the letters on the combination lock, ducking away from the spikes and bending lower to escape the ceiling that was about to flatten them.

"Kate, get out of here, now! I don't know how much longer I can hold this up!"

She glanced over her shoulder at him and finally saw that he was using all his strength to hold up the spiked mechanism.

His face was beet red with the strain, his arms shaking. He could feel the veins bulging in his neck, the deep strain in his elbows. The pressure on his joints was enormous. "Get . . . out," he wrenched out.

"But then *you* won't be able to," she whispered, aghast, as she grasped his situation.

"Please, Kate — if I mean anything to you, just go."

"And you say you are unfit for love," she breathed. Then she spun around, making her stand to finish the code — or die with him.

She ducked down between the descending spikes, still entering letters on the dial while Rohan was driven down to one knee like Atlas with the world on his shoulders, fighting to buy them a few extra precious seconds.

Kate kept working feverishly, dialing in the final letters of the combination. "R, e, t!"

The spikes suddenly stopped; at the same time, the iron door swung open ahead into the inner sanctum of the Alchemist's Tomb. Chest heaving, Rohan dropped his quivering arms to his sides and hung his head.

"Wait for me next time," he panted in reproach.

"I will. Sorry." She gazed somberly at him and did as she was told, not venturing over the threshold of the room that had now opened.

As a clatter of unseen gears and pulleys began pulling the spiked ceiling back up to its original position, he straightened to his full height once more.

"Look, we did it! We found Valerian's burial place!" Kate stared at him in girlish uncertainty, as though wondering if he was angry at her, as she pointed into the next room. "I can see the coffin!"

He heaved a slow, measured exhalation, then joined her at the edge of the burial chamber.

Obediently, she had remained outside the inner sanctum but pointed to the large stone sarcophagus that sat on a slightly raised dais in the center of the tight, low-ceilinged room. The sides of the chamber were packed with Valerian's odd alchemical accoutrements.

"I don't see any scrolls." From the safety of the doorway, she began scanning the walls of the chamber, then glanced warily at him. "Are you all right?"

He grumbled in the affirmative.

"Don't be angry at me, my love! It was for the best. You were being overprotective again. We had to press forward. We couldn't go back —"

"I'm not angry," he muttered, but it wasn't her nearly killing them that had disturbed him. Her words from a moment ago still echoed in his head.

And you say you are not fit for love.

Maybe, just maybe, he was. With the guilt for killing the father of those Promethean children lifted, and the Kilburn Curse revealed to be a superstitious sham, what could stop him now?

"Can I go in, please?" she cajoled him. "I have to find those scrolls!"

He growled, but after studying the room for a moment, he nodded. She tiptoed in ahead of him and began poking around in the ancient piles of her ancient ancestor's personal effects, waving away a cloud of dust with a small cough.

She turned to him and shook her head. "I don't see them."

"Maybe they're inside the coffin," he murmured. "Should be weathertight. They might've put them in there with the body to help preserve them."

"So." Kate looked at him. "Let's crack it open."

Rohan eyed her uncertainly. Having only just recovered moments ago from his superstitious leanings, he still did not relish the thought of disturbing the dead.

Especially a dead warlock.

Nevertheless, he took a deep breath and went over grimly to the sarcophagus. He began lifting the heavy stone lid. His arms and shoulders still ached from the strain of holding up the spiked ceiling. Kate saw him wince and quickly hurried to help.

They exchanged a glance, confirming both were ready. By now, they both knew they might have to jump back fast if another nasty surprise sprang out at them, rigged to dispatch any would-be tomb robbers.

"One, two, three —" They shoved the lid hard. It slid off the side of the coffin and crashed away from the dais onto the floor of the Tomb.

"What was that?" Kate murmured, glancing around as the rumble started.

The open door to the burial chamber slammed shut. The whole room began quaking, and the dais began to descend into the floor, while fine dirt like sand began pouring from the ceiling from a hundred small cascades.

"This isn't good," Kate remarked, while Rohan glanced down into the coffin, his heart pounding.

Valerian's flesh had long since wasted away, his skeleton draped in the rotting wizard's robes in which he had been buried. In his bony fingers, clutched to his chest, was a large, ornate key.

"Rohan, the roof's caving in!"

"I know. Just a second." With a grimace of disgust, he reached into the coffin and pried the key out of the skeleton's bony fingers. Whatever case or chest it opened, the scrolls Falkirk was after were probably inside it.

"Um, Rohan, any ideas?" Kate asked more insistently, looking around. "How are we going to get out of here?"

The dirt was coming down faster. Rocks were starting to tumble in. It seemed the final trap in this mad labyrinth was that anyone disturbing the Alchemist's eternal sleep was doomed to share his grave. The whole structure was beginning to come down on them.

They were about to be buried alive.

"There!" He pointed to where light broke through. He could barely see Kate through the pouring clouds of dust.

He tucked the key into his waistband,

reached his hand out blindly in the direction of the sound of her coughing, and hauled her to him, making his way toward a break that suddenly opened in the roof.

He rushed toward it across the collapsing Tomb, pulling Kate with him. He knocked aside rocks crashing down on them and lifted her toward the hole in the ceiling. She pulled herself through while he tried to find a foothold.

Pure chaos and choking dust now filled the Tomb. He could not see. He could barely breathe, but he managed to stand on top of a large rock that had dropped down into the chamber. Fighting his way toward the surface, he began struggling frantically as the dirt began filling around his chest. Damn it, he was too big to fit through the opening.

Dust filled his eyes and ears and tried to fill his nose. Everything was shaking; he couldn't breathe; but through the deafening rumble, he could hear Kate screaming.

He felt a sudden burst of cold air above, then both her hands clasped one of his, guiding his grasp to a solid ledge so he could pull himself up.

His scrabbling fingers locked on stone; below, his foot found one more solid surface on which to raise himself. Clawing, frantic, toward the light, he suddenly emerged from the waist up, then dragged himself away from the sunken hollow of the Tomb. The ground had given way, caving in on the now-covered burial chamber.

Kate and he were covered in dirt and frozen in the snow, but they had both reached solid ground. They were alive. He sat up and began coughing violently as his lungs cleared out the dust he had inhaled.

"Are you all right?" he asked Kate between coughs.

She nodded, looking extremely shaken, but they were both out of the cave, and he still had the key.

She came closer on her knees, putting her arms around him with a small sob. "I thought I'd lost you."

He touched her hand, not wishing to let her know that he, too, had thought he was dead there for a second. "I'm here," he panted. "It's all right. Don't cry, love. Where are we, anyway?"

They both glanced around, then looked at each other in awe. They had come up in the center of the ancient Dragon Ring: The mighty standing stones loomed all around them in a circle.

CHAPTER 20

Kate was shaking with terror from nearly seeing Rohan die in front of her. Fighting back tears, she hugged him again, tenderly brushing some of the dirt out of his hair.

"I'm all right," he assured her, glancing back toward the sunken hollow. "Let's just get our bearings, now. Damn, I lost the compass. My knapsack didn't make it."

His words arrested her. She suddenly whirled around with a gasp. "The book!" She began searching frantically, to no avail. "I've lost it! *The Alchemist's Journal*! I dropped it in the Tomb!"

"Kate, it doesn't matter. Calm down. You're alive. That's all I care about. And I still have that key."

"What good is the key going to do us when whatever it opens is buried under all this dirt? The scrolls must still be down there, in a box or a chest or something! But we'll never get it now. The whole trip was a waste!"

"Slow down," he soothed. "What makes you think they'd put the key in the same location as whatever box it opens?"

She eyed him uncertainly. "You think the scrolls might be elsewhere?"

"Come, you're smarter than that," he teased in a low tone. "Were there any more clues we didn't get to?"

"One, but I have no idea what it means."

"Perhaps I can help. How did it go?"

She recited it to him: " 'Secrets kept where no thief can purloin, wisdom waits in shadow for the trial of the coin.' " She gave him a bewildered shrug.

"The trial of the coin?" he echoed.

"Gibberish, isn't it?"

"No, I know exactly what that is," he said abruptly, then he shook his head. "Damn, I should have known!"

"What does it mean?" she exclaimed.

"It means we need to get back to London."

"The scrolls are — *where*?"

He flashed a roguish grin.

"Don't you dare keep me in suspense!" she cried.

"Westminster Abbey," he relented at once.

Her eyes widened. "Are you sure?"

"Entirely. Come on, let's get moving. I'll

explain on the way. Right now, we need to find our way back to civilization before it's dark. I think I see a village that way." He nodded over his shoulder as he stood. He offered her his hand, pulling her up, but Kate winced as she gained her feet. "Are you all right?"

"I wrenched my ankle a bit scrambling out of that grave. It's not bad. Lord, we look a fright!" She began laughing ruefully, glancing from herself to him.

In their long sealskin coats, completely covered in dirt from the Tomb caving in — their faces, their, hair — they surely resembled two of the pagan barbarians who had built the stone ring centuries ago. "Honestly, we look like two ancient wild people who haven't yet figured out how to make fire!"

"You speak for yourself. I look good." He grinned, shook his long mane, and sent fine brown dirt scattering everywhere. Casting her a smile, he turned away and began trudging off through the snow. "Come. We've no time to dally!"

Kate lingered a moment longer, fascinated by the ring of towering, silent stones in all their raw, craggy power.

Nobody knew where these enigmatic monuments all over Britain had come from, but they were as old as the tales of Merlin, ancient even in the days of the Romans. The Dragon Ring stood atop a dramatic hilltop overlooking the sea. In all directions, the treeless expanse was dusted with a light layer of snow.

All of a sudden, a deep boom reverberated from a few miles out across the sea. Kate turned, drawing in her breath. Then she pointed. "Rohan, look! Papa did it! The Promethean ship is sinking!"

He quickly returned to her, narrowing his eyes toward the water.

"It looks like he's leaving," she said. "He's not waiting for us?"

"That wasn't your father's ship that fired the last salvo. See, out there? The Coast Guard's on their way."

"The Coast Guard again!" Kate immediately thought of Caleb Doyle and his trouble with the Coast Guard after the smugglers' shipwrecking activities. It was part of the reason she had ended up with Rohan in the first place.

"Don't worry," he said. "We'll be in contact with your father later. We must go to London, and he had better get out of here to avoid arrest."

"I hope Papa was able to rescue Mr. Tewkes."

"Knowing your father, I'd wager he did. Wish I hadn't dropped my telescope, or I might've been able to see something."

"I suppose all we can do now is hope for the best. Goodbye, Papa — again," she murmured, shielding her eyes as she looked out across the shimmering water and watched the frigate slipping away toward the horizon under full sail.

"You'll see him again," Rohan promised her softly.

His kindness was a comfort to her now, just as it had been when he had first stopped her from flinging herself off the Cornish cliff. She was so glad to be near him.

Then she smiled. "Look down there, on the beach." She pointed to some shaggy sheep with curved horns grazing on the long strands of seaweed that had washed ashore.

After all the dangers of the past few hours, she savored the tranquil beauty of the Orkadian landscape, with its delicate pastel wash of lavenders and blues.

"This is a beautiful place," she whispered, especially charmed by the flock of hardy swans honking and clacking on the hillside, and by the shaggy black pony that was staring at them from the edge of a barren meadow nearby, its long mane blowing in the breeze.

"Beautiful?" Rohan had turned to her. She could feel him staring at her. "You think so?"

She looked at him. "Don't you?"

He shrugged, then shook his head. "Bleak and harsh and difficult."

"Perhaps." She smiled gently, gazing at him. "But there is an exquisite sensitivity in the color of the light. And the sweep of these hills bespeaks a calm strength," she said slowly, her gaze traveling over the landscape. "Noble, but unpretentious. It is what it is. A hard land, maybe. But plain and honest." She glanced at him. "I could live here."

The morning light matched the soft blue shade of Rohan's eyes as he gazed at her, sensing she was not talking only about Orkney. His wordless stare was so over-whelmed with emotion for her that although she was covered in grime and dressed like somebody's footman, the way he looked at her made her feel as beautiful as a princess.

He suddenly lowered his head. "We should go," he mumbled in a voice gone slightly husky. Turning away, he started marching ahead again while Kate followed at a slower pace, trying to force herself to walk without too much of a limp.

When she slipped on a little snow, how-ever, she cursed under her breath in a puff of steamy air. "Any idea how far it might be to that village?"

He stopped and pivoted, his face instantly darkening when he saw her limp. "You're hurt." He strode back to her. "Damn it, Kate, why didn't you tell me? Is it bad?"

"It's just my ankle."

"I'll carry you."

"Don't be silly! I can walk on my own."

He scowled, but turned around, scanning the whole area. "Wait here."

"Where are you going?"

"Just stay there a moment. I have an idea."

Keeping her weight on her uninjured foot, she watched as Rohan crossed the snowy meadow and approached the pony.

He began speaking softly to it, taking out a length of rope that had been attached to his weapons belt.

The pony's ears pricked up. Kate smiled, charmed. Well she knew the persuasive power of that deep, velvet voice. The pony stretched out its nose and sniffed Rohan.

He edged closer and began stroking its fuzzy neck. Kate's smile broadened as he slipped the rope over its muzzle, fashioning a loose halter. She watched him, enchanted, as he led the docile pony over to her.

"Look what I found." As he joined her, Rohan put his arms around her. Kate stared into his eyes, tongue-tied with adoration, her heartbeat quickening. If it were not so cold, she'd have laid him down and loved him in that snowy field.

Then he lifted her onto the horse. She let her legs dangle down astride and took hold of the pony's long mane. Rohan clasped the makeshift lead rope, clucked gently to the creature, and began leading them toward the distant village.

Neither of them spoke as he walked the horse for about ten or fifteen minutes. They were only about halfway to the village when the church steeple showed above the next rise.

Rohan suddenly stopped.

Kate furrowed her brow. "Is something wrong?"

He turned around abruptly and looked straight into her eyes. "Marry me," he said.

Her eyes widened. *"What?"* She nearly fell off the horse.

"Marry me, Kate," he repeated. He swallowed hard. "I need you in my life. Please. Say you'll be my duchess."

"Rohan . . ."

He took a step closer. "I know I said some boorish, stupid things that day in the music room. You were right. I was scared. I didn't know how it could be between us, but I see it now. And that night on your father's ship, I acted like a brute, telling you to prove your love by sleeping with me. It was wrong."

She shook her head. "You needed me."

"I did. I still do. I always will. I don't know what I'll do if you say no." He lowered his head. "I know you've reason to be wary. That I can be a thoroughgoing bastard sometimes. I've had too many women in the past, but, God, I don't want that anymore. And it is true, I, er, kill people now and then, but just to safeguard England. And if you can live with that —" He shook his head with a tempestuous fire in his eyes. "On my word, I will be true to you, and I will love you until the end of time."

Kate had lost the power of speech. Indeed, she could barely breathe. Tears rushed into her eyes.

Lord Byron himself could not have uttered more romantic sentiments.

"There can be no other for me, Kate, but you." The Beast walked over and stared hard into the depths of her eyes; sitting on the pony's back, she was on eye level with him for once, and the whole tumult of his soul was there in his eyes, discovering love for the first time, setting his heart free at last. "You . . . make me feel things I've never experienced before. You've been so patient, and I've been such a fool."

"No, you haven't," she breathed, wonder-struck by him. Was this just a dream?

"Stay with me always," he implored her in a confidential whisper. "And love me . . . as I love you."

"You — love me?" she echoed, her chin trembling in the most embarrassing fashion.

"With all my heart," he vowed in a soft but fierce tone, looking as deeply moved as she. He touched her hair, tucking a wind-blown lock of it behind her ear. "Kate, you and I were meant to be together. I'm still superstitious enough to know when I have found my destiny. It's you. You're the one who broke the curse."

"I thought you don't believe in that curse anymore," she chided tenderly.

"But I'd still be trapped in it if it were not for you. Give me an answer, Kate. You must be my bride."

"Still giving orders?" she whispered with a tremulous smile.

He bowed his head with an almost humble half smile: "Please."

"Of course, I will," she breathed in a shaky voice. "You are everything to me!" She threw her arms around him and pressed her cheek to his as she held him in a clinging embrace. "Oh, Rohan, I'm so in love with you. I can barely stand it."

"I know what you mean." His arms were wrapped tightly around her waist. "I feel the same. It's maddening, isn't it?"

She nodded, laughing and crying at the same time.

"Is there any way to ease this feeling?"

"Yes," she told him with a sniffle, pulling back again a small space to look into his eyes. "You must kiss me. That will help."

With a tender smile, he wiped a tear off her dusty cheek with the pad of his thumb. "Gladly."

But instead of the hearty kiss she had expected, he caressed her lips with his own in tantalizing softness until she moaned. "Oh, I need you to make love to me."

"Before we're married?" he teased in a very naughty whisper. "Shocking, Miss Madsen."

"You really are a Beast."

"And you love me for it."

"Yes. With all my heart." She trembled with sheer happiness. He was impossible — and she wouldn't have him any other way.

Rohan rested his forehead against hers. They remained like that for a moment in wordless bliss. In truth, she had not realized how close they had grown after all they had been through, but she could feel it now.

Their love surrounded them, wound them together with great invisible ribbons of devotion and delight in each other. A commitment to each other's good.

There were no words for this moment, just the wind and the surf and the distant calls of seabirds.

"I love you so much," she whispered again, breathing him in as he remained in her embrace.

"Oh, Kate, I'd be lost without you. You must know you own my very soul."

"My love." She closed her eyes against fresh tears and kissed his lips, then his forehead.

"I'll always be here for you," he promised.

"And I, you," she answered.

"Well, then." Taking a firmer tone, he pulled back slightly. "Let's get on with it, shall we? Let's go get married."

"What, now?" She straightened up in surprise.

"Of course! I don't want to wait a moment longer," he declared. "As soon as we get to that village, I'm marrying you, by God."

"Are you?" she exclaimed.

"We might as well make the most of our visit to Scotland, eh?" he added with a wink.

She laughed gaily. "You want to get married like this, looking like two barbarians?"

"Well, we are, aren't we? Oh, come, Duchess, you'll have your whole life of drawing rooms and finery ahead."

Kate stared at him in amazement, then laughed. "I suppose I will! In that case, Duke, lead on — to the blacksmith's forge, by Jove!"

"That's my girl." He grinned at her in unabashed pride. Taking the pony's lead rope again, he strode the rest of the way to the tiny hamlet.

Any outsiders in so remote a place at this time of year would have been cause for local gossip, but when the two of them paraded into the one-street village, their odd appearance drew something of a crowd as they walked through the tiny island town.

They were such a mess that they did not even attempt to go to the little church, but went straight to that other august establishment where a Scottish marriage could be easily procured — not as respectable, perhaps, but every bit as legal.

The village blacksmith.

They found the "anvil-priest" hammering out a horseshoe. The leather-aproned giant had a wild orange mustache, massive forearms, and a considerable belly.

"Morning," Rohan greeted him as he led

her on the pony up to the smoky, open forge. "We'd like you to marry us, if you're free, sir."

The blacksmith eyed them warily and set aside his hammer. "Ye two have aught to do with that sea battle out yonder?" he asked, nodding toward the coast.

"What sea battle?" Rohan echoed with an innocent lift of his eyebrows.

The big Scot snorted, but they soon convinced him to do the honors. Since their gold had been left behind along with most of their supplies in the Tomb's collapse, Rohan had to barter with what few items he carried on his person. He offered the blacksmith his favorite dagger in exchange for his services as wedding officiate.

Kate's eyes shone with eagerness as the blacksmith tested the dagger, examining it with a skeptical eye. At length, he nodded to Rohan, accepting the trade.

"Ye must 'ave two witnesses."

Rohan turned around and surveyed the crowd of onlookers who had gathered around the opening of the forge to watch the proceedings of these odd-looking outsiders. "You. And you there. Would you do us the honor of being our witnesses?"

"Me?" a scruffy shepherd asked, brightening.

Kate fought laughter, exchanging a twinkling look with Rohan as the two country fellows joined them.

Rohan put them in place on either side of them while a village child fed a carrot to the pony.

An old lady shuffled over and handed Kate a tiny purple flower of some sort. "There you are, dearie."

"How kind, thank you!"

"Have ye got the ring for ye bonny lass? 'Tis a requirement," the blacksmith rumbled with a great Scottish rolling of his r's.

"Oh, right. I, ah, don't suppose there's a jeweler's around here," Rohan mumbled with an awkward glance at Kate.

She brightly offered him the flower. "You could tie the stem into a knot!"

"Ach, we can do a wee bit better than that." The blacksmith shot her unprepared fiancé a disapproving look, but she sensed his amusement. A festival atmosphere was coming over the growing crowd. To be sure, this was the most excitement the tiny town had seen in months.

The blacksmith reached into one of his rugged, dusty containers, took out a long, thin nail, and showed it to them. "Consider it me weddin' present to the lass. Let's hope she knows what she's doin,' " he added dryly.

Rohan scowled, but Kate laughed as the blacksmith carried the nail over to his forge. Taking it between long black pincers, he held it in the fire until it glowed red.

When he pulled it out again and brought it over to the anvil, Rohan joined him. "May I? I've got a bit of a knack for this, as it happens."

"Oh, do ye, now?" the blacksmith asked in amusement, but he let him try his hand.

Rohan picked up the hammer and whacked the little nail flat with a few well-aimed blows. She watched him in startled delight as he quickly changed to a smaller tool and began shaping the flattened scrap of metal into a circle.

The man never ceased to amaze her.

When he had joined the two ends of it, the blacksmith took over to refine Rohan's work, smoothing the edges into a neat little ring. He let it cool in a vat of water, but within a quarter hour, they had the necessary wedding band.

"This is only temporary," Rohan assured her as he came to stand beside her, showing it to her.

"Nonsense. I adore it." Her heart danced.

"It's a nail, darling."

"It's my wedding ring!" she protested mildly. "I don't care that it's not gold. My husband made it for me. I shall treasure it always." She took his arm and stood beside him, beaming.

"If everyone is ready!" the blacksmith bellowed sternly, coming to the edge of the forge.

"I am," Rohan said at once.

"Me, too."

"Me, three," their shepherd witness chimed in.

The other nodded with an eager smile.

"All right, then."

The quick and tidy ceremony ensued.

Kate narrowed her eyes, listening for all she was worth. She had to strain her ears to understand the blacksmith's speedy, mumbled words with his Scottish burr. In fact, she was not entirely sure just what she was agreeing to, but as long as it meant that Rohan would be with her forever, she was all in. She loved him with all she had, and joining her life to his this way, in this adorable place at the edge of the world couldn't have been more perfect for, well — the way it was with them.

"And do ye pledge yer troth to be married for a year and a day?"

"No!" they both exclaimed at once.

The crowd hurrahed.

"Year and a day, my foot," the bride huffed in playful indignation.

The blacksmith glanced from Kate to Rohan with a flicker of surprise in his bright blue eyes; it was only then he seemed to realize that they were actually serious. This was no trial marriage or some juvenile game, as Scottish elopements frequently were.

"Aye, then. For as long as love may last?" he ventured, another common pledge.

"No." Rohan looked at Kate. "I pledge my troth to you, Miss Katherine Fox, forever."

"Well, then," the blacksmith murmured. "And you, young lady, do ye pledge ye troth to 'im?"

"Forever, yes, I do!" Kate said breathlessly.

"Then, I now pronounce ye man and wife!"

Their witnesses and whole country crowd cheered as Rohan drew Kate into his arms and planted a big, dusty kiss on her lips. She returned it, giggling, and wrapped her arms around him. Joy tingled along her nerve endings as he lifted her off her feet in his embrace and twirled her around in a circle, holding her up like she was his greatest prize. His pale eyes shone with his utter adoration of her as he set her down gently on her feet again.

Tucked under his ever-protective arm, she kept her own around his waist as someone produced a bottle of the local malt. Shot glasses appeared; Kate, dizzy with happiness, barely noticed as one of the cups was pressed into her hand. One sip made it apparent how these hardy folk descended from the Vikings kept warm in winter at this latitude.

Then the toasts began, the villagers showering them with blessings for their health, and shouting well-wishes of long life and many children.

Somehow, the drab day in that remote village, with its thatched roofs and single muddy road, became the warmest and brightest day of Kate Kilburn's twenty-two years.

At length, Rohan asked if the village had an inn.

The whole crowd laughed knowingly, a thunder of merry innuendo. The scarlet blush that rose in Kate's cheeks was due to more than the cold northern air and the few celebratory sips of whiskey.

Rohan put his arm around her and pressed a kiss to her temple with a manly laugh.

They thanked the blacksmith again, then the whole band of their new Orkadian friends escorted them to the local inn at the other end of the village.

Kate and Rohan bid the crowd adieu and ducked inside, where the landlord, unaware of the impromptu festivities outside, furrowed his brow and puzzled over them.

The landlady nearly had an apoplectic fit at the dust they trailed in, thrusting them back outside to have their sealskin coats shaken out.

Only then were they allowed back into the establishment, though the innkeeper looked perplexed by Kate's footman costume, even more so when Rohan asked if he'd be willing to barter.

Before long, he had traded two of his finest pistols for a night's stay, some food, and tickets for the morning stagecoach. "We'll need a bath sent up," he added.

"Ye think so?" the landlord answered dryly as he handed them a room key.

Within an hour, they were both lounging in the large bathing tub, a bit cramped, but enjoying sharing the warm steaming water after half a ton of dirt had rained down on them in the Tomb's collapse.

The bath was set near the fireplace in their quaint little bedchamber on the inn's second floor. A stack of fresh towels waited nearby, along with a cozy tea service and a plate of bannocks and cheese.

"I think I'll take a break from adventuring for a while when all this is over," Kate mused aloud, leaning her wet head back against the rim of the tub.

"To concentrate on being a duchess?" He watched her with a lazy smile as he ran the soap up one gorgeously muscled arm.

"It may take some study," she admitted. "I do hope one can *learn* how to be a proper duchess."

"Kate. The Fibonacci sequence? Backwards Greek translation? Decoding rhyming couplets out of the bloody chart of elements? Trust me, you will have no trouble with the occasional charity ball and a ladies' tea. And if you do, just ask Daphne, Rotherstone's lady."

"Was she one of the women in the carriage when we were leaving London?"

"Yes, and she happens to be a reigning expert on all things ton."

She was silent for a moment. "Your friends are in the Order, aren't they?"

"A fact that I must ask you to forget, my darling."

"Of course," she murmured. "Will it be like that much, do you suppose? That you'll have to keep secrets from me about your work? I trust you, you know. I will understand."

"I do trust you, completely," he answered, gazing at her with gratitude. "I prefer to be open with you, but it might not always be possible. I'm glad you understand."

"I'm proud of you," she said earnestly. "But what do you think the Order will do when they find out you've married a woman with Promethean bloodlines?"

"Half-Promethean," he reminded her, then he shrugged. "I suppose we'll soon find out. I'll just have to remind them that Count DuMarin paid the ultimate price for helping our side all those years ago. Surely he redeemed himself in their eyes. It's not as if you're Falkirk's granddaughter. I'm sure they'll want to ask you some questions to make sure they can trust you," he added. "But you're my wife. We're a matched set now. If they want me, they take you, and there's an end to it."

She stared at him in wonder. "You'd give up the Order for me?"

"I've already lied to them for you. But don't worry, I am fairly sure they'll be appeased when we present them with the treasure trove of the Alchemist's lost scrolls."

"Which you say are in Westminster Abbey? I've never been in there."

"Well, you'll see it very soon. We leave for London on the stagecoach in the morning."

The water rippled as she moved closer, draping her arms around his neck in steamy affection. "How ever shall we while away the hours until then, husband?"

He laughed softly, wickedly, but he soon carried her over to the bed. Moving under the covers, fully naked, their bodies still warm and damp from the bath, Rohan laid her down with endless kisses full of tender passion. As he made slow, deep, gentle love to her, he kept whispering, "I love you," and it was so worth the wait to hear him say it at last.

Kate was in heaven, his strength covering her, his vulnerability safe in her hands. She yielded herself to him gladly, giving him all she was. As he urged her body toward completion, her heart was so full of helpless love for him that she wept with release.

They lay together afterwards, spoon fashion, in spent, glowing silence. Rohan was behind her, his arm draped over her waist, his palm resting on the mattress. She slid her hand atop his, idly comparing the size of their hands.

His was so much larger than hers, and yet,

for all his power and strength, she knew he needed her in a way that was more than physical. She closed her eyes.

He nestled closer, nuzzling her neck, which he then kissed. "Happy?" he murmured.

"Oh, Rohan, yes. And you?"

"More than words could ever say, my precious wife. Get some sleep," he whispered, leaning near to kiss her cheek.

"But it's barely evening. How early do we leave?"

"It's not that," he chided in a whisper. "Rest up now, because I am going to want you again. Soon."

She laughed and reached back to caress his face as the Beast bit her lightly on the shoulder.

The next morning, the stagecoach took them to the Orkney coast, where they caught the ferry to Aberdeen; they took passage the following day aboard a packet ship, which, in turn, brought them down to the port at Great Yarmouth.

Back on English soil, they hired a post chaise and traveled southwest, passing through the refined streets of Cambridge, and swiftly on to Town. They reached London after nightfall and went immediately to Westminster Abbey, where Rohan called on the Dean.

He had explained that since Westminster Abbey was classified as a Royal Peculiar, the Dean answered directly to the sovereign — as did the Order.

The Dean was a very powerful man. After all, it was he who would assist as second only to the Archbishop of Canterbury when the time came for the coronation of the Prince Regent. A very learned and well-connected man, he was, Rohan had told her, one of the few in London who was aware of the Order and its purpose.

For that reason, the Dean promptly dispatched an unsmiling verger to take them at once into the darkened cathedral and let them into the mysterious Pyx Chamber.

"So why do you believe the Prometheans hid the scrolls in here?" Kate whispered as the verger led them into the huge, silent, candlelit Abbey.

"It's one of the most secure buildings in England," Rohan murmured, "especially the Undercroft."

Hurrying past the numerous gilded side chapels, one more ornate than the next, Kate gawked at the magnificent stained-glass windows, only feebly lit by the winter moon.

Countless monuments loomed eerily in the shadows, honoring the thousands of dead buried within the Abbey.

"The Pyx Chamber has been used as a treasury for centuries by the Crown and the Exchequer," he continued, holding her hand and hurrying her along. "You'll see how thick the walls are. Double-reinforced doors. It's been solid since the eleventh century. Down here, watch your step."

Rohan went down the stone stairs ahead of her into the oldest part of the Abbey. The verger crossed to a massive Gothic door, which he began unlocking.

Hauling open the double-layered entrance, the Dean's man let them into the Pyx Chamber, a low, vaulted room with an ancient tiled floor and wide rounded arches between the massive pillars holding up part of the weight of the great cathedral above.

By the light of the verger's lantern, Kate saw rows and rows of wooden shelves lining the walls. They were filled with small wooden chests, each identical.

There were scores of them.

"Those are the pyxes," Rohan told her. "They hold samples of all the coins ever minted in England. Each year they have an official trial to make sure the proper weight of gold and silver are being used to mint the coins — that there's no cheating in the value of our currency."

" 'The trial of the coin!' " she exclaimed, recalling the last line of the final couplet from *The Alchemist's Journal.*

"Exactly. Those scrolls are somewhere in this room," he said grimly, glancing around. "There are other priceless valuables stored in here, as well. Crowns. Deeds. Charters. Not everything's kept in the palaces or the Tower of London."

He pointed to another wall of shelves piled with assorted old chests, boxes, cases, and caskets of all sizes and descriptions. A mass of documents seemed to accompany every one.

"There are so many. How are we going to find it?"

He shrugged. "We look for one of the right size. From there, it's just a matter of whichever one the key fits into. We'd best get started."

She nodded. For the next two hours, Rohan pulled down one aged box after another, while Kate tried Valerian's key in each. The verger stayed on hand as a necessary witness to their presence in the high-security room, and finally lent a hand.

At last, Rohan slid a long, weathered case off the top shelf and brought it down to her.

It looked about right — two feet long and about six inches deep.

They exchanged a determined glance, then Kate once more lifted the key that Rohan had taken from the Alchemist's coffin. "Here goes nothing," she murmured.

But then, she drew in her breath as it slid neatly into the keyhole. She turned it. "It works!"

"Let me lift the lid — just in case."

"Careful," she whispered, moving back. She turned her face away, ready to dive for cover in case of any nasty surprises like the many they had encountered in the Tomb.

Rohan stood back, poking the lid open.

Nothing happened.

No explosions, blades, or puffs of poison dust rose up to harm them, so he lifted the lid the rest of the way.

They both peered into the long wooden box.

It was filled with ancient parchment scrolls, each tied with a ribbon. They exchanged a victorious look.

Rohan picked up the top scroll, but did not need to unfurl it to note the strange occult symbols, runes, and other Promethean markings. "This is it, all right."

"Unbelievable." Kate shook her head in amazed resentment that the Prometheans had had the audacity to put the dark, occult scribblings of a medieval sorcerer in this holy place.

Rohan closed the box again and locked it. "This is what we came for," he informed the verger.

The man nodded. Rohan headed for the door. Kate was right behind him. Once more, they were hurrying through the giant Abbey and out to the street.

Carrying the box in one hand, he hailed a hackney with the other, got the door for Kate, and ordered the driver to take them straight to Dante House.

They were silent, both well aware that something of a confrontation awaited them at the headquarters of the so-called Inferno Club. Kate was a bit nervous, knowing she was going to be questioned, but with Rohan by her side, she was ready. She had nothing to hide.

Before long, the hackney came to a creaky halt. Rohan told the driver to wait a moment for the butler to come out and pay him, while Kate handed Rohan the case filled with Valerian's scrolls.

She glanced up at the darkly eccentric Dante House, but after the Alchemist's Tomb, the spooky strangeness of the place hardly made her lift an eyebrow.

Rohan led her through the spiky black gate and down the crooked front path, but the instant the front door opened, a raucous clamor of big dogs barking instantly filled her ears. Kate jumped back in terror when she saw the giant guard dogs leaping on Rohan just ahead of her.

But at his curt command, they dropped obediently to their haunches and went quiet. Only one regarded her with a low, uncertain growl.

"It's all right," he told her as she inched in. "Gray, would you go and pay the driver? Sorry about that, I'll owe you."

"But of course, Your Grace. Does, ah, Master Virgil know you were to bring a guest?"

"She's not a guest, Gray." Rohan reached for her hand. "This lady is my wife."

Astonishment froze the butler's heretofore-expressionless face for a second, but then he masked his shock, offering Kate a low bow. "Your Grace."

"Oh — that isn't necessary," she mumbled, blushing.

"You'd best get used to it," her husband murmured. "Are they here?"

"In the parlor, sir." Gray sketched a bow, then stepped out to pay the hackney driver.

Rohan turned to her. "Ready?"

She took a deep breath, nodded, and prepared to meet his fellow agents. Her heart beat faster as she followed him into the mysterious club, down an extraordinarily gaudy red corridor.

"Warrington! There you are." The two good-looking men who had come to his house on the night they had left London were already in the room when they walked in, along with a brawny, older Scotsman.

"Where the hell have you been?" his black-haired friend, Max, asked.

The sandy-haired Jordan stepped toward them. "Are you married or not?"

"Who. Is. This?" their handler demanded, staring at Kate. Earlier, Rohan had told her that the blustery Scot's name was Virgil.

He reminded her of that blacksmith up at Orkney.

"This, sir," Rohan answered, laying his hand protectively on the small of her back, "is my duchess."

"Hullo — I'm Kate," she said with a nervous little wave to them all, though she felt as small as a shrub in a forest of trees standing among all these towering warrior males.

"So, the rumor *was* true!" Max exclaimed.

"You look a little different than the last

time we saw you," Jordan remarked with a smile.

"Your *wife*?" Virgil echoed incredulously at last. "And you thought it wise to bring her here?"

Kate winced, but Rohan met his stare evenly. "She is as much a part of this as we are, Virgil. You see, Kate is the Count Du-Marin's granddaughter."

Thus it began.

They sat down, except for the Highlander, who leaned by the window with a stunned expression. They spent the next two hours answering a barrage of questions. Rohan told them the whole story, from the reason Kate had been kidnapped, all the way through to their successful mission to the Tomb and their subsequent visit to the Pyx Chamber.

"It's because of Kate that we were able to get to the Alchemist's scrolls and keep them out of the hands of the Prometheans." He took out the key from Valerian's tomb and opened the case.

At once, Jordan was on his feet, crossing to the trove of scrolls, crouching down to view them in fascination.

"You'll have your work cut out for you now," Max remarked to him.

"They're all in code," Kate spoke up, "but

I-I made some progress on that from my mother's book. Maybe I could help."

They all looked at her. Virgil eyed her as if she were some manner of rat that had crawled up from the river.

Kate finally took umbrage at his hostility, knitting her eyebrows together. "I know I have Promethean bloodlines, sir, but I-I am a good person!" she asserted firmly, her heart pounding. "I love Rohan, and I will do whatever I can to help your cause, just like my grandfather did. My own mother was a victim of Promethean evil, too, you know. I understand your skepticism, but I hope you will at least give me a chance!"

Max stared at her, a faint twinkle of approval in his eyes at her refusal to be intimidated. "Well, well," he murmured. "She certainly sounds like a Warrington."

Rohan smiled ruefully.

"Come, gentlemen," Max said. "We've been rude to the lady for long enough, surely. Congratulations are in order." With a fond smile, he rose and crossed to where Rohan and Kate sat together.

First he bent and gave Kate a respectful kiss on the cheek. "Brave lady, I wish you happy. Well done, my friend." Then he clapped Rohan on the shoulder. "You must allow Daphne and me to give a ball in honor of your marriage."

"A ball?" Kate breathed. "Well, you are very kind, I'm sure, but —"

"But, what, Kate?" Rohan asked, smiling.

She glanced swiftly at her husband. "I've never been to a ball."

They all began laughing, though not unkindly.

"Well, you've got a lot of catching up to do, then!"

"Thanks, Max." Rohan shook his hand.

"Accept my congratulations, too." Jordan bowed to her, pressing a gallant kiss to her knuckles. "Though, sadly, I must point out, you two have left me the last bachelor of the lot."

"I believe there will be several ladies in Society who may need comforting on that point, my lord," Kate reminded him.

They laughed, but Jordan glanced at Rohan. "You didn't stand a chance with this one, did you?"

"Not at all," he agreed with a smile, but their brooding chief had not yet given a response.

Kate eyed him anxiously. Virgil's arms were folded across his chest. "So, you say Drake was with Falkirk aboard the ship her father sank?"

"Yes, sir," Rohan answered in a more serious tone.

"Do you think Drake's dead?" Virgil asked bluntly.

"I asked Captain Fox to rescue him, and he said he'd do his best. But I don't think the crew had much time to look for him in the water. The Coast Guard was on its way, and Fox had to set sail. They wouldn't have had much time to look for him." Rohan shook his head grimly. "The temperatures were freezing, not to mention we spotted a lot of big sharks in those waters. Still, if any man could survive that sort of situation, one of ours could. But, Virgil, surely you noted what I said? I had a clear shot at Falkirk, and Drake protected him. I think we have to face the real possibility that Drake is no longer one of us. That they've turned him."

Virgil drew a deep breath, then exhaled it, shaking his head. "I refuse to believe that."

"As do I," Max murmured.

Jordan and Rohan exchanged a skeptical glance. Neither of them knew Drake as well as Max did, but Rohan knew what he had seen Drake do, and he could not think how else to explain it.

He shrugged. "Captain Fox will be in contact with me. I will certainly pass along any news he has to report as soon as I get it. If he did manage to pull Drake out of the water, he'll let me know. Then we can go and collect him."

When he glanced at Kate, he found her covering a yawn. He furrowed his brow and glanced at the mantel clock. "Midnight. Come on, you. Time to take you home. We've been on the road all day," he explained to the others.

He stood, captured her hand, and tugged her to her feet. Max and Jordan exchanged a glance, as though they could not believe their eyes at the Beast doting on her.

"I'm coming," Kate said with another yawn. "Gentlemen, it has been a pleasure. And thank you — for what you all do here, for England."

His friends looked startled by her words as they stood and bid her a gallant good night. Finally, Virgil added his gruff congratulations.

Rohan shook his hand. "Thank you, sir."

"But don't bring her here again," the Highlander warned him in a low tone, though Kate suspected she was meant to hear it, too. "It is too dangerous." Then Virgil sent round for his coach to drive them home.

Kate breathed a sigh of relief a while later when Virgil's coachman finally dropped them off under the lighted portico at Rohan's grand town house in Mayfair.

"Am I ever glad that's over," she mumbled.

Before they even reached the door, however, Eldred threw it open in surprise. "Your Grace! You're back! Miss Madsen."

"Hullo, Eldred!" Kate said with sleepy cheer.

"Eldred, old boy," Rohan greeted him, as he closed the door behind him. "She's not Miss Madsen anymore, nor Miss Fox. Allow me to present to you — the Duchess of Warrington."

Kate raised her hand, giggling. "Me."

Eldred gasped, his eyes widened. "Oh, Your Grace — Your Graces! What happy, happy news!" The butler quickly recovered his deadpan demeanor and cleared his throat. "I am overjoyed," he said gravely.

"As are we! But there is much work to be done," Rohan said heartily as he swept Kate off her feet.

She let out a small shriek of delight, throwing her arms around his neck. He had missed carrying her over the threshold, but he now traipsed up the staircase with her in his arms.

"Work, sir?" Eldred asked.

"The modiste, my good man! We must have the finest mantua-makers from Bond

Street here tomorrow. Loads of 'em. And what else? Some fashionable shoemakers, perhaps, and er, millinery, whatnot, and — well, what other dashed things do you females require?"

"The hair dresser, sir?" Eldred suggested.

"Right-o. Hair dresser, too."

"What's wrong with my hair?" Kate protested in feigned indignation.

"And the jeweler!" her husband added pointedly, casting her a smile. "No duchess of mine shall have a blacksmith's nail for a ring."

"I love my ring," she said softly, guarding it with her other hand.

"We can do better," he whispered with a wink. "I told you I was going to spoil you, didn't I?"

"Well . . ." Her smile widened.

"Tomorrow the project begins! We'll make my wild Dartmoor girl into a duchess. No, don't argue. You can't go around dressed like a footman all your life, Kate. It won't do. We must get her something suitable to wear, a new wardrobe for her new life. You will arrange it, Eldred, will you not? Her Grace and I have got other business to attend to."

The butler smiled knowingly as Rohan carried her up the sweeping staircase.

"Gladly, sir. Good night, Your Graces."

"As for you, my lady . . ."

"Hmm?" Kate murmured, a flirtatious twinkle in her eyes.

"You're not *that* tired, are you?" he whispered.

"Never," she breathed.

He let out a hungry growl of laughter, kissed her soundly, and carried her into what would henceforth be their shared bedchamber — then he kicked the door shut behind him.

EPILOGUE

A few weeks later

"Their Graces, the Duke and Duchess of Warrington!" the butler announced from his post beside the entrance to the ballroom, and at once, the whole glittering crowd paused and eagerly turned to look.

Kate still was not used to all the attention, but she was told from those in the know, that from the first whispered rumors of their secret marriage, she had charmed the ton.

The Society pages praised the excellent taste of her enormous wardrobe; the hostesses of the aristocracy were pleased with her French noble blood; and at the ball the Rotherstones had given in her and Rohan's honor a few weeks ago, the ton's haughtiest dandies, the cruelest arbiters of taste, had pronounced her the rarest of finds: a great beauty with a sharp mind, a spirited wit, and a bold sense of style.

In short, she had been proclaimed "all the kick."

Kate found her sudden celebrity slightly disconcerting, but she wasn't about to let it go to her head. While she liked to believe there might be a grain of truth to some of their praise, she knew full well her overprotective husband would have torn the dandies' heads off if they had said otherwise.

Apart from that, she was enjoying herself immensely in her new life. She was no longer alone. She had friends now, a place to belong. And most of all, she had Rohan. They fell deeper in love with each day that passed.

Not everyone was happy about that, of course.

As they proceeded into the ballroom, her white-gloved hand resting in the crook of her husband's arm, she noticed the band of lascivious ladies who had come to the house that day. Tonight Lucinda and Pauline and the rest had found a new male plaything with which to amuse themselves.

There were now swarming around Sebastian, Viscount Beauchamp, the leader of another team for the Order.

Rohan had told her that Virgil had been waiting for the other team's return from the Continent for some time.

"Beau" was leaning against a column in the ballroom with a crowd of lovely women around him. The tall, good-looking viscount appeared more than happy to oblige each and every one of them.

Rohan noticed the clamor around Beau and sent Kate a sardonic look askance. She shook her head just as Lucinda and Pauline glanced over.

Flanking Lord Beauchamp, the two ladies nodded to Kate in begrudging respect. They might not like having lost the Beast to her, but they did not appear to want to cross her.

"There's Max and Daphne," Rohan murmured.

Kate smiled as their friends waved.

As they started toward the other couple, Kate caught a glimpse of them in one of the room's large, gilded mirrors.

They had come a long way since Orkney. Arm in arm, they certainly looked a part of the crème de la crème of Society. Rohan, as always, was mouthwateringly handsome, clad tonight in formal black and white.

Kate had donned a rich pink gown with a low, heart-shaped neckline that left plenty of space to show off the brilliant diamond necklace that he had given her. It matched the dazzling rock of a blue diamond ring that he had presented as part of his promise to spoil her.

Under the diamond ring, however, on her left hand, closer to her heart, she still wore the blacksmith's nail he had fashioned for her on their wedding day. She always smiled to herself when she thought of it, the two of them dressed like dusty barbarians in seal-skin coats, but madly in love.

Come to think of it, she was already beginning to grow a little restless for their next adventure, wherever it might lead.

"There you are!"

Greetings were exchanged as they met up with Max and Daphne. Kate let go of Rohan's arm as she received a small hug from her golden-haired friend.

Daphne, as well as her best friend, Miss Carissa Portland, had welcomed her into their friendship with such warm acceptance that both had quickly become as dear as sisters to her, while Max and Jordan were now like her own brothers.

"We finally heard from my father!" Kate told the Rotherstones in excitement, keeping her voice down. "His message just arrived today."

"What news?" Max murmured, glancing at Rohan.

"They got old Mr. Tewkes back safely!"

Kate chimed in.

"Drake's alive," Rohan told him. "Captain Fox doesn't have him, but saw the Coast Guard pick him up. Unfortunately, Drake managed to rescue Falkirk, too."

"He saved that blackguard again?" Max asked, narrowing his eyes.

"Apparently so. My father-in-law didn't know where they are now, though."

The news was repeated to Jordan when he joined them a moment later, followed by the petite, auburn-haired Carissa. Noticing those two together, as they often were these days, Kate nudged Max confidentially in the side while Rohan turned to greet Jordan.

"See? Carissa and Jordan are together again."

"No, trust me," he murmured. "She's like a sister to him. I've known Jordan since we were lads, and all that time, there has really only been one woman for him."

"Who? Is he courting her?"

"No," Max said dryly. "They hate each other. Besides, I think Carissa has got her eye on somebody else."

Meanwhile, Rohan began telling his friends how he had finally procured the licenses for the fishery he wanted to start in Cornwall to make honest men out of the smugglers.

Kate noticed that Jordan seemed a trifle detached or distracted. She supposed he was probably still on the lookout for that Promethean assassin Rohan had warned her about.

The men and the ladies separated for conversation. Carissa joined Kate, scowling like an angry fairy queen at someone across the ballroom.

"What's wrong?" Kate asked in amusement. "Who are you sending those dirty looks?"

"Ugh!" the redhead huffed. "He is the most horrible man on the earth."

"Who is, pray tell?" Kate exclaimed in amusement as Daphne moved around the men to join them.

"I think I know!" she chimed in with a smile. "She's fixated on *Beau.*"

"Are you joking?" Carissa scoffed. "The man's a jester. An utter fool!"

"But a handsome fool," Daphne teased her while Kate folded her arms across her chest and nodded in amusement.

"Look at him, eating up all their attention. He is shameless."

"Didn't he ask you to dance a few nights ago?" Daphne asked innocently, folding her arms across her chest.

Carissa rolled her eyes. "I shouldn't have said yes. I've never met anyone so annoying. He thinks he's clever, but he doesn't seem to grasp that one is laughing *at* him, not *with* him."

"Oh, come!" Kate laughed.

"I don't understand why he bothers you so much," Daphne said. "He's not so bad!"

"He's a coxcomb!" Carissa vowed. "Why can't he act more like Lord Falconridge? Jordan, now, he is too much of a gentleman to let women fawn on him like that."

"Are you gossiping about me, Miss Portland?" the earl in question drawled, overhearing. When he glanced at Carissa with a brotherly smile, Kate realized Max was right. Theirs was just a friendship.

"No, my lord," she answered. "I am praising you as a paragon of chivalry."

"Ha!" Max replied to that, but Jordan tugged his own coat with an air of satisfaction.

"You hear that, boys? I'm a paragon."

Rohan scoffed. "Any progress with those scrolls?"

Jordan nodded. "A little."

"Don't forget, I offered to help you!" Kate reminded him, but just then, Jordan's light eyes narrowed on a distant quarter of the ballroom. He suddenly went motionless.

Maybe he had spotted his "one and only" lady in the ballroom, whoever she was, Kate mused. But then she noticed that Rohan and Max had also come to attention, following his gaze.

"If you'll excuse me." Jordan withdrew from their midst without another word.

The other two exchanged a sober glance.

"Is it Bloodwell?" Rohan murmured, but Jordan had already gone ahead of them.

Daphne drew in her breath bravely as Max nodded in answer and followed Jordan with a dark look.

Rohan stayed by the women to guard them. "Don't worry," he told them softly.

"What's going on?" Carissa asked in confusion. She had not been made privy to the true nature of the Inferno Club, as the two wives had.

"Jordan should have stayed. He's the code man. I should be the one to do this," Rohan growled under his breath, but Virgil was still disgruntled at him for not following protocol; he had given the job of killing the Promethean assassin to the earl.

"I am sure Lord Falconridge is equal to the task." Kate gave her husband an even look, but Daphne glanced at someone who was approaching from the other side of them.

"Lady Rotherstone," a haughty male voice greeted her.

Kate turned around as Daphne's usual smile thinned, her posture stiffening. "Your Grace."

Kate moved closer to her friend, having already been introduced to Daphne's insufferable former suitor, the haughty Albert Carew, Duke of Holyfield.

"So formal? Come, my dear, we were once engaged. You can still call me Alby, as you used to."

"Our 'engagement' existed only in your mind, Albert. If you recall correctly, I never agreed to it."

Albert snickered, glancing toward the door. "I notice your husband ran off when he saw me coming."

Rohan raised an eyebrow at the smaller man in the dandified clothes.

"Warrington," his fellow duke greeted him. "Damned fine filly you've got there, eh? All the kick, so they tell me."

Kate's eyes widened as Rohan's narrowed at Albert's breezy tone. She shook her head firmly at her husband.

No, darling. No lopping off heads in the ballroom.

He scowled in answer, but Alby was oblivious.

"Yes, I say, a most excellent wife. I should get me a lady like yours, what?" He sent Daphne a reproachful look askance, then regarded Kate again with admiration. "Wherever did you find her, anyway?"

Rohan glowered at him. "Let's just say she was given to me . . . as a gift."

Albert laughed heartily. "A gift, eh? Right. Ah, here comes the Prince Regent!" He brightened. "His Royal Highness will be wanting my company, no doubt. If you'll pardon me."

"Gladly," Daphne replied.

Albert dashed off into the crowd, then Kate went to Rohan and put her arms around his waist.

"Given to you as a gift." Daphne shook her head at Rohan. "You shouldn't encourage him with such jests. That's going to be all over Society in about ten minutes, you know."

Kate laughed. "Let them talk! We are too pleased with each other to care."

"That we are." Rohan leaned down and kissed her forehead. "Best present I ever got," he added in a roguish murmur.

Just then, Max returned, but as he joined them, he was still glancing behind him rather warily.

"Is everything all right?" Daphne asked,

going to him.

He nodded as he put his arm around her.

"Does Jordan need any help?" Rohan murmured.

"He's already got some," he replied. "Beauchamp."

"Help with what?" Carissa exclaimed, perking up at the mention of the viscount she supposedly couldn't stand.

"All those dreadful women," Rohan replied indulgently.

Kate scoffed and shot her husband an arch look. *You mean your former harem?*

But the hungry look of pure devotion he gave her now reminded her she was the only woman in his life.

He gathered her hands into his, kissed each one, then tugged her toward the dance floor. "Come, I want that waltz you promised me."

Meanwhile, outside, Jordan's eyes gleamed in the darkness, his breath steaming in the cold air of the late February night. He bent smoothly and slid a dagger out of the ankle sheath concealed by the leg of his trousers.

Beau signaled to him from the other end of the dark, silent garden, and they both began moving stealthily in the direction that Dresden Bloodwell had gone . . .